THE SCORCHED HUNTER

ANDREW JOHNSTON

This novel is dedicated to my mother.

BOOKS BY ANDREW JOHNSTON

The Discarded Knight

The Iron Frost Universe:

The Ignited Moon

The Scorched Hunter

CONTENTS

MUTAFAKARA

CRIZALBOLT

NEMA

NATLENDT

HAUSARA   CILLNAR   I

BR

NIEV

THE WORLD OF
IRON FROST

◇ CITY
◎ NOTABLE TOWN
•• COUNTRY BORDER

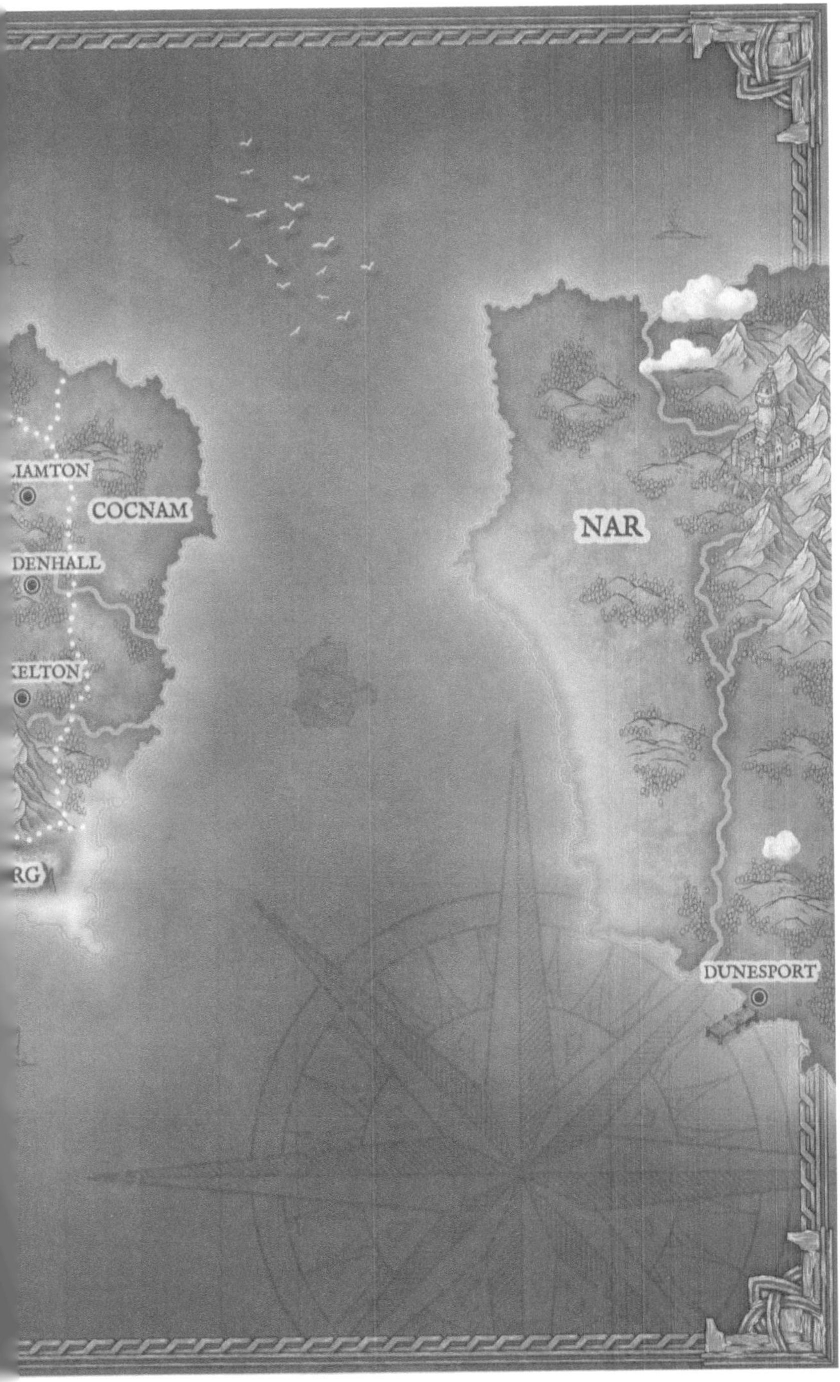

IAMTON
COCNAM
DENHALL
ELTON
RG
NAR
DUNESPORT

ONE

The mountain's narrow path always felt like a balancing act. Cole pressed himself close to the mountainside, his mass leaving a foot from the path's edge. It slowed their progress, but Anna would rather her friend used caution. The day had been long. Longer for Anna after the time it took to drag her kill through a mile of undergrowth. She groaned, lifting her arms, the reins loose in her hands. Her muscles felt like jelly after heaving the deer onto the storm bison's back. It hung end to end over his thickly muscled shoulders and dark silver hump.

Grass hissed across Cole's hooves once they reached the mountain's bottom. There was a sudden slowing once the ground leveled off. Anna leaned past her kill to find her friend panting. Her lips curled into a frown. Cole let out a low groan, his nostrils manifesting spritz of rain and thinning clouds.

"Come on, old friend," she said, rubbing his side. "You're too brave and swift to stop now."

She urged Cole onto the trail they used before. His pace increased, and his clouds thickened from her encouragement. Lightning clapped in the distance, jarring her from her bent position before she could draw in the scent of wet grass. Raindrops from Cole's clouds tapped the ground as the lightning faded from sound. The heat from the waning sunlight pressed against Anna's cheeks. Her hometown of Williamton was a good distance away, hidden by the forest.

Trees not yet ready for winter clung to their leaves, giving some shade. Scurrying rabbits broke the near quiet; wind shifted the branches. A light, almost relaxed feeling resonated when she'd return from a hunt. One akin to rolling in snow. Anna wished she could bring the woods sounds home.

Anna smiled, running her fingers over the thick winter fur of her kill. She hoped that if the servants cooked it well, her lord grandfather might join her on a hunt. She licked her lips, already tasting the tenderness of deer meat. She pictured her grandfather on his esant, in riding cloak, flying low with the wind. His words would be about the present and not about what troubled Lampara. Sharing time with him in the woods mattered more to her than who governed. No lecture on the prime's ten-year governance or their proving worthy of being in charge for so long.

The main path was in sight, all the snow of last night gone, leaving behind damp smells and darkened leaves. She was still at a respectful distance from Williamton. The town had renamed itself to honor her grandfather after he saved her from the dragon. *I had wanted it for more than just a mount.* Anna grimaced and then reflected on Cole's silver hooked horns. Storm bison held near boundless energy in their youth, but when she purchased Cole, he already had been ancient in her eyes. A smile crossed her lips. A dragon wasn't kind, like a storm bison anyway. Dropping her hand to Cole's reins, she gripped them fiercely and then snapped them. They made it to a good speed as the wind bathed her cheeks and carried Cole's clouds into the—

Flames tore through Williamton's rooftops. Anna yanked at Cole's reins, dirt churning, slowing them until they came to a stop. Fear gripped her throat to see the towering smoke grow thicker and higher with each second. The cabbage field before her filled her nostrils with a raw, earthy scent, tainted by smoke. The small, quiet town beyond the field had been her home since the age of fifteen. It was an oasis amidst the legions of trees making up the Greethumb region. The town's high walls and thick gates grayed in the late afternoon light and thickening smoke.

Dark clouds drifted northward at an unusual speed, lashing out with lightning bolts. Pouring out of the north gate at great speed was a man upon a creature of black. Trailing behind him like a comet's tail were men in ever-green and scarlet armor.

Anna jabbed her muddied boot into Cole's side. The old storm bison bolted onward. She narrowed her singular eye and clenched her teeth. She found the men possessed too great a lead to follow. Anna pinned back her long, shimmering black hair with a thin metal stake. The riders grew clearer with the speed of Cole's powerful legs. Their leader rode a black storm bison. Whoever he was, only great wealth could provide someone a beast that rare. *Crack.* Lightning struck beside him. Anna gasped, but the man crouched, jabbing his heel into the bison's side.

She shook her head at the thought of how aroused a black storm bison would have to be to create lightning.

Toward the distant woods ahead of the riders, there were no other storm bison. Without a source of motivation, Anna wasn't sure how the black storm bison created its lightning.

Cries of pain filled her ears as she neared the west gate, but Williamton's thick walls should have made that impossible. Anna's senses heightened when she drew near danger or became stressed. She released a breath, hoping that this time what drove her mad might be of use. *For once.*

There were no guards manning the west gate's octagon towers. Anna moved on with the cries fading from her ears. She urged Cole to the north gate, where the riders made their hasty exit. It like the other gates was layered with names of past citizens in copper over its oak surfaces. The tradition kept the memory of those dead or moved on alive. The height and smooth surface of the town's walls made the north gate hard to spot.

Anna licked her lips, her tongue withdrawing swiftly from where her burns had healed part of them shut. She drew in a breath. The town was like a barrel full of kindling, its homes crafted from wood and dry stone. Another scream struck her ears, as if someone was being chased. She reached for her quiver, counted its arrows, eyeing the way ahead for the north gate. 28. Anna held on to hope there were no more armored soldiers. And that her hearing had just deceived her.

She passed through the gate, smoke consuming it like a foggy narrow gorge. It teased her nostrils as she swiped at the smoke's unrelenting gray. Flames stretched out ahead of her, torturing homes and shops the deeper she went. The trading post groaned from her left, its weakened timbers cracked and bent.

"Grandfather," Anna called. Footsteps answered, growing closer and faster. A man clutching scrolls to his chest burst forth from the smoke. The trading post released a final creak, crashing in a heap. "Norman? Where is Lord William Brighton?"

Norman spun with his hair a mess and ash on his cheeks. Amidst the surrounding chaos, he bowed to her, an ink bottle slipped from his pocket, smashing amongst the slush and mud. His lips trembled as he stood erect.

"He's guiding people out of the south gate, Lady Anna."

Relief filled her belly like cool water to know her grandfather was safe. She secured Cole's reins around the horn of his saddle and slid down from his back. Her cloak caught on his thick gray coat, crackling with static.

"Thank you for this news," she said. Norman looked at her, and her heart quickened. The accountant's blue eyes were reddened from the smoke. His finely tailored crimson doublet smelled of ash. "Take Cole to where grandfather has led the others. Do you know why those riders came?"

Norman stuffed his scrolls into a saddlebag, straining to pull himself up. The blacksmith's forge belched out a great blast of flame behind him. Anna flinched as Norman lost his grip and then regained it, clamoring for balance. Anna held Cole close, his bleating boomed within her ears. She stroked his head, feeling the storm bison clouds rush over her cheeks. Cole stomped in place. Norman hugged against his heaving back, gagging at the deer's open belly over the bison shoulders. The storm bison clouds grew, rising swiftly over the town before they released a torrent of rain. The droplets quenched flames lingering across the collapsed trading post.

"I don't know why they came," said Norman, swallowing hard, readying Cole's reins, "but I know how we can save Williamton."

"Are you certain?" Anna said, remembering the accountant's struggle to mount Cole. "Maybe you should leave by the south gate and—"

Snap went the storm bison reins. Anna leapt back, stumbling close to the blacksmith's shop. Its heat and flames jarred her memory, adding haste to her steps. Anna collapsed to one knee, gasping, her fear of fire consumed her. Great canals of sweat ran down her back. She peered over her shoulder, finding her cloak was on fire. She ripped its pale bear brooch off, holding tight the white-stoned guardian. She staggered to her feet, pressing the brooch close to her chest. At a distance, rain pattered upon the road and struck at homes. Below the rising nimbuses Norman sent Cole down a narrow alley.

The sky filled swiftly with clouds, sending rain over what burned. An inn nearby Anna wished had seen more business this past autumn burned. Visitors of her grandfather had stayed there, but in recent weeks the inn began hosting fewer and fewer guests. Smoke billowed from the roof and lower levels. She moved closer, hearing no commotion from its windows. The smoke jabbed at her eye, stinging it before a sold sign tore away from under the inn's timber awning. Wind sent it spinning into flames, devouring it in seconds.

Clouds gathered over the inn, its rain falling with significant force. The inn's flames hissed, vanishing, the roof like a marble of black and brown. She sucked in a breath, wishing Gwen Mindal had kept the town's oldest residence. *Perhaps whoever she sold it to will not want it now.* She eyed the structure once again and then drew in her lip.

She grew weary of Cole. His breathing had become more rampant once reaching Williamton. Her kill had evaded them over rough terrain and was still tied over her friend's back. She pressed the brooch to her chest, whispering a prayer to Simdorn for her friend. Stuffing the guardian away, she turned her head westward.

"I must find where those screams came from before it's too late."

CHAPTER
TWO

A damp and muddy path stretched out behind Norman. Ahead of him, lit by the remaining sunlight, Williamton's two main roads filled his line of vision. He had been coming from the east end of town, where the fires had begun an hour earlier. His heart pounded almost in rhythm with Cole's heavy panting. Gray swirling clouds blasted from the storm bison's thick black nostrils. The ground before them grew muddy and sucked at the mount's hooves. Norman chewed his lip as raindrops raced down his brow. A grinding pain filled his chest, distracting from the abundance of sound. *Damn my cowardice.*

The moment had been there, but he was too afraid to tell her. Anna would never forgive him for his silence. He had heard what wasn't meant for his ears. *Damn myself for being caught,* he thought, snatching a scroll before it slipped from a saddlebag. Clenching his teeth, Norman wished that scoundrel with his long, thick chin whiskers had refused his lordship. He wished he had returned later for the scrolls. As the sun sank, and his way grew darker, there was no use traipsing back to the past. There was no use in wallowing in regret.

Norman pressed his legs against Cole's sides. He yanked at the saddle horn as his buttocks slid to the beast's gray furry behind. The saddle was far longer than a horse's, and from where he used to live, a cobraswift's dome saddle required no need for balance. He'd never ridden a storm bison until today.

He caught sight of crusted blood from where the deer had been gutted. Norman gagged as a rush of bile filled his throat. The deer flopped up and down on Cole's back. Blood leapt from its belly, tapping, and running down the storm bison horns. He sent the mount east, where the flames grew worse and roared loudest. The house Norman had long lived in was nestled at the neighborhood's center. His heart felt lighter to know Samuel was safe. The guard and the accountant had been at their posts before the fires began. Samuel had taught him to do things in measurements as one would a man's savings. Norman cracked Cole's reins, keeping to covering quadrants of the town.

The unpleasant taste formed again in his mouth, this time of sour milk he realized too late was spoiled. The dead beast from Anna's hunt made the taste seem worse. Norman spat and rummaged through the saddlebags for a knife. Norman felt the leather of a hilt and withdrew his hand, ignoring the loud gurgle of his stomach. *I will not cut loose what Anna worked hard for.* He re-buttoned the bags, jerking the storm bison reins, turning him west.

Clouds swirled and gathered as he passed homes and shops. Some were engulfed in flame; others crashed and boomed as if the rain had given a last nudge. Norman pressed a heel to Cole's side, making certain to turn up every alley. Women and children slipped past them, narrowing things, slowing the progress of extinguishing. Screams rang out as people scrambled from doorways.

"Hurry everyone," he urged. "Head for the south gate."

Shutters crashed open as a man barreled through a window. He scrambled to his feet and vanished amongst the smoke. Norman eased up on Cole's reins. The poor beast was panting harder than ever; his clouds combusted before they could rise. Norman eased their pace to a trot, pity swelling in his stomach for the mount.

They'd made it to the town's center. Rain battled with the roar of flames for supremacy. Williamton was gray in places, with roofs up and strong, while others were black, collapsed, churning up vast towers of smoke. Toward the north, west and south, rain clouds drifted and gathered, releasing thick droplets. The wind shifted the storms ever so slightly. Norman held on to the hope that it was only a brief breeze. It was said a storm bison's clouds were easily carried. He climbed off Cole as another breeze ruffled his hair. Norman slipped the beast's long black reins and led him into the open.

At a distance, people gathered beyond the south gate. Many were huddled close to the woods. Amongst them, Lord William Brighton sat upon his esant. The lord wore a black leather tunic and a flowing crimson cloak. A long sword hung across his back, its silver pommel in the shape of an eight-pointed star. He raised his thick eyebrows at Norman. The years hadn't been kind to his lordship. Where once he sat tall with his ginger beard cut short, now he was hunched with bushy, prickly chin hairs.

"Norman Tilt." His lordship jerked his esant's reins. The long, swift bird strutted up next to Norman, running its thin tongue across its sharp, hooked beak. "Why are you in possession of my granddaughter's mount? And where has she gone?"

Norman bowed to Lord William as he watched his lordship survey the town. His lordship's esant possessed fierce glowing eyes. The feathers on its head were scarlet and jetted back like talons tipped in black. Lord William narrowed his gaze at Norman, turning up his nose.

"Lady Anna remains within the town's walls, my lord," said Norman.

Lord William raised an eyebrow. His lips trembled for a moment, retreating to a solid, firm line. His lordship huffed, snapping the esant's wide decorative red reins. Norman yanked Cole forward. They stumbled out of the lord's way as the esant squawked, its razor-tipped talons tore at grass and dirt as it gained speed.

"Remain with Cole and the townsfolk," Lord William called over his shoulder. "I will find her."

"Will you tell her about—"

Norman fell silent before Lord William took to the air. He pressed the storm bison reins to his back and clamped his mouth shut. Among the townsfolk, mounted men in scarlet plated armor and evergreen chainmail surveyed the people. Upon their breastplates a badge rested, one of the Brighton eight-pointed star inside the jaws of Lampara's governing crest. A silver horse shaded in black. The horse seemed to clamp down hard on the star. One word would have placed him in trouble with Lord Brighton and the law.

Cole huffed, easing down, dropping with a thud. Norman knelt beside him, eyeing Williamton. Flames vanished with the wind and speed of Lord William's esant. The bird was barely a blur to his eyes, and then, all at once, it vanished.

"I hope he is honest with her." Norman stroked a dark

gray furry patch on Cole's immense face before removing his scrolls. The storm bison dozed, bleary-eyed, "as I should have been. She deserves as much for coming home to such terror."

THREE

The western half of town was a shifting orange and black. Her friend's storm clouds encroached from behind, stretching and manifesting, outpacing every step she took. The air filled with rain, meeting the coming darkness. Dampness filled her nostrils, weak against the scent of smoke. Anna stopped short of the west gate, panting, running a fist across her brow. With the flames vanishing under the rain's onslaught, Anna's hopes rose. They rose higher as it appeared her hometown would survive the harm thrust upon it. Her ears caught cries for help, distant and faint. She scanned every home. Foundation stones had cracked, given up to the strain imposed by the heat, weight of their houses. The rain became a downpour, and when she shifted her stance... Her eye widened. Anna dashed with all her speed, the screams crashing upon her senses.

Sweat blurred her vision as a mother, and child raced out onto the street. Their hovel caved quickly, tongues of flame and chunks of debris chasing their steps. Clouds overshadowed the small structure. Rain ripped at its timbers and quieted the flames. Anna pressed a hand to her pale bear brooch nestled in a pouch on her belt. *Thank you, Simdorn, for sparing them.* Pounding snatched at her senses as she turned to find the goddess's temple before her. At its steeple, Simdorn stood atop its bell tower, strangled by a serpent-like stretch of rising smoke. The goddess, wreathed in blackness, had long streaming red locks. Her face was ageless within the open jaws of a bear helmet. About her slender figure, white robes hung, halting short of the vacant belfry.

Anna's heart went into a sprint. The temple's diamond-pane windows glowed angry yellow. The entrance between the pale bear statues supporting a crescent moon was chained shut. Anna searched for her knife, trembling, exhaling to center herself. Never had she picked a lock like some thief, but it was worth a try. *Dammit!* The knife was far off in one of Cole's saddlebags.

Pounding rattled the temple's doors, overshadowed by the pleas of priests. A thin shadow ran across her sight. Anna dashed to the temple and slipped the long, thin stake from her hair. Her hair tumbled over shoulders, settling inside the folds of her hood. She snatched the lock, twisting and turning the stake. Anna winced from the heat pressing at the dark brown of her hunting leathers.

"I'm here," Anna said.

"Please free us," said a priestess. Her voice was shrill and uneven among the priests that pounded and bellowed for help. "Men came for her while we worshiped, but we refused to give her up. They've doomed their souls setting fire to Simdorn's house."

Anna wanted to ask more but continued to pick at the lock. *What madness is it to set a town ablaze for one person?* The stake was thin, but sturdy, navigating the lock with precision the more she tightened her grip. Anna twisted and pushed, clenching her teeth, until the lock clicked and tapped. Her grip lessened, every finger taking a turn on the lock's metal. She composed words to reassure the goddess's servants, but nothing came of her efforts. Such madness of the chains sealing shut the temple was a ritual begun three days previously. It was meant to provide Simdorn's devout with unbothered prayer. *Should I learn who they protected, that man will owe them his life.*

Heavy humming shattered the din of flames and caving roofs. The light from the setting sun flickered for a moment, then shone fully before a shape passed overhead. Anna wiped her sweat away and gasped. The cries tormenting her senses had fallen silent. She dropped both lock and stake. A long, painful groan sounded from the temple roof. A rush of wind erased the flames on nearby homes, whipping her hood against her back. Hope rekindled in her chest. Crowing lashed at her ears. It came from the only bird she knew to be so swift. The esant touched down, stones snapping under its talons, dust filling the air. The bird settled its wings over a length of muddy road. The esant was longer than two carriages. Its wings hummed, shuffling as her grandfather slid from its back.

"Why did not you leave with Norman?" he roared. His esant flashed its crimson head, blinking its glaring eyes with lightning speed. "Out of the way." Her grandfather brushed her aside. "I have lost the damnable key."

She pressed herself against the hind leg of a pale bear guardian. Lord William drew his sword, raised his brow to the crescent moon, and whispered a swift prayer. *"Forgive an old lord's foolishness. Grant me strength in the days ahead, oh goddess."* He drew in a deep breath and faced the chains sealing the temple. Lord William swung and severed the chains. Sparks hit and hissed against the temple's brick-work. He drew back his sword and slipped it back into its sheath. Anna eyed the crescent moon, thanking Simdorn for sending her—

"Why do you stand there?" her grandfather said, pointing at the chains. "Help me free Simdorn's servants."

The screams rose again, but Lord William quieted them with assurance. He spoke of their plight being over soon. Anna tugged at the chains, seething at the stinging heat. The core of her palms swiftly radiated pain through her muscles. Her grandfather helped remove the first layer from the long brass door handles. He pulled swiftly. His hands retreated and then grasped another chain link. It seemed his reflexes hadn't lessened since she was a child. Even bent by age, his height nearly doubled her own. He switched places along the chains with her.

Anna untwisted the last chain and then nodded to her grandfather. He yanked it free, spreading his cloak wide, resembling a nutsnatcher's fleshy wings. They yanked open the temple doors, stumbling behind the pale bears. Shouts led a stampede of priests in robes blacker than the smoke chasing them from the temple. A crack and snap sent Anna trailing at the cloak tails of her lord grandfather. The temple folded in on itself, coughing up a tower of smoke. The smoke consumed the white marble of Simdorn's guardians.

"Go swiftly to the south gate, priests of Simdorn." Her grandfather turned back to her. His bushy gray eyebrows knitted together. His steel-blue eyes narrowed. "Where have you been all day? And why was Cole with Norman Tilt?"

"I... Norman rode on Cole to put out the flames with—"

Crash. Across the way a home collapsed. Anna fell silent before she eyed the esant.

"Can we leave and find them?" Anna bit her lip. "Please."

Fear crept down her spine, teaming with the heat and the slow darkening of the day. Lord William looked down his nose at her. He sighed, resting his hand on her shoulder.

"Let's go then," he said, giving her shoulder a squeeze. "I can guess where you have been by the blood on your boot."

Anna eyed the collapsed temple once they climbed onto the esant's back. The priestess's words troubled her mind. Her grandfather tugged at the esant's thick red reins, emblazoned with their family's silver eight-pointed star. The esant took off at a sprint. Wind whipped her hair and hood back as the bird cawed. Anna wrapped her arms tight around Lord William's waist. The town blurred, and like lightning the esant lashed out its wings. They launched them into the air, trailing mud and streaks of dust. She felt weightless as the clouds brushed against her cheeks. The sun resembled a ripe fruit in the distance. Its brightness stored away all she had seen and returned her happiness. Such feeling fled from her heart at the sight of ash smeared across grandfather's cheeks.

"We are away from danger," he said. "I know fire remains a fear of yours, sweet girl."

The heavy rain tampered Lord William's words down. The whole town was under gray, swirling clouds, leaving narrow openings. She looked through them and bit her lip. Cole was nowhere to be found. She wrapped her arms tighter around her grandfather's waist. He patted her hand and then strengthened his grip on the esant's reins. Her eye searched every alley. A horse rushed east, making her believe it was Cole by the color of its coat. Her mind raced to whether Norman had driven the old storm bison too hard. She swallowed and refused to believe her worst fears.

"I must ask you something," Anna said.

The esant banked right until its wing beats brought them beyond the south gate. She strained for a sign of Cole or Norman but found nothing.

"A priestess said the riders wanted a girl, but none of them gave her up."

Lord William slouched. His posture resembled a fishhook. His face was unreadable with the relentless wind in her eye.

"They were here for you."

Anna gasped.

"Why?"

The rain slowly subsided as her fear quickened, chilling her like a winter wind. She couldn't remember doing anything wrong, or at least nothing that would drive someone to set Williamton ablaze.

"Three months remain until a new prime or primnoire will earn governorship of Lampara. Prime Luther has done more ill than good since coming to power." Lord William grinned. A crowd appeared at the forest's edge. "He has two sons of his own campaigning for Lampara's favor." He grumbled, snapping the esant's reins. "The lads must desire to remove any rivals for the position. You are trained well enough, and our family name inspires—"

Anna rested her hand on his shoulder and squeezed it.

"I know where your words go," she said. "I... I can't do it alone... I can't live up to the Brighton name."

"You can, Anna," said Lord William. His voice heightened; worry removed its usual depth. "Our family founded this country and can save it," he sighed, beginning their descent. "I'm sorry. We have spoken of this on many occasions. What the dragon did to your face has robbed you of courage. The courage to see beyond the woods to the troubles of our people." He smiled. "I know you have strength, Anna. You need only put it to a good cause."

She shook her head of the memory, grabbing at her hood to hide inside it, but the wind possessed greater strength than her own.

"I made my choices that day, Grandfather," Anna said, "and I will forever regret them." Tears ran down her trembling lips. They were bitter, like the elixir her grandfather's physician provided when her burns grew too painful. "The woods are the only world I wish to know. And though you want me to continue our family's legacy, my answer remains... No."

Her grandfather let out a low hum, returning focus to flying. His silence left no space for her thoughts to find comfort. She gasped and pointed. She caught sight of Norman kneeling beside Cole. A smile stretched across her face. And from what Anna could tell, the storm bison was asleep. The grass grew brighter, greener, and closer. The esant grabbed at the ground, but caution had vanished from her mind. Anna leapt from the bird's back.

"Cole! Norman!" Anna cried. Her legs begged to give way, but she tucked and rolled up in seconds. "Thank the goddess you both are safe."

Anna embraced Norman, his doublet a darker shade of red than earlier. His short chestnut hair a soggy mess, like the scrolls under his arms.

"I pushed him for as long as I could," said Norman, turning to the deep, labored breaths of the storm bison. "But he needs rest, and I'm unable to remove the deer."

The esant cawed, followed by her grandfather's low,

angered breaths. The conversation concerning campaigning wasn't over. Anna felt guilt heave itself onto her shoulders, but she shrugged it off. She caught sight of the saddlebag her knife was in. She unbuttoned it, slipped free her knife, and cut the rope. Her shoulder went numb before the second rope brushed her fingers.

"Anna Brighton!" her grandfather said, pulling her around to face him. "The priests of our fair goddess knew where you would be. They ... protected you."

He squeezed her shoulder so tight, Anna dropped to her knees.

"Will you make such a sacrifice a waste?" he growled, releasing her. "I require an answer."

Anna climbed to her feet and rubbed the pain from her shoulder. Williamton's people were out of earshot, which raised her spirits. Any misstep would go unheard, but there was still Norman.

"I cannot do it alone, Grandfather." Her face tensed with rage. Her hold on the knife tightened. "I... I cannot thank you enough for your lessons, but I am far too damaged. No one wants a primnoire like me."

Turning the knife in her hand, she cut the second rope. The deer's fur hissed against Cole's as it thudded upon the ground. She stuffed the ropes in a saddlebag, grabbed her kill by its brow tines and dragged. Sweat met their smooth-ness, slipping, the points dug into her palms. She was a hunter, one with ties to Lampara's first governing family. But after coming of age at fifteen and the poor choice of a dragon, to have authority, a role in her people's lives... It was all for another Anna whose senses didn't drive her mad under pressure. *And no one will follow a woman who is incomplete.*

"I'll campaign at your side, Lady Anna," said Norman,

his tone firm with confidence. "I've learned much about Lampara as an accountant."

Dryness tormented Anna's throat. Her lips fumbled with one another, itching to thank Norman. She shuddered, resting a hand on her face. Lord William grasped the accountant's shoulders with his gnarled, tested hands and uttered what words finally came to Anna's mind.

"You're not a fighter, Tilt, and that is a key requirement of a prime," said Lord William. "Though I must thank you for your courage on this day. Williamton would be gone without it."

"I'll learn to fight, Anna." Norman looked at her. "Lampara's finances will always be balanced." His eyes were soft, reddened from the smoke. Anna could repay his eagerness only with apprehension. "I can be of great help to you, my lady."

"I appreciate your offer, Norman," Anna said, "but leading Lampara isn't where a burned woman belongs."

Anna focused on Williamton for a moment. The forest's tall pines peaked over its walls and between its homes. Echoes of the black storm bison lightning met her ears. She caught sight of its clouds, though the evening sky soon made them invisible.

"This deer was to convince you to take up hunting, Grandfather." Anna dragged it before him, rising, strain fleeing down her back. "Give it to our people if you find its meat not to your liking."

She pulled a small handful of berries from a pouch on her belt. Anna dropped to one knee and fed them to Cole. Neither man said a word as the storm bison sniffed. Cole gobbled the berries. He licked his lips and rubbed his wet nose against her cheek. She smiled. Her friend stood upright as Anna climbed atop him. She sought to ride north to town, but pressure closed fast upon her ankle. Anna looked to find her grandfather, brow furrowed and knuckles white about her boot.

"You had best reconsider your actions," he said, pointing to the priests draped in their heavy, layered robes. "They will not forget your unwillingness to repay their silence. I shall not forget."

Her heart retreated into the depths of her stomach. Lord William narrowed his eyes, reminding her of their discussion within the sky. She formed her lips into a solid line, releasing a firm breath.

"I have considered my actions, Grandfather."

He released her ankle and folded his arms.

"And?"

"I'll do what I am best at. I'll go on a hunt."

CHAPTER
FOUR

Anna shut her eye tight against the chilling northern breeze that countered the heat of quieted flames. She feigned a smile. Being half-blind had at least one use. It kept hidden much of the destruction tormenting her heart. Her eye lost sight when the healing went wrong, forcing the eyelid shut forever. Her grandfather's physician offered to perform surgery, but at such a time everything scared her. Night was upon Williamton. The fading embers in the west half of town prevented total darkness. Cole's clouds were gone from the sky. The air was musty and drenched with the scent of mud and burnt debris.

She patted her friend's massive hump, his breaths labored and deep. Faint remnants of her kill's blood met her nose, crusted beyond her hand in thin streaks across the storm bison fur. He lengthened his strides, ignoring his fatigue, keeping the drive within him going. She rubbed his side, admiring him for his focus. She peered up at her hometown.

Anna sucked in a breath. There was no use ignoring what damage her quarry had left behind. Homes deep in neighborhoods stood tall, their roofs solid and peaked. But the ones meeting Williamton's two main roads were collapsed and blackened. Their thatched roofs lay in heaps, protruding from dry stone windows. Voices breathed out from alleys of those venturing to salvage what they could. A tear ran down her cheek as they waved, then went about sorting what remained of their lives. She waved, hoping to reassure them and herself, swallowing her sadness.

"Neither grandfather nor Norman must have mentioned my refusal," she said, keeping her voice low. "Williamton would expect me to campaign after aiding the priests."

Carts littered the road home, smoking or collapsed inward. Hoofprints crossed from one part of town to another. Norman had covered a lot of ground. And though his offer was tempting, his ability to ride unquestionable, she found accepting it too much to handle. Anna opened a saddlebag and tied her hair back with a length of cord.

Anna kept Cole at a slow pace, avoiding an assortment of deep muddy patches toward the north gate. Faint echoes of the black storm bison lightning met her ears. She rested her gaze on the woods its rider sent it through. The reasoning for its rider and soldiers was clear, but setting the town ablaze with its lightning made no sense. *Especially with no lady bison to entice it.*

Once beyond the north gate, Anna took in Williamton once more. Aiding everyone in rebuilding crossed her mind, but it would have to wait. *Will you make such a sacrifice a waste?* Anna shook her head. Coin was needed to travel and gain support throughout Lampara.

"And grandfather would give it to me without question." She focused on the south gate. Darkness kept it hidden except for the torches on either watchtower.

She tugged at her bow, counting the arrows in her quiver. Anna slouched in her saddle and rubbed the sweat from her brow. Her grandfather may have trained her to wield a sword, throw a knife, and strike true with an arrow, but to kill a man was different. Anna put a heel to Cole's side, sending him into a trot. Storm clouds raced over his cheeks, encompassing them like the task ahead of her mind. They needed to move faster, but to delay the death to come felt right. *I'm a hunter, not a soldier.* Her attention fell on Cole's struggle to keep pace. Delaying what needed to be done by allowing her friend rest felt right too, except under the current circumstances, impossible.

"You'll have a long rest, Cole." She patted his side. "I promise."

Will you make such a sacrifice a waste? She pressed her lips together. Her grandfather's words churned over and over in her mind, but that did not mean they needed heeded.

"I will find those soldiers." Drawing her hood over her head tight, raindrops tapping its surface. "And if able, I'll stop them from telling Luther's sons I am alive."

Anna snapped Cole's reins and felt his immense legs propel them up a steep grassy hill. He blazed through bushes, crushing roots and small stones. Williamton was gone in moments as all her focus went to listening. Once she had come to a field, Anna tugged at the point of her hood. She prayed to Simdorn for a swift end to this adventure and a return to a quiet life.

THE LIGHTNING HAD long since fallen silent, and her nervousness slowed from a jabbing to a prickle. Anna sniffed, the scent of charred meat ebbed in her direction. It meant the riders were close, relaxed, and she hoped in the mood to make a deal. Leave her and her hometown alone. Rain droplets clung to her hood as she narrowed her focus. Anna slowed Cole until they were several feet before a clearing. There was a divide at its center too wide for her friend to overcome. Anna dismounted and rested her hand on Cole's shoulder. She sighed, knowing his part in this hunt was over.

She spotted a tiny flicker of orange and red through the crack of a downed tree. She removed her bow, strung it, and then shouldered her quiver. The strap of her quiver held tight to her person. Anna ran two fingers down her bow's string, clearing it of rain droplets.

She crept to the divide. Jagged rocks littered it all the way down to a muddy bottom. Anna leaned back, gripping her bow firmly. Twigs snapped and bushes rustled as starlight and moonlight highlighted a man stumbling toward her. Nocking and drawing, she trained her arrow on him. He was at such a short range he might as well have been standing still. Plated armor protected only his legs. The soldier wore a yellow tunic with brown laces drawn tight at the collar. Over his heart within a spade-shaped badge was a black badger. His head was shaven but for a tuft of red hair down the middle. He froze in place and spat. A twitch in his upper lip rustled his long, thick chin whiskers.

"Who the fuck are you?" He belched, hovering a hand over a bollocks knife at his hip. "Can't I piss in peace?" His eyes grew to the size of apples. "Lower that thing before I call my men."

Strain ran up Anna's arm, pinching her shoulder. The fletching chafed against her cheek with her eye fixed down the arrow's shaft. Anna adjusted until the arrow met between his eyes.

"You've caused great hardship to many for one girl," she said. "Why is Lord William's granddaughter a threat to the prime's sons?"

The soldier drew in his lower lip and bit it; his hand danced slowly over his knife.

"Lady Anna is of age," said the soldier, "and by law our prime can't govern a third time. Those boys need all the help they can get."

Two lights rose from the distant fire, meandering toward them. Anna brought her attention back to the soldier. She swallowed. Every muscle strained the longer she kept her bow drawn.

"You best hurry, girl," he said. "My men travel in pairs like good little soldiers."

"Let us," she said. "Let us strike a bargain."

"Oy." A deep voice bellowed from the trees. "Where you at, Lord Barden?"

"What do you have in mind?" Lord Barden smirked. "Hurry up now."

Her arms shook in sync. Anna wasn't used to being anchored for so long. Being alive may keep all she cared for in danger, but if she could persuade this stranger to leave, there might be hope. Shouts and stomps of the smirking lord's men banged at her ears. She shook it off.

"What if I convince her not to campaign?" said Anna. "And you can tell the prime that she is dead."

Lord Barden lunged. Anna released. Flesh and clothing tore, releasing blood from the lord's shoulder as his blade whooshed overhead. Anna rolled to her feet, dashing for the woods. The lord whistled. It pierced the air and rattled her senses. Twenty men at most burst forth into the moonlight with torches in hand. Their stallions flooded the tree line as the thunder of hoof strikes kicked up dirt.

"You won't make it far, girl." Lord Barden groaned. "And we'll be paying the town another visit."

Nocking another arrow, Anna squinted through shadow and moonlight. Horse after horse leapt the divide one after another as she sank deep into the undergrowth. She darted behind a thick pine, sweat enveloping her cheeks. Her every breath fled for safer quarters. She glared at her bow. Anna thought back to her grandfather's rants. What these men wished upon her violated campaign law.

Yells and hoof strikes drew closer. An immense wall of storm clouds charged toward Anna. Cole's dark marble-shaped eyes held concern; his panting breaths. Fear for her friend warred within her. She drew back a heavy breath with her bowstring, released, then took off at a sprint.

Thump. The arrow punctured a horse's chest, toppling it headfirst. Its rider cried, crushed, the torch in his hand snuffed out. Anna sent another arrow between the steel mouth shield and arrowhead helmet of another. The man shrieked like a frightened nutsnachter. All the others drew their swords, swinging them every which way.

Sharpness ran up her arm after she loosed her fifth arrow. Her wrist guard hurtled into the brush as pain lanced through her arm. Anna cursed through gritted teeth. She wanted to rub where it hurt, to hide once again, but with her senses in torment, and Cole drawing near, she cracked another arrow to her bow.

The storm bison brushed against her back and then raised his leg. Anna climbed onto her friend, hanging her quiver over his saddle horn. Anna sent Cole into an arc around the men, leaning low, releasing more arrows. Upon a finger count, ten arrows remained. The soldiers gathered their wits and followed, wielding torches and swords in combined rage.

The clouds parted, and in her rush to conserve arrows, silence fell. Anna pulled up on Cole's reins, reached, but found her hood must have slipped off. Her lips parted to draw in breath, but it left before touching her tongue. The men remained rooted like the towering sentinels behind them. They looked at one another, pointed, and began laughing. Anna rested a hand to her cheek. All of their amusement struck her emotions so hard tears fled her eye, doubling. She fumbled to find another arrow. The laughter stole her courage and blinded every thought. Anna grew dizzy on her friend's back. The strength fled from her muscles like a pair of frightened doves. Footsteps followed labored breaths until Lord Barden emerged amongst his men.

"What's all this?" He clutched his arm like it was ready to fall from his body. "Surround this girl this instant, you..."

"Go ahead, my lord," said Anna, begging deep down for the clouds to cover the moon and hide her in darkness. "Have your laugh before carrying out your orders."

The lord's lips remained a solid, unwavering line. He snarled, then barked an order for silence. Her bow arm fell to her side, the ability to hold her weapon fleeing with her courage. The bow felt as if it had tripled in weight. Cole huffed and snorted at the men the closer they came. There was no way to hide anymore. She could see in their eyes a boundless mockery, even with their cruelty silenced. *I must escape for Grandfather.* Anna drew Cole back, his mass striking an immense oak. He snapped and snarled at the closest man.

"I know who you are now." The lord called his men to halt. "If not for your hood, I'd have remembered you sooner," Lord Barden pulled a tiny chain from under his tunic. A pendant dangled from his blood-tipped fingers. It was a "W" encircled by a ring of storm bison, esants, horses, and dragons. "I once worked for the Wayne Trading Company. I... I sold you that dragon."

A cold sweat broke over her brow like a smashed egg against a rock. The once well-mannered man, who had accepted her grandfather's coin, commanded his men to put away their swords. Anna rubbed away tears to find confusion in the eyes of men once captivated by the extremes of her disfigurement.

"Are you going to finish what the dragon started?" she said.

Lord Barden rested the pendant against his chest and then clasped his wound once more. Silence built upon itself as a breeze toyed with his chin whiskers. Cole remained restless, stomping in place, eyeing the lord's red and green ranks.

"No," Barden waved. Soldier after soldier began the short jaunt back to their camp. Their slow departure put Anna's mind at ease. "I won't be. The prime's brats can win on their own."

"But, my lord," said a soldier with thick eyebrows. "We have orders. You'll lose your title and..."

"Damn my title." Lord Barden barked. "I have done enough to this poor girl."

Every tense muscle loosened; the misery cleared from her mind, but the thick-eyebrowed man continued to protest. Her breath flew in quick succession from the confusion in his eyes.

"Enough," said Lord Barden. "I got the title only because my former prime father died."

"Thank you, my lord," said Anna, bowing. "But I am not campaigning."

Lord Barden gave her a sour look. He untied a pouch from his belt and tossed it to her. It slipped through her fingers, the drawstring catching on her thumb.

"That's for what we did to your grandfather's town."

"I thank you for this, but if the prime will break campaign law for someone like me... What of the others wishing to govern?"

"Prime Luther would have entire armies to contend with. Last I saw, Williamton had enough blokes to guard its name gates. And only one peasant lord has put his neck out. A lot of folks support him. He's become something of a legend with his bow."

Anna secured the heavy purse within Cole's saddlebags. She ran a hand over his heaving hump. He hummed and grunted, settling, his nimbuses drifted over the grass like a morning mist. The thought of another archer intrigued her, but her anger at the lord's actions took precedence.

"You should not have endangered Williamton," she said, making a fist. "I am no threat to anyone. I did not enter my name."

"Well, some bloke entered it in the final calling."

Thud. Her bow struck dirt.

"Who answered the final calling in my place?

"Your ... grandfather."

There was no greater darkness than the fur of the sleeping black storm bison. Streaks of lightning danced over its nostrils, overshadowing the crackle of the campfire. Anna ran her fingers slowly through the mount's well-groomed fur. Lord Barden spoke of Roland being the last to have been bred successfully in one hundred years. Even before the Lampariens' took an interest in the rare beast, few roamed the country. Anna met his eyes; her fascination vanished. Her lips formed a solid, hard line. A deep cavern of disappointment opened in Anna's chest to have witnessed this poor creature being used for destructive means.

"I must return home," she said, turning from his gaze. "You have not redeemed yourself with me. And my grandfather has much to answer for his deception."

"You be right in your words," said Lord Barden. "I don't think your grandfather or I deserve any forgiving. I'm near the end, by my guess." He tore free his sleeve to find his wound had stopped bleeding. "Once I return to the capital with news that you're still breathing... The ax will be my fate."

Anna hesitated for a moment. Regret lowered the lord's ginger eyebrows as he pressed thumb and forefinger to his brow.

"I thank you for allowing me to see Roland." Her eye fell to her feet, "for sparing my life, but I mustn't remain with someone willing to harm so many."

"I don't blame you, my lady," said Lord Barden. His chin sank into his chest. "I deserve what's coming and can't hide. I'm too well-known in Cillnar."

Anna turned back to find that amongst tents, grazing horses, and a low burning fire, all eyes were upon them. The man with his thick eyebrows muttered something to the others, kicking up laughter like embers fleeing a dropped log. *Bastards.* She drew away from Roland and shouldered her bow, leaving for the divide.

"You thinking about campaigning with a target on your back?" Lord Barden asked. "By now, it's too late to back out."

"No," she peered over her shoulder, shrouding her self-pity with a scowl, "there must be a way to relinquish my place in the running." Anna pulled her hood over. It felt like a shield against the soldiers' amusement. "I can't win Lampara's favor alone. No one wishes for a broken prim-noire to govern them."

"We need one who won't drain the coffers faster than they're filled. By my guess, you're wanting answers more than anything."

Anna nodded. Her grandfather had to know how to end her struggle before it gained strength. With such a secret kept from her combined with Williamton's suffering, the desperation in her heart was unbearable. *He must answer to the town too,* she thought. *His decision cost them greatly.*

"I thank you again for sparing my life," said Anna. "If you wish redemption, confess your guilt to Simdorn. Turn yourself into someone not aligned with the prime's sons."

Lord Barden's face darkened for a moment as he untied Roland's reins from a tree.

"Those folks will be hard to find. But," he spat, giving her a worried look, "you're right. At least allow Roland the honor of helping you across the divide."

Anna shook her head, tempted by the offer, wanting to ride so rare a beast. Deep down she hadn't forgiven his lordship enough to be swayed by the opportunity. The black storm bison gave a disgruntled huff, sending crackles of lightning clouds from his nostrils. Anna made her way to the clearing's center. She took off at a sprint. Twigs crunched and grass squashed under her footsteps. She leapt, keeping her eye straight as she waved her arms.

Her boots found purchase, thudding against the soggy mud. She staggered for a second but kept her feet going. She turned back to the tree line, to the faint flicker of the soldiers' fire. Relief poured down her chest to be free of their rudeness. She had experienced nothing like it before. They had been less than willing to spare a horse for her to cross the divide earlier. Anna pushed through the under-growth to find Cole dozing, heavy-eyed. A large puddle stretched out from his nostrils. He rose at the sound of her footsteps, bleating as she stroked his back. Emerging from the woods, Roland followed his master out into the clearing.

"I want to redeem myself with you, Lady Anna," said Lord Barden. "I know a way to fix those burns of yours."

Anna mounted Cole and sat up straight. The moonlight gifted a softness to his lordship's green eyes.

"I have tried physicians."

"No," he chuckled. "Those quacks are useless. I'm talking about a wizard."

Anna grimaced, picturing an old face of mist, glowing eyes, and black robes containing secrets.

"Grandfather says wizards always take more than they give."

Lord Barden scoffed, pulling at his auburn chin whiskers.

"Why bother trusting what he says?"

"I have no way to find one," she said, contemplating it until finally understanding where he was leading her. "And I am uncertain whether I can trust you either. Despite your offer to mend things, my wish to stay away from Lamparien affairs remains unchanged."

With a snap of leather, Cole turned about at great speed, sending them both deep into the dark woods. Anna peered over her shoulder to the lord and his missing sleeve. A stiff breeze tugged at her hood. The lord rubbed his bare arm against the breeze's chill. She shivered as he did, sympathy tugging at her heart. To accept his offer was more tempting than anything in the world. Temptation, though, was one of many sins Simdorn frowned upon.

It wasn't just her grandfather who had warned her about wizards. Townsfolk older than even Lord William himself spoke of how wizards played on your wants. That no coin was demanded with their services, but if your words were not measured, a great price would come of it. A price outmatching the worth of a man's conscience.

Anna secured her bow and quiver, ducking low under a

collection of branches. As she eased into Cole's gait, she thought back on her actions. She saw blood run from the bodies of those she had killed. Every emotion sank to the depths of her stomach to find she had brought these men down. She hoped to avoid killing, even when in the presence of Lord Barden for the first time. There were arrows in the sword master's quarters, should more men be sent to kill her. But if her grandfather repaired his wrongdoing, more killing wouldn't come to pass. Snapping Cole's reins, he turned his head and bleated. Anna patted his side and rubbed until he accepted her apology. She wanted to trust in Lord Barden's regret, yet an eagerness for a possible change of mind plagued her thoughts. The eagerness clawed like the bear once on her heels a year back. Its immense paws had almost left her back a bloody mess if not for Cole catching wind of her screams.

"I'll see you have a rest, Cole," she said, bending low, whispering in his ear, "before I confront grandfather."

She envisioned what to say to him. Wondering now with his secretiveness had her grandfather lied about her parents. Lord William once told her they had died fleeing a band of robbers when Anna was a babe. That some young milkmaid who found Anna shortly after her parents were murdered. After seven years, when her grandfather became lord over Williamton, the truth became not of two robbed innocents, but of casualties in a battle too brief for history to record. *Can I trust him anymore?* she sighed.

Anna came to the river she had rested beside hours previously. She slid down from Cole's back and led him to drink. Pulling off her gloves, she splashed water on her face. Cole's deluge ceased while he drank; a faint mist glided across the water as he lapped and gulped. The water sent a chill up her arms and into her chest. It reminded Anna of the coming winter, her favorite phase of the year, when game was easiest to track. Running her hands down her face, the cool water didn't soothe. *The battle was probably a lie.* Anna bound her hands into fists, dropped to her knees and brooded, sinking into the depths of her hood. However many miles remained until home, her grandfather owed her more than a removal from politics.

Rising, dirt clung to her knees as she watched water slosh from Cole's lapping. Lord Barden's wish to make amends dwelled in her mind's eye. *His intentions are noble, but I still do not trust him.* Pulling her gloves on, she felt water trickle over the tight sleeves of her leathers. They clung to her arms like a shiny layer of skin. Anna took Cole's reins, leading him into the river, its waters halting at her hips. Rain tapped at the river's surface, urging her to move faster. It made Anna fear the coming chill before illness of throat and nose. Water sloshed and splashed against Cole's shoulders as they waded to the southern shore. The sky thundered before they reached solid ground. Down the river, many of the stars disappeared behind the clouds, leaving the moon alone in the night.

"Stop!" A deep voice roared. "Stop, in the name of Prime Luther."

Anna turned to find the eleven who remained of Lord Barden's men. Swords hissed from their scabbards as every man lined the shore. The thick-eyebrowed soldier unfastened his mouth shield. He sneered through yellowed teeth.

"What have you done with Lord Barden?" said Anna, urging Cole until they made it to shore. "He gave direct orders to stand down, and leave me—"

"We don't listen to traitors, girl." He snapped his mouth shield closed with a *click*. "After her, men."

Anna climbed onto Cole, cursing herself for unstringing her bow. It was wedged in its place across her saddlebags. Dirt kicked up, roots snapped, and the ground disappeared beneath her. Nimbuses rose in great sprints from Cole's nostrils, blanketing the earth behind them. Heavy rain filled the air until the trudging from the river fell mute. Shouts reached her ears, scrapping like a knife at her nerves.

Faint flames dotted the tree line, growing distant behind her. The old storm bison panted heavily, slowing, but pressing onward. Anna half wished to hide them both, but only trees and thickets provided any source of cover. She gasped. A hand clamped down on her arm. A torch flooded her vision with heat and light. Piercing eyes under a sharp helmet shattered the brightness. Her friend bleated and roared as another soldier seized him by one of his horns.

Anna yanked and punched, shaking her hand from striking the man's breastplate. He chuckled, then cried out, dropping his torch, and clawing at his face. Her fingers released the arrow's thin shaft. She spun, snatched the falling torch, and struck the other soldier. He released Cole as embers scattered and poured into his eyes. Anna grabbed and flicked her friend's reins. The remaining soldiers gathered speed, plowing through thickets.

Nine soldiers remained to plague her, waving their swords, cutting through raindrops. Their torches struggled against the wet onslaught. Light weaved through legions of trees until Anna found the steep hills leading home. Beyond them, her heart leapt to see Williamton again, lit by flames not bent on destruction. She searched for the trail, grinned, then steered Cole toward it. Rocks gave way, the trail wide enough to hold them, but slick and runny from the thick rainfall. Anna pulled Cole's reins, urging the immense storm bison to hug the steep bramble hillside. Trees reached overhead, curving like a set of ribs.

"Stop." the thick-eyebrowed soldier called. "You are marked for execution."

Anna rummaged through a saddlebag. She drew out her knife and hurled it. It scraped a soldier's helmet and then skipped into the rough. She kept forward, every breath a struggle, the trees were beginning to spin. Cole stumbled over a root, regained his balance, and huffed in exhaustion. Anna pressed her boot into his side, but her oldest and only friend was spent. Seizing every ounce of pride, she slowed them before reaching flatter terrain.

"You made the right choice, my lady." Removing his mouth shield, the thick-eyebrowed man dismounted with sword in hand. "Now get off that beast."

Cole tugged at his reins, snorted, and charged, but Anna slipped off him. The storm bison huffed, maneuvering his great mass like a shield, her bow within reach and quiver dangling.

"Move your beast, woman," one man called. "Or we'll cut him down."

"Please leave him be," she said, shielding Cole with herself. "He only wishes to protect me."

Her head rang with pain as if being struck. Every noise was enhanced from the strain of the soldiers pressing in. Anna clenched her teeth and eyed her bow, the men growing ever closer. This could not be her end, death on the run. She wanted it to be at an old age, when life no longer granted her strength to hunt. A time when she could walk amongst the trees and truly listen to their sound with no time for worrying. By then her grandfather would be long gone, and though her trust in him had been corrupted, a care for him remained ingrained within her soul.

Lightning struck so close she covered her ears. Screams rang out. She peered past the startled men and gasped. Two lay charred and splayed across the ground, their arms and swords aglow. Some men ran to their side, crying their names while horses dashed for the woods. Another crack went off, throwing several men from their mounts. They rose in time with a third strike, and then a fourth came but closer this time. Anna placed herself between her pursuers and Cole. Those who remained made a mad dash for her but stopped short at the thunder of hooves.

"Leave her be you gits," Lord Barden exploded from the woods. He thrusted and jabbed, yanking free his sword from a man's throat. "I won't allow harm to her."

Roland rammed into a soldier, forcing the man's sword free, summoning a scream and crunch as the black storm bison trampled him. The other soldiers charged but backed off as the bison blew thunderclouds from his nostrils. Anna swallowed her fears, removed, and strung her bow. She drew and aimed at the thick-eyebrowed soldier. He made for the hill's steep side, clawing at exposed roots.

"That one's yours, my lady," said Lord Barden, cutting a swathe across a man's throat.

The arrow flew, shattering raindrops, ignoring wind, striking the soldier in his back.

"Thank you, my lord," said Anna. "I owe you twice for saving my life."

"You owe me nothing," he said, flicking blood from his blade. "I'm the one in debt to you. And I know where we've got to go to repay it."

"And where shall you find a wizard?"

She slung the bow across her back and mounted Cole. She heard the lord swallow. It was as if he were afraid, but when their eyes met, he showed only courage.

"South to the mountains where they've been banished."

T he rain stopped tapping against her hood, cool
droplets clung to its fringe. Roland's lightning had
diminished from the sky. Howling winds replaced
them, which was a noise Anna welcomed over all others.
His lordship's last words robbed her of her own. A stretch of
bushes and narrow tree trunks kept Williamton's northern
gate at a distance. It was closed, and men paced back and
forth within its towers. She was thankful for the darkness.
It kept the outlaw lord hidden. Anna swallowed her
nervousness, the words finally coming to her.

"You didn't command the dragon to attack me," she
said, tugging her hood point at a stiff breeze. "I was foolish.
Foolish enough to seek the approval of a few lord's sons."

Her mood grew dark from the memory. She held still to
avoid the compulsion to shudder from it. Lord Barden bit
his lip and spat, stroking his beard while holding strong to
his silence.

"I was desperate for coin. I needed to sell it quickly," he
said. "Had I not, the Wayne family would have smeared my

father's name. They'd say the Bardens were bad for business. I guess I did the smearing, burning a town and all."

She clasped his shoulder. The storm bison beneath them were in a conversation of their own, bleating and snorting nearly in sync. Anna relaxed her shoulders, releasing a pent-up breath. She found her anger toward the lord slowly melting. *He should turn himself in.* The moonlight passed over the wrinkles of his face, revealing the slouch in his posture. She shook her head, deciding something she hoped not to regret.

"Your guilt warms my heart, my lord," she said, firming her grip on his shoulder. "I shall ask my grandfather to pardon you."

Lord Barden looked up at her, rubbing sweat from his brow and cheeks.

"Good luck," he snorted. "We didn't quite get along last I saw him."

"He is a man for whom the law is second to Simdorn," said Anna. "Will you be okay while I am gone?"

Lord Barden chuckled, hugging his stomach as if what she said were a joke.

"I ride a living lightning storm. Remember?"

Anna failed to find humor in his words, realizing the meaning behind them a moment later. Roland, though gentle toward her and his master, possessed great potential for destruction. She smiled back at his lordship to make it appear as if she understood. Pressing her heel into Cole's side, she headed for Williamton. The darkness disguised its lingering smoke, but the smell remained. Once within earshot of the towers, a guard leaned over and gaped.

"She's back!" he called over to the other tower. "Lady Anna has returned!"

"Open the gate," said the other guard, calling over his

shoulder. "Your lord grandfather will be pleased you're back, my lady."

Rumbling ran down the gate's surface, rattling its names of metal. They eased back foot by foot, the gap forming wide enough for them to pass through. She gave the reins a slight jerk. Their pace hastened as she firmed her grip. The rein's leather whined, but doing this fought the building worry. The smithy's shop was like a gaping black wound. *How will he recover from...?* At the edge of the shop's ruin, amongst all the fallen timbers, the smithy's anvil lay on its side. She found a small sense of hope. Anna smiled knowing someone could start again.

As she drew closer to home, lantern light flickered on windowsills. The lights marked houses fortunate enough to survive Barden's attack. She peered up at her home ahead. It was made of evenly cut granite blocks like those holding strong Lampara's capital. Thick oaks stripped of bark and branches formed the roofing of different sections. Calm took her in its arms to be home again. Banners hung from every window, presenting her family's crest. The lowest window belonged to the study. Light faintly streamed through its diamond windowpanes. Anna dismounted and led Cole onto the grounds of the house.

With a three-finger salute to their dome helmets, her grandfather's guards opened the gate. Ahead, torches graced the stable entrance. The doors were open, with straw crossing under the entryway. And as she entered it crunched and hissed under her boots. She unsaddled Cole. She realized that, had Lord William made known their conversation, a prepared stable was unlikely. Anna watched her friend settle into his stall. She closed its door, thankful she'd kept her promise to him.

———————

TENSION RAN up into her chest with each minute she gathered what to say. Light crept from under the study door. Anna raised her fist and brought it close to the door, its oak, old and knotted in places. Her grandfather had to know how to pull her out of campaigning. Although she wondered if he could stomach the embarrassment of doing it. Withdrawing was not unheard of for Lampariens wanting to govern. Anna bit her lip, daring to believe Lord Barden was wrong, that it wasn't too late. She hoped to bring up the subject of pardoning him, and that the result wouldn't lead to his banishment. Anna clenched her teeth, the burns on her face tensed. She knocked.

"Enter."

Anna eased the door open, prolonging the moment, loosening the tension in her... She gasped, slamming shut her lips. Her kill's antlers rested on the mantelpiece, polished, illuminated by the fire below, twelve points in all. On the small table beside her grandfather's chair, a plate was slick with grease. In its center, like an island, was a small piece of meat. Anna spun to face the bookshelves, every breath fleeing from her lips. Her grandfather peered over his shoulder, smiled, and slid a book back in its place.

"My obvious guess is you were successful," he said, strolling toward her. He embraced her as if she had been gone a month. "I'm glad you are safe." He kissed her brow. "I have decided with our town's recent tragedy to no longer push my interests on you. I shall instead embrace yours," he smiled, parting for his chair. "Seems much more productive."

"But." Dryness enveloped her throat with his willingness for change. "What of the prime's sons? What about another attack? More of the prime's men may come for me."

Lord William sat weaving his fingers together, pressing his brow to his knuckles.

"I must confess something to you, sweet girl. I——"

"You entered my name in the final calling," said Anna, the anger too strong to contain any longer. "You risked everyone's life over a responsibility I possessed no desire to take on."

"How was I to guess Prime Luther would risk breaking campaign law?" he said, raising an eyebrow. "And how do you know I entered your name?"

He rose, leaning against the mantelpiece. The firelight splashed over the whiskers on his stiffened chin. His cloak puddled on the floor.

"I was successful. Enough so that Prime Luther will not know that I draw breath." Anna yanked down her hood, pointing to her face. "And I shall say this one last time. No one wants to look upon their primnoire and not see beauty. I am not strong enough to govern anyone. We must find a way to withdraw——"

"You were strong enough to take on nearly twenty men." Lord William pointed to her bow, strung across her chest. "And those men cared more for avoiding death than for the face of who was bringing it. I'm glad you left no one alive. But I know of no way to withdraw your name."

"I did ... leave one man alive," Anna sighed. "I ask you to deliver justice upon him instead of what Prime Luther may do for his failure."

"And who is this man? Where is he?" Lord William snapped. "How do you know he hasn't already sent word for reinforcements?"

Anna turned away from him to a shelf packed with

scrolls. *I had not thought of... No, he wouldn't.* Her breath blasted from her nostrils like an enraged storm bison. Lord Barden saved her life and twice for that matter. Anna saw no reason for betrayal in him, yet she was never the best at reading people. She shook her head, remembering the lord's offer, his wish to mend the burns upon her face. Telling her grandfather this may alter the twist of disappointment in his eyes.

"His name is Lord Barden," she said, facing her grandfather. "He is the one who sold me—"

"I know who he is," Lord William roared. "He is the reason I cannot convince you to campaign" He took her hands into his own. He held them firmly, releasing the deepest of sighs. "I knew I could not trust him."

"What...? What do you mean, Grandfather?"

"He didn't tell you." Lord William withdrew from her, eyeing the fire's glow. Her fears compounded with his silence. "Lord Barden came to our town with the intention you already know." He shuddered. "But I offered him coin to spare you, and to remember what happened with the dragon. And most importantly, I asked him to help me bring you to your senses."

Her heart was in freefall, remembering the pouch at her hip. Its contents swayed Lord Barden to arson, yet why use such an extreme. Anna felt her knees buckle. Two thousand lived within the walls of Williamton, and her grandfather was prepared to risk them all for a world she knew wouldn't accept her.

"You're both mad. You won't help me," she said, wiping her eye of tears. "You love me but will not help me. You'd risk innocent lives so I may do what? The farthest I travel daily is to the borders of your lands. It has been five years since I saw the capital."

Lord William dropped his chin. His neck bulged from his stiff high collar. The hunting leathers he wore were worn and brown. Its gauntlets covered the tops of his hands in an arrowhead shape, embroidered with the family crest. He buried himself within the depths of his cloak. His heavy brow sank, smoothing the wrinkles above.

"There is much at stake. You were my only chance of stopping what's coming," he said, swallowing and looking her straight in the eye. "I cannot govern a third time by law. You were Lampara's last hope, and I could not convince you. You may stay the night, but before sunrise I best not see you in this house."

Anna backed away, bumping against the open door. She clasped a hand over her lips as her mind ran through a thicket of thoughts. His words cut deeper than thorns in a briar patch. Lampara was foreign to her besides what woods had become like a second home. Even with Lord Barden's wish to make amends, it was apparent why she still needed to be angry with him. And yet he possessed enough regret to make her feel as if he were her only ally.

"I will be off to bed." She eyed the antlers, the lone piece of meat on its plate. "I would beg you to use what influence you possess... But I guess I will have to withdraw myself, since I am no longer a part of this family."

"You most certainly are not." Lord William sneered. "You have thrown all I have given you—"

She slammed the door, cutting short his words. Marching to her chambers, Anna cared not to hear another word from him again. Lord William had put her in an obligated position, and with it, set all she knew ablaze. She dashed up a set of spiraling stairs, meeting a long hall lined with braziers and littered with rushes. The rushes' scent tormented her senses, and the more she dwelled on his words, the worse the smell became. The rushes crunched underfoot. She made it to the hall's end and flung open her door.

On her bed lay two quivers crafted from fine black leather. They were filled, to her surprise, with arrows containing fletching from red goose feathers. She reached out, stretching and bending her fingers. Her anger for her grandfather sent tremors through her hand. The fletching was soft and smooth, closely trimmed to pierce the wind. She removed an arrow, laid it against her bow and drew. The balance was unquestionable, like no arrow was present, and the fletching kissed her cheek. Returning the arrow, Anna reasserted herself in the present. A final answer was needed, and she reasoned before dawn's light to have it.

EMILY PASSED her at the crest of the steps, nodding, putting broom to stone to remove old rushes. "I wish you'd listen to me like you did as a child, my lady," said Emily. "Your grandfather is a reasonable man."

Anna peered beyond the darkness of her hood.

"If he were reasonable, then Williamton would not be in ruin."

The chambermaid rested her hand on Anna's, giving it a light squeeze. Within the pit of her stomach, Anna felt as though her grandfather had changed. Why send her away for not sharing his concerns? He had taught her all she knew, so why had he not given her lessons in governing? Anna possessed no idea how to improve the life of another.

"Grandfather is too eager to change what he believes is wrong," she mumbled, withdrawing her hand. "I know I can fight if needed, but if more is required of me, I'm... I'm no leader."

Emily nodded, pressing broom to stone.

"Good luck, Anna."

Anna took each step two at a time. A pang of guilt pained her chest to see Emily sad. She meandered to the study, knowing that, being the week's sixth day where her grandfather was going to be there. Easing the door open, he sat slumped in his chair asleep. The hunting leathers on his person were like a crinkled leaf. To wake him to say her goodbyes would have been proper. A good enough reason to ease the ache of her heart, but her anger thundered too loudly. She rested the pouch on the mantel between her kill's antlers. The deer possessed a swiftness Cole could barely match.

The arrows in both quivers rattled. She paused before the door. Anna peered over her shoulder to see if it had broken the rhythmic pattern of Lord William's snoring. He shifted slightly, crossing his feet. The heels of his boots dug into the old bear rug. A tear readied itself in her eye. Deep within her grandfather's aged bones was a man with good intentions. But somehow such good intentions found a misguided reason. She pressed her hand to the boiled leather of her fresh hunting garb and whispered a brief prayer for his good health to Simdorn.

Out across the grounds, Cole's barn sat, its torches were nearly spent. Beyond it was a towering pinecone-shaped aviary that housed her grandfather's esant. It had a cage-like structure crowning its summit. The servants had tried housing it with chickens and geese, but they were eaten before midday. She opened the barn doors and breathed in the smell of wet straw. It smoothed her senses. She applied Cole's saddle and stroked his furry head. He licked her hand. His eyes captured her reflection, soft and heavy-browed. It was as if he knew this was a time for change. She mounted him after securing her quivers to his saddle horn. Their arrows were like flames erupting from his back. The butts of both quivers hung close to his shoulders.

Along her way, stable boys, the smithy, and her grand-father's personal guard gathered with lit lanterns like an ensemble of lightning bugs. Anna cast her gaze up to Lord William's balcony, finding its doors closed. She unbuttoned the high collar of her tunic, exhaling. It felt as if the next few steps taken would be the hardest. She had Cole by her side, and he'd followed her wherever. Except this time there was no certainty of where they might end up.

"Lady Anna."

Anna turned to the servant's quarters. Emily held thickly folded furs close to her chest, taking off at a sprint, her skirt hem tucked into a sleeve. The guards eased the gate open to the vacant alley beyond. They buried their chins against their chests, one wiped a tear from his cheek. Emily made it to her side, panting, raising what wasn't more furs, but a long black cloak. It matched the leather of Anna's hunting garb. She had promised not to wear another cloak after fire had claimed her green one. She hesitated before slowly accepting Emily's gift. The old chambermaid folded her hands and bowed.

"Wherever you may go," Emily said, meeting Anna's gaze, "winter will follow soon."

The cloak was lined with nelka fur found only in Lampara's mountain-covered south. Rutoe tradesmen bred and worshiped the immense feline after banishment to the south. They halted the trade of its fur, slowing the near extinction of the red and green streaked beast. Anna bit her lip and unfolded the cloak. It was heavier than her old one of silk and bearskins. *If anyone but Emily had given it to me...*, she swallowed the lump forming in her throat, wiping a tear from her cheek, *keeping my promise would have been easier.* Emily bowed, brushing back her long, graying brown hair. As the gate fully opened, the air grew cold. Before Cole's silver hooked horns pierced through to the alley, the guards bowed their heads. She turned back to everyone. Their faces shone brightly in the light of their lanterns.

"I cannot promise a return," she said. Her voice grew soft and clear. It drew out comfort from what she could see, yet she was unable to feel it herself. "But I put all of you in danger the longer I remain here."

There was silence among them all, even Emily, who leaned on her husband's shoulder. The smithy held Emily close as she smiled a small smile. Anna flicked Cole's reins, filling the gate with his swirling clouds. Their rains overwhelmed the fresh morning dew. Anna swung the cloak over her shoulders. To bid them all farewell pained her too much. She shut her eye and whispered a prayer Emily had taught her long ago.

"Whether parted or together," she said. The gates whined and clattered shut. "By war or treacherous storms, every deed and smile from you has been sewn into my heart. May Simdorn send her pale bears to guide your remaining days' steps, and may the moon for which the goddess governs from never allow you to travel in darkness."

After passing through several neighborhoods along the town's main road, the north gate was in sight. Fresh guards climbed ladders leading up to either guard tower. The sky was growing lighter. Crisp, cool wind raced over the street, summoning creaks from shutters and hanging signs. She drew the cloak close about her shoulders, deciding to be firm with her fear. *I will tread with care next time,* she thought as footsteps came from far to her left. Anna gave Cole's reins a jerk. She didn't want to say goodbye to another person she cared for.

"Lady Anna."

Her heart stopped. Every finger strained until she found herself bringing them both to a stop.

"Norman," she whispered.

He was bundled in a coat matching the leather of his doublet from yesterday. She had checked if any more scrolls in Cole's saddlebags. *There were none left.* Norman stroked Cole's head. The storm bison rubbed his wet nose against the accountant's cheek.

"Did you forget a scroll, Norman?"

"Oh, no, my lady," he said, smiling. "I received word you were back from my father when he returned home. I thought you might be parting for one of your early hunts. I wanted to speak with you about a matter."

Anna gulped. "I'm keeping to what I said yesterday."

"I understand." His face grew dark despite the growing light of morning. She worried that her grandfather might have changed his mind. Had he decided to do far worse than banish her? She smiled, realizing Norman wouldn't be sent for such things. "I saw something that no one was meant to witness."

"And what was it you saw?"

"I had been at your home, He rubbed his hands together, then stuffed them behind his back, "balancing Lord William's accounts whilst you were gone. His lordship and a man with thick chin whiskers entered the study."

Anna fixed her gaze on the north gate. Its doors were shut; both guards had finished their climb and were conversing with their comrades. A shudder ran through her as her guesses about what he might say next compounded.

"I was asked to leave." Norman continued, sucking in a nervous breath. "Before I had taken my leave, I remembered I had forgotten to give my report. The study door was open slightly when I returned. There were whispers of your name being—"

"Grandfather entered my name in the final calling." Anna interrupted. "And he asked the man you speak of to set Williamton ablaze. He used his black storm bison to do it."

Norman raised an eyebrow, tilting his head.

"Whoever the man was he must have confessed before you killed him. Your grandfather did ask the man to burn Williamton. He was given coin, and some bottled substance. I believe it aided in creating the lightning."

Anna nodded. Her heart quickened as she folded her hand into a fist. Norman's words would have held more useful had he said them yesterday. She knew of the bribe, but again, if Barden regretted his past deed, then why not just leave? *His regret is a lie.*

"Why did you not tell me this before, Norman?"

Norman turned away from her, tucking his chin against his chest.

"I was discovered before the man took on the task." His breath caught in his throat as he met her eye again. "I was forced to remain silent, or see my father killed. I ... know I should have stayed out of business not my own."

Anna explained what she had learned since leaving yesterday, adding that whatever danger remained for his father, Samuel, that Norman's secret was safe. With a shudder down her chest, she cleared her throat and finished with her grandfather telling her to leave town.

"I go now to the capital to remove myself from campaigning."

"But Lady Anna," Norman gasped, "the rules have changed on withdrawals."

"What are they?"

A chill ran down her spine as the wind failed to carry her heavy cloak. Norman rubbed his hands together before summoning up his words.

"Word came by cheefox months previous of public shaming deemed too childish for those wishing to withdraw." Norman's lips trembled as he rubbed his fingers more. He drew in a breath finally and stiffened his chin, though his eyes were downcast. "Anyone who withdrawals, peasant or noble, must fight in the arena and win. If you lose, campaigning is your best choice, and should you refuse, you face..."

"Norman," Anna cried. "Please tell me what will happen."

"You face execution for cowardice."

CHAPTER
SEVEN

E very feeling went numb after Norman's last words. Anna swung her leg over Cole's back and slid until her boots thudded against dirt. Any strength she possessed before had abandoned her; every muscle gave way, dropping her to her knees. The dirt coated her fingers as she clenched them into fists. Norman knelt beside her, every word from his lips mute to her ears. She blamed herself for ignoring so many of Lord William's rants. Anna seethed at what she decided wasn't her concern. What else was different about the country so many wished to govern?

"I have two choices, Norman," she said, licking her lips, tasting sweat. "I must take on what I feel is impossible or fight to free myself from it."

His hand rested on her shoulder. Voices rose from distant houses as her senses buzzed so loud that her head hurt.

"I believe in you, my lady." He gave her shoulder a squeeze. "I know your choice will return your life to what it was. Let me go with you, and see it done."

She scoffed. Success would grant her freedom from her rising. Anna rose and pulled down her hood.

"You know I have no life to go back to," she said, mounting Cole. Norman's eyes dimmed at her words. "I will go and fight because I am able. I've heard of someone who is campaigning. This man has skill with a bow. He might be able to do what I cannot."

"Who, Lady Anna?"

"I don't know," she said, "but there is someone I know who does."

LORD BARDEN WAS NOT where she had left him. Once they were well beyond the gate, and through a series of bushes and brambles, the outlaw lord emerged. He held the reins of a horse belonging to one of his men. The Lamparian governing crest emblazoned upon its saddle's center, faded, and worn in the leather. Snow fell in slow, heavy flakes, their cold bringing no calm to Anna's frustration. She turned over in her mind what she had learned. Piecing each part together bristled with her growing curiosity. Norman dropped his hands from her waist and slid off Cole.

"Why does this man still live, Lady Anna?" he snapped.

"Oh, bother," said Lord Barden. "What's the pretty boy doing here?"

"He's my friend, my lord." Anna rode up close to Lord Barden. The cut on his arm showed slow signs of healing. "He spared me, Norman." She gave the accountant an assuring nod. Her senses went into a fit once focused again on Lord Barden. "I must still know why you set Williamton ablaze. You knew who I was beforehand. What made my grandfather's coin worth such suffering?"

"You can stop calling me lord," Barden said, slipping a tiny vial from a pouch on his belt. "Urine of a lady storm bison." Barden handed it to her. "My house name is Barden, but I feel my birth name, Nathan, is what I deserve now." Nathan glanced at the morning sky. He sighed. "I do regret my recent misdeeds. Can you find your way to forgive a blockhead like me?"

Every muscle in Anna's face tightened with anger. It felt as though someone wearing an iron glove had punched her in the stomach. She had been taught since fifteen by Simdorn's priests about the power of forgiveness. The difference came when laws were broken, but deep down she couldn't fight her pity for him. She turned to Norman. Someone she knew to be the wisest man in her life.

"I'm lost, Norman. I'm uncertain what I must do." Anna pressed a hand against her head, raking her hair for answers. "You were caught overhearing what wasn't for you to know. What made Nathan burn our town? Why did he take my grandfather's money?"

"It doesn't matter now, my lady." Norman stammered. "The town is safe, and you can—"

"Answer me!" Anna said. "You must know."

Anna brought Cole around. The storm bison sensed her frustration and charged. She pulled tight on his reins, churning up grass and mud. Her friend released a wall of rain clouds from his nostrils before coming to a halt. As the clouds and hammering raindrops cleared, the accountant stood shaking and rooted to the spot. Norman pressed his hands together, eyes wide, and teeth chattering.

"His lordship ... took your grandfather's coin because," he said, "I'm not permitted within Lamparien borders. Lord William bribed him not to report my existence." Norman pointed at Nathan. "He used the storm bison urine to bring down the lightning. He did not do so for the reason you know, but to show that his mission had succeeded."

"That is mad logic," Anna said, sneering at Nathan. "And what warrants Norman not being permitted to live where he was born?"

"He ain't what he seems, m'lady," said Nathan, pointing. "That copper counter ain't even human. Look."

Anna spun to find that Norman's face was green. He had high cheekbones and a well-defined jawline. His ears were pointed, like thorns at the tops and lobes. His hair flowed down to his shoulders, shimmering black like her own. Norman's skin phased to a darker green as he meshed his lips together. He backed away slowly from Cole's huffing fury. The accountant's lips parted to reveal teeth sharpened to intricate points.

"I can no longer hide." Norman met her eye, raising a hand. Flames formed over it in a flash. "I am a rutoe of the ignited clan. We are gifted with fire, and by my speech, I did long ago live like any other Lamparien."

"Do you go by a name other than Norman?" said Anna.

Anna clenched her teeth. She patted the bison's hump, whispered calming in words, but Cole growled at Norman's flames. The rutoe maneuvered his fingers as snowflakes vanished within their retreating flames. She was unsure if he shook from nervousness or the growing cold of the morning.

"Norman is far easier to pronounce than the name I chose for myself." Norman focused on his feet for a moment. Anna let the tension ease from her jaw, finding his honesty refreshing. "I am thankful you came when you did. Cole's storms were Williamton's best—"

"Let's go, Norman."

Anna urged Cole up beside him, finding the storm bison

had sensed her rising trust. Norman mounted Cole, grunting from the saddle's narrow seat. Anna felt a deep warmth in his hands once they rested on her hips. Her heart danced in her chest for a moment to have him so close.

"Lady Anna, please!" Nathan cried. "I want to redeem m'self."

The fur around her collar brushed softly against her nose as she craned her neck toward him.

"You would have been of greater help had you refused to pursue me."

Nathan Barden glared at Anna for a moment, spat, and then covered himself in a cloak from Roland's saddlebags. He pressed his heel into Roland's side.

"You even know the way to Cillnar?" said Nathan, catching up to her. He thrust his hood over his head. "I can at least be a guide. I'll leave you be after that."

Anna pulled her hood tight to her cheeks against the blasted bitter wind. The cold usually soothed her, but this time it reddened her skin and forced a shiver down her spine.

"You're right," she said. "Allow Norman the horse and whatever its saddlebags provide."

"Oh, you're kinder than your granddad says," said Nathan. "I will find you a wizard m'self once you've freed yourself from campaigning."

She drew back slowly on Cole's reins. Nathan handed the horse's over to Norman. It was growing more and more difficult to remain angry. The man was persistent, more so than anyone she had ever met. Anna pulled her cloak closer around her shoulders and led them west at a steady pace. Nathan and Norman didn't speak to one another, which allowed her to focus on recent events. One had been where he should not have, and the other she found to be mad, unpredictable, but most of all her only way to become complete.

———

It was in the shadow of a tall stone pillar that Anna's ability to lead ended. The pillar was gray, moss covered and marked with the Brighton crest. Several more pillars of the same size towered left and right at great distances. They marked the borders of her grandfather's land. Beyond Nathan Barden and the prime's soldiers, only tradesmen entered them. The outlaw lord slipped a flask from his belt and downed some of its contents before offering it to her. Anna waved it away.

"Which direction will take us swiftly to the capital?" she said.

"We can head straight as we 'ave been," he said, wiping his lips. "Or wait since we pressed on night and day."

She found herself in the web of a coming yawn. The sun was setting far east of them. Norman was on her right, in line with her blind eye. He remained still in his wrinkled wet clothes and hadn't searched his saddlebags for a cloak. Anna realized his fire ability must keep him warm.

"Can we stop for a rest, Lady Anna?" said Norman. "Cole appears to need it."

Cole had slowed before they reached the end of her grandfather's lands. With the cold growing more prominent, his rains had turned into snow. The added flakes slowed his steps and forced a weight on his breathing. Anna guessed that if he were younger, the journey, and change in his storms would have been easier to manage.

"Let's take shelter under that tree," she said, pointing to

a thick pine. "I thank you, Norman. My eagerness has pushed all of us too hard."

"You've got the right thinking," said Nathan. "Let's get some—"

"I was speaking of Cole and Norman," Anna snapped.

Anna dismounted, leading Cole to the tree. Its green leaves and long branches held the weight of snow, leaving the ground about its roots grassy. She needed Nathan's guidance for the journey, but finding complete forgiveness remained distant. Norman joined her as she wrapped Cole's reins around the tree. His face spoke of disappointment, perhaps for how harsh she was, but he had to understand.

"You did not start the fire." She whispered, watching Nathan find another tree for Roland. "I must keep control over him if I can. He might be of use later."

"You're right," said Norman, eyeing her burns. "Though I can't help feeling sorry for him. He saved me with his greed in a way. And if I'm not mistaken, you are beginning to sound like a primn—"

She shot him a fierce glance from the shade of her hood. Norman raised his hands in surrender.

"I'll get us some firewood," Nathan said, crunching snow underfoot after securing Roland's reins. "I'll be back in a snap."

Norman sat against the tree, drawing out a stone from under his bottom. Anna removed her hood, replacing it with the one from her cloak. It was as if her anger was a dark, untraveled road. Anna had not felt much anger. Frustration with her grandfather's bickering about politics. Mortification from her encounter with the dragon five years ago, but anger was something only witnessed.

"I am grateful to be here, to be of help," said Norman.

"You are angered by my assumption, but can an agreement be made concerning your use of strategy?"

Anna found no answer for him at first. Outside of his recent words churning eagerness in her heart, a reason to be authoritative was necessary. She wanted to be complete again. Nathan knew how to give that to her. It felt wrong to use him, but his guilt felt far more real than she thought.

"I can find forgiveness for Nathan," she sighed; stroking Cole's brow as tiny clouds wafted from his nostrils. "I still feel anger concerning Williamton, yet my heart tells me he is truly sorry."

"I must agree with your conclusion," said Norman, biting his lip. "Do you still intend to use him after freeing yourself from campaigning to find a wizard?"

Anna folded her arms. She sat next to him beside the tree.

"Yes," she said finally. "And I will forgive him and discard my doubts."

Norman nodded. "I must beg forgiveness then. Despite taking coin to keep silent, I find his willingness to send me south offensive."

"I understand." She rested a hand upon his own. "How did Grandfather know you were a rutoe?"

"He is the only lord who provides work for them."

Anna leaned against the tree; sweat trickled down her cheeks from the cloak's warmth.

"I'm satisfied then," she said, finding his heat was the source of her sweating. "What must I know before we reach the capital?"

Norman let out a breath, meeting her gaze. He explained what was required to remove oneself from campaigning. A duel with everyone no longer willing to seek the role of leadership like herself. Anna gulped, refusing to guess the number of Lamparians who entered their names. Many lords and peasants were relations of previous primes, and it was a tradition for their offspring to campaign.

"You will not be fighting them to the death," Norman continued. "But if you lose, we both know campaigning is your only choice."

Anna bit her lip, studying the grass poking through the snow. She shook off the thought of execution, knowing how one proceeded.

"I mustn't lose then," she said, looking up at Norman. Anna tucked a lock of hair behind her ear. "I thank you for your knowledge." She licked her lips, hesitating where the burns began. "You were always the wisest one in our class."

Norman's cheeks went a light shade of green.

"I must be fair in telling you," he said, "when we were both only fifteen, I realized—"

She rested a hand on his lap, finding her heart in some sort of race. The snow falling around them slowed with each passing moment. Anna removed her hood, slightly hesitant, fumbling with the strange feelings swirling inside of her.

"You were always beyond all of us." Anna smiled. "Your fa... I mean, Samuel told me he wished he had enough coin to send you—"

"I consider him a father," said Norman. "He's a good man."

They both fell silent. Conversations of the past and present melted away. She could feel Norman guiding himself to within a breath of a kiss. She brought him slowly into an embrace, finding the accountant sturdier than his slender frame suggested. He pressed his lips to her own. They were smooth, unlike her cracked and chapped ones.

Snap!

Anna cocked her head left, doing so more from half-blindness than fear. Nathan emerged from the brush, poorly disguising a smirk. *He was watching us.* She ignored the burning within her chest and the flush in her cheeks. Nathan had an assortment of twigs and branches under his arm. He dropped it beside Roland, removed the mount's saddle, and placed it on a fallen tree.

"My guess is pretty boy stays, and I go?"

"This *pretty boy* never had a lord's resources for education," Norman brushed wet grass from his legs, and stood up. "And can still weave words better than you."

Nathan stormed toward Norman. Anna stepped between them as Norman puffed up his bony chest, flashing his pointed teeth.

"I need both of you for what's ahead," she said. "Stand down!"

Both man and rutoe pressed at her hands as she splayed her fingers like strands of a web. Norman nodded, backing off as the snowfall slowly stopped. She eyed Nathan, who had retreated without her noticing. Nathan snatched her hand and rested a soft, flaky heel of bread in it.

"Here! Eat up, my lady," Nathan said. "You've got a proper fight ahead."

She raised the bread to her lips, hesitant at first. She wondered if she should remain awake tonight, ripping the bread in two and handed half to Norman. He nibbled at it. His diamond-shaped eyes fixed on Nathan. They were redder than the sun's remnants weaving through the forest canopy.

"I forgive you, Nathan," Anna said. "You and Norman call a truce."

The crickets answered her first.

"Samuel once said an accountant's conflict is with numbers, not men," said Norman. "I will accept a truce."

Anna smiled. Sometimes when Norman spoke, it was like listening to scripture sent from the goddess herself.

"I've got bigger worries than some illegal like him." Nathan spat. "Get to eating, you two. We've got ourselves a month's ride before winter takes hold."

EIGHT

Rising above the thousands of homes beyond the city walls stood swirling towers supporting oval structures. Cillnar possessed clean-cut brick-work, flags whipping in the wind at intervals across its wall. It was less like the ancient city Anna remembered and more like a monument. One dedicated to Prime Luther and his primnoire. A crescent moon arch of smooth granite balanced end to end atop the heads of snarling white marble bears. The bears' front paws were raised to defend the thick black wooden doors between them. The wall encircling Cillnar held more than guard towers. Looming likenesses of both governors stood back-to-back, one in armor and the other in a flowing dress. Neither statue was carved from a plain stone, but of a crimson marble and something that couldn't be jade for there was none in Dar. The governing couple's second term was near its end, and just as Nathan had said, the country's coffers had stood no chance of remaining full.

The capital was also far larger than when Anna first saw

it at fifteen. She pulled gently up on Cole's reins. Norman and Nathan slowed until aligned with her. Neither had tried to settle their differences, keeping to a silent truce. Norman had returned to the face she knew growing up, with curly chestnut hair and eyes the color of a mountain stream. The way Norman truly looked impressed her more, like it was a form of honesty shown instead of told. There was a familiarity to it she couldn't place, an old dream that felt more like a distant memory.

"I haven't been this far west since I was a child," said Norman, his voice high, filled with joy in its pitch. "Prime Luther has been busy."

Nathan grumbled. "More like he allowed his coin-gobbling primnoire to turn the city into a circus."

"I rather like it. It was plain and crowded before," said Anna. She smiled before rediscovering what she took to be ridiculous. "The wall about it could do without the statues though."

"It's no less crowded. Them statues are why taxes you can get an apple of less than five nardans." Nathan checked his person and then surveyed their surroundings. "You'll need to surrender your weapons at the entrance."

Nathan pointed to a sign poking out of a bush. It read,

NO WEAPON MAY PASS. CONFRONTATION COMES WITH NO SHARP EDGE IN CILLNAR. VIOLATION OF SUCH A DECREE WILL BE MET WITH PUNISHMENT.

Anna returned her eye to the capital, recalling the city's layout Nathan had gone over last week. A lump formed in her throat at leaving him behind. It was necessary should Nathan be recognized and questioned about her, but that didn't remove the guilt churning in her stomach.

"Do you know what the punishment is?" Anna asked.

Nathan sighed and stroked his thick chin whiskers.

"An eye for being dim enough not to read the sign and obey."

Anna gulped, refusing to imagine what complete blindness was like. Her right eye knew darkness too well thanks to the burns over it, the skin rough and warped. She led them on, finding the snow was well over Cole's hooves. His storm clouds filled the hoof prints of previous travelers with fresh snow.

"What will you do while I am in the city? We didn't pass any taverns or hovels nearby."

Nathan took a nip from his flask and wiped his lips on his sleeveless arm.

"There's a town some miles north of 'ere called Natlendton," he said, belching. "They serve a fine brew, and nutshatcher races run from morning until midnight. Head that way when you've won."

She watched him raise an eyebrow at Norman. The former lord sent his storm bison into a gallop down a road overgrown and neglected. Anna rested a hand to her chest, finding some comfort from his confidence. They went down a slight hill until the road leveled out once more. The ground had frozen over the wagon tracks to and from the capital's distant doors.

"I don't understand that man, Lady Anna," said Norman.

"He feels guilt for his past deeds, Norman." Anna pulled her hood forward until only the tip of her chin met sunlight. "I'm uncertain of my chances, but whatever happens, I know he will be there for me."

Norman pursed his lips.

"That fills pages for itself. I don't see how someone can be both a scoundrel and a man of his word."

Anna found no answer to Norman's riddle. She was more familiar with the men of Williamton than with those of the outside world. Perhaps small-town men were easier to read than those from cities and distant lands. Anna and Norman eased to a halt within a sprint's distance of the city gates. Men in green plated armor and thick red under-clothing asked them to part with their weapons. She sighed, removing her quivers, and with reservation in her grasp, handed her bow over. It was a gift from a traveler she had met at fifteen. The traveler showed apprehension and a hint of fear when seeing her face, but both relented when Anna admired his bow. He advised her to wax the string routinely to prevent weather damage. The guard received it, running his fingers over the wood of its riser. He rested it carefully within a small shack. She smiled a small smile, finding her bow was beside another, clean and well-treated like her own.

"Does the young lad require a search, or will he surrender his weapons willingly?" said one guard.

Norman rummaged through his horse's saddlebags for weapons or whatever else could have belonged to the dead soldier. Leather flapped against the horse's flanks until his hand settled. Norman's eyes grew wide with delight as he drew out a quill, a small abacus, and several rolls of parchment.

"Just don't be poking anyone at a 'slap and stroke,' establishment." The guard chuckled at the quill's sharp copper nib. "Or keeping a tally of it."

The second guard raced to the bell beside the shack, rang it, and waited. Its dinging rattled Anna's senses. She clenched her teeth, bracing when a distant bell answered. She let out a frustrated breath as the doors slowly eased open, both far thicker than the name gates in Williamton. They rode through as the sky grew gray with clouds. Snow fell with heavier flakes, more deliberate once they were both through, placing the city under a winter siege. Cole bleated at a storm bison pulling a wagon piled high with hay. Anna was uncertain if he was more excited for the hay or seeing another of his kind.

To her right, she heard a faint growling and found a store displaying wooden cages in its windows. A cheefox lived within each, the bars leaving streaks of shade across the face of some curled up comfortably in sleep. The awake cheefoxes played a game of some kind with their fluffy spotted tails. Above hung a sign in bold letters claiming the store sold the fastest cheefoxes in western Lampara. The slender dog-like creatures with their short round ears and long narrow muzzles were large enough to carry packages of great weight. Anna felt a burst of passion in her chest, wishing she were a child again, riding one of these creatures of messages, racing through an open field with the sun at her back.

They continued down streets of cobblestone. Anna recited the directions Nathan had given under her breath, leading Norman up long stretches of storefronts. Droppings of nearly every kind dotted the streets. Some were fresh, but Anna had grown used to such smells from the woods. She heard Norman swallow his vomit and caught him draping his tunic over his nose.

They passed alleys of dirt, walled on either side by buildings with bricks too old and many to count. A man lying motionless outside a side door to a pub occupied one alley. A strong smell like that of piss drifted from him, but the odor was shadowed by decay. Anna gasped, urging Cole onward and wincing at the man's sunken face. A series of arriving and leaving rats nibbled his fingers. He was half buried in slush, shoeless, falling snow covering exposed flesh. Anna pulled both her hoods tighter over her face until she rounded a corner.

Her heart slowed its dashing beat as they passed a gathering. The people surrounded a man standing proud on a large barrel marked Wine of a Northern Vintage. The lettering was old and faded, unlike the bright smile on the man's face.

"Have you lads and ladies heard of the archer, Lord Arthur?" he bellowed with hands spread wide. "It's said he fought for our prime when the rutoe began their rebellion. Our prime and his lordship bravely fought off those monsters. They halted one of many intrusions onto our lands only a fortnight ago."

Norman halted his horse and scowled. Anna jerked him back by the collar.

"He calls my people monsters," Norman whispered.

"I'm sorry for it," said Anna, "but I don't want the crowd harming you should you act."

Both were at least ten heads back from the man on his barrel as a tale of battle sent whispers throughout the crowd. Norman glared, a faint red surfacing in his eyes, slowly dying away to blue.

"You're right." He sighed.

"His lordship is said to have released three arrows at once," said the man among the city folk. "He struck true three raging rutoe in the chest. He sent another arrow through a quiet one viciously on the heels of our prime."

"Let's go, Norman." Anna patted his shoulder. "I wish not to hear any more."

They continued until the man's words faded into the distance. Anna half hoped some tragedy might befall the archer, finding the man's tale brutal. To think in such a way was a sin against Simdorn, but for Norman's sake, she allowed herself to go against the goddess.

Noon's sun broke through the clouds after some time. A bell rang in the distance, deep and commanding. Anna exhaled slowly and ignored its chimes. She spotted an age-eaten sign directing them toward the arena. A line of carriages narrowed their way until a bridge led them over a narrow frozen moat. Anna's eye grew wide as her lips parted.

Beyond the bridge, walls were stacked one upon another. They towered a mile each, with the lowest constructed of the oldest granite blocks. Thick oak supports surrounded the arena, holding fast the next level. The ground surrounding the lowest level was sinking; cracks reached up from the dirt. From what Anna guessed, the arena was of little concern to the primnoire. Each added level possessed no polish to its stone. Poles lining its top bore torn and weathered flags. An archway held firmly by two iron supports marked the main entrance.

In an illustration Anna once saw, two pale bear statues had manned the entrance at odds with one another. They symbolized Lamparians battling for power. Above both bears, Simdorn held for the victor a medallion carved from finished oak held inside a gold full moon. She knew from her grandfather's rants this place held the Tournament of Primes. The last chance to prove worthy of governing Lampara and her people. The medallion, like the goddess, was missing.

The bears lay on their stomachs, no longer locked in combat, but their long iron claws dug deep into snow and dirt. Under them burned braziers with guards huddled around them, shivering, clutching spears to their chest. A man exited from under the left paw with the grace of a bird.

"Welcome to the Proving," the man said, casting his hand to the arena. He was bundled in white furs that looked familiar. "I'm Simon Anderson. Are you both here to fight your way out of campaigning?"

There was a hint of mint on the man's breath as it came and went in faint bursts through his smile. Black piercing talons from an esant buttoned the brown leather of his coat. Around the coat's collar, the fur puffed against his cheeks like fresh cotton. Anna's eye widened. *He wears fur from a … storm bison.* She bit her tongue.

"I'm here to do so," she said, watching her tone. "The man beside me is my companion."

Simon pressed two fingers to his chin and then rested his hand to her shoulder, widening his smile further.

"You, my lady, are just in luck. There remain only five left out of the twenty-four to fight. Those who won exemption from this year's campaigning joined the spectators. The men and women destined someday to govern Lampara have gone to earn the people's favor."

Norman rested a hand on her shoulder and whispered. "You will be fine, Anna."

He must have sensed her nervousness. So much of what she had experienced since entering Cillnar was new to her. Anna bristled at the thought of people judging her from on high, and in great numbers at that.

"Where must I prepare for my fight?"

"I'll show you," Simon said, casting his hand to a tall pair of doors half open at a distance from the guardians.

Their hinges were rusted, and the wood desperately needed sanding. "You, my lady, have evened out the remaining competition. You'll have the opportunity to fight until only two remain, and trust my words, all of them are more than desperate at this point."

What   do you—"

"Time is at its most direr now." Simon wagged a finger. "Follow me at a persistent pace if you will," he eyed Cole with a hint of interest, "and you may leave the storm bison behind."

"But Cole is my—"

"The Proving is wet enough from snow and blood. He will be fine with your companion I trust."

Anna huffed. Frozen breath bellowed from her lips like a flustered dragon. She dismounted, bringing Cole close. His clouds coated her hood with their light snow. Anna fumbled with his reins and then offered them to Norman. Cole licked her cheek, washing away her worrisome thoughts.

"Take care of him, Norman." She frowned. "He's the closest friend I have."

Norman took the reins with a look on his face she didn't understand.

"Good luck, Lady Brighton."

She crossed between the bears through snow littered with hundreds of boot prints. Anna wanted Cole to be with her like he had against Nathan's men. She thought too that she would be permitted a mount for the duels in the arena. Each step felt heavy. Soon, the darkness of the entrance hall enveloped her. Distant burning braziers kept away complete darkness, but their light was not enough to see clearly. After some time, Simon turned right down a musty hall. She drew back her hood, discovering the darkness allowed a break from hiding her face.

"Did I hear that handsome lad call you, Lady Brighton?" Simon said.

"Yes, my lord," said Anna, sucking in her breath, wiping sweat beads from her brow. "I am Lady Anna Brighton, granddaughter of Lord William Brighton."

"Fascinating!" Simon chuckled. "I'd never expect a withdrawal from a descendant of the first prime."

"I fail to understand the humor in it."

"My apologies."

Simon spun on his heels before Anna could shield her face, but then she remembered the darkness.

"I laugh, my lady," he said, "because twenty years have passed since last the Brightons showed interest in Lamparien affairs. Why retreat into silence after all this time?"

Anna sensed the humor in Simon's last words. She clenched her teeth, ready to take a step forward, yet found herself confused. How had he wounded her feelings? Never had she embraced her family's past, and until recently, only wanted to have her life remain the same. Anna made a fist, releasing her pent-up breath.

"My name was entered without my consent," she said calmly. "I've not the knowledge nor the will to govern."

Simon clicked his tongue. His boots crunched on the straw littering the brick at their feet. Anna continued to follow him. The mint on his breath grew distant with his steps.

"And yet, like the others, you possess a strong enough will to fight your way out of responsibility," said Simon. Grimness firmed his words as his pace increased. "I believe our prime made a poor choice in altering the rules for these fights."

"How so, my lord?"

"Because, my lady," Simon peered back. "Public shaming is far more deserving of those who do not care for their country."

The air was growing colder. Snow fell once more as the wind took hold of it, covering Cole's massive hump and legs, giving the old beast some of his youthful white back. The bison shook it off, groaning and huffing. Norman noticed the slowness in his movements as he did. They needed shelter with there being no certainty of when Anna might resurface from the Proving. Norman decided they'd return when morning came, knowing Anna would scour the capital. *He is her closest friend.* He sighed at her last words. Snow nipped and bit at his cheeks. He couldn't feel the cold, but Anna's devotion to Cole made Norman wish he did. He wrapped the horse and bison reins around his hand. A faint hope was all he had to mean something to her. She had spent nearly all her time with Cole since his accounting apprenticeship began. They even rode to Simdorn's temple for lessons in scripture.

He led Cole and the horse over the bridge. Their hooves clopped casually upon the bridge's stonework. Norman moved a few paces ahead. The carriages narrowed the street so much that there was barely room for them to pass through. There were no horses tied to any of them. It sank his hopes of an inn having room in their stables.

The Proving climbed higher and higher until its levels blended with the coming night. Deep within his heart, Norman hoped Anna would succeed. But from Simon's words and what he knew about the rule changes concerning withdrawal from campaigning... *Anna doesn't possess the same desperation.* There was strength in her, and bravery, and a swiftness like those of his clan in the south. He half wondered if a rutoe had trained her as a child. Lord William's willingness to give his people jobs made such a theory a possibility.

Norman shook his head, leading both mounts up the street. The shops, inns, and abandoned structures reached high enough to blot out the ever-present height of the Proving. He had said nothing of it to Anna, but upon their arrival earlier he had mistaken the arena for a mountain. Norman's thoughts drifted back to when they had reunited outside Williamton's southern gate. There was a fear behind Anna's eye, one that enhanced her misgivings concerning her being fit to govern. And yet when she found him amongst the smoke, his arms overwhelmed with scrolls, she had given swift instruction on finding safety. *She doesn't believe in herself,* he thought. *Not in the way I or her grandfather do.* He tied the horse's reins to Cole's saddle horn and led them onward.

The street was paved with cobblestones, with snow piled in places it hadn't melted. Norman chose this direction because the other possessed a series of brothels. He remembered a fine inn not far away. Cole huffed behind him. The horse was quiet in comparison, which, by Norman's guess, had been bred that way for a fight. He hoped the inn possessed a room for them both.

Reaching the inn, a sign above it that read,

RESTFUL TRAVELS

The door had a knocker shaped like a man sound asleep. He gave it three raps, and upon the third, a woman opened the door. Warmth filled his nostrils, woven with the scent of roasted duck.

"I'd like a room for the night, my lady," said Norman.

The woman was at least two heads shorter than him. And that wasn't counting her finely made brown curly wig reaching a foot high. Faint gray hairs sprouted from where her wig met her ears.

"A room for a handsome man like yourself is no problem." She pulled her flower petal collar tight to her spotty neck as a stiff breeze. The sign above swayed, setting free a piercing squeak. "Will you be in need of lodgings for the mounts as well?"

"Oh, yes."

Norman stepped aside as the woman squinted, raising a monocle ringed in gold to her left eye.

"The horse will do nicely in my stable around back," she said, letting the monocle drop from her eye. It dangled from a black thread pinned to her chest. "That rainmaker will have to be settled elsewhere."

"I must keep him where I go," said Norman. "The storm bison belongs to a … dear friend of mine."

"I see." The old woman raised her monocle back up to her eye. "You're determined to honor your friend. I honor coin. And those rainmakers cost nearly as much as an esant to house."

Norman frowned. His shoulders sank as he led the mounts away.

"I'll be on my way then," he said. "Your honesty is most appreciated."

He passed almost an entire house, its windows filled with hearth light. A crunch mixed with heavy panting chased his disappointed footsteps.

"You might give Leo's a look-see."

Norman turned back to the old woman. She held her wig firm against the wind.

"Does he feel the same about my friend's mount?" said Norman.

"Yes. And he is more vocal about such things than I am. However, I know he tends to reward those who help him." She winked.

Norman looked to the sky for a moment. The afternoon was gone from it, and the light blurred the appearing stars. Winters in Lampara hastened the night's unyielding blackness. He ran his fingers through his hair.

"I shall give him a try." Norman grinned, waving to the old woman.

It took a short time to find *Leo's*. Several of the carriages trailing toward the Proving remained, lessening his confidence, but stashed away the feeling. *I must try nonetheless.* The tavern possessed a far more spacious look at its front. Off to the right of its entrance, an orb lamp hinted at a fenced-in alley, but the space it showed was filled with the backside of horses. The tavern's sign was far larger than most and one with the establishment.

Norman eyed the subline below the owner's name. *Poke and tickle? What shall Anna think of me?* he thought, tying off Cole's reins to a ring by a window below the sign. Formed in the windows purple panes was a woman half exposed, eyeing a bearded man on a bed sporting an erection. Norman rolled his eyes and raised a clenched fist to the door. Light flickered through the small diamond panes of the window. A clopping echoed in the long empty street, doubling, tripling, in pitch. A patrol of ten men wearing polished arrowhead shape helmets and steel mouth shields thundered by. Their capes were of a fine silk, the Lamparien governing crest was stitched down it in intricate detail. Norman released a breath, allowing his fist to fall slack. It was wise not to bring Nathan. Though the man was a scoundrel, the outlaw lord was seeking what Anna called redemption. Something he never expected from anyone who thought Norman's people didn't belong.

The door creaked slightly, straw hissing and crunching under his feet. He decided to mention the storm bison instead of showing it to him. Perhaps measured words would be better. Heat washed over his face from the twin hearths. They were wide and possessed many bricks, rising like massive supports to the tavern's open beer hall. Men sat at full-moon tables; their laps kept warm by women possessing long auburn hair. The girls' flowery perfumes combined with their overuse of eye makeup made him wish to keep his distance. These women had their 'talents,' as he once heard them called. *I do not wish to know what they are.*

For himself, Norman wasn't sure what he could offer Leo concerning talents. There was too great a risk in using his clan gift to remove unruly patrons. And changing form may further heighten the city's distaste for rutoe. It pained him to admit such a thing, but the humans of Lampara had embraced the bigotry of their leader.

"What 'ill it be, young lad?"

Norman looked up to a man possessing a cleft upper lip below a full head of short curly hair. He went up to the bar, resting his hands on its aged, chipped surface.

"I need a place to stay for the night," Norman said,

swallowing back his nervousness. "I have two mounts in need of shelter."

"Well, first thing, lad," the man said. "They call me Leo. What be your name? I run a friendly business for lads and ladies alike." Leo chuckled.

"Norman Tilt," he said, noticing the sign above the dozens of bottles behind Leo. "I will require only one room. I have tied outside a horse and—"

Leo raised his hand, peering past Norman to the window.

"It hasn't been foggy in Cillnar for months." Leo folded his arms. "If you be thinking I'm gonna house a storm bison, then you best have a wagon stocked with straw."

Norman eyed him curiously, but then it dawned on him, remembering the damage Cole's rains had done to Williamton's straw. Wagon loads were soaked, and there hadn't been enough to cover the muddy alleyways. It was a shame that an act meant to minimize damage had created more.

"Is there any way I can convince you otherwise?" said Norman, stemming a rush of anger at the bottom line of the sign,

Quiet One, 2,000 nardans

Leo was using rutoe women to earn coin in a way unbecoming of his people. "I'm proficient with numbers, for my profession is accounting."

"A copper counter, eh?" said Leo, returning his focus back to Norman. "Well, if you can," he heaved a ledger large enough to crush him onto the bar. Papers protruded from its sides like the fan feathers of a turkey. "Sort this mess out, and then I might allow a storm bison this one time."

A deep, throbbing doubt swelled in Norman's chest. He fought for focus to keep from reverting to his rutoe self. Norman slid the ledger, rubbing his fingers together from something sticky. Leo licked his upper lip, cracked his knuckles and folded his arms once again. Norman slipped his hand into the deep pocket of his coat. He drew out the quill and ink bottle. *I must try. Though Anna considered Cole more a friend than me, my care for her remains.* He rested the quill on the bar, untwisting the ink lid.

"Let's get started."

"Good luck, lad." Leo grinned, slapping the bar. "I'll have my boy settle your mounts. Yell should thirst plague you."

Leo snapped his fingers as Norman opened the ledger. The door creaked open and then slammed shut. Norman removed the loose papers from between the ledger's pages. He settled on a stool topped with sheep's wool. There was a faint scent of cinnamon making its way through the heavy cigar and hearth smoke. A creak came from his right as he pored over the pages. Leo's handwriting was, to Norman's surprise, finer than the pleasure house owner's appearance let on.

Hands, long and slender, rested on the bar. They were gloved in leather, but the gloves were absent their fingertips. A familiar clattering rattle sent Norman's attention to a hooded figure. Curly blond hair streamed down the woman's chest as she drew back her hood. Norman noticed the sharpness of her green eyes, and the youth in her face placed her a few years shy of himself. As she ordered her drink, the dimness of the room made her gray leathers like a shadow upon her tall figure.

"Admiring my arrows?" she said. "Or do you think me part of Leo's talented selection?"

Norman shook his head. The archer winked at a woman sitting at the bottom of a set of stairs. The woman smiled, aiming her thumb to the rooms above. The archer raised her drink and then whispered something he faintly heard. *"Allow me to finish this first."*

"No. It's just you remind me of someone. I'll return to my task," said Norman, regaining his composure and straightening the loose pages.

The woman took a sip of her drink. A red wine with a fine bouquet by its aroma.

"Is she an archer with a good aim like me?" the woman said. "If so, I welcome her to campaign at my side so change can finally be made. Lampara sorely needs it."

There was a great need for change in what he had witnessed of late. Straw was far cheaper before his father's farmhand job was taken from him. The rutoe were seen with better eyes before Norman was brought to Williamton. And now assassination was being done on the order of someone unable to give up power.

"My friend wishes to withdraw from campaigning," he said.

"I see." The woman scoffed. Her eyes widened at the state of Leo's accounting ledger. "I suppose that is your storm bison outside. Leo was always willing to exchange a favor for a favor." She offered her hand. "I'm Emilia."

"Norman."

They shook hands before Norman drew out the last loose page from the ledger.

"May I ask what business brings you to the capital, Emilia?"

Emilia sloshed her wine in its glass, drawing in its scent.

"Tell me more about your friend," she said. "Why would she enter her name only to withdraw it?"

"She has her reasons," said Norman, resting his hands upon his lap. "And I am here to support her in what way I can."

Emilia chuckled, finishing her wine. "A man of numbers possesses a great mind too, right? Why not convince her to change her mind?"

Norman repressed a gulp, setting aside the straightened papers, plugging the cork in the ink bottle.

"She is stubborn," he said. "If I were born a quiet one, convincing her to reconsider would be easier."

"I agree." Emilia rested her glass on the bar, pulling a handkerchief from inside her sleeve and dabbing her lips. "But I hear it's painful to have a quiet one in your head."

"What do you suggest? I sense your bravery, and I know my friend has potential."

Norman began searching for where his mind was going, making marks in the ledger, and totaling where he could. He'd not intended to change Anna's mind, but Emilia was right in every regard.

"Potential is good. I'd convince her of its existence."

"You have convinced me to try," said Norman, catching sight of the waiting woman. She tapped her foot on the step. "Our conversation is making your friend impatient."

Emilia peered over her shoulder, parting her arrows to one side. She turned back with a slight smile on her thin lips. "My wife, actually. We stay at Leo's when we wish to be away from the norm of our lives."

Norman rested his quill on the ledger. He began to long for the life he had. One without a rebellion and in the company of his father. The traditions and rituals done left his mind at ease. Too much had changed for any of it to be more than a memory.

"Where I'm from, the norm is built on old ways."

"That sounds a tad boring," said Emilia, "if you don't mind me saying."

"I miss it a great deal. Work wasn't limited to certain folk as it is now."

Emilia rested a hand over his own, slipping off the stool to the hardwood floor.

"I hope to make work plentiful again. Life won't be as you see it for long."

She made her way toward the steps, receiving her wife's hand in her own. Norman admired the smiles on their faces.

"Be without worry, Norman Tilt," she said. "You won't be hated for much longer."

Norman gasped. *How? Was it the last thing I said...*

A nna discovered there were fewer people in the arena than she expected. She set foot on what Simon called the champion's platform. Others occupied parts of its lower levels, but her interest was trapped by the vastness of the Proving. A door lay below at its center, large enough to house a town. Straight ahead, what seemed like an immense spit cast a long black shadow across the door. Thick ropes hung loose at either end. The entire contraption towed high enough to align with the champion's platform.

The ropes were wet from more than snow, judging by how dark they were. Anna noticed that those who had won their way out of campaigning dotted the steep, inclining seats. The wealthiest sat in colorful pavilions set against a large portion of the seats that were chiseled into the arena. They aligned with a viewing box of white marble and pristine wood columns. Simon told her it was the primnoire's last gift to her prime before her recent death. Anna focused her attention on the dusty stonework at her feet. Her heart sank at first, but it was hard to feel sorry for the primnoire.

She saw no point in the woman's immense spending, or the finery of Simon's coat.

"My lady can wait here if she wishes," said Simon, a bit out of breath from the stairs both had climbed. "Mingle with the other unwilling, as they've been titled," his voice went to a whisper. "Although I don't recommend the one behind us."

The man's garb was unlike any she had ever seen. He wore a helmet in the shape of a full-moon that shaded his steel-blue eyes. There was a small dome at the helmet's center, making it appear snug to the man's head. His beard was close cropped and from his lips hung a thin unlit cigar. Upon his shoulders was evergreen plated armor, hammered to resemble the leaves of a spade tree. His boots possessed spurs that shone brightly in the sun. Anna's eye shot to his belt. Unlike those on the rest of the platform, there were identical knives on either hip. They contained a crescent moon where hilt met blade. Tightly bound around their hilts was leather from the hide of a pale bear. A third less ornate knife peered from his boot. Its pommel was a red orb gem.

"How is he permitted weapons, but not I my bow?" Anna hissed.

Simon motioned back to the man with his thumb, retracting it like a frightened turtle into its shell.

"Ordermen are not ones to be separated from anything sharp."

Anna glanced over her shoulder to find the man leaning against the railing. She had never seen an orderman. He crossed his arms, sighing as if he had been on the platform for some time. Simon let out a deep shuddering breath, then regained his composure. The arena rumbled. Crackling followed until the ropes below went taut. Clouds emerged slowly from the doors as they separated. Emerging through the rising, rolling nimbus was a field of grass, fenced by tall posts wrapped in a black chain-link net. Anna shuddered. Rising at once from beneath the field, a unified bleating came to her ears. *Storm bison.* By the growing sound, there must have been hundreds, all tasked with the purpose of raising the field she would fight on.

"Why make slaves of storm bison?" she said, sneering. Anna grabbed Simon by the collar. He shielded himself with his well-kept fingers and gasped.

"I don't choose what beasts keep the Proving in motion, my lady," Simon said. "If I did possess such a choice, dragons, to me, are far better suited. I believe from the burns on your lips and chin you would agree."

She released him, gripping the smooth wooden railing of the platform. Every sense was on fire as she drummed her fingertips. The storm bison tasked with raising the field were white beyond that of a cloud, their hooked horns a shining black. *They are so young.* She thought. A boom led a ring of granite around the field, quieting the bison beyond. Anna squeezed the railing tighter as if turning knuckles white might free the poor creatures.

Anna stirred restlessly as two of the unwilling made their way to the Proving's center. They were small to her eye, but the shortest one's gold armor glinted in the cascading afternoon light. The other wore armor possessing so great shine it rendered him nearly invisible once he stepped within the sunlight. The preparing duelists made her wish she had kept the nardans Nathan had given to her. Wearing only hunting leathers made her feel vulnerable. They were of better use against thorns than swords.

"You planning to win your way out of this, girl?"

Anna spun to find the man with his disk helmet staring

at her. There was a sharpness in his steel-blue eyes, like she was a target for his knives.

"Yes," Anna snapped. "I want to win and go back to my quiet life."

What life? she thought. *I've no home or coin to purchase one.*

"I doubt you've what it takes," said the orderman. "The desperate tend to fight harder than most."

He removed his helmet, revealing hair slick with sweat and black like his tunic. The stranger brushed snow off his helmet and replaced it on his head.

"I assure you I am as desperate as you and the others," said Anna, firming her tone. "I do not wish to campaign. I'm no leader."

The orderman raised a burning coal using the tip of his knife, lit his cigar, and then flicked the coal into the brazier beside him. *I did not even...* Anna blinked.

"Your focus is off balance thanks to your love for them rainmakers." The orderman drew in a long drag of his cigar, leaving it to rest between his chapped lips. "And before you go asking how desperate I am, *my lady.* I've more to lose than peace and quiet." He withdrew his cigar, appraised it, then placed it between his lips. "You see. Folks like m'self, take no pleasure in protecting someone who doesn't give two shits about his people. The boy's and I didn't want assassination on our conscience, so we played a round of 'outpace the cheefox,' and well, my horse threw a shoe."

"Why did you come here if replacing Prime Luther was your intent? Sir?"

"My name ain't your concern unless you become prim-noire," the orderman said.

Anna turned away from him, unsettled by the man's demeanor. She knew her reason for being here mattered, and that her desperation existed. A gong rang out from above, rattling her teeth with its deep thrumming. Cheers from those seated below followed. The unwilling clashed, slow in their steps somehow, every blade stroke a chore. Their sword blows echoed like a knife dropped against brick in an opposing room. Anna admired their determination, tapping her fingers on the railing.

"Duels were fought on mounts for many generations," said Simon. "Our Mistress of Duels and Debate decided horses made them too easy. If one is going to fight their way out of responsibility, one must rely on oneself and no one and nothing else."

The movements of both unwilling grew clearer, the traveling clouds removing sunlight, turning their armor to a darker silver and gold. Simon's explanation for excluding Cole made sense, but she still didn't like it. A weak, distant cry rang out. A chill ran up Anna's spine as she saw the man in gold clasp his arm. His opponent knocked his sword from his grasp. The sword tumbled across the ground. His gold-armored opponent collapsed onto the lush grass. He cast up his arms in surrender. The gong reverberated once more, and a faint creak below it drew Anna's attention.

A woman wearing a flowing dress of green and silver emerged. Her hair was bound back tight with a small pale bear pin. Anna felt her brooch within its pouch on her belt. It was made of stone instead of the bright white ivory the woman's bear was crafted from.

"Would Ronald of Flood Street and Lady Anna Brighton make their way to the Proving's center," said the woman. Her voice was sweet and clear.

On Anna's blind side, footsteps clicked up the steps to her section of the platform. She faced Ronald, finding like herself, the young man wore no armor. He was shorter than her, yet there was strength in his shoulders. The calluses littering his fingers provided a hardened look. Anna gasped. His face was burned too, but on the opposite side. His eye wasn't sealed closed like her own. He gave her a look she had never received from a man. It was lustful. His tongue moistened his lips as he saw Anna as a meal. She shivered. She began following him and Simon under the balcony where the woman stood poised. Words wisped from the woman's painted lips. Anna couldn't hear them, but their movement was clear. *Watch that one!*

THE FAMILIAR SQUISHING of grass put Anna's mind at ease. Ronald entered from the opposite end of the arena. His sword's dull side rested upon his shoulder as if its weight was familiar to him. The blade's sharp edge caught light from the mid-afternoon sun. Anna had seen a similar sword when last in Cillnar. It was cast from one solid piece of metal. It had a screeching eagle pommel molded from gold, and its hilt was bound in brown leather. She held its twin. Both aged well, except the pommel on hers was vigilant. Anna found the sword came up to her shoulder. She had never learned the purpose behind the two swords, but she knew that neither was for open battle. Perhaps the situation before her solved the five-year-old mystery of their purpose.

"Are you ready, love?" said Ronald. "How about I beat you and then we leave for a go under the sheets?"

Anna dry heaved. She ushered the bubbling squeamish feeling he gave her behind a blank face.

"What? Am I too crispy for you?" He chuckled. "Got m'self an idea. How about I call it quits, and in two months when I win the tournament I'll 'ave a wizard make m'self pretty for you?"

"I'd rather," Anna swallowed her bile and gagged. "Bathe in horseshit."

Ronald readied his sword with a wide grin. His teeth were rotten, broken, and one dangled by its root. The gong rang out, collapsing its noise onto her nerves like an avalanche.

"I guess we'll see who ends up on top then."

Anna raised her sword as Ronald charged. His arms remained steady unlike her own as he swung at her side. She sped forward using the sword's weight to carry her momentum. Her blade chimed against his as she tried to firm her grip on the sword. Every thought focused on what he had said earlier. Anna blinked and cried out, pain shooting up her leg as it gave and twisted. She dropped her sword, rolled on the ground, rubbing out the pain. Laughter from the seats hammered in her ears. The Proving wasn't full, but the amusement rattled Anna's confidence. She gulped at the sound of hastening footsteps.

"I can rub your leg for you," said Ronald, bending low enough for his breath to splash against her face. "Ah," he smirked, "I guess I'm not the only one needing a good patch-up."

She climbed to her feet, pulling her hood forward, ignoring the heat beating against her cheek. She suppressed her attention to the laughter to find her sword. Time for shame and dwelling on her past stalled as she realized something. The crowd knew Ronald and favored him despite his burns. His wielding of the dueling sword was skilled. *He's done this many times before.* She picked up her sword, charged, and he caught her strike near the crossbar of his sword. Compulsion demanded she hide her face, but Ronald's pride-sharpened smile jabbed at her like a needle stitching an open wound.

It pulled at her mind with every blow she gave, and everyone she blocked, of what might give Ronald more glory. If she lost, earning Lamparien favor remained ahead before the tournament. And if she won those in the crowd cheering for him will have their favor already won. Those in their ornately decorated pavilions could lend coin to his campaign. Anna collapsed on her back from the dull edge of Ronald's sword against her calves. The pain rattled its way up her back, worsened by the crowd's laughter. She straightened her legs and groaned as a cramp gripped them. She ground her teeth, rolled to her feet, and stabbed her sword into the grass and rose.

"You're a tough one, love," said Ronald, firming his grasp over his sword's long hilt, "but tough don't always make the fighter."

Ronald swung downward. Seconds split in two, the sharp edge aligned with her shoulder. Anna spun her sword in the dirt and heaved with all her strength. Ronald cried out, spittle lashing from his lips, his dangling tooth flying from his mouth. A crack sounded from his side as he collapsed. Ronald gasped and heaved, raising his hand to his sword but then waved it off.

"Guess I better learn to block, huh, love?" said Ronald, wincing.

The gong rang to signal the end of the fight. Anna's nerves eased to a simmer. Those unwilling spread throughout the arena were silent, as if the man on his side were dead instead of injured.

"You fought well." Anna said, a bitterness on her tongue. A shuffle against grass made her turn to find men running to Ronald. They carried a stretch of fabric held taut between two wooden poles. "By Simdorn's grace," she swallowed, forcing what needed to be said. "I hope I didn't wound you to a great extent."

She backed slowly away from him and made to leave. To ignore Simdorn's teachings concerning forgiveness was tempting because of Ronald's foul behavior, but she wasn't about to go against her beliefs. The men carefully helped Ronald, lifting him using the item she had never seen before. He clutched his side, further wrinkling the boiled leather of his garb as they lifted him. Her blow had sliced through tunic and trousers, leaving a long purpling gash.

"Guess you'll find out when I'm in charge," he said. "I'll be making sure you know it." Anna bit her lip and, for the first time, hoped for someone to fail. Ronald winked at her, drawing a line across his throat with his finger. "I think making you suffer will be my first act as prime."

"You will not have the chance," Anna barked. "There are others better to lead, and I shall win my way out of campaigning."

"Keep thinking so, love," said Ronald. "You got someone special up on that platform left to fight."

It dawned on her, dropping her courage to the depths of her belly. *The orderman.*

TENSION SLOWLY LEFT her chest knowing Ronald was gone. It was no comfort that now he was possibly to become prime, or that many who watched their fight left with him afterward. But what robbed her of complete relief was the orderman. She knew little of him except that he protected the prime, was swift in his movements, and worst of all, feared. There was time permitted before her next fight to refresh.

Anna stripped down to her bare skin and rested her hunting leathers and cloak upon a bench. Her feet clapped against the old, cracked tile toward an immense steaming bath. A chambermaid took her clothes, eyeing her burns, withdrawing her lower lip. She promised to provide whatever Anna needed. Anna sighed once the woman's footsteps faded away.

It wasn't until beyond her grandfather's lands that such aversion to her appearance had shown itself. Anna placed one foot into the bath, seethed at its heat, then placed the other in. *Grandfather was right,* she thought, *about Williamton.* The bath was large enough for several women to wash in. Braziers stood like glowing sentries along the walls. A shaft of light touched the bath's center from a stained-glass window to her left.

Anna applied soap to the washcloth, scrubbing away a month's worth of filth. She turned over and over the next fight in her mind. Simon said a former prime's grandson would fight the orderman first. She remembered him from the champion's platform, dwarfed by a man servant at his side. The boy was rail thin, possessing short red locks. He wore pitted armor that hung heavy upon him, its gauntlets large enough to house both her hands.

She drew in the water's heat, watching wisps of steam rise from it. Anna pressed the washcloth to her face. No matter her burns being long since free of pain, there was something special about having a cloth against them. A soft, slow breath eased from her lips. It was as if she felt complete, and all that remained was for sight to return to her eye.

"Congratulations on your victory, my lady."

Anna gasped, spun, pressing herself to the side of the

bath. She sank neck-deep, searching for where the voice had come from.

"My apologies for startling you, Lady Anna." There was a clopping of heels before a figure loomed above. The blondness of her hair turned to gold in the window's light. "I'm Evelyn Wayne, our prime's mistress of duels and debates. I'm pleased you bested the street rat."

Anna crossed her arms, pressing them to her chest. She kept the woman's family name in mind, uncertain if it belonged to the owners of...

"But he will campaign with many to support him," Anna said, then wondered. "How can someone like him be—?"

"Loved by so many?" Evelyn interrupted. "He plays to the interests of the people. Lampariens were far more companionable and civilized twenty years ago. Some still are, but life changes, and now bad is seen as good. I will never fully understand the reasoning behind it."

Anna moved to the steps to find her hunting leathers were still gone. In their place, new ones of an emerald green lie folded neatly on the bench.

"I'll have your cloak returned to you," said Evelyn. "The garb you came to Cillnar in will be returned, so if my gift doesn't—"

"No," said Anna, excitement swirling in her voice. "I'm most grateful for your gift."

"Good."

Evelyn sat on the bench, pressing her legs together. The mistress of duels and debates possessed high cheekbones. Her eyes nearly matched the gift resting beside her.

"True," Evelyn continued. "The scum has a head start on many who've gone off to win the hearts of the people. I can tell you though, Prime Luther's sons won't allow victory for Ronald."

Anna stepped out of the bath, taking a towel near the top step. Evelyn had an admiration in her eyes Anna was uncertain of.

"Why do you look at me as you do?" Anna asked, drying off and then wrapping the towel around her chest.

"Tis nothing," said Evelyn. "You remind me of my daughter. There is a spirit about both of you Simdorn gives too few."

Anna smiled. A jolt went off in her head about something she neglected.

"Before I came to Cillnar, a man came with soldiers to kill me. He reconsidered and spared me. He said that Prime Luther sent him to lessen competition for his sons."

Evelyn gasped.

"Why would our prime go to such extremes? He knows campaign law. His sons possess far too much support to warrant law breaking."

Anna bit her lip, pondering whether she should tell Evelyn more. She wrung out her hair. It was irrelevant to mention her grandfather's actions, being he could not run for a third term. She dressed in the new leathers to further buy time to think.

"My logic was the same as yours," said Anna, finding the leathers snug but for good reason. "I thank you again for your gift. There is fur lining from its feel."

"Simdorn's high priest says winter will be longer this year." Evelyn smiled. "You'll notice the metal sown within it too."

Anna patted her shoulders and stomach to find thin yet heavy plating.

"I must ask despite my acceptance of these leathers. Why give it?"

"Let's not drift further from the previous topic." Evelyn stood, folding her hands. "Once the sun has set, the next fight will begin. If what you've learned is true, the Council of Affairs must be called to meet. I can send word before your next fight."

"Can the council find the truth before then?"

Evelyn raised an eyebrow, placing a hand on Anna's cheek.

"You have my daughter's impatience too, Lady Anna. Investigations aren't as swift as an esant in flight."

"But I'd rather avoid another fight," Anna snapped, backing away. "This is all grandfather's fault. He entered my name, and now I'm involved in affairs not my own."

"Affairs not your own?" Evelyn grabbed Anna's shoulder, the fur and plating shielded against the woman's strength. "There is much at stake if campaign law is being broken. Are you not concerned about what may happen to Lampara should one of the prime's sons win?"

"I..."

"They're popular in appearance only. Neither has a mind between them for governing."

Evelyn stormed off past the bench to the door. Anna stepped forward but froze at the frustration in Lady Evelyn's eyes.

"Lady Anna, there is much that has happened since Luther became prime. Traditions have been broken, and now potentially laws. The prime is meant to lead by example. I will call upon the council and begin an investigation."

"I told you he is breaking them. Can he not be arrested on suspicion until proof is found of his guilt?"

Evelyn yanked open the door and narrowed her eyes to slits.

"The council not only enforces laws but also safeguards tradition. We are protectors and advisors to the prime. Our laws require proof before accusation or imprisonment. Why do you not know this?"

"I was never good at remembering such things."

"You had best improve your memory."

"Why?"

"Because" Evelyn stepped into the hall passing the chambermaid. She turned to Anna with what seemed double the disappointment in her eyes. "Prime Harry Brighton shaped our laws."

CHAPTER
ELEVEN

There was no purpose at present in hiding her face. Both the hood of her new hunting leathers and the one from her cloak hung limp and heavy down her back. All unwilling and city folk gone with Ronald knew her face. Her worry compounded more for Evelyn. The mistress of duels and debates had summoned the council. She learned this through Simon. They looked down from the champion platform.

"Where is she now, my lord?"

"Above us as is her duty, my lady," said Simon. "If I were you, or anyone for that matter, I'd give the council's most respected member time alone."

"I must give my apologies. I had no intention of upsetting her."

Simon chuckled.

"I believe the orderman was wrong concerning your desperation. You wish to avoid campaigning more than anyone I have met."

"What does Evelyn have to do with it?"

Simon Sanderson leaned against the railing. The darkness over the champion's platform swiftly vanished as large braziers lining the rim of the Proving were lit. Their flames were immense, outmatching the light from the stars. Those braziers upon the posts holding the net taut flickered to life as the orderman and noble's son moved onto the grass.

"Were you to test already raw nerves," Simon said, "your life would end faster than the fight before us."

Anna raised an eyebrow, laughter bubbled in her throat and then went flat from the concern in Simon's eyes.

"She doesn't appear a skilled fighter to me, my lord."

"Anna," Simon whispered. "She is more than a council-woman or overseer of fights. She's an orderman."

Anna stepped back from the railing. She wanted to curl into a ball and hide within her hoods.

"But what about the man down...?"

"He is deadly. There is no doubting it by his reputation, but his skill with a blade does not compare to hers."

Every sense pounded at her skull as Anna hugged her stomach. She found herself short of breath. Simon moved to her in one swift motion, resting his hands gently upon her shoulders.

"You had best leave her be," he said, offering an encouraging smile. "Focus on the fight and learn what you can."

Anna swallowed her panic. She jumped out of her skin from the gong rang out. Both unwilling stood their ground; the former prime's grandson took two steps back. He applied his mouth shield. Anna grasped at her chest, remembering the absence of her pale bear brooch. When she looked up, the orderman was pressing down on his opponent. He held his sword nearly parallel to his chest. The boy's sword soared downward, colliding with the crossbar of the orderman's sword. They pushed off one another. The orderman leveled his weapon once, winding back in an arc. The boy in his cumbersome armor had his blade dug deep in the dirt.

The former prime's grandson slumped over it like a rag, panting, and then he threw up his fists. Anna leaned hard on the railing, brooch in hand, whispering every prayer of confidence she had learned. One for strength. One for willingness. And finally, one for believing in one's abilities. She drew in a breath to find the orderman matched the boy, fist to fist. The boy swung, but like an angered serpent, the orderman delivered a blow to the lord's son's temple. The boy spun and tumbled to the ground.

Anna set free her breath, knowing at least, her prayers kept the young boy confident. Yet the strength and speed that the orderman possessed made her realize something. The fight ahead was going to take more than just her faith.

AN ABUNDANCE of relief washed over Anna's chest. Her last fight would begin at high noon tomorrow. She made her way out of the Proving, both hoods over her head, doubting word had spread about her burns to the city. From the pale bear statue to her right, a hint of meat, seasoned and charred, reached her nostrils. Fresh snow fell in sheets. The wind pressed them against her hoods, folding and closing them, lifting her cloak like a curtain before an open window.

She paused beyond the bears. Their cracks and fading detail erased by the fresh snow. Fear crept down her spine, and for a moment, she'd forgotten how to breathe. Cole and Norman were gone. Anna dashed to where the smell had come from, finding the guards huddled around a fire. One of them turned a spit, the meat skewered by it dripped grease. She skidded to a halt, feeling the heat from the fire press over her face.

"Did you see where the man and storm bison went?"

One guard looked up with a sliver of meat between his teeth. He gobbled it up like a dog, grease smearing all over his chin.

"We ain't responsible for who leaves this dump." He rested his plate on the ground. "They've probably gone somewhere you can't freeze your coin purse off."

"Which way have they gone?" Anna said, eyeing the ground before the bridge. There were tracks from and to the Proving, but the snow was too tossed about to be certain which belonged to Cole.

"The hell if I know," the guard said, thrusting his thumb back to the arena. "We protect the Proving, not rope pullers and pretty boys. Now run along."

Anna grumbled, pulling her hoods tight against a blast of cold air. She gave the Proving a good look before crossing the bridge. Temptation mounted the further she went to leave Cillnar and the orderman behind. The hot bath from earlier hadn't eased the ache in her muscles from the first fight. There had been no time to enjoy the bathwater. The conversation with Lady Evelyn saw to it. She sighed. It seemed that following through with her duel was the only way to apologize. She traipsed down the street, shaking her head to focus on finding her friends. Many of the carriages were gone, revealing shuttered windows with a faint glow seeping from some.

Above, an argument broke out, and then a window slammed open. Anna leapt out of the way as a steaming brown liquid splashed onto a snowdrift. A warm surge ran up her throat, lapping at her tongue. She doubled her pace. The stench was worse than rotten cabbage. It was worse than storm bison dung. She swallowed and felt her eye water.

Ahead, laughter rang out from on her blind side. A creak came from the sign over its ajar entrance.

LEO'S POKE AND TICKLE TAVERN

A bleating came from behind a wooden gate around the corner from the tavern. Anna's eye widened with her lips curling into a smile. She broke into a dash, grabbed the gate, and heaved herself over it. A wall of clouds lingered between the tavern and a bakery. Her balance vanished as her boot met ice. Anna swayed her arms, sliding into the snow, forcing her to her knees. Something wet lathered her face with affection, but she knew it to be only one thing.

"Cole!"

She embraced the storm bison, relief overpowering her. Anna rose with her friend's furry gray head in her arms.

"Where's Norman?"

Cole's black marble eyes darted to a door where light flickered from a red orb lamp. Anna gave him another tight squeeze and then checked the door, finding it locked. A moment later, she slipped into the tavern and closed the door. Dread filled her chest at the wave of noise, the sheer number of people. The cacophony of voices jabbed at her senses like thorns to her cheeks. Anna thought this must have been the place the city guard mentioned. Norman was too civil for a place like this yet since learning he was a rutoe, new questions had surfaced. How could he wield fire and change form? She knew little about his people. Anna half wondered if his abilities were the reason his people weren't permitted in Lampara. *He is kind. There's no reason for anyone to fear him.*

Anna made her way to a long bar with stools topped with sheep's wool.

"Sir," Anna said. The scrawny, curly-haired man behind the bar peered over his shoulder. "Have you seen a man named Norman? He was traveling with a horse and a storm bison."

The man draped a stained rag over his shoulder and then wiped his hands on his equally stained apron. He squinted at her despite both being within an arm's reach.

"I don't recall the lad's name but am not too pleased with his mount. The bugger is soiling the stable with its rain. He'd better be a one-night stay, cause he's costing me coin."

Anna dug her fingers into the leather of her gloves. It wasn't Cole's fault, and yet it was never her burden to bear the cost of straw in his stable.

"He's a friend of mine, and I can assure you his stay will be brief."

The man smiled, giving a hint of a gold tooth from under his cleft upper lip.

"Good to know," he said, resting his hands against the bar. "What will you be having?"

"Water."

"We've no water for drinking. Unless of course you're eager to share with the horses."

A chorus of chuckles made its way from the end of the bar. Anna's throat was dry. She guessed he was joking. She wasn't certain the laughter was approval of his jest or not.

"I shall pass on a drink then." She swallowed. "Do you have any memory of where my friend went in your establishment?"

Another round of laughter stirred up as the man behind the bar folded his arms.

"I feel high and mighty enough to call m'self, prime. I had no idea my whorehouse was nice enough to be called an establishment."

A woman came through the door directly behind the man. Anna averted her gaze from the woman's prominent breasts, long flowing black hair, and alluring green eyes. The woman embraced the bartender from behind and smiled. Her teeth were pointed and yellowed. Anna focused her attention on the smooth wood of the bar's surface.

"Meet my leading moneymaker," said the bartender. "Rutoe have the prettiest women in Lampara." The woman kissed his cheek. "This one doesn't make a peep, otherwise good-bye the block."

Creaking came from Anna's blind side beyond a cluster of tables. The surrounding men had begun singing an old tune. It was of Simdorn on her quest for land. Anna's eye brightened with delight. Norman peered over the railing, scanning the patrons below. The men were upon a verse about how the goddess had found herself in a fog. They went to a lower pitch when the goddess decided fish would be her only sustenance. Anna, like other Lampariens, never found a taste for fish. They allowed the scaled creature to be at peace should the goddess travel the seas or venture up Lampara's rivers to the lake, Crisuldon.

Anna made for the stairs. She rested a hand on Norman's shoulder and told him she had found Cole. He removed his gaze from her, hinting at what Anna thought might be disappointment, but for what reason she couldn't tell. They climbed the stairs to a door cracked open at its top. A fire snapped and popped in the hearth near the window.

"Why leave the Proving, Norman?" Anna said, splaying

her fingers over the fire and rubbing them together. "And how are we paying for a room when—?"

"When we have no coin," Norman said, resting in a leather-bound chair. Gray plumes of stuffing puffed around its top. "I saw that Cole required rest, and we knew not when you'd be back. I offered my accounting services in exchange for a room. There's only one bed, unfortunately."

She saw the bed was sunken and threadbare in places. Its sheets were wrinkled, and the blanket folded at the end was frayed and moth-eaten. Anna tightened her stance, thinking of that moment with Norman in the woods.

"I will be fighting tomorrow at noon." She swallowed, keeping her eye on the bed. She drew in a breath. "It will be against an orderman."

Norman gasped. His eyes went wide enough to capture her worry like a butterfly net.

"I wish I could say you'll win. Except, ordermen are said to be legends before being given their norlstrell disk helmets. Anna! Their training comes from century old lessons. I have been told that no one in the world can match their speed."

Anna removed her hoods, dropped onto the bed, raking her hair. She clasped her face with both hands. *Legends!* she thought. Laughter and song breathed their noise through the floorboards. Legend was something she believed was just a word to draw attention to characters in a book. *Is it the same for Evelyn? And why have not such legends reached my ears before?*

"Is there no other way to avoid campaigning, Norman?"

Norman sighed. "There is one way, yet if you even tried, such a choice may lead to imprisonment if unsuccessful."

There was no need to ask what he meant. The beginnings of sadness showed itself in the trembling of his lips.

Anna rose, moving to him with a speed an esant would pale at. She held him close, feeling his nervous breaths against her chest.

"I will keep faith in Simdorn, Norman," she said. "Death at my own hand will never be my road out of my problems."

He rose from where he had been sitting. The accountant was a little taller than she was. His breathing slowed to a crawl. Anna bristled at first as Norman kissed her forehead. The kiss tossed aside her worries about tomorrow. She returned his affection with a kiss she had been saving since last they parted. He drew in a breath through his nostrils as Anna loosened the string of her cloak. She took a step forward after it piled like a snowdrift around her ankles. He guided her to the bed as kiss overlapped kiss.

She had only felt such passion abound in her chest before for another. He was the one Anna wanted to impress with her purchase of the dragon. Pushing past old memories, Anna felt Norman's chest, absent of its coat and tunic. It was smooth and barren of hair, unlike the smithy's during the summer months. She slipped out of her new hunting leathers, resting flat on her back and receiving him. Every motion snatched the breath from her chest as she pressed him deeper with her heels. It drew out excitement from her like an eager soldier marching off to war.

Anna pressed his face to her chest, finding the crackle of the hearth's flames overcome the noise from downstairs. The straw in the bed's mattress swished and crunched with their motion. She pressed him deeper with her arms. She clenched her toes at the hint of chill from the window. A shiver raced to her chest as her nipples hardened from Norman's movements. And with a last thrust, the cold became a faint memory to the warm swelling inside her.

Norman rested beside her. They searched for words among one another.

"I waited long for us to do this," said Norman. "If Simdorn doesn't favor you tomorrow, we could both—"

She sat up and pressed her feet to the cold, dusty floorboards.

"Leave now," she said, knowing exactly where his words were leading. "Count more coin for the barkeep, Norman."

"Why?"

The nerve of him! she thought, snatching, and pressing the blanket to her chest. *How can he lose faith in me after our moment of...* Anna wasn't sure what it was. She thought of the orderman with his disk helmet. The sureness of him believing she didn't have what it took to win. Anna shot Norman a hard look. Her frustration puzzled the accountant.

"Because Norman Tilt, you know why we're here. I cannot and will not lose tomorrow. Now out!"

CHAPTER

TWELVE

T he sun was near its highest point over the Proving,
but during a Lamparian winter its heat seldom
possessed the strength to melt ice. Anna stood
with her ankles submerged in snow and her calf-length
boots dotted with heavy flakes. The dueling sword in her
hand was heavier somehow, as if her anger at Norman
added strain to her aching muscles. Much of the pain in her
back came from her bed. There was a weight on her eyelid
from the noise below her room. Norman sat in the crowd
behind her. He had thrown away his usual good posture,
and his eyes begged to the point of barely containing their
human guise.

As high noon approached, her mind shifted from anger
to Cole. The storm bison remained outside the Proving, tied
to one of the claws belonging to a fallen pale bear. Leo told
her no more straw would be lost to her friend's rains. It
seemed something so basic as straw had become precious
like gold.

She held back a sigh as the orderman made his way

onto the field. The sun's rays struck his helmet for a moment before making a retreat. He rested his sword, with its calm eagle pommel, on his shoulder. Anna kept her sword ready, its weight sending tremors up her arms. The gong rang out.

Anna charged, wound up, swung for his shoulder. He knocked her sword away and then punched Anna in the cheek. She fumbled with her sword. He swayed out of her way, watching her stumble with grimness in his eyes. He yanked her cloak. She landed hard and flat against the snow, launching jolts of pain through her back.

Shaking her head, Anna undid her cloak and rolled onto her chest, shoving both hands into the snow. It crunched under her weight as she realized the sword was missing. She reared back as he came at her with his sword held high over his head. Anna's eye widened. Grabbing her sword, she heaved it up in time. Blade scraped against blade, launching sparks and tiny metal shards. Anna clenched her teeth so hard her molars whined, and jaw clicked. The orderman snarled, forcing Anna to blink, but she kicked his leg. He fell to one knee, drew back his blade, and swung, cracking Anna in the knee.

Pain surged like a fire gaining strength. The strike sent a strain into her throat. She gagged and crawled away as the crowd jeered and called for more. Every rushing sense coursing through her head made her wish to yield, but that meant greater dangers ahead. She placed weight on her foot, wincing when upright once more.

"You're beaten, girl," said the orderman, getting back to his feet. "You don't want me to make you a cripple."

Anna eyed her sword. Its enraged eagle was only an arm's reach away. The scent of wet grass rolled in her nostrils; blood lingered on her tongue. The temptation to lunge for it snatched her every breath away. She concentrated on the sword, battling back the ringing in her ears. The crowd called out again, but their voices sounded muffled.

"I won't yield, not when I must campaign alone. Not when I've neither the skill nor coin to lead."

The orderman chuckled. He raised his sword, resting the dull edge against his shoulder.

"Your confidence is hunkered in an open grave, my lady. You want someone to bury you while you crave open fields."

Every muscle ached as the air grew crisp enough to start a nosebleed. Anna shifted in her stance. She found herself almost in agreement with the prime's bodyguard. She did wish to hide from the world. It was so different from the town she had grown up knowing. And with her drive to win her way out of this mess, open fields felt like freedom to her.

She rushed for her sword. The orderman grimaced, sprinting with his blade held high. Anna heaved the dueling sword in time to catch the razor-sharp edge of his. He pressed on, the stench of his cigar hailing from his breath. Anna blasted a breath from her nostrils. She interlocked the crossbar of her sword with his and yanked. Both swords flew free as her eye followed them through the sunlight. All at once she fell, groaning from a quick, massive blow to her face.

THE ROOM WAS NEARLY pitch black except for the candles on either side of the bed. They gave hints of a high ceiling and rushes across the floor. For once, the scent of rushes didn't agitate her senses. The stands supporting each tall candle were of bronze, guiding each tiny flame upward like a spiraling staircase. Anna eased her head from the pillow, a blanket of dizziness wrapped itself about her eye and mind.

At a distance sat a slim figure with his elbows pressed to his knees, folding his hands in prayer. The figure let out a low sigh. *Norman?* Anna thought, propping herself up with both elbows. He looked up at her after some time.

"Lady Anna."

Her lips teetered on the edge of anger and relief. He moved to her bedside, dropping to one knee. His hair was a mess, brightened by the candlelight. Even alone with her, Norman held to his human form. Anna suddenly wished he wouldn't, finding herself ashamed of her anger toward him. A lump formed in her throat before her lips had time to form a word. Her previous feelings about campaigning made... She gasped.

"I ... lost."

"Yes," said Norman. "Yes, you did, my lady. I'm sorry."

Anna shook with soreness and worry, collapsing against her pillow. Her last effort for victory had been snatched away. Anna rested a hand on her blind side, shuddered, but then found herself lost.

"Where are we?"

"You're safe within my home."

Emerging from the distant darkness, Evelyn's heels clicked against polished tile, rustling through the furs surrounding the bed. She wore a breastplate of gold, shaped to her figure with a letter formed from two 'V's' to become a 'W' between her breasts. Below them, shaped from emerald, were the same animals that graced Nathan's medallion. *The Wayne Trading Company.* Anna guessed. A dress of yellow silk flowed from the base of the mistress's breastplate. Within Evelyn's arms were the hunting leathers Anna wore in the Proving. She hadn't noticed the soft nightclothes on her person. They were light, sweet-smelling, unlike any she had worn as a child.

"I thank you for your generosity, Lady Evelyn." Anna bit her lip. "Yet you seemed angry with me before my last fight."

"I possessed disappointment, not anger, for you," said Evelyn. "Your family began it all. Choosing to make laws against governing through authoritarianism and dictator-ships. Many like me have fought to keep it this way." Evelyn cleared her throat. "I've news from the investigation. We have learned—"

A door opened on Anna's left, its hall light stretched across the room. *Click.* Anna gulped, firming her face as if a battle were to begin. *Click.* The door closed, and soon within the flickering candlelight the orderman appeared.

"What do you want?" said Anna.

"Ease that temper, my lady," said the orderman. "And go back to sulking over your mistress, kid."

The orderman turned, revealing Norman with a clay pitcher raised above his head. Norman's ears were pointed, and teeth were clenched. The red eyes of his rutoe form flared and then settled, resembling dying embers. Anna gave him a nod. Norman slipped back to her side, morphing into human form once more.

"Leave us be, sir. And go back to protecting the prime," said Anna, pushing herself up to feel less like a rabbit trapped in its hole. "I must now do what I know I can—"

"Please cease your self-doubt," Evelyn interrupted. "It

will get you killed long before your two months have expired."

"That isn't enough time to earn favor with anyone." Anna snapped. "I'm nothing to Lampara. A—"

"Again with this poor-me song and dance," said the orderman. "Your someone now, my lady. Word is spreading about you. You'll be worse than a nobody if you don't survive the coming tournament."

Anna fell silent. She'd forgotten about the tournament. She folded her arms, pressing them to her chest. Everyone kept their gaze fixed on her. The orderman slipped a cigar from his breast pocket. He sheathed it slowly, from the sharp look Evelyn sent him. Norman's lips moved to say something, but he looked to the others instead.

"What is it, Norman?" said Anna.

He backed away from the bed, stopping mid-stride before his chair.

"What if we search for the man, lord, ugh, our friend Nathan spoke of?"

Her eye widened slightly. A faint smile crossed her lips. It could work, and she would not be alone during the tournament. This mysterious man sounded strong and, by Nathan's vague description, clever. And yet, she sighed, neither Nathan nor any of them knew where this man might be.

"Who do you speak of?" Evelyn asked. "Time is swift, and if he can campaign with you, my men will find him."

"We do not know his name or where to find him," Anna said. "I know he isn't someone in the sights of Prime Luther. His prime-ship wants me dead."

"Wait." The orderman gaped. "That old man's killing of campaigners for those pretty boys?"

Evelyn turned to him, crinkling her nose, raising an eyebrow.

"An investigation is underway, Phillip. You and I may be protectors to our prime, but I fear he seeks to be in control indefinitely."

"What do you mean?" Norman said, at Anna's side again.

"It means Prime Luther has found a way to govern beyond the limitation of two terms," said Evelyn. "He needs only to stay alive, and with his cunning anything is possible."

"He wishes to be a dictator, using one of his sons as a vassal." Anna gasped. "Either would be their father's mouthpiece.

"Yes, in some twisted way," Evelyn said, flashing a grin. "So, what shall you do, Lady Brighton? Allow our prime to keep his hold on us all, or campaign, and become our next primnoire?"

Anna released a deep sigh. Life beyond what she had grown up knowing was desperate and cruel. The capital couldn't trust Lampara's people to be armed. Dead men lie in alleys unattended, rotting amongst the living. What was in abundance for someone like her grandfather was in short supply for others. It reminded her of the crudeness in Leo and the guard protecting the Proving. But what churned her stomach most was the treatment of storm bison. A creature she knew from scripture, once prized for its strength and kindness.

"I will find a wizard and become Lampara's primnoire."

THE RED GOOSE fletching glided across Anna's palm. She inspected her quivers and slung them over her shoulder. A rich, earthy aroma met her nose from their leather straps. The sun was at its earliest light, giving a darker shade to the white shafts of each arrow. Letting the final one drop into her quiver, Anna and Norman made for Natlendton. Evelyn had arranged for her bow and arrows to be returned, giving her and Norman food, water, and other supplies. Anna halted them outside the city entrance. She asked Norman whether he remembered what direction the town was located. The accountant shook his head. She looked down from Cole at the guard beside her.

"Do you know in which direction we will find Natlendton?"

The guard looked up with a raised eyebrow and then spat at Cole's hooves.

"You're pulling my ear, aren't you, love?"

Anna leaned back a bit, keeping her face plain, ignoring the huge boil above the man's brow.

"It's my first time this far west," Anna said, half lying, wishing five years hadn't separated her from traveling across Lampara. "I am Lady Anna Brighton. I'm in need of direction to find a friend while I campaign."

Using her family name to garner respect left Anna uneasy. Although in Williamton everyone knew who she was, which made such a gesture pointless. The guard clapped his hands together and blew into them, rubbing both to remove the red forming in his fingertips.

"Head north toward them trees." He pointed with a shaky finger. "Now be off with you. I don't waste my breath on rain riders like you."

"Come, Norman," Anna said, giving Cole's reins a flick. "We won't keep these men from freezing."

Norman chuckled, following her as a strong wind sent the guard's teeth into a chatter. Anna pulled both her hoods tighter to her face. *If I become primnoire, such despising of storm bison will be forbidden.* She gulped at the thought. What she never wanted was becoming more personal by the day. From the harshness of the city to distaste for the peaceful creatures, the country her family found felt dismal.

They went north, facing a vast gathering of trees doused in white. Hints of green could be seen in the distance, and before long, the pine caressed Anna's senses from branches reaching to greet them. Being amongst nature once more removed her from the close stone and mud confines of the capital. She thought of what Nathan had said about Natlendton, reminded of the swiftness of nutsnatchers. Once when eighteen, she saw two during what the master of arms called the mating season. Both leapt from branch to branch, performing twists and spins, the male with a dark streak of brown down his back. The female a light brown with tiny white spots.

Anna smiled as Cole's clouds released sleet in place of rain. The cold weather possessed power over a storm bison's clouds like it did over the ones of the sky. She reached, gathered a handful of flakes and drank some before they froze. The snowflakes were light and soft like Cole's fur.

She remained quiet as they maneuvered through the overgrowth. The anger at Norman had only subsided a little. What she knew to be right pulled at her heart. Anna could not help but want to forgive him. Norman never wavered in his loyalty, always helpful, and though nervous at times, wanted to see her happy.

"I'm sorry for allowing myself to become angry with you."

Norman brushed snow off the top of his saddle horn.

"I care for you," he said. "The affection we shared was something I longed to do. I'm uncertain why I ruined it."

There was a sadness in his words that melted the chill in Anna's chest. To weep felt right, yet she wanted to remain strong for him. She found herself caring for him more than she had at sixteen, admiring only his appearance then.

"I...," she said, dragging on Cole's reins. "I overreacted. I should have said it before, but I trust you. You want what is best for Lampara. And now that I see what has become of our country, someone must change it."

His eyes brightened to a swirling, yellowish red. The ends of his ears formed points as his skin returned to its original dark green.

"Does this mean you wish for me to campaign at your side?"

"If the law permits an entry so late," she said, warmth filling her to see him happy. "But I wish to find Nathan first."

Norman parted his lips but then closed them. She knew he understood the fear still warden over her confidence.

"Understood, my lady."

"You may call me Anna."

He smiled. The wind played with the treetops, shaking free a light dusting. They went on for some time with Anna keeping low. Cole's size gave her one disadvantage in the woods, but time had taught her to avoid shallow branches by instinct. Early morning's remaining light met them before entering a clearing. The clearing was short, opening to a frozen lake in the formation of a horsetail. Toward the tail's tip, a stone bridge linked a road to a gathering of homes. Chimneys topped them, and a wall of disheveled bricks surrounded the town. Gray smoke drifted from the chimneys belonging to the tallest homes. Atop the wall, like the spines of a porcupine, oak spikes shot up in all directions.

Anna and Norman followed the shoreline to the bridge. The shoreline below the wall provided little footing for two mounts. The air grew warmer by a few degrees as they neared the bridge. Anna's nose ran from holding still the tears of earlier. Her heart was still burdened but lighter knowing she wasn't alone. She slipped her hand within her first hood, feeling the burns across her cheek. *If he can accept me, then why cannot others? Why do I still wish to seek a wizard?* Anna swallowed, aligning her eye with the cracked stone of an arched sign over the bridge.

NATLENDTON

the sign read and, below in twisted writing, it said,

WHERE YOUR COIN FINDS A HAPPY HOME

She crinkled her nose at such odd words. She wanted to ask Norman what they meant, but if she was to win the town's favor, learning on her own was needed.

The town entrance was shut and manned not by men but by two pale bears of Simdorn. The goddess rode on the back of both guardians. The paws were raised in defensive poses. Neither statue was of stone, but of worm-eaten wood. Anna slid off Cole's back, giving him a good rub behind the ear. She pushed open the doors. They creaked and whined, and along their bottom wood slivers chipped off. The doors were uneven, made of an older wood she had never seen before. The street beyond was empty except for a gray tabby cat licking its paw at the street's center.

"The town appears abandoned, Anna," Norman said.

"The cold might be keeping everyone inside," she said, mounting Cole. "Winter has only begun by the pure white of the snow. A month from now, it will grow colder and hold hostage the sun in early evening."

"I see." Norman panned his vision. They approached a choice of streets. "Which way do you believe Nathan has gone?"

"I'm uncertain. He was easier to track by Roland's lightning."

They decide to head where they saw wagons shallow with straw, and others piled with fruit under canvas. All forming a caravan down a narrow muddy street. A rush of icy wind scattered some of the straw strewn across it. Two men came from an alley, leaning against one another, sharing a bottle made of clear blue glass.

"Look what wandered into town, Paulberd," said the man, pinching the bottle by its neck.

"An ignited one and a storm bison," said Paulberd, letting off a fart. "Oh! Pardons, m' lady. It came from the cellar, not the attic this time."

Anna gave the man a puzzled look but then made the connection.

"Have either of you seen a black storm bison and a man with blond chin whiskers?"

The man in charge of the bottle downed its remaining contents, burping loud enough to send the cat sprinting from its spot.

"Pardon m'self, m' lady. The last I saw another storm bison was at Liza's."

He pointed past them to a street beyond the town's

center. Its homes leaned toward one another with open shutters. The gloom of it gave Anna a feeling she didn't like.

"My thanks, Paulberd," she said. "We will be off now."

Paulberd snatched the empty bottle, raising it to her.

"Don't let Slick Street frighten you, m' lady," he said, slurring. "The last bum snatcher was strung up by his acorns. We tolerate only thieves here."

Anna left the two men with Norman trailing her. She snapped Cole's reins so hard it left the storm bison glaring up at her. He snorted heavily and plowed onward. She had never heard talk such as that. Anna felt a tug at her cloak, but she believed it was the wind. She crouched low until her eye peered above Cole's hump. The homes and boarded-up shops narrowed. In the distance, there remained no place left to run. Cole had far outpaced Norman's horse. It was as though the whole time she believed someone was about to snatch her from his back.

"Anna." Norman called, trotting up to her. His horse panted as he dismounted. "Are you alright?"

"I ... was unfamiliar with what he said. The look in his eyes, as if he were this bum snatcher himself."

Norman sighed, resting a hand upon his horse's head, stroking its mane.

"Lampara has changed," said Norman. "Or it may have always been this way and neither of us knew it."

Anna sniffed back the urge to allow her nerves to overcome her. Everything teetered on the tip of a needle. A warmth ran over her, but Norman was out of arm's reach. She removed her hoods, yet the warmth died only a little. She found that the anger and fear from before had lessened. Creaking came from above like the murmurs of a waking bat.

A sign hung half-rotted and eaten by age. Neither of

them was certain it was Liza's until finding a notice on the door written on yellowed paper. It was stained with something fresh and foul-smelling. Anna slid off Cole's back, tying both him and Norman's horse to a crossbar below the tavern's window. The window was dusty, but it held beauty against the decay the town was in. Its diamond panes were small, purple, with gold roses at their center. Norman opened the door for Anna, bracing himself for what might come. Nothing. And then a lady, hunched and bundled up to her cheeks, came to the door.

"Are you here for the nutsnatcher races?" she said, peering up at Norman. "They've been outlawed since the prime's last visit." The old woman spotted Anna, smiling a smile of browning teeth. "I'm sorry to disappoint, m' lady."

Anna wished to ask what became of the nutsnatchers, but time was short.

"We are searching for a friend," she said. "He has blond chin whiskers and rides a black storm bison."

The old woman's face sank into the nest of scarves about her neck.

"Poor lad," she sighed. "He kept going on about a Lady Anna."

Norman raised his hand to announce her, but Anna cut him off.

"I'm Lady Anna."

The old woman brushed past Norman, taking Anna's hand gently in her own.

"He's been taken to the chopping block."

Anna gasped.

"What for?" Norman said, eyes flaring. "Anna is here with us. No death came from—"

Anna shot him a look but then realized her hoods had

been down. She bit her lip, finding no repulsion had risen from the old woman.

"Why?" Anna said. "Why do you not recoil with me like this?"

"I live in a place far worse than the burns on your face. Your friend got himself drunk and spilled his guts to me. Sad thing is, the soldiers at a table away congratulated him on serving some cause. I heard that part before they carted him off to be arrested."

"Why arrest him at all?" Anna said. "I wasn't..."

"I'm sorry for not stopping them, m' lady," said the old woman. "Those soldiers made it seem to all m' customers that your friend ordered the dragon to kill you. Your friend was so drunk he couldn't bring himself to protest."

Anna patted the old woman's hand and untied Cole. Cole raised his leg, clouds drifted from his nose to the shuttered windows above.

"Come Norman! We must save him. Where will they be executing him?"

The old woman pointed down the street, instructing them to head opposite the town's entrance. She said to look for the head of a bear with its mouth open wide. Anna recalled her grandfather finding execution unjust. It was before Williamton had been named after him. Anna took off ahead of Norman, leaving the old woman in the midst of a storm. Norman mounted his horse, catching up with her this time. His horse and garb were wet from the trail of Cole's clouds.

"How will we save Nathan, Anna?" he said, his face returning to human form. Pinkish flesh replaced the green, and the black of his hair lightened to brown. "We might be outnumbered."

She turned to him, wishing to do what he could. To

alter her appearance to her unburnt self despite what the old woman had said. *Why can I not accept myself as others have?* Anna shook her head and thought about Norman's concerns, pulling up both her hoods.

"I must consider too that people know I am campaign-ing," she said. "It will not do well to harm the government's soldiers."

"You are right, Anna," said Norman, "but I fear that may be impossible to avoid."

CHAPTER

THIRTEEN

T hey turned right, cobblestones clicking and clacking under Cole's hoof strikes. Anna tightened the straps of her quivers and shouldered her bow. She hoped words might prevail over the use of violence. Whatever was meant by "cause" must have meant removing competition for the prime's sons. She ran her fingers down the string of her bow to heighten her courage. A bend came in the street toward the sound of gathering voices. Pulling lightly on Cole's reins, Anna led Norman down an alley, stopping before a door. The alley ended at the town's outer wall. She needed time to think of what words might save Nathan. She slid off Cole's back and handed his reins to Norman.

"Why have we stopped?" said Norman, dismounting. "We may already be too late."

"We aren't," said Anna, realizing what was missing. A sound that would come to them before they reached Natlendton. "The temple's bell hasn't rung. A bell would have rung at the capital too."

"You know more about Lampara's customs than you

claim credit for." Norman smiled. "What do bells have in relation to execution?"

"A bell signals a man has been punished for his crime," Anna said, blushing at his admiration. "My grandfather outlawed executions in Williamton. He believed that through banishment, a man deprived of all he knew could be punished justly. The bell was removed from the town's temple when I was sixteen."

"The bell is rung from a Simdorn temple to announce an execution?"

"Yes. The goddess is a believer in cruel justice, and a bell signals its completion."

Anna turned down a narrow alley. There was good reasoning behind her grandfather's defiance of Simdorn's brutality. There was much she knew concerning forgiveness, prayer, and remembrance of promises, but to take a life for a crime seemed to counter those teachings. Perhaps she thought, the goddess had her limits for the misdeeds of mankind like anyone else.

The further she went, her shoulders touched building to building. Every nerve raised the hairs on her neck. She kept her bow across her back for the time being. At a distance within the center of a platform of crumbled brick, Nathan slouched and shook. One man in armor of the capital guard restrained him. Anna stopped short of the crowd, her heart pounding. The bear's head was like the one from home, open-mouthed and pointing to the sky. The bell announced an ultimate sin had been committed, and an axe was Simdorn's hand passing final judgement.

"This man shall be made infamous," said the judge, dressed in dark green robes. "Murder is the highest sin to dishonor of our goddess." He pushed Nathan face first into the bear's open mouth. "May Isbran hold steady your worthless neck, Nathan Barden. May you receive punishment with pride and dignity."

Anna pushed through the crowd, receiving curses along the way. She raised her hands once at the edge of the platform.

"This man is innocent," she said, climbing until eye to eye with the green-robed judge. "I am who you believe has been murdered."

Her fingers tensed, every nerve at the boiling point as the crowd demanded an explanation. Many had only cloth wrappings to warm their feet, others were garbed in a mishmash of coats. Nathan looked up and winced. The bear's teeth had left cuts up the sides of his neck. Streams of his blood dripped into a funnel below his throat.

"Anna. You found me." Nathan swallowed. "I guess you won yourself out of the mess of campaigning."

She knelt before him, resting her hand on his cheek. It was wet and cold. The hairs of his chin whiskers were dark as if he'd been dunked in water.

"I failed, Nathan." Her throat filled with emotion. Every beat of her heart made it hurt to admit it. "I must campaign. And there is corruption above it all."

Fingers pinched deep into her shoulder. She spun toward the pain as her hood shaded her from a flash of sunlight.

"Did I hear right, or am I both delirious and daft?" said the judge.

Anna yanked herself free. The heels of her boots tasting the platform's edge.

"You heard right, my lord." Anna huffed. "I am Lady Anna Brighton."

"Can you confirm this, Barden?" The judge kicked Nathan in the ribs. "Be quick, because if I don't remove your fat head." The judge pointed to the angry crowd. "They will."

Shouts boomed from the crowd. Each demanded of Anna to move, and the axe to fall.

"She is who she claims." Nathan shouted. "Now, get me up. I'm still a lord no matter what the prime says."

Anna swallowed her nerves, yearning to relieve the pain in Nathan's eyes.

"I know of your cause against me," Anna said, lowering her voice to a whisper. "I'm to be killed to aid chances of victory for our prime's sons."

The judge took a step back, his face reddening with rage. He clasped the medallion around his neck. He leaned in close, raising a ringed finger displaying the Lampara governing crest. Its sapphire features marked his professional status.

"We'll let him go, but," he eyed the crowd. Soldiers on horseback came in from the main street, "you will come with us. A life for a life or I'll gut him here and now."

The judge drew a bollocks knife from his belt. It had a thin, triangular blade with two orbs above a long brown leather hilt. Anna looked at Nathan, with his hands bound behind his back. Nathan straightened his neck, easing out of the bear's mouth, but dropped into a coughing fit.

"I will go with you," said Anna. "But I must see that Nathan is tended to first."

The judge gave the chain of his medallion a tug and then nodded.

"Fair enough," he said. "Lampara's lawmen are above all else understanding."

Anna went to one knee, the soldiers aiding her with Nathan. The crowd protested and questioned as Nathan went into another coughing fit. The bear's teeth scraped against skin, widening, and teasing his existing cuts. Once they had him up, Anna guided Nathan back to the alley she had come from. Norman emerged in his human form, concern aging the youth on his face. Anna slipped an arrow from her quiver, severing Nathan's bonds. She smiled to see both her friends safe. A thin shadow raced down Norman's face.

"Anna!"

She jerked back, dropped the arrow, and collapsed to the ground. A horse whinnied as the crowd parted behind her like grass from a fleeing rabbit. The rope pressed her arms hard against her sides. The horseman dragged her out into the street. Anna rolled and kicked, churning up slush.

"Norman!" she screamed. "Help!"

Anna twisted and turned as the horse increased speed. Her arrows rattled in their quivers and her bow's string pressed deep into her neck. A change came over the crowd as if the anger from before was nonexistent. Some chased after the soldier, calling out and pleading for him to stop. More soldiers met them on horseback. Anna could feel her cloak tugging and tearing. Its hood swiftly slipped from her head. The hood of her hunting leathers yanked at her scalp. She struck her boots against the ground, finding no purchase, wanting to scream, fear blurring the townsfolk chasing after her.

A loud tear ripped the dangling half of her cloak. She felt for her knife, seized it, but a loose cobblestone knocked it from her grasp. Soldiers followed on either side with no emotion on their faces. A rush of heat raced overhead in the form of a lashing tongue of flames. They flashed across her face. The rope went limp. She reached up with both hands and painfully slipped the rope off. Anna turned to find a wave of clouds flashing orange and red filling the street.

Screams rang out as she maneuvered herself onto her knees.

A face emerged from the clouds as she stumbled to her feet. At first, she thought Nathan had recovered somehow, but at such a speed it was impossible. The face was high above her, wet with snowflakes and engulfed by clouds. She waded through the storm blanketing the street. Flames flashed away from her summoning, unleashing ungodly screams. Something wet touched her cheek, and by the heavy breathing beyond it she knew it was Cole. Anna embraced him and then looked up. Her jaw dropped to see Norman. His face was still human, brown in hair and absent of green in face. He gave her a nod before pressing on.

Readying her bow, she burst forth from Cole's storms, sliding across the snow. She nocked an arrow and released it. Her heart brightened in spirit to see Norman showing his bravery again. Three soldiers charged her, towering on their horses. The wetness of the snow on the metal of their helmets brought a shine to them. She released arrows in rapid fire, striking two men in the chest and piercing a third in the eye. Shouts came from her blind side, but no clop of horse hooves followed them. Another roar of flames flashed out of the corner of her eye. Soldiers leapt from their horses into the snow, failing to put themselves out. The metal rings of their chainmail glowed red hot. Their screams were loud and shrill. Anna refused to allow them to get to her. She had heard the screams of men before when Nathan was her enemy. And though it sent her senses into a race, it was live or see Prime Luther rule long into the decades. Foot-steps grew in pitch behind her. Anna drew an arrow, pulling back as she spun, but she didn't release.

"Where's my mother?" The little boy had a cut above

his brow, grasping a wooden sword. "Are you going to kill me?"

Anna eased her arm until her arrow and bow were in one hand. She knelt with her hood shading all but her chin.

"I aim for the soldiers, young one. Let's—"

"Got you," said a voice, followed by arms tight about her shoulders. "We'll 'ave you out of the prime's way in no time."

The little boy screamed as the man pulled Anna back. Anna waved her hand at the child as he raised his sword, and then a woman came, kneeling and embracing the boy.

"Let her go," the woman cried. "You're breaking campaign law. She's in the running."

"Oh, we know," said the soldier, "and she's gonna find out she crossed the wrong people."

Anna twisted and turned, thrusting her head back, but the man was too quick. He dragged her into the alley where she had left Cole and Norman. Its darkness outmatched the midday sun, a rotting smell she hadn't noticed made her gag. Anna thrust her head back again, striking true. The man's grip loosened, removing the press of chainmail against her arms.

"Lucky shot, rich girl," he said. "Try that again! I dare you."

A sharp pinch went through her leathers and bit her side. Anna seethed. Never had she felt the sting of a blade. It dug deeper as she forced her screams deep down . The woman and her son dashed to the beginnings of the alley, calling for someone to help her. Anna kept her footing, but as the blade dug, her knees grew weak. *I can't give in. What about Cole? Nathan? What about ... Norman?* She slammed the heel of her boot into his ankle. The man let out a yelp, losing his hold on the blade. Anna grabbed his wrist and slid out the blade. She thrust her head back, cracking him on the nose.

Collapsing to her knees, Anna pressed her hand to her side, seeing he had dropped the blade. Her head throbbed as she leapt and grabbed it. The man drew his sword, raising it high, charging like a bull angered by the fresh brand from his master. Anna lunged and then spun, thrusting the blade into the man's gut. She collapsed onto her side. The man dropped, letting out a shuddering breath before his face struck the ground.

The woman returned with her son at her side. She dropped to her knees and slowly turned Anna over.

"That monster wounded you. I found help, m' lady. They'll be here soon." She rested a hand on Anna's shoulder.

Anna winced, finding every breath, every movement painful. The woman hoisted her son into her arms, headed out of the alley and pointed in her direction. A shadow blotted out what light Anna could see.

"Anna."

The shadow shrunk in moments. The voice it belonged to was deep and quick, but Anna welcomed it.

"Nathan?" she said. Her voice was wet and weak. "I am glad you're safe."

"Same for myself," he said. His breathing was no longer labored, faint streaks of red ran down his neck. "You're bleeding."

"A woman has gone for help. Has... Has the fight ended?"

"Yes." Nathan sighed. "But one of them soldier's got away."

Anna pressed her hand to her side. Her fingers were

slick with blood as she realized what was to come was her fault.

"I've doomed Natlendton." She coughed. "The prime will punish its people for helping—"

"He won't do a bloody thing," said Nathan. "Now rest. I hear someone coming."

The alley grew darker, filling with clouds and snow. Anna felt herself being raised by firm hands. They rested her on high, her head found a familiar furry hump. *Cole.* She grew tired. Her sight played tricks on her as the sun streamed against her face. The homes looming on either side blurred or stretched. Anna breathed easy knowing at least she had saved her friend from the sharpness of false justice.

FOURTEEN

Nathan held her arms to her chest. Anna's shirt was raised where the blade had pierced her side. The man's strike had slipped between the armor plating. A stranger held her legs down while another held a red-hot poker. Anna meshed her lips together, forcing herself to remain calm. The hot poker would seal the wound and halt her bleeding, but to feel intense heat against her skin was an unbearable reminder of her past. Light filled the barn they were in from the open doors ahead. Cole's clouds drifted out of them from a stall beside it. She placed all her focus on the outside, the rising clouds and falling snow.

Hissss

Anna screamed. Her lips lashed open as her pain rose in vocal pitch. It felt as if she had shaken the dusty rafters of the barn. Nathan and the stranger released her, clasping their ears. The poker clanged against brick, its user covering his ears and rushing out of the barn. She drew in a deep breath, clenching her teeth.

"You got yourself some powerful lungs," said Nathan,

releasing his ears from the pressure of his hands. "You're lucky that bastard nicked nothing important. You did bleed quite a bit."

A faint crackling and popping came from a stall near the barn entrance.

"Roland." She smiled. "I'm glad he is well."

"And the old boy is glad you're okay too."

She searched the barn, finding some straw wet from Cole's clouds. Nathan stood with a feeding bag in hand and opened Roland's stall. Cole's creaked open.

"Norman!" Anna grinned.

He held a bucket with a reddened rag slumped over its rim. Her eye was more on his smile, the long black hair framing his face. She sat up to receive a bow from the man who had held her feet down. His bow was low as if she were already primnoire with no need to win his support.

"Your heroics have brightened the town's spirits, my lady," he said, standing up straight, folding hand over hand above a ragged lengthy tunic. "Natlendton has agreed to back you as our potential primnoire."

"But... I've brought the prime's anger upon you."

"I said he won't try nothing," said Nathan, wiping his hands on his sides. He rolled his shoulders and winced. "The whole town knows he's breaking campaign law now."

"He will have the escaped soldier's words to stew over," Norman said, kneeling beside Anna. "Raising a hand against his own people will confirm he is guilty."

Anna gulped. She knew about the man escaping. The prime may be more discreet. He may send assassins after her next. Her worries raced through her head like papsa fish up a river during spring. They spawned, asking if she should continue her search for a wizard or campaign to earn the people's favor, further pressuring Luther. Soldiers and wild game she could handle, but trained killers, ones possibly deadlier than an orderman, were another story. She found her bow and quivers behind Norman on a long bench.

"I feel I must still head south." She rested her gaze on the man. "I'm honored for your support. I ask you to prepare Natlendton should my concerns come true."

The man bowed again, heading toward the door, then paused.

"I don't know what lies south, m' lady, but you and your mount are welcome in my barn any time."

Anna smiled, propping herself with one hand to wave him farewell. He bowed a third time, heading to a house yards from the barn. A child emerged from its open door, leaping into the man's arms, whispering something. The man turned to her with a smile, urging his child forward.

"And who are you?" Anna said. The child hesitantly entered the barn, halting below the beginnings of its hayloft. "I'm Anna Brighton of... Williamton."

The child took two steps back. He eyed Cole, whose silver hooked horns caught the dying daylight. She was uncertain whether it was the hitch in her voice or the burns on her chin that caused his uncertainty.

"He wants to see your storm bison, m' lady." His father called from the house.

She forced a smile, but it sent the child another step back. His lips trembled. His eyes shot over to Cole, then to her once more.

"You may see him," said Anna, pulling her hood further over her face until only the steam of her breath showed. "Cole loves children."

He took a step toward the stall. He looked at Cole and then at her as if she were a dragon guarding its master's castle. Anna offered her hand to him, but the boy shrieked, taking off for his father. She clambered to her feet, gasped, and then dropped. The barn spun, and her focus was off before she shook her head. She gently eased back against the hay bale.

"We head south," she said. "I do not wish to frighten anyone again."

NATHAN AND NORMAN moved at a steady pace behind her. Roland's electric-like breathing crackled and popped amongst the howl of the wind. Anna pulled her cloak tight about her shoulders. The little boy's mother had mended its torn end. She peered back at Nathan, his saddlebags packed. The town had given them bread and cheese for their journey. Anna drew up her cloak's hood, keeping her eye on the bridge. They passed under the sign, and in that moment she allowed herself to breathe. She was thankful for Natlendton's support, but she could not accept the feast they offered last night. The thought of another child being frightened of her was too much.

The air had grown so cold it bit at the tip of her chin. Icy rain replaced snow, with Cole's storm clouds following the sky's lead. She ran her fingers through the fur atop his hump to relieve the distress of yesterday's experience. It didn't erase the look on the boy's face from her mind. As if sensing her misery, Cole let out an immense blast of clouds from his nostrils. The clouds blanketed the frozen river below the bridge. She smiled, giving his reins a light flick and scratching behind his ears.

"I believe I understand now." Norman put a hand on her shoulder. His horse challenged his reach being smaller than Cole. "I don't know the Rutoe lands in the south well, but a wizard may reside in my home city."

She rested her hand over his. She winced. The movement jabbed at her side, summoning its tenderness. The soldier's blade felt as if it were still there. She released a low breath, shifting her weight. The cloth bandage bound over the wound shuffled and rubbed.

"I thank you both for joining me. It has not been without risk," she said, reflecting on the cuts around Nathan's neck. "I'm grateful for your understanding of the unease I have toward my burns."

Nathan rubbed his eyes and nodded.

"And I owe you more now for saving my life."

The black storm bison snorted, breaking up the gray of the day with tiny yellow lightning bolts.

"I would say what debt you feel exists has been repaid," she said.

Nathan shuddered as if about to weep, though he blamed it on the cold. The woods brought a darkness to his face the deeper into them they journeyed. Heading south would take weeks, Anna guessed. She urged the others to increase their speed and cut down on time. Wind grabbed at her hood as Nathan led them south. Each of them agreed to follow his direction. Nathan, once employed by the Wayne Trading Company, had traveled the length and breadth of Lampara. The Waynes were one of the oldest families, employing lords and peasants from and beyond the country's borders.

After reaching a clearing, Anna saw it was midmorning and had them give the storm bison and Norman's horse a rest. She slid off Cole's back with slight unease, biting her lip once her feet hit the ground. Anna pressed a hand to her side, then told Nathan and Norman she'd fetch wood for a fire.

Light snow crunched with ice under her feet, her thoughts on all she had experienced since leaving Williamton. She found herself ready for a fight if needed, and able to place others above herself, yet she longed for the solitude of her old life. The child's face made her wish to remain hidden no matter the looming threat of a dictatorship. With Prime Luther willing to go to great lengths for his sons, there seemed no way to remain hidden for long.

The responsibility of gaining more favor may only take good deeds. Deep down, she didn't feel it would be enough. There may be people from Williamton at the tournament, and she half wondered if they had learned what happened at the Proving. From what she recalled of her grandfather's ranting, Williamton hadn't had a potential primnoire they liked since her great-grandmother. *Will they do so now?* Anna pushed a strand of hair out of her eye. She gathered stick after stick until her mind fell upon Nathan. *Should I win, will they demand I bring justice to him?*

She took her time heading back to the others, treasuring the feeling of being around nature again. There wasn't much snow on the ground. Roots divided the ground where patches of grass were doused in pine needles. She drew in a breath, finding the air damp and musty. Anna went to one knee, setting the sticks on a fallen log and closing her eye. An overpowering wave of nerves crashed upon her shoulders. Her head perked up, eye opening.

"If not for Grandfather, none of what I have faced would have existed. No child would see my face and flee."

Anger compounded in her chest. She rose to her feet, finding the pain from her wound dull in comparison. She knew she wasn't alone. Norman would campaign at her side whether his name was entered in the final calling or not. And that Nathan, like Norman, would go where she did. None of them would have been in this position, though. Had her grandfather allowed her to live out her life, neither would be at risk. Anna balled her fists, the leather of her gloves whining from her rage. The wish to retreat into prayer came and went. It would have been for strength, except now, it felt as if she could split a boulder with her fist. She exhaled and gathered up the sticks.

A blast of flame sent her stumbling before reaching the others. Cole and Roland bleated, filling the air with clouds and frequent flashes of light.

"She's one of us." Nathan roared through the chaos, a whoosh from that of a sword. "I've made girls scream like that cus they love—"

"You are a foul man," said Norman.

Anna gathered herself up, discarding the armful of sticks, pushing through the clouds. The sun revealed Nathan at Roland's side. Norman crouched feet from him, manipulating a grow ball of flames.

"What is the meaning of this?" said Anna. "We don't have the time for you both to be at odds again."

Norman swirled his hands, absorbing the flames into his palms.

"You're a rutoe, Anna," Norman moved to take her hand, but she backed away, "and the scream you released within the barn proves it."

Anna laughed, slapping him on the chest.

"Your scream may be just as loud if you had a..."

Norman raised an eyebrow. She frowned, remembering how the barn's rafters shook.

"It means nothing," she said. "Cuts and bruises I can

manage. It's burns," she pointed to her face, "that cause me the most pain."

Norman's eyes fell to the grass piercing the snow. Nathan's sword hissed back into its sheath as he cleared his throat.

"And I's telling him that even badly wounded men can make you think the world is collapsing. It's called pain, and sometimes you find yourself feeling theirs."

Anna thought back to the hot poker pressed to her wound. The pain was instant and terrifying. Somehow her throat vibrated in rhythm with her emotions in that moment. She had no memory of the same feeling when the dragon threw her from its saddle. Nor had it happened when the dragon's fire seared her face. Her grandfather had lodged an arrow in its neck, cutting off its rage.

"I must side with Nathan on this, Norman." Anna said.

Norman looked up with a flicker of yellow in his red eyes.

"It may have been my worry for you confusing my judgement," he sighed. "I know not what made me think you were a quiet one. Quiet Ones cannot utter a word without destruction to whatever stands in their way. You clearly have not that issue, or you would be an outcast like me."

Anna took his hand.

"Your worry for me brings me comfort." She kissed his cheek. "I worry about you too."

Norman embraced her. Anna felt her anger from earlier drain away.

"Let's make camp." she said, smiling. "On the morrow you can point us in the direction your home city lies."

FIFTEEN

The snow was high enough to bury oneself in, crusting both Roland and Cole's chin whiskers. Two weeks had passed like the crack of a whip to a team of horses. The only scent in the air was pine. Anna shared her saddle with Norman, his warmth soothing about her waist. His horse had taken a misstep. It pained her to end the steed's suffering. It was different with a horse versus a deer or other game, and with the oats running low she had to choose between a wounded horse or two storm bison. A storm bison's winter fur and plow-like hooves managed snow and ice better. They were originally from the southern mountains, where snow remained like a bad memory.

They crossed cautiously into the lands belonging to the Kardans. An old house, whose time governing spanned three generations over a divided two hundred years. Norman had told Anna about Lampara's great houses after they passed a tall pylon. At its top, engraved in the limestone, was a snarling serpentine dragon. It possessed horns that stretched back to the sky and, along its back, a rapid arrangement of spines. Unlike most crest markers that represented the limits to one's land, this one was plated in solid gold. Anna diverted her focus to the brush, so much gold led her to believe there might be patrols. Nathan followed her lead.

"We're near the center of Lampara," he said, riding on ahead. He rested a hand firm to his sword. "The Kardans rival the Waynes in coin. It's said their nardans keep Lampara safe."

"And from what I'm told," said Norman, "this will be the first year no Kardan shall be campaigning. Nathan is right. Without the Lord Kardan's wealth, our country would face invasion."

Anna gulped. Invasion was a word she rarely heard and was taught to fear. She was familiar with the countries surrounding Lampara, ones her grandfather cursed the existence of in his rants. Hausara, Pepnar, and Cocnam were said to be well-armed and jealous of Lampara. She pulled the point of her green hood forward and refocused on where they were going.

A great flapping breached the tree canopies. It was familiar, raising every sense to full alert. Anna nudged Cole's side with her heel, catching up with Nathan and Roland. The black storm bison moved at a greater pace than Cole. His nostrils puffed a lightning-laced black cloud, melting a wide path through the snow.

"That sounded like an esant, Norman," she said, receiving a nod from Nathan.

"I've never seen another other than Lord William's." Norman peered toward the sky, branches covering it like grid lines over a map. "Could other great houses have their own, Nathan?"

There was a faint snap. Nathan pulled up Roland's

reins, edging his sword from its sheath. Anna aligned with him. Another flap came and went in a flash. The hair on the back of her neck stood on end. She removed her bow from over her shoulders, nocking an arrow. One of her two quivers remained full. Anna did not expect to kill so many people at the start of her journey. It wasn't the use of arrows possessing rare fletching that bothered her. It was the need to kill, something she hoped never to grow comfortable doing.

Something zipped past her head, striking a thick oak behind her with a *crack*. A man in black furs and boiled leather rose from the bushes. He clapped another arrow to his bow. Anna loosed her own, striking where the man's hand met his bow. He collapsed, screaming as he yanked the arrow from his wrist. From all directions, icy snow crackled, and men in black boiled leather closed in. Nathan drew his sword. Norman slid off Cole's back, igniting his hands. He sank into the snow as his flames reflected off and turned it to steam. Anna urged Cole toward an archer drawing back. The bison bleated as she nocked another arrow and clenched her teeth. Heads appeared from the brush, raising drawn swords.

A clang rang out. A roar of flames summoned screams, filling the chilling air. There was a closer and more concentrated flapping followed close behind by a booming voice. Anna could make out the word *stop*. The esant remained hidden amongst the treetops. She loosed another, but before she reached for another, her heart dropped to her stomach. They were surrounded. Her arrows numbered twenty-six. Norman was backed against Roland. The fight was over faster than it had begun. She pinched the nock of her arrow, seething through her teeth.

Branches snapped and gave way, falling in a random

arrangement of jagged points. An esant landed in the deep snow before her. Its wings and tail feathers created a wide breadth as it settled. The bird's head was masked in pounded iron, resembling a dragon's head. She breathed a sigh of relief. The mask had been so convincing at first.

"Halt your advance, men. This is the woman we've been searching for," said the man astride the esant. "Lady Brighton." The mounted soldier gave her a slight bow. "I suggest you tell the rutoe to extinguish his fists."

The man wore black armor with a shine to it that captured the light. Gold ringlets made up his chainmail. The pommel of his long sword contained the crest of House Kardan. The man's helmet made his deep, commanding voice appear as if trapped within a deep cave. He unbuckled its mouth shield and removed it. His closely trimmed beard and his combed hair held a blond hint at the beginnings of graying. Anna held her tongue about it, but the man's jaw rested at an awkward angle.

"I suggest he do so with haste," the man said. "For when I do favors for a friend, no lack of casualties is beyond my drive to see things through."

"What makes you believe I am Lady Anna Brighton?"

The man rested his helmet over his esant's saddle horn and chuckled.

"My friend said to look for a burned woman riding a storm bison. Her mount would be advanced in its years. Those poor loyal creatures tend not to live past their white coats these days. Thus, you can only be her."

Anna looked at Cole, reflecting for a moment on the storm bison from the Proving. Each was young by what she remembered, pure white in their coats, and their horns showed no sign of a change to silver.

"And is your friend a prime?" Anna grimaced, straightening her posture. "My life and those in my company have been at constant risk. Prime Luther wishes no competition for his sons."

The man raised an eyebrow and then motioned with a wave of his hand. A collective hiss filled the air as swords were sheathed. The man cleared his throat when Norman remained on guard. Anna nodded to Norman, and his flames went out.

"You may know this, dear girl, but campaign law demands no assassinations. As lord of House Kardan, I, Lord Martyn, would be a fool to deliver on such treachery. I'm also not campaigning. I am old and without heirs to take my place."

Anna released a tense breath. The lord tried to ease her mind with a smile. It appeared difficult to manage, as if a smile wasn't something the lord did often. It left her with slight unease. Lord Martyn slipped a gold handkerchief from his gauntlet. He dabbed a thin stream of spittle from the corner of his lip.

"My companions and I are traveling south," Anna said. "Who may I ask, is the friend you have mentioned?"

Lord Martyn released himself from smiling and massaged his jaw. His eyes softened, a hint of tears surfaced in them.

"I was told not to reveal his identity," said Lord Martyn. "Although..., I assured him you are welcome in Kardanhall. It is the ancestral home of my family."

Temptation rested its assuring hands on her shoulders. She needed food for Nathan and Norman, rest for Cole and Roland. Losing Norman's horse forced them to take only what food the saddlebags could carry, and there had been little game the last few days.

"I have my suspicions as to whom you speak of," she

swallowed, stemming the tide of her building anger, "because he placed me in danger from the start."

The lord rested a hand on his helmet. It had narrow eye slits reaching from the nosepiece, and above the brow golden horns reached over its crown. Trailing from where the helmet met the nape of the neck were hammered platelets in the form of a dragon's tail. The mouth shield hung from the helmet by long leather straps possessing gold stitching, and across its surface snarled silver teeth.

"Come to my castle and warm yourselves at the least," said Lord Martyn.

Anna looked at Nathan and Norman.

"I follow you, Anna," said Nathan. Norman cleared his throat. Nathan rolled his eyes. "You ain't technically campaigning, green ears."

Anna nodded to the lord before Norman could utter a retort.

"Good," the lord said, straining as he smiled again. "Follow my men, and I shall have a feast ready before you can get settled."

The lord aligned his teeth. His face braced slightly as he applied his helmet and fastened the mouth shield. Through the slits of his helmet, his discomfort disappeared from his eyes. Anna didn't understand why the lord was in pain. She turned Cole in the direction in which Lord Martyn's men went. The lord snapped his esants reins, launching the long brown feathered bird into the air. Norman mounted Cole behind her and whispered.

"Something plagues his lordship, Anna."

"I know," she whispered. "And I believe it has nothing to do with us."

TOWERING beyond the woods stood a castle built from black stone. Neither she nor Norman knew the stones' origin, but it was black enough to pass for a shadow. Williamton, Natlendton and Cillnar were built using a gray stone quarried from the mountains in the south. There was a sheen to the castle's stone, and in the gray light of winter, all of it was a blur. Anna rubbed her eye, but no matter how close they came, the Kardan's ancestral home remained out of focus. It had guard towers along its thick curtain wall. The center structure spiraled up and up amid a fortified keep. A gold dragon roared on banners of black from every window.

The tall, studded doors before them rumbled open. Hundreds of wing flaps buzzed overhead, vanishing behind the castle. Anna took in the acres upon acres of trees lining either side of the dirt road. The dirt was muddy but free of snow, with large puddles that narrowed their way. With a great thundering boom, the doors closed, but Anna was calm somehow, as if she could trust the lord of Kardanhall. She wondered if, like her, the lord's deformity had been from an accident. Or had he angered Simdorn? The goddess was fair to the faithful, she told herself. *If so,* she thought, *why allow the dragon to burn me as it did?*

"It will take us until nightfall to reach the castle," said Norman. "Lord Martyn could have a feast ready before we find the dining hall."

"I have to agree," she said, urging Cole to be faster. "There are fewer than two months until the tournament. I've only one town to support me."

"Place your words and actions in step, and his lordship's bound to support you," said Nathan.

Anna set loose a restrained breath, hoping Nathan was right. They came upon the crest of a hill as the sun sank behind the mountain. The mountain protected the rear of the castle like a malformed shield. The air grew colder. Snow slowly dotted the road until brown turned white, rendering the puddles invisible before they found flatter ground. The hill behind them had not been natural but of a gathering of earth and roots. Cole let out a low puff of clouds, telling her his nervousness had subsided. Her own remained. Not for the time they were losing, or for Lord Martyn's plight, but for who she believed waited for her.

"I believe my grandfather is the friend Lord Martyn mentioned." She peered over her shoulder and grimaced. "I know it."

He drew her in close, wrapping his arms softly around her waist.

"I'll burn him if his words bring you harm."

Anna swallowed, shaking her head.

"I shall deal with him in my way."

"But he is the reason you can no longer go home," Norman said. "He is the reason you are in danger."

Anna meshed her lip together, finding a fact countering her and Norman's feelings.

"And yet without him no one, not even the council, would know of the prime's plan."

"True," Norman sighed.

The castle's doors opened, its drawbridge met the end of the road. Lord Martyn's men immediately entered; their boots clanked against the wood of the drawbridge. Its rusted chains rattled and swayed. Beyond the gates, Kardanhall's height went on for what seemed forever. The ground before them was muddy, littered with small stones, and liberally covered in straw. A stable to her right stood two stories tall, emitting no odor unlike the ones in Cillnar. Anna pulled on Cole's reins; the storm bison groaned at how hard she had done so.

"Anna. Why have we stopped?" said Norman. "Is there something that troubles you?"

Anna gaped, stroking Cole's muscled hump to calm him. The doors in the distance were lined with gold studs. Their wood possessed a shine to it, not of gold, but a finish that captured the graying light.

"I have never seen such splendor," she murmured, barely noticing a stable boy offering to take Cole's reins. "It robs me of words."

"I possessed the same reaction on my first visit here as a child."

Lady Evelyn Wayne stood at the top of a set of oak steps. She descended them in a polished metal corset that hugged her slender frame. A fur collar formed the summit of a cloak streaming from her shoulders, trailing at great length. The dress she wore was fringed with fur as well. She stopped at the bottom step.

"My apologies for the choice in secrecy, Anna," she said, a soft, reassuring smile on her lips. "A member of the council must not leave the capital unless commanded."

Anna shook her head, rubbing the amazement from her face. Deep within her heart, she wanted to explore the entire castle. Its keep stood out amongst the rest of the grounds, a cylinder of brick, partially ringed in places by rows of catapults. She slid off Cole's back and slowly handed his reins to the stable boy. Norman joined her along with Nathan. The mistress of duels and debates looked upon her with admiration.

"I expected another in your place," said Anna. "Where?" She panned her vision across the courtyard, finding men pulling carts filled with firewood and another carrying two limp chickens. The distant *ring* of a blacksmith's hammer stood out amongst the bustle. "Where are Lord Martyn and his esant?"

Lady Evelyn hovered at the edge of the bottom step, then stepped down, bracing for some reason. Her hand rested on Anna's shoulder. A slight discomfort ran across her face until it regained the earlier poise.

"They are at the castle's aviary." She swallowed, eyeing her surroundings. "You've ... more pressing matters. Now we shall join his lordship. I have much explaining to do."

Anna nodded. Lady Evelyn spun on her heels, striding ahead, unease coming and going in her steps. Anna parted her lips to say something, finding the councilwoman's abruptness rude, but held her tongue.

"Something smells like horse piss with these high on the coin lords and ladies," said Nathan.

"For once we agree, Lord Barden." Norman stepped up beside Anna. His eyes narrowed, taking on an orange resembling the sun's light gracing the mountainside. "First, his lordship and now a woman we believed to be a cunning warrior."

"I feel we can trust them," said Anna. "But as the scripture of Simdorn says, Norman, 'The guilty always fall under the strain of time, and time is unyielding.'"

CHAPTER

SIXTEEN

T he Great Hall possessed six hearths below an immense banner of the Kardan crest. The banner flowed across the entire length of the ceiling. At the hall's center was a long, wide table with two cooked geese resting on silver trays at the center of a long wide table that overwhelmed the room's center. Steaming potatoes orbited the geese in bronze bowls, as well as carrots. The bread was baked to resemble large coins. Anna sat beside Lord Martyn, who remained in his armor, and once his food was placed before him, reluctantly removed his helmet. An urge to ask what caused his pain came, but she thought better of it. *I must not pry.* The lord slowly began eating, wincing a little.

Across from her, Lady Evelyn's earlier discomfort was absent. She neatly cut a small potato in two, then took a small bite. Norman and Nathan sat at the far end of the table at the request of his lordship. Anna protested at first, but then Lord Martyn said.

"The fewer ears for what must be discussed, the better."

Lady Evelyn swallowed, dabbed her lips with a gold silk napkin.

"Word reached the council of your acts in Natlendton. Prime Luther has fed everyone in Cillnar a line of snail leavings about it."

Anna ignored her food, though its aroma lured her. Salted pork and stale bread had kept her full along her journey.

"What does he say about it?" she said.

The mistress of duels and debates rested her knife and fork down. There was a calmness in her eyes bordering on sleep. Anna felt the same warmth splashing onto them from the hearths.

"He has declared you an agitator of the people," said Lady Evelyn. "Prime Luther has begun a countrywide seizure of all bows. He permits only soldiers to use them."

Anna gaped. The consequences of such an action were immense. She knew Lampariens could still defend themselves with a blade, but a bow possessed a greater use beyond that of combat.

"You will have a greater target on your back, Lady Anna," said Lord Martyn, finishing cutting his food into tinier bites. "Many favor the Lampara's government guard. You will lose many to that event in Natlendton."

"What if I told everyone the truth?" Anna squeezed the armrests of her chair. Its soft leather back brought her no comfort. "They must know what happened, how I was attacked after agreeing to come peacefully. I don't need another reason to be feared. Some ... already do."

She pressed her elbows into her knees and slid her chair back. Anna pressed her face into her hands. Anxiousness rode the length of her spine. Creaking and footsteps broke up the crackle of the hearths. Beyond her plate of steaming carrots and goose, both lord and lady wore faces of sympathy, but there was an edge to it. An edge telling her they wanted her to summon the courage growing distant from her heart.

"What 'ave you two done?" said Nathan. "She's got loads of pressure on her. You've got no cause to bring her mood down."

"Stress is but a minor annoyance for someone wishing to lead a nation," Lady Evelyn said, rising from her seat. "Lord Martyn says you seek a wizard in the south. May I ask, did the people of Natlendton care if you were disfigured?" Did it distract them from witnessing your struggle to save your friend?"

Anna looked up, removing her hood before wiping her eye of surfaced tears.

"No," Anna mumbled.

"I must say then, Lady Anna," said Lord Martyn, his kerchief pressed to his chin. He drew it away, firming up his face. "That I took a blow from a horse in my youth. My father didn't trust wizards, said a price came with their magic. I went against his wishes after a physician was sent for. I did not want to be disfigured. I did not wish to be reduced to lying in bed, surviving on broth. I was selfish. My father never spoke to me again. The wizard warned me of this and punished me with eternal pain."

"But you may have been bedridden like you—"

Lord Martyn raised a hand, halting her words.

"My father died without," he winced, massaging his jaw, "a final word, a last act of love for me. I didn't allow him to be a father." Lord Martyn wiped spittle from his cheek, tossing the kerchief aside. "I refused to allow him to do the best with what he had."

Anna looked about the room, but before her lips parted, Nathan stepped forward.

"Your father had enough coin for a wizard. There's no bloody reason he couldn't have fixed you."

"Once an ignorant lord's child, forever will you be an ignorant lord's child," said Lady Evelyn.

"I'm sorry, Miss Mud scares me." Nathan chuckled. "Some orderman you be."

Lady Evelyn's lips quivered and then formed a firm straight line. She grabbed a knife, but Lord Martyn slammed his fist on the table. His anger sent his plate skidding down the table.

"She's right," he said. "And despite my current wealth, none of it existed when I was struck by that horse."

Anna gasped. She scowled at Nathan.

"I'm sorry, Anna," said Nathan, storming off to the Great Hall's entrance. "I got to go before I get blood on someone."

Lord Martyn nodded to the men manning the doors. Anna watched her friend leave. She decided to deal with him later.

"What must I draw from your story, my lord?" said Anna, meeting Lord Martyn's eye. "You don't frighten children like I do."

Lord Martyn signaled for another kerchief, slumping back into his chair. Lady Evelyn placed the knife beside her plate. The mistress of duels and debates narrowed her eyes. The candlelight barely reached them, yet it left Anna unsettled.

"The point of his lordship's story was coping." Lady Evelyn ate a small sliver of goose, dabbing away the juices on her lips. "You have gone how long without seeking a wizard?"

"Five years."

"And ...," Lord Martyn sat up, leaning close to her, "why in all that time did your grandfather not summon a wizard for you?"

Lord Martyn received his fresh kerchief and ate, chewing slowly at length.

"He believed as your father did about wizards."

Norman cleared his throat. Anna turned to him, finding in all the trading of words that she had forgotten him.

"I think your deeds in Natlendton and Williamton," said Norman, "are proof your burns have no influence upon people."

"No influence?" Anna snapped. "You saw how that boy reacted, Norman. You saw how he fled from me."

"A child is new to this world," said Lord Martyn. "They are not meant to understand at first." The lord massaged his jaw, setting down his fork. "His elders will support you at the tournament."

"But." Anna sighed. "I want to feel whole again."

Lady Evelyn rose again, but this time, amongst the dark and candle flames, her eyes were soft.

"Time as you know is short. I," Lady Evelyn hesitated, then leaned in close, "shall send for a wizard."

Anna turned to Norman, every muscle begging her to leap into the air. But her eye went to the mistress of duels and debates, narrowing until thin like a knife's edge.

"You have spent this time convincing me to *cope* with my burns," she said. "Why make such an offer, Lady Wayne?"

"I want you steady in your feelings and focused for the coming dangers. You have my backing as our future primnoire."

THE ROOM LORD MARTYN offered her was half the size of a stable. Anna watched the chambermaid cast long, slender shadows after building a fire within the hearth. The hearth was so tall and deep it could house a couple comfortably. She recalled the hearths of her grandfather's house; none were nearly so huge despite his wealth. No matter her constant anger towards him, there was something to be admired in his passion for simplicity. No matter the guest, grand or small, Lord William never held feasts, preferring a small meal of meat and potatoes.

Anna sat on the bed, facing the double doors of her room. Above them, two pale bears in a smoothly etched tile stood on all fours in opposite directions. They remained vigilant under a full-moon crafted of pearls that captured the hearth's light. She removed her quivers, bow, and cloak. Joy rose in her heart as she reached to remove her hood. She had left it down for once. The knowledge of being complete, of her confidence no longer wavering because of a foolish mistake, was a relief she never expected. Anna smiled. She would no longer be half-blind.

There was a rap at the door. Anna reached for her hood but allowed her hands to fall to her sides. It would be over soon. The hood would no longer serve as a shield against judging eyes. A way to hide from the world while amongst its people became irrelevant.

"Enter."

The doors opened to reveal Norman, followed closely by Lady Evelyn. And as the doors closed, neither possessed a hint of emotion. Anna chewed her lip. The feeling that life was about to begin anew wavered.

"A cheefox has been sent out," said Lady Evelyn,

easing into the chair beside the bed. Her arms shook as she did. "Many wizards have taken residence in Echnumbard."

Anna raised an eyebrow. Norman explained that Echnumbard was a rutoe sanctuary where many went to learn control of their clan gift.

"Prime Luther had all wizards banished to the south," Norman continued, "in the first years of his second term. He did so after one left his niece with a stutter for joking about another girl's speech troubles."

Anna felt tempted to reach for her hood as a wave splashed over her. It seemed all her grandfather had said about wizards was true yet...

"I'm neither rude, nor do I intend to be so in my pursuit of being complete."

"True," said Lady Evelyn. "And my hope is once a wizard arrives, no choice of yours will result in a harsh lesson."

Anna's eye fell to the bearskin rug beneath her bare feet. She wished Lady Evelyn Wayne hadn't said that, for it seemed in her life, when someone spoke of hope, the opposite occurred. Peering up at her ladyship, there was a slight twitch in her eyes.

"I will keep myself on the smooth path then," she said, searching for the right words, noticing the shaking the mistress failed to hide. "What troubles you, my lady? Nathan's words bothered you. I see pain in your movements."

Lady Evelyn intertwined her fingers, resting them on her lap.

"My balance isn't what it used to be." She looked to Norman and then to Anna. She feigned a smile. "I was told at my age the Quake was impossible. Such an illness is supposed to occur in older women of my mother's family. I can only hope that it stops with me."

Anna raised an eyebrow, though she hadn't meant to.

"How can an illness end if within the family?" she asked, looking for anger on Lady Evelyn's face, but finding only calm. "My tutor said that illness is—"

"An endless fight shared in bloodlines," Lady Evelyn finished for her. She placed her hands on the chair's armrests and rose. Both arms gave, but Norman caught her. "Thank you. Your friend, Lady Anna, would have been a fine prime had he entered his name."

Norman eased Lady Wayne to her feet. His lips grasped for words as his eyes took on a bright orange.

"I'm part of the council of affairs, remember?" said Lady Evelyn, changing the subject from her illness. "We receive a list after the final calling has ended."

Anna licked her lips, curious whether an illness plagued her own family. She dared to hope it wasn't what put her on edge so often. Or something far worse than what tormented the woman whom she admired.

"We've been working side by side since our journey began," said Norman, grinning. "Haven't we, Anna?"

"Yes," Anna said. "And I have learned much about the recent happenings in Lampara thanks to you."

Norman nodded. His eyes went from orange to cherry red. Anna wished the rules for campaigning were different, that she had the power to enter his name, but to do so would require her to be a man. She let out a low sigh, remembering what Evelyn had told her. It would have required her wanting to campaign in the first place, so follows her choice to make Norman a *prime at my side*. None of that could be changed now.

"If only the rules were different," Lady Evelyn grimaced,

assuring Norman she could stand. "A woman of any social class can govern, yet none possesses the rights and privileges a man does when campaigning." She moved closer to Anna and whispered. "Perhaps you can change that when you win."

Anna looked down at her feet again, both within a forest of the bear fur. She found her confidence in the balancing act upon a rope. One end led to a future where she must fight not just for Lamparien favor but for no chance of dictatorship. And the other to a fear long upon her mind, one Anna hadn't been able to shake since her journey began. *Will I cave under the weight of what's expected of me?*

"I thank you for your faith in me, my lady." Anna hid her apprehension behind a small smile.

"You will have me at your side, Anna," Norman said, as if reading her mind. "I can make certain the coffers stay—"

"Everything will ultimately be on her shoulders." Lady Evelyn cut him off, her face stern, yet there was a hint of sympathy in her eyes. "You will have to be chosen by Anna if she wins the tournament."

Anna frowned at this, finding herself for once hoping for her own success. She shook the thought away for now. Norman sighed; both his eyes faded from their cherry red to a dark dying orange.

"Beyond what we've told you, has proof been found, Lady Evelyn," said Norman, changing the subject, "of campaign law being broken?"

The mistress of duels and debates moved slowly to the fire. She leaned on the mantel. The fire highlighted the sharp features of her face.

"None. He rides with his sons to every city and town. He uses his name to gain them favor. He," Lady Evelyn faced them, rising to full height. The hearth's light reached around her like long gold fingers, "has been in power long enough to know how to hide and deny if needed."

"How many support his sons?" said Anna.

"Without wizards to read the minds of the people, there's no telling. Perhaps the capital and Sponernar. Both are quite large."

"What of the town called Rockelton?" Anna knew the names of Lampara's towns and cities from her tutor. It was the land beyond her grandfather's that was a mystery. "I've always wondered where it was."

Lady Evelyn's eyes brightened. A short, thin smile crossed her red-painted lips.

"You must have Simdorn on your side, Lady Brighton. You have only to step out onto your balcony. The town you seek lies at a distance behind Kardanhall."

"What will you do there?" said Norman.

Anna strolled to the door, realizing what was missing from the plan at the tip of her tongue.

"Where are you going?" Lady Evelyn said. "It's night now, and you are without your boots."

"I've traveled this far with two friends." Anna snatched up her boots from the rack left of the door. "I will need them both if I am to win Rockelton."

STRAW CRUNCHED as Anna entered the guest stable. Its high ceilings and smooth stonework felt unnatural. A mount in her mind needed a more earthy home. It sat within sight of the keep. Horse droppings, fresh straw, and a hint of oats from a loft above filled her nostrils. A calm claimed her when inside a stable. It was a place you could go where nothing else mattered but the animals in your company.

Cracking and popping broke the pattern of snorting and hoof clopping. Soon the thick rafters grew cloudy and damp. Cole sniffed against the gate of his stall, dousing it with snowflakes. Above, moonlight lit the grays of his clouds through a skylight. Nathan sat affront his mount's stall. Roland lapped water from a trough. The outlaw lord had abandoned his armor, his chin whiskers were longer too. His cloak was wet, and his tunic was a darker yellow than when she first met him.

"You here to lecture me for insultin' her delicacy?" said Nathan. "I'm not taking it back, nor do I care about his lordship's dribbling problem."

Anna sucked in a breath through her nose, half tempted to set loose her frustration over his rudeness. To lecture about what he had just said was tempting, but she reminded herself of the delicacy of time.

"You've got enough age on you to apologize when ready." She bunched her nose. The odors were many, but the one rising from her friend overshadowed them all. *Did he soil him...* "I will head for Rockelton to gain its favor until the wizard comes."

Nathan looked up at her with bloodshot eyes. The flask he kept in his boot lay against his thigh, open and lip end in the straw. He sniffed, turned, but then shrugged.

"Good luck," Nathan hiccupped, "cus that town's full of tricksters and blockheads thinking they know magic."

Certainty escaped her what a trickster could be. Anna guessed Nathan meant a thief. The people who knew magic sent her imagination churning. She watched Nathan reach for his flask. With a hint of hope, she wanted to believe a wizard lived amongst what sounded like pretenders.

"Will you come with me?" she asked. Anna hid her excitement under her lingering frustration with him. "You have guided me this far. We may find a way to remove your lingering guilt."

Nathan shook the flask, then tossed it aside.

"I'm willin' to take the chance then. I just got one request."

Anna smiled.

"Name it."

"Kick that Wayne bitch off the council when you win the tournament."

CHAPTER

SEVENTEEN

It took until the sun was at its highest to reach Rockelton. The town was tucked within the shadow of the mountain, and unlike other towns, no wall protected it. Every home was of the same stone as the distant crumbled base of the mountain. Their roofs were of dark wood over a thatched one. It explained the long, wide stretch of land pockmarked with tree stumps behind them. The cleared land formed a natural road from Kardanhall to the town. The snow had all but stopped falling, resting heavily on the rooftops. The stumps left behind had been many, making maneuvering the bison a chore.

Anna and Nathan led Cole and Roland at a steady pace once away from the stumps and roots. Norman strolled between them, calmer than she felt at the moment. The town resided further from the others than Williamton. Her tutor once said the people of Rockelton were of a different mind than most. Keeping to daily struggles, unburdened by the changing times while connected to the world through trade. A distant ringing drew her attention to a smithy.

Splash. Beside the smithy under an awning, a man

scrubbed in an outdoor bath. A sign above the building the tub belonged to said,

Baths, Three Coppers for a Soak

Far off among the homes stood a likeness of Simdorn. A heavy-bronze bell hung below it. Anna hadn't visited a temple of Simdorn since the fire in Williamton. Guilt swelled within her like a fire out of control. Her reason for coming to Rockelton was to win its people, but her faith was something she couldn't neglect. Recent events taxed it to almost no end, leading her to question much of what scripture told.

Anna rested her eye on the people roaming the streets. From how her grandfather had described a wizard, they were old, possessing a face of mist, glowing eyes and wore black robes. A steady procession of robed men streamed from the street to her left. She sighed. Theirs were the gray of Simdorn's priests. They moved in single file in the direction opposite the temple.

"How you plan on winning over these folks, Anna?" said Nathan. His mind seemed clearer after breaking his fast this morning. Lord Kardan's servants had provided him with new garb and a bath too. "They ain't what I expected. Maybe the tricksters got bored and left town."

"I haven't decided on a plan," she said, chewing her lip. "None was required before do in part to the fight we won. Gratitude was abundant after we learned the judge had fled with that soldier."

"And from what we've been told, word of your bravery has spread," said Norman, smiling. "I will wager it has even reached a remote town such as this one. There are sure to be some here who wish to see you govern."

Anna blushed, guessing he was right. The crackle of Roland's lightning-like breathing grew suddenly faint. Nathan had wandered off. She saw him and Roland below a tall vertical sign that read,

WAYNE TRADING COMPANY

"Why have you stopped, Nathan?" she asked, resting her hand on his shoulder.

The outlaw lord pointed at a poster beside the entrance to the trading post. Anna gasped. On it was a rough portrait of Nathan and below it a ten and several zeroes.

"The prime is offering ten thousand gold nardans for his death," said Norman. "I think you may want to leave for the safety of Kardanhall, Lord Barden."

"Norman is right." Anna gave Nathan's shoulder a reassuring squeeze. "I will find a wizard and discover a way to win Rockelton."

"I know there are eyes out for me, but I can't abandon you 'cause some old bastard wants my head."

"Please, Nathan." Anna said. Her worry rendered her throat dry. "I have had so few friends in my life, and to lose you would be too much."

Nathan let out a breath that rustled his chin whiskers.

"I'd hate to give you one more reason to be sad," he said.

Nathan gathered Roland's reins, mounting the black storm bison. A chilling wind whipped back his cloak, rustling his gray tunic. Anna found her strength fleeing when she raised her hand to wave him farewell. The last time they had been parted, it had nearly cost him his life. Nathan rode off until there was no trace of Roland or the lord himself to be seen.

"Let's see if a wizard lives in town," said Norman.

Anna sighed, turning from the edge of town.

"Let's." she smiled, more so for him than herself.

They chose the road opposite the trading post. It was crammed with shops, and far to their left, conversation breathed its way from a pub. Above its door, etched on a plank of gnarled wood, it read,

No Rutoe. No Dogs

Anna huffed. Norman bit his inner lip and then smirked.

"What's so funny, Norman?" Anna asked.

He returned to his human form, with chestnut hair and blue eyes. As his skin matched the color of those inside his brow wrinkled. Anna hadn't noticed it before, but when Norman changed, it pained him.

"I'm glad I kept to my studies and learned the trick of skin."

Trick of skin? Anna thought as they entered the pub. She frowned slightly, curious whether that was how Williamton's citizens could accept him. It was another complex issue she wondered if she could change should she become primnoire.

"Me too," Anna said, a hint of worry in her tone. "I don't wish for you to be excluded from this journey at any point."

She took his hand gently in her own, finding it warm as always. Sparsely filled round tables were scattered throughout the room. The bar was shaped like an immense drum with one small section allowing the barkeep to leave it. At the center was a vast support column ringed with shelves. Stacked on them were bottles of wine and small kegs. Their labels were in Lamparien. Many others were in languages from countries that bordered it. She choked back some bile from the foul scent rising out of a brass spittoon.

"Come on over and slip off those hoods, wonderful lady," said the barkeep. "Have that lad of yours buy you some brisolnut. I just got a few bottles this morning."

Anna rested her hands on the bar, splaying her fingers. Drinking wasn't something she normally did, yet she wondered if it might earn the favor of others. She held her breath, then slowly answered.

"I haven't any coin, good sir," she said. "Do you know whether there are any wizards in town?"

The barkeep ran his thumb and forefinger across his thick mustache.

"What if may I ask," he turned his head to the side, then flinched a little, "can a wizard do for you? Their services come at a price higher than what I've got in stock."

Anna grimaced, bending her fingers until they were the hooked talons of an esant.

"You have been decent in saying nothing of them." Anna removed her hoods. The barkeep's eyes went wide and then softened, his lips parting. His chin sank deep into his chest. "I'm Anna Brighton. I wish to return my appearance to what it was and become your primnoire."

With a slight bow the barkeep met her eye, offering a small smile from under his yellowing mustache.

"The Brightons are why we have towns, my lady," said the barkeep. "I'd not have my family's pub or a place to do business without your ancestors. I must make my apologies, though. The lord in charge doesn't allow wizards in Rockelton. The last I heard, the prime banished them to the mountains. The mountains lie south of here."

Deep throbbing anger ran through Anna. She would need to wait for the cheefox to deliver its message. And from what she remembered about Norman's explanation of Lampara's lands, a creature possessing great speed may take days to reach Echnumbard on land. *If only a cheefox were an esant,* she thought.

"We'll be going then," she said, replacing her hood over her head. "I will have to win your fellow citizens in the meantime."

She bid the barkeep goodbye. Norman trailed behind her, slower in pace. His human face lacked the deeper emotion of his true self, Anna thought, as his shoulders slumped.

"There may be a family requiring an expert hunter, Anna," Norman said, eyeing her remaining arrows.

"You may be right, Norman," she said, running her thumb down the string of her bow. "My grandfather once suggested it, and I...."

A brightly colored poster with three rings across its center caught her eye. Arrows flew through them, loosed by a handsome archer. At the top in bold letters it read,

WITNESS YOUR FUTURE PRIME.

Below the archer, in even bolder letters it read,

PERFORM WONDERS WITH A BOW AND SOLVE YOUR DAILY WOES.

"I know what I shall do." Anna unslung her bow, testing the draw of its string. "This must be the man Nathan spoke of. I'll challenge him to an archery contest."

They left the pub briskly, Anna noting the archer would be in a place where crowds were massing. A lightning strike sent her nerves into a frenzy for a moment. Dark clouds were forming in the direction of Kardanhall. It seemed strange for lightning to be so close and concentrated above the forest, but her mind was narrowed on finding the archer.

The gathering of townsfolk took little time to discover. A familiar thump reached Anna's ears, stirring up a resurgence of memory. From morning until noon, she had heard such a sound after surviving the dragon. The swift, sharp brush of fletching against her cheek became a way to find peace. It wasn't until after years of practice that she was sharp enough in sight to knock a pot from a post. Anna smiled as she and Norman halted short of the edge of a vast crowd.

Beyond the people of Rockelton, on a stage of dry stone stood a man. She could make out his beard, sharp and pointed like a sword tip. His hair appeared short and well-kept with black curls. A target stood across the stage with a black dot at the center that emitted thin expanding red rings over a stretched white canvas. On top of the archer's head, a helmet or, more so, a hat shined in the bright sunlight. Three thumps came at once, each arrow from what Anna could tell had struck within one of the rings.

"He's quite skilled," said Norman. "Have you the arrows to spare for this?"

"Their points will be penetrating only paper, Norman," she said. "Targets aren't people or animals where damage can come to an arrow."

Norman chuckled.

"We rutoe have our magic to hunt or fight, but I'd be pleased to learn how to use a bow someday."

Anna kissed his cheek, finding more and more a deeper care for him.

"I will need to show you how when time grants it."

She handed him Cole's reins, wading through the crowd. Her heart pounded like the hoofbeats of a horse, but this time it wasn't from fear or nervousness. She found herself forgetting her manners as she pushed past, all her focus on the accountant behind her. They had been in classes together and spent time in her grandfather's study. Upon her eighteenth year, Norman became one of her best friends. Her heart grew heavy for a moment. She finally understood the look he'd given her before she lost to the orderman.

Lightning clapped far behind her, disrupting the hopefulness she was feeling. Anna gulped, momentarily losing sight of the archer, growing lost among people of greater height than herself. Another thump sounded louder than the previous, giving a hint of how close she was to the stage. It came into full view with a set of aged wooden steps leading up to a deck covered in straw. Anna gaped. The archer stood on a stool. His head and shoulders had convinced her he was of a great height. She bit her tongue to stem the gathering questions in her mind. The archer's boots were half the length of his legs. His doublet was belted tight to his waist, and the laces at his collar were lined with gold thread.

"I've just demonstrated what skill I possess," the archer said, his voice deep and smooth. "As prime, I will do the same to our foes." He looked down at Anna and then grinned. "And I assure you, my policies are as true as my aim."

Someone snickered beside her. Anna's gaze shot up to a man with a disk for a helmet. He was draped in a long coat of black leather and wore a breastplate bearing the badge of a silver horse shaded in black. She choked on the cloud of smoke tumbling from his lips. The orderman plucked his thin cigar from his mouth. He gave her a wink as the archer raised his thick eyebrows.

"Does the orderman among us doubt the word of a lord's son?" the archer shouted. "The word of myself, Arthur Manderlin?"

Around them the crowd gasped, backing away, and bowing. Many had a look of fear under a layer of respect. The orderman tipped his helmet to the people closest to him. He placed his cigar back between his teeth.

"It takes more than fancy shooting to govern folk, your lordship." There was a hint of mockery in his tone Anna just barely caught. "That big talk of yours only makes you sound richer than you are. You sounding fancy doesn't mean squat when it comes to knowing a damn thing."

Anna thought back to her own way of speaking. Her grandfather was among the wealthiest lords in Dar, but from what the orderman was inferring, it seemed she wasn't the showman he believed Arthur Manderlin to be. The lord gave off the feel of a performer, and neither herself nor her grandfather ever acted in such a way.

"Hey, girl. Haven't seen you in a while," said the orderman, releasing smoke from his nostrils. "Heard you've been earning favor of late. Not so much with the prime, of course."

"What does he mean, my lady?" said Arthur.

She took a deep breath, climbing the stage one step at a time. She met the lord eye to eye as he stood up straighter on his stool. "I'm Anna Brighton." Whispers wisped through the crowd as she balled her fists. "And I have come to challenge you."

EIGHTEEN

The sky opened slowly to the blue of spring Nathan missed. Gray clouds faded to white as Rockelton grew distant and small. He ran a hand through his beard and smiled. He knew Anna possessed the skill to defend herself, and even the pretty boy, he admitted, could hold his own. The rutoe helped save him from the chopping block with more guts than Nathan expected of a coin counter. *Guess I was wrong to want him banished like the rest of his kind.*

Snow surrounded every stump in Nathan's way like islands in a sea of white. Hints of grass broke through the white as the warmth of the day rose. Such a break in the winter was temporary during Lamparian winters. He hoped Prime Luther's existence in this world would be just as short. If not for his men sending a crimsigil hawk, the old man would never have known Anna still lived. There would be no price on his head either. *They paid for their backstabbing.* He spat, chuckling. Roots snapped under Roland's heavy, thick hooves. Nathan eyed the town and then switched focus to Kardanhall. The castle was a towering dark blur in the distance, its magic a mystery, but he'd be safe from Luther at least.

He found it strange that Rockelton wasn't the same as he remembered. Its streets were cleaner. The Wayne Trading sign painted and pristine for once. He half expected his pocket picked, but everyone he saw kept to themselves. Wind raced over Roland's hump, ruffing his well-trimmed fur. The town was heaven compared to the sorry excuse from twenty years back. There was a mile or so left before reaching the castle. He wondered if Lord Ransom Wayne's wife planned on giving him grief for leaving Anna.

"That shaky highborn better have the skills ordermen got if she plans to chomp at my ear."

There was a faint fluttering in the wind, familiar to his ears, something he had heard twice in recent months. Nathan looked to his left. A glimpse of brown racing over the trees caught his eye. It rose higher within seconds before he eased Roland to a stop. A crunching, then crack-ing, leapt at him from his right. Within the shadows of the tree line, a gathering of armored men advanced at a deter-mined pace. He knew there had to be Lamparien soldiers patrolling these lands to keep the peace. How could they have known he was in Rockelton? Nathan's thoughts raced, slipping the vial of storm bison urine from a saddlebag. He popped the cork and leaned close to Roland's nose. The storm bison stomped in place; immense clouds blasted from his nostrils. Nathan urged him back to town, churning up snow, grass, splitting roots in two at a full gallop. The clouds rose and gathered from his friend, trailing them like an immense reaching shadow.

Thunder boomed all at once as he edged his sword from its sheath, firming his grasp. Lightning struck rapidly, sending up bursts of snow and mud. The faint fluttering went to a whisper the more the lightning raised its voice. Roland galloped with unwavering speed, blasting blackened clouds into the air, bleating in agreement with their thunder. The soldiers gained but barely, their horses cowering and backstepping from the flashes of light to follow the lightning. Nathan caught sight of the esant and sneered. Upon it, Lord Martyn drew his sword, the shine of his armor catching the lightning's deliberate anger.

Nathan jerked Roland's reins left. He realized he'd be leading them to Anna if he headed for town. The soldiers followed him into the woods. Trees rustled, and some split in two from the lighthim,ning, scattering branches. He eyed the sky. The drooling lord zipped back and forth like a fly over a corpse. Behind him the soldiers had managed the chaos trailing him. The badges on their breastplates showed the Lampara governing crest. To think he had once led the prime's men, been a semi-respectable lord with a place to put his feet up in the capital. Nathan spat, drawing his sword, turning him and Roland about as they circled a massive stump.

"You won't be catching' me kickin' and screamin' to that bastard you lick the boots of," said Nathan.

One soldier stopped ahead of the others, unclasping his mouth shield.

"Who said he wants you alive?" said the soldier.

A lightning bolt struck behind Nathan. The flash blinded the soldiers, making his ears ring incessantly. He rolled his shoulders and cherished the crackle of his stiff neck.

"Let's go then."

Nathan jabbed his foot into Roland's side. He aimed his sword at the lead soldier. The soldiers beyond their leader, charged upon their white stallions. They kept their distance as the lightning struck at rapid points. Nathan swung, shearing off the head of a soldier. Roland bleated and swung at the horses with his hooked black horns. A horse screamed as it was gored in the chest. Nathan drove his sword into the throat of a man, using his friend's storms to keep the others off his back. The noise was unbearable because he had always been at the head of the lightning. He meshed his lips together, sliced a long red line across another man's throat. He brushed aside the time he'd used the lightning to break the heart of a friend.

He hoped Anna was safe, proving herself with that bow of hers. Nathan sliced the laces of a man's gauntlet, cutting deep into his wrist. The man cried out and tumbled from his horse. Nathan focused beyond the trees to Rockelton, counting his blessings for Anna's forgiveness. He charged, taking off a man's hand as the others chased him. The world opened up to legions of stumps and fallen snow. The soldiers split up as the snow fell about them before he roundabout in the field.

In a flash the lord upon his esant struck, toppling Nathan from Roland, throwing the bison off balance into a cress crossing of upturned roots. The black storm bison regained his footing, circling back to where Nathan had landed. Before Nathan was on his feet, a sharp pain lodged itself into his side. He cried out to see soldiers looming over him, eyes narrowed above the rim of many mouth shields. Nathan reached for his sword, finding it nowhere, eyeing Rockelton again. *I should 'ave stayed with her.*

Roland bleated and charged at Lord Martyn. The esant pounced on the mount like a cat to a mouse. The storm bison toppled over, but snorted, rolling back to his feet.

"Leave him be, you drooling twit."

Another sharp pain in his gut led to a towering soldier

drawing back his blade. Nathan seized hold of the sword and pulled. Its edge sliced at his palms. He coughed, tasting blood. His eyes blurred and finger grew weak. He felt the cool steel of a blade raise his chin. Nathan gazed upon the sky, never one for religion, but he hoped Simdorn would protect Anna. The best the ginger goddess could do at least.

"Go ahead," he coughed. "Shave me pretty when you're done."

The blade went deep across his throat. The fight with the sword in his stomach ended. Nathan rested his eyes on the shifting clouds and blue of the sky, wishing he'd have lived to see one more spring.

NINETEEN

The wind had changed direction with the lightning fading slowly from both sound and sight. Anna focused on Arthur, waiting on the edge of her breath for his acceptance of her challenge. He folded his arms. His bow was longer than he was tall and appeared as lopsided wings in his grasp. The quiver at his back didn't possess red goose fletching like her own. They were of a silver swallow. It was a fine fletching, as was the bird by what Anna knew, yet it wasn't highly prized since the swallows weren't as rare as they once were.

"You challenge me, Lady Brighton?" Arthur chuckled. "Can you even hit the broadside of a deer with that tradesman bow?"

Anna looked down at her bow. Its shaft was dark brown, smooth, and sturdy. The string had been replaced, but the leather of its grip was worn and possessed a craftsman's mark. She'd never questioned her grandfather about it.

"I'll show you my skill," she said.

Drawing an arrow swiftly from her quiver, Anna nocked

it, and then drew, releasing, hitting the bottom of the target. A roar of laughter filled her ears like the buzz of bees from a disturbed hive. Arthur had to steady himself to keep from falling off his stool. His laughter leapt from his lips.

"So much spirit in you," he said, clearing his throat. "You'll really frighten our enemies that way. Come every-one! I shall buy you all a fine brew."

The laughter faded around her as the people left. Anna peered over her shoulder to the orderman. He dropped his cigar on the ground, stamped it out with his heel, then tipped his helmet to her. Anna faced the target once more, drew three arrows and released. Three *thumps* halted Arthur before he reached the edge of the stage.

He turned back. "I don't believe it."

Anna let her arm drop. The arrows were in perfect alignment with Arthur's. Her confidence rose. He moved beside the target to admire her placement. The crowd returned too, each in awe of her skill.

"Challenge accepted, my lady," said Arthur, tipping his hat to her. "Remove your arrows and mine, if you please. I've a challenge I'm sure to best you at."

His last words robbed her briefly of confidence. She removed each arrow; the heads of his lordship's were rounded below the points. Her own arrows had a fine four-bladed point. Arthur snapped his fingers. Men raced from the ends of the stage, replacing the target with three tall plinths. Atop them were thin-shafted rings open enough to act as bracelets. The crowd cleared the way behind the rings, opening things up to a vast stretch of cobblestone bordered by distant houses.

Moving beside Arthur, every nerve tensed her muscles. He mounted his stool once more and kindly received his arrows. She pretended it was no different from hunting, that the rings were rabbits, or pheasants, yet both were larger than the rings. Anna placed her arrows back in her quiver, finding twenty remained.

"After you, my lord," she said. "I suppose the challenge is to send an arrow through each of the ten rings?"

"Correct, my lady," said Arthur, grinning, each tooth a moon white. "But you will have to be swifter than the speed you displayed earlier."

He drew an arrow, releasing it and then another in quick succession. The clack and hiss of each arrow shaft found Anna's ears. Arthur readied and loosed one final arrow, but it rattled the ring, deflecting high into the air. The crowd scattered like doves at a sudden noise.

"Damn," said Arthur, snapping his fingers. "A bit slow on that one."

"Well shot." Anna gulped. "I barely noticed your hand to quiver."

Anna nocked and drew, releasing arrow after arrow. No sound of fletching brushing a ring came, but upon the final ring the arrow missed an inch above it. The crowd clapped. Some young boys ran to retrieve the arrows. She permitted herself to relax for a moment, flexing her fingers over her bow's grip.

"It appears we are at a draw," said Arthur, with a strange look in his eyes. "We can't have that, can we?"

She shook her head, remaining still and emotionless. She noticed the awkward hitch in his smile. His eyes admired her in the same way Ronald's had in the Proving. It left her wanting to hide. She pursed her lips to stem the rise of her disgust.

"No," she said, putting on a smile for the boy handing over her arrows. "Shall we go again? I consider these rings a challenge and feel Rockelton values my skill with a bow."

"Ha. Is your aim your only way of winning the people? I suppose that was how you did it by what the orderman said. If wizards weren't banished, I could have one show you the minds of our audience."

"The challenge isn't over," said Anna. "You've not won them. How could a wizard tell you that? They cheered for both our performances."

Arthur rubbed his eyes, the leather of his gloves riffling against his eyebrows.

"I've been in this town for over a week. A fine wine from my family's vineyard sits on the shelves of every pub."

Anna thought back to when the barkeep offered the recently received wine. Keeping Nathan's money would have made campaigning easier. She'd need to work with what she possessed.

"I will outmatch you," she said, squeezing the grip of her bow, finding her strength. "And win them on merit in place of money and," she looked to find the orderman had returned. He nodded, lighting a fresh cigar, "not use big talk despite my grandfather's wealth."

Arthur looked her up and down again, cackling, before placing his arrows back in his quiver.

"Let's make things interesting," said Arthur. "I like you. Enough to want you as primnoire at my side."

The crowd looked on with whispers on their lips. One she caught speaking of why she wore her hoods, of not trusting someone that hid their face. Another wanted to see both her and Arthur govern Lampara together. A third again spoke of not wanting her if she refused to allow others to look upon her face. She had expected this to happen, to be wanted as primnoire at someone's side. Lady Evelyn had mentioned the subject at Kardanhall, but Anna wanted it to be with Norman. Someone who didn't look at her in a strange way. She readied to remove her hoods, wanting those whispering about them to stop. Anna hesitated. Performing such an act to earn the people's trust might also give Arthur an excuse to mock her further.

"If you can bring down a deer," Anna pointed beyond the town's limits. The dark clouds replaced by ones of white, shading the woods below, "before I can then I will become primnoire at your side."

Her final words were like a strike to the chest. It pained her to have said them, but hunting was her greatest strength. Some relief came in knowing Norman wasn't within earshot, believing he may get the wrong impression.

"I ...," Arthur took tiny steps on his stool, the crowd cheering his name, shouting what great feast he could bring them. "I accept your challenge, my lady. And let it be what wins Rockelton."

THEY MADE their way out of town to the east. Anna took in the breeze, drawing in the scent of wet leaves, the vibrance from nature lying dormant from the cold. Beside her, Arthur stepped delicately around mud puddles, keeping a sharp lookout for roots. At a distance behind them the orderman followed, volunteering to be the eyes of Rockelton, to see which of them killed a deer first. He had told Anna before entering the woods that she needed to win this. A man declaring a woman to be primnoire at his side was binding if she lost. Anna swallowed her nerves, making a face inside her hood as if such a fate were porridge lacking cinnamon.

She turned back to the orderman. His footsteps were soft but purposeful through the mud and overgrowth. It was as if he were a ghost. Her mind narrowed itself back to hunting, placing focus on smells, the direction of the wind. An animal's droppings lay at a distance between two barren bushes. Steam rose from between them, as did a scent. She saw Arthur turn his nose up at its potency.

"I must confess. Lady Brighton," he whispered. "I rarely hunt not on horseback."

Anna faced the bushes again, daring a smile. She spotted faint tracks from where the droppings had been left. It was easy to understand his need for a horse, but for some reason she felt nothing from his words. They were pained as if in a state of uncertainty. She knew comforting him was what Simdorn would do. His earlier actions doused all feelings of sympathy.

"Keep close then, my lord," she said, listening for hoof thuds. "If you find any game first be prepared to fight for it."

Following the tracks beyond the bushes, she kept her pace slow. Snow faintly crunched from her steps, overshadowed by the quick, erratic pace of his lordship's footwork. She peered over her shoulder and glared at him. He offered a faint smile, stepping lightly, creating a distance between them. His head cocked right, flashing a grin, disappearing into the overgrowth. Anna panned her vision to where he had gone, catching the sun's rays flashing off his hat.

Trudging through underbrush, Anna found herself at the advantage, knowing Lord Arthur's norlstrell hat was a giveaway. The shine from it was sure to frighten a deer. A faint wet squashing led her to find the orderman gone. She wondered if he saw the uncertainty in his lordship and decided to keep track of him.

Branches snapped to her left, followed by a thudding familiar to Anna's ears. It was heading directly past her, hindering her vision with trees and falling snow. Anna dashed close to the sound, catching the flick of a tail. There was a faint yelp, as if someone had fallen. Anna readied an arrow and ignored it, careful not to get caught up in bushes.

The thudding ceased with a head rising, ears pointing outward. The deer took in its surroundings before sniffing the air. She grinned, finding a tree thick about the trunk to hide beside. The deer's tail wagged, then rose erect as if it were about to bolt. Long ago, Anna had deciphered that hunting meant you needed to catch an animal in the calm. The deer was large and without antlers. Its thick winter fur matched the barren bushes. A faint glint caught the sun streaming from an opening in the treetops. Through the light, a grin flashed across the orderman's lips. He faded into a wall of twisted briars and low, bare branches, trailed by his long black coat.

Drawing back she rested the arrow's fletching against her cheek. The deer turned broadside as she sent her sight down the arrow's shaft. A voice rose from beyond the deer, startling it to take a step forward. The voice was more a laugh than words, sending Anna's nerves into an inferno. The deer shifted its head at the sound, drawing back a step, its front shoulder trapped between light and shadow. She released. The arrow struck just before it, drawing blood like sap from a tree. The deer bolted toward the laughter, panting, blood dotting the ground. Anna raced to keep sight of the deer, spotting that her arrow had gone straight through.

Blood trailed thinly across the snow, flecking onto the bushes. The deer was quickly outpacing her. Off to her blind side, there was the hiss of low branches against fabric and metal. Anna took her focus from where the deer was going, noting where blood lay. Arthur emerged with a blunted arrow in one hand, and in the other an open flask.

He downed its contents. The lord eyed the blood and licked his lips.

"You are as well-shaped as you are skilled at hunting, my lady."

The orderman joined them, lighting a cigar with something Anna had never seen. A silver vial containing a small button that rubbed two tiny pieces of flint together. She met his lordship's gaze once more and shook her head.

"You'd have won if your intention wasn't hunting me," said Anna, smirking at the disappointment forming over his face. "I will find my kill and then be done with the way you look upon me."

Arthur pressed the flask to his lips and then tossed it into a bush. He unshouldered his bow, cracked an arrow to it, and loosed it. Her eye grew wide before a swift yank brought her onto her side. Anna rolled over in the snow as the arrow whizzed past. *Thunk.* The arrow struck a tree; its shaft shattered, scattering thin splinters. Arthur dropped to his knees and belched.

"Are you both mad and lustful?" Anna snapped. "You almost struck me."

She staggered to her feet, drawing her vision upward to find the orderman. He snarled at her. His steel-blue eyes were on the kneeling lord.

"You may be right on both accounts, Lady Brighton," Arthur said, searching for the flask before meeting her gaze. "My apologies for giving you a fright. Can you forgive my drunken jealousy?"

Anna turned away from him, heading to track her kill.

"You lusted after me and nearly violated campaign law. I've no forgiveness for you."

She felt a firm grip on her wrist. The orderman yanked her back, releasing a cloud of smoke from his lips.

"You won," he whispered. "I don't condone sore losers either, but you've got to be the better person."

"He disgusts me," Anna said, struggling to break free of the bodyguard's grip. "He looks upon women with what Simdorn calls *a thirst*." She stuck out her chin, pulling wrist back before matching his fierce gaze. "I think our goddess will agree someone *almost* ending my life negates forgiveness."

The orderman sighed. He flicked ash from the tip of his cigar.

"He wasn't in his right mind, being drunk and all. Isn't part of being true to Simdorn pitying those in their moment of weakness? It don't make sense to me either, but *almost* isn't a thing with that goddess."

The orderman released her wrist.

"You're right," she said, shouldering her bow. "I have won. But with matters concerning my life, I have no pity for men like Arthur. Now, I have a deer to track."

"You aren't the girl I fought," said the orderman. "You'd better fix what's broken in that head of yours."

She pressed her lips firmly together, every breath like pushing an immense stone.

"I have only one thing to repair," said Anna, "My face."

TWENTY

He watched from a distance as Anna took to the stage. Norman's heart pounded, every nerve on the rise for her. Resting a hand on Cole's fuzzy head, he found the storm bison digging his hooves into the mud and snow. *He is worried too.* Norman thought. His sight was keen, like all rutoe who wielded flames. The diamond shape of his eyes were narrower because of it. He saw the man unsettled Anna, who appeared not to be as tall as he thought. He let out a breath and found himself calm. He hoped Anna would find some calm before challenging the archer.

Thump.

The crowd roared with laughter. Anna let her arm fall to her side. Norman couldn't see where her arrow struck the target, but it mustn't have been good. He had no way of seeing Anna's reaction with her hoods, but he felt her embarrassment. As the crowd slowly parted from the stage, the man jumped off a stool. Norman's heart leapt as three arrows hit the target. He grinned, and with it, his chest felt lighter. Dryness overwhelmed his tongue as he cheered. He slipped a hand into his pocket, fumbling with the small coin pouch. Norman shivered at a strong breeze, finding Lampara's winter bothered him for once. *It is not enough to have helped her.* He released the coin pouch.

Norman shook his head, returning attention to the stage. The target had been removed, replaced by thin rings atop plinths. They were faint even to his own eyes. Each was placed before Anna and the archer. It was easy to tell the man's ego by his two-cornered hat and its black plume feather. Cole grunted, blasting swirling clouds back toward the castle. Lightning clapped in the distance. The storm over the trees nestled in the shadow of Kardanhall faded and shifted. Norman turned back to find Anna and the archer leaving the stage. He thought of following them, but the dryness crusting his tongue grew worse.

"Shall we revisit the pub, Cole?"

The storm bison gazed at him with his black eyes. He motioned with his massive head to where Anna had disappeared. A man with something round and metal on his head followed her.

"If that is who I believe," Norman felt a pinch of uncertainty in his chest, but he couldn't allow Cole to know it, "then Anna will be fine."

Norman mounted the storm bison, giving him a good scratch on his hump. He rode back to the pub with only Cole's clouds filling the sky. He went down one street, and then another, passing the same line of priests from before. He had been too busy under Samuel's apprenticeship for Simdorn's teachings. And from what he learned in his travels, most seemed too black and white. The priests merged onto a side street, chanting as they did, in a language perhaps only the goddess's faithful understood.

Finally reaching the pub, Norman slid off Cole's back.

His shoes landed with a click against the cobblestones. There was no place to tie off a mount's reins. He wrapped Cole's around a post steading the pub's awning. Norman sighed. The whine of the reins spoke for him as he finished the knot. The sign about rutoe and dogs bothered him more than he had allowed Anna to see. It was an insult to his kin and one more reason for their rebellion.

He entered the pub wishing he could shed his disguise. It took most of his focus to keep up such a farce despite five solid years of practice. Few rutoe learned such a skill. Until their recent banishment, such magic belonged to only one clan. He chose a table near the door. Clouds filled the windows beside it, drifting skyward, and trailing snow. He ran his fingers across the table's smooth surface, its wood spotless, unlike his recent adventures. He and Anna knew what was at stake, but when sharing a saddle, Anna confessed she wished for another way. A better way to stop Prime Luther beyond winning the coming tournament.

"What you'll be having, young sir?" said the barmaid, shuffling up to his table. "We've got a wide selection, including Lord Arthur's family wine." She gestured to the bar with a pencil in hand. "I hear it's an excellent vintage on account of how old his lordship's family is."

Norman licked his inner lip. His mouth watered at the thought of such an old vintage.

"I would like a glass of that," he said.

The barmaid smiled, scribbling on a scrap of parchment. She blushed like Anna did the first time they met.

"You're the first to sample it," she said, tucking the pencil behind her ear. "Be back in a snap."

Norman cast his eyes to the rest of the pub, finding many people had taken tables close to the hearths. The hearth resembled the snug huts from the mountains around his home city of Lardenfall. The huts were used to house rutoe youth too overwhelmed with emotion to contain their clan gift. Smoke drifted over the dry stone of the hearths from their openings.

Running a hand over his chin, Norman shuddered at the thought of being so alone. Those secluded in the mountains did, however, receive food drops from crimsigil hawks monthly. Click went the glass on his table, and a dark purple liquid splashed within its shallow bowl. Norman raised the glass to the barmaid, nodded, drawing in a slow, smooth sip.

The barmaid cast up her arms and screamed. The bottle crashed to the ground, wine seeping between the floorboards. Norman spat and made a face. The taste was something between vinegar and pond water. He felt a ripple down his cheeks, a thrumming rattled his mind, heightening the barmaid's scream. His eyes burned, flashing red as his ears lengthened to their pointiness. Norman seethed, the roundness of teeth sharpened, nicking his tongue.

"You're a rutoe!" the barmaid screamed again. "Someone, help!"

Norman shot out of his chair. Men around the hearth rushed toward him. He tripped over his fallen chair and released a torrent of flame that righted him up. He burst through the door. Shouts struck his ears, calling for his imprisonment. He untied Cole's reins and climbed onto the bison's back.

"Forgive me, old creature."

He jabbed his heel so hard into Cole's side that the beast's clouds combusted. At a speed Norman never knew was possible in so old a beast, they took off. Yelps came from behind as the men slipped on the snow. Others came from an alley on horses, slowly gaining, but both snow and clouds crashed upon them. Norman spat again, wiping his lips with his sleeve. Whoever this Lord Arthur was, he had swindled the barkeep. A snap went off in his mind that the man on his stool might be his lordship. Norman clenched his pointed teeth, passing the Wayne trading post. *Anna is with what Nathan called a trickster,* he thought, squeezing the reins tighter.

The edge of Rockelton was within a hair'slength as Cole's hooves pounded dirt. Behind them men were caught up in the snow. The sky itself joined in on the storm bison winter releases. Norman gasped. A faint glimmer leapt over the edge of the woods. His suspicion about who had followed Anna had been right. The orderman was dressed differently, though with a breastplate that sported the Lamparien governing crest. Both he and Anna dragged a sizable doe, followed by who Norman guessed was the Lord Arthur. The taste was gone from his mouth, but he still wished words with the lord.

Thundering hooves filled his ears once he reached the woods. Anna looked up and smiled, rising to full height, waving. Her hand fell slowly once he dismounted.

"Why are you being pursued, Norman?" she said, taking him by the shoulders. "And why did you return to your rutoe self?"

"That," Norman swallowed, regaining his breath, "is from suffering through the taste of Lord Arthur's wine."

His lordship waddled from among the trees. He slumped his shoulder. His bow loose amongst his fingers, trailing through the mud. The horses snorted and whinnied as the people of Rockelton reached them. Riding with the barkeep, the barmaid dismounted first, bowing to Anna, the orderman, and Lord Arthur.

"I saw your ladyship earlier, Lady Brighton," she said.

Her auburn hair was dotted with snowflakes. She rose to full height, pointing at Norman. "Why do you travel with this rutoe?"

The faint despair on Anna's lips disappeared.

"He is my friend," Anna snapped. "I saw the sign outside the pub. What cause do you have to pursue him?"

"I discovered Lord Arthur's wine to be foul," said Norman, eyeing his lordship and Anna. "I reacted poorly and thus exposed myself."

"I am insulted, Lady Brighton," said Lord Arthur. "I know I'm more a showman than a hunter, but I worked hard to bring Rockelton my family's wine."

"That was no wine," Norman snapped. "If it were, the townsfolk would not have needed to chase me."

His lordship shrugged, raising his hands in a surrendering pose.

"I cannot help if man and rutoe alike have weak palates."

Norman's eyes burned with rage; rings of flame encircled his hands, hiding their green in yellow and orange. Anna pressed a hand to his chest, raising the other. The people of Rockelton gasped and backed away. He felt a firm grip on his shoulder, finding the orderman at his side. A piercing gaze shot from the bodyguard's steel-blue eyes.

"His lordship's been through enough today," the orderman said. His words went to a whisper in rutoeis. His speech was swift and fluent, with a hint of the Eastern dialect. He spoke of the lord nearly breaking campaign law, and of Simdorn and forgiveness. It made no sense to Norman, but what was said next sent shock down his face.

Norman gasped. *She has never allowed her feelings to trump her beliefs.* "This is most unlike you, Anna."

"I need not guess what he told you," she said. "I didn't

appreciate the way his lordship looked at me, nor his jealousy." Anna turned to Lord Arthur and frowned. "Can you forgive my behavior?"

"I'm not ashamed of my desires," he chuckled, leering at the deer. "And now that I truly think about it, my actions were justified. I had this town eating out of my hand."

Both Norman and Anna stared at him, sharing their confusion. The townsfolk on foot and horseback looked at one another aghast. His lordship slowly grew, hair turning to short sharp quills. His nose narrowed to a point as the clothes on his person morphed into a coat of chainmail. A long black lumao sewed itself into existence about his waist.

"The perfect guise to fool humans and have a country for myself ruined by a green matchstick," said the Trickster.

Norman drew back from Anna, bounding his fist in flames. Anna cracked an arrow to her bow and drew back. The orderman slipped a pair of long knives from his belt and then spat out his thin cigar.

"Everyone, run!" Anna cried.

A piercing roar erupted from the Trickster's jaws. The people scattered, running for the town, clasping their ears. Norman winced, stumbling back, plugging his ears. Through the glow of his flames, the Trickster's needlepoint teeth captured the sun's light. A gray like that of early day raced over the skin of the once stunted lord.

"You'd have won over many within the mountain's shadow with those burns, girl," said the Trickster. "These humans are most sympathetic to deformed folk."

Norman heard the shuddering in Anna's breath. She aimed for the creature's throat and stepped forward, but each step was a shuffle. Norman sensed the creature's words had struck deep. He thrust his fist, releasing a sphere of flames. The Trickster bent and twisted into an 's' shape. It pounded the ground as the tips of its quills fell, burning up before striking the snow. Anna released an arrow, yanked down her hoods, nocking another. The burned half of her face stretched and tightened as she released again. The arrow bounced and sparked off the Trickster's head. It yelped and scratched at its face, tangling its fingers within its quills. Norman lashed out with his flames, boiling a stretch of skin across his lordship's cheek.

"You bloody green bastard!" Arthur yelped. "I'll kill you for that."

The Trickster's feet rooted to the dirt as his body stretched. He freed his fingers, splaying both hands as every fingernail sharpened. He snatched Norman from his feet. Norman shook with ferocity, feeling blood rush to his ears. He reached forward, the air fleeing his lungs. A faint tear formed in Anna's eye as she called his name. A glimmer shot across his line of vision as he felt his strength leave him. His focus faltered and faded with the flames in his hands. Suddenly, he fell, hitting the ground with a thud.

"Norman," Anna said, running to his side. "Are you?"

"I'm well, Anna," he said, chest heaving the more he tried to reclaim his breath.

He glanced up as the trickster reared back. Blood black like ink rained upon the grass and snow. A blast of light blinded him for a moment. Norman shook it off, finding the orderman straddling Lord Arthur's back. The bodyguard plunged his long knives into the creature's sides. The Trickster spun and seized the orderman around the shoulders. Anna released an arrow. It pierced through and out the back of Lord Arthur's throat.

Norman steadied himself until afoot again. Leaping from the Trickster, the orderman landed, churning up dirt.

Repetitive thuds kicked up snow as the Trickster shrunk, changing both skin color and clothing. The snowfall increased slowly, erasing the black of Lord Arthur's blood.

THE STENCH from the lord's corpse filled his nostrils. It wasn't potent enough to rob Norman of the relief that it was over. What remained of the Trickster lay face down in the snow. His blood was almost erased from sight by the persistence of winter.

Anna ran up to Cole, taking the storm bison's massive head in her arms. Norman watched the creature welcome her, licking the burned side of her face. A faint *snick* of the orderman's knives caught his attention. He stood watchful over the Trickster's body as if suspicious its death wasn't permanent.

"I'm uncertain what to do," said Anna, parting from Cole, taking Norman's hand. "Rockelton will not trust me now. All over our friendship."

He held her hand tight in his own. Heavy snowflakes pummeled the tangled locks of her hair. *If only all Lampara were like Anna,* he thought. That was one thing about Lord Brighton no one instilled better in others. The acceptance of everyone. He wished the lord of Williamton had spread that kind of thinking abroad. And with that, Norman found his anger toward the lord less worth dwelling over.

"We shall have plenty to eat then," said Norman, gesturing toward the deer. He smiled to stem the tide of her worry. "Nathan must have gained an appetite by the time he reached Kardanhall."

He felt his words were falling short. Anna's hand was warm and wet from the deer's blood. She let go, replacing her hood over her head, facing Rockelton like a lone sentry. Norman took her hand in his again and brought her close.

"It's only one town, Anna."

She met his eyes. His own low flickering spheres, telling her without words that he understood how she felt.

"It's not losing the town that troubles me," she said. "It's what Lord Arthur said. It reminded me of home, of a time when my hoods weren't needed."

TWENTY-ONE

Anna took the return to Kardanhall at a slow pace. Her kill hung over Cole's back, tied tight with what remained of the rope from her saddlebags. The cold kept its stench at bay as Norman walked beside her. They thought of giving the deer to Rockelton regardless of recent events. Before she could mount the deer on the storm bison's back and bring it to town, the orderman offered to help. He told her in a hushed tone. "The people are gonna think Tilt cursed it for chasing him." He tipped his helmet to her before she could question the absurdity of such a belief.

Anna caught a brief flash of light from his helmet. She scratched her chin and returned her focus to the castle. *Nathan would not like a servant of the prime joining our journey,* she thought before considering calling the bodyguard back. Lady Evelyn was one too, but no matter the mistress and lord's differences, Nathan had nothing to fear from her. She worried Nathan's attitude might change the council member's mind, though.

The falling snow pounded her shoulders, more so than

when the hunt ended. Cole's own snow tacked on more, making Anna wish it were spring. His storms let loose rain during that year phase. And when alone amongst the trees beyond Williamton, Cole's rains brought her mind peace and covered her scent on long hunts.

Pulling her cloak tight to her chest, she let her thoughts flow to the recent hunt. Her behavior felt justified. The proof of his lordship being a trickster made it so. She released a low breath. The orderman was right. Scripture contained lessons for her childish deed too. *Words are noise-filled emotions capable of pain,* she thought. *Actions are blades with true intent to deal such pain.* She was relieved the trickster would no longer harm anyone, but should something similar occur, her emotions would be better measured.

The towering sight of Kardanhall emerged from amongst the woods and relentless snowfall. Its strange brickwork made it appear more distant than was true.

"There's a creature large and black ahead, Anna," said Norman, pointing.

Anna shook her head. The creature's pacing was erratic, halting in one spot, and then circling it. The wind rushed, closing her hood over her face like flaps to a tent. She drew them both back as the cloud opened a little, allowing thin beams of sunlight. The light raced across the creature's hooked horns.

"It's Roland." Anna's heart went into a sprint. She leaned over her kill, squinted, then leaned back. "Why would he be alone?"

Anna and Norman increased their pace. The wind died down, allowing the snow to fall straight and orderly. She heard the faint crackle of lightning from Roland's breathing. A mustiness emitted from his fur, telling her the bison had been among the elements a while. Nathan's mount bleated and stomped toward something. Three ravens scurried away and launched themselves skyward from a mass feet away.

"Anna," Norman cried. "It's..."

She leapt to the ground, racing with all the strength she possessed. Her heart dropped within her chest.

"Nathan!" she screamed. "No."

Every muscle within her stiffened, the cold having no part in it. She collapsed to her knees, warm tears filled her eye. She crawled to him. Anna rested a hand on Nathan's chest. All that remained of his chin whiskers was a twisted stub. Her hand went to his cheek, wet with blood from the wound near his chest. She drew it back and covered her lips. In their greed, the ravens had robbed Nathan of his eyes. A faint rush of heat clasped her shoulder. Words lapped at her ears as a lump formed in her throat large enough to rob her of breath. Rubbing the tears from her eye Norman's words grew clearer.

"This explains why the orderman was in Rockelton," he said. "He was hunting for Nathan."

Anna glared up at him, forming her lips into a sneer.

"All Nathan wanted was to make amends for what he believed was his fault."

She took in where her friend lay. The snow eased in its downfall. There was something long and brown woven among a cluster of tree branches. Her heart pounded with anticipation and hope that what she saw wasn't a... *Feather.* It was the width of both her hands combined, resting out of reach. She turned back to Nathan. There was a wide wound across his neck, black lining its edges from the cold.

"An esant was here," she said. Norman knelt beside her, resting his hand on her shoulder. "Lord Martyn attacked our friend."

Norman brought her close. Her chest heaved up and down. She ran a thumb along her bowstring to ease her nerves. Nothing. Neither the comfort of his arms, or what steadied her mind most often brought her comfort.

"I... I sent him away. I thought his lordship would protect Nathan. This is my fault."

Norman was speechless for the first time. It left Anna's thoughts to wander. Could they even return to Kardanhall with what they had found? Just like some villain in a book, the lord would play things off with ignorance. Her grandfather told her once that books draw from the world we know. She swallowed, resting her head on Norman's shoulder.

"You possessed no knowledge of what could happen, Anna," Norman said, kissing her brow. "Nathan crossed his lordship, but not enough for blades to be drawn."

She kissed his cheek, parted from him, wiping her cheeks with her fist.

"We must leave my kill for the crows," Anna said. "Nathan deserves a proper burial under the instruction of a priest of Simdorn."

Norman rested his gaze on Nathan. The cold had preserved the former lord's final feelings. His mouth agape and body twisted in struggle.

"And what if Lord Martyn refuses to grant our friend a proper burial?" Norman swallowed. His eyes faded to a weak, whitish red. "We cannot storm a castle with just the two of us."

Anna spun on her heels and went to untie her kill from Cole's back. It slid off, striking the snow with a collective crunch.

"Help me with Nathan, Norman," she said. "We must bring him to the castle."

"You have a plan then?" he asked.

She guided Cole over to where Nathan lay half buried in snow. Some of it had melted from Roland's attempts to chase off the ravens. She stroked Cole's side, and he eased himself down. They struggled to rest Nathan across Cole's back. Snow tumbled from his lordship's limbs in large clumps. The accountant grunted and strained, clenching his teeth until their friend was properly settled. Anna applied the ropes and cursed. Her fingers shaking, she'd dropped the rope. Snatching it up, she made several knots and then made for the castle.

"No matter what comes next," she said. "If Martyn Kardan wants a fight, it will not end in his favor."

PASSING across the drawbridge into Kardanhall, its moat was a solid sheet of ice doused in snow as it disappeared around the castle. Guards met them as they passed under an archway shaped at the point like a spade. Anna told them the truth, that her friend had been attacked, leaving out her suspicions.

"Where is the castle temple of Simdorn?" she asked. "My friend must be properly buried. I will need to speak with the temple's priest."

The guards led her along the curtain wall, their numbers increasing little by little. Anna looked at Norman. One of his hands firmly held her own while the other flexed, forming a faint glow. She tugged at his hand, mouthing no, feeling the heat through her glove. His teeth were clenched, and from where his eyes went, he was counting their odds. Her eye grew wide as she realized for the first time that it was she who was calm. It felt unnatural. Norman nodded, whirling his hand until the glow faded into his palm.

At the end of the curtain wall beside the keep, the temple sat. Its bell tower was stunted, and the temple below was smaller than Natlendtons. Anna kept facing forward. Long shadows reached over the surface of the keep. The guards numbered in the dozens, as if they were an armored audience at the beginnings of a dangerous event. Anna looped Cole's reins tightly about her hand and wrist. The storm bison remained calm, his clouds covering their tracks in fresh snow. Roland wasn't so at ease, matching the frustration on Norman's face, fiercely eyeing the soldiers. After what happened to Nathan, Anna didn't blame one of the world's rarest creatures for his lack of trust in armored men.

Two figures emerged from a door below a set of stairs to her left. The second stumbled forward after the first kicked him in the thigh. Anna realized the figure struggling to regain footing was bound at the wrists. *Evelyn,* she thought, seeing the mistress of duels and debates clamor to one knee. Snow dampened her dress, and her long blond hair hid her face.

"I see you've found the traitor's body," said the man, pointing his sword to Lady Evelyn's back. "You are all under lordship arrest. Prime Luther was wise to make the rich commanders of Lamparien soldiers. The law of their own lands"

Lord Martyn's breastplate bore a silver horse shaded in black. He wiped his cheek with a kerchief stitched with gold thread. Spittle dripped onto his family crest. The golden dragon snaked its way around the horse's neck. Its head rested over the horse's in a dominating way.

"You cannot arrest someone campaigning," said Anna,

recalling what Norman taught her, containing her anger behind her teeth. "I committed no crime against another in the running or have done damage to property."

Whether she had done anything was irrelevant to how she felt. The dribbling lord had taken her friend's life, and for what reason she intended to find out.

"I don't allow hunting on my lands without," Lord Martyn swallowed and then wiped away more spittle, pressing his sword to the cords of Evelyn's corset, "great need. Therefore, damage was done to my property. A lord's granddaughter should know better." He coughed and wiped his chin again. "Your punishment began just before your arrival. The cheefox has been seen to. There will be no wizard."

Anna clenched her teeth. *Does he know about the trickster?* she thought. She balled both hands into fists. It was all she could do to hold on to hope. *There must be another way. I must find a wizard.* She felt a deep wish to lash out, but held her ground, keeping an eye on Lord Martyn. He grinned at her anger and unease. Anna cursed herself for not guessing the woods belonged to him. Lord Martyn was likely lord of Rockelton too. It should have been obvious. To hunt on another's land without permission was equal to stealing.

"You're right," Anna said, eyeing the council member. Evelyn shook where she knelt, but Anna knew it wasn't from the cold. "I ask you to let Lady Evelyn and Norman go free. Take me in their place."

Lady Evelyn made it to her feet. Lord Martyn drew back his sword and kicked her legs out from under her. The mistress crashed against snow and mud, losing something silver and gold from around her neck. Anna took a step forward, but his lordship's blade pressed to Lady Evelyn's back again.

"Remain beside your green friend, Lady Brighton," said Lord Kardan, rubbing his jaw. "You will both be shackled before being sent to Cillnar. You've both pressed your noses into business not your own."

Anna gazed down at the council member. Blood ran swiftly to Evelyn's lush lips from her nose. Anna tensed, lessening the anger bound in her fists to calm the urge to act too quickly. She was eager enough, yet what that might mean for Norman she dared not imagine.

With a great stretching of her neck, Lady Evelyn seized the item beyond her nose with her lips and blew. Cole and Roland roared, stomped, pulling their reins free from her and Norman. The storm bison charged after the men behind them. An almost agonizing roar reached from far beyond rumbled where they stood. A chill raced down Anna's spine. Lady Wayne blew again. Howls echoed from cheefoxes locked in a kennel by the drawbridge.

Anna was too familiar with the roar she'd heard. A crash erupted. Thudding followed in the dozens from what she couldn't guess. The air grew colder, clasping at her throat like the hand of a vengeful phantom. Her breath formed short, thin clouds. Another roar lead a collective crackling as if thousands of windows had been struck at once. She spun to the curtain. Far beyond the woods, the sun sank below the mountain. Something fast and huge briefly eclipsed its burning disk.

"What have you summoned?" Lord Martyn dug the tip of his sword into Lady Wayne's back. "Tell me!"

Evelyn gasped, dropping what was some kind of whistle. It had a silver shaft, clasped over the center by a golden tongue. Over the tongue roared a multi-headed beast. Evelyn grinned as blood mixed with the blondeness of her hair.

"You'll see, my lord." Evelyn said. "Just wait."

A great boom rattled the bricks of the curtain wall. Anna's heart pounded so fast her ears hurt, every breath grew short and hot. The crackling came again before four long claws of ice grabbed hold of the wall's battlements. Men drew their swords but soon dropped them as an immense head rose. Great wings of ice and flesh retracted to a long slender body. Anna readied her bow, fumbling with the arrows in her quiver. Norman's hands flickered, flames swirled into being, then vanished. Her friend paled and curled into a shaking ball.

"I came here on a dragon of ice," said Lady Evelyn. "Relinquish your intention to arrest Lady Brighton."

Lord Martyn clasped his sword with both hands and raised it. "Call off the ... creature!" he snarled. "Or I shall feed it to your—"

Anna released her arrow. His lordship cried out, dropping his sword, her arrow splitting and splintering the flesh of his hand.

"Kill the dragon and the traitors!" Lord Martyn roared, clutching his hand. "End them for your prime."

"No," Anna said, readying another arrow.

The lord fled for the keep, yanking free her arrow, wrapping his hand in his cloak. The dragon mounted the wall, cracking its brickwork, jabbing its head toward Lady Evelyn. Men thrusted at its belly with their swords. Ice cascaded down their blades, falling in small flakes from the dragon's scales.

"Anna, drop to the ground with your friend," said Lady Evelyn.

Anna raised an eyebrow, then turned to the dragon. It flashed its pale fangs as they glowed blue, releasing a heavy white mist. With a roar, the dragon spewed ice-blue flame from its jaws. Anna dropped and rolled beside Norman as the flames soared overhead. Lord Martyn screamed. His feet left the ground as the flames smashed him against the keep. His scream faded fast. The air grew so cold Anna had to huddle against Norman. He gasped at her touch, shaking ferociously. The heat she expected from the flames was a blistering, piercing cold. She wrapped herself around Norma and draped her cloak over them.

The dragon ceased its flames, roared, then devoured a man whole. The other guards cried for Lady Evelyn to show them mercy. With an immense swipe, the dragon cleared the wall of soldiers with its tail. Their cries were long but faint amongst the wind as the dragon crawled on its belly to Lady Evelyn. Anna untied the laces around her neck, then covered Norman with her cloak. She raced toward the mistress, readying an arrow. Lady Evelyn rose as Anna drew back her bow, aiming for the dragon's black heavy-lidded eye.

"Quiver your arrow, Anna," said the mistress, turning her back on the dragon. "You will only prolong my time bound at the wrists."

Lowering her bow, she kept the arrow nocked. Conden-sation lined its string, and a thin film of ice captured the condensation against its riser. Anna held her focus on the dragon. It released a tiny puff of mist from its long, narrow nostrils. The ropes about Lady Evelyn's wrists froze, shat-tering as she yanked them apart. She took up the whistle again as men gathered in the hundreds with swords drawn. Anna spun, bow at the ready, to find them with long spears wrapped in cloth, dipped in flaming oil.

"Surrender," Anna said, eyeing Norman. His breath was steady. The cloak was doing its duty. "Your lord is dead."

There was a hint of uncertainty in her words. She still

found herself afraid of the dragon and wasn't sure of its loyalty to Lady Evelyn. She didn't wish to relive the past.

"We've got your storm bison," said a guard among the others. "Send the dragon away and turn yourself in."

Anna craned her neck to the dragon. The long, serpentine creature curled up behind its mistress. A faint icy mist streamed over its teeth as it growled. Cole meant more to her than most, but as the cold remained unrelenting, Norman worried her more. She swallowed her nervousness, barely able to keep it down, not sure how to end all of this.

"You will not harm them. If the council's mistress of duels and debates orders the dragon to destroy Kardanhall," she winced, bracing against the sharp piercing wind. The metal plates of her leathers tacked on a chilling burden to her skin. "She will bury you along with it."

Some men eyed her with unease, squinting through the constant winds between domed helmet and gold cloth wrapped against their mouths. Clouds rose among them at a distance with a faint crackle and snap. Anna kept her eye trained, her bow slightly anchored. Her body shook more from the dragon's presence than from the tension in her arms.

With great organization, the men parted and then aimed their flame-tipped spears. Cole and Roland huddled close to one another. Her heart throbbed as the storm bison pulled and twisted, bound by half a dozen ropes, each with men digging their boots deep to hold them steady. She allowed her arm to rest for a moment, knowing there was no use in keeping her bow anchored. Lady Evelyn remained motionless below her dragon's head. It draped the mistress in shadow.

"I... I will go." There was no choice, Anna thought, none but to be brought before the prime and...

A roar erupted. Anna spun as the dragon rose on its hind legs. The air grew so unbearably cold she dropped her bow, collapsing beside Norman. Her body folded into a fetal position against him. All strength to remain awake fled like villagers from a flood.

TWENTY-TWO

The chill on her skin was replaced by the warmth of something Anna knew only briefly and in a less spacious room. Beside her, Norman slept softly, his clothes missing like her own. She climbed swiftly from the bed, wrapping herself in a cloak draped over a tall, leather-bound chair beside the bed. They were back within Kardanhall, yet why was she in bed with him, unclothed, her hair free from the string it had been in since Williamton.

She brushed aside the confusion forming a storm in her mind. Before her, Norman lay half exposed in her rush to be separated. They had lain with one another in Cillnar. Her heart was with him, but to awake in bed after the standoff between the dragon and the hostage storm bison was jarring. Last she remembered, she had been in a hurry, so Norman would suffer no more from the cold. The dragon's chill bit worse than any winter wind she had experienced on a hunt.

Beside the hearth, cloaked half in light and darkness, rested her leathers on a manikin. The sleeves hung like folded wings of a bird, casting thin shadows on the floor. Anna released her breath and covered Norman with the blankets. As her fingers brushed his shoulder, a faint coolness remained on his skin. He shivered. *Sleep well.* She drew back his long dark hair, kissed his cheek, and dressed.

Finding her way to the Great Hall from the day previous was difficult. Lord Martyn's servants cast stern eyes upon her in passing and increased their pace. She thought, with the sun stretching its beams through every window, that Lady Evelyn would have her midday meal. Thick oak columns supported the corridor; some appeared as if trees had been yanked free from the ground and turned upside down for roots clawed at the ceiling.

She reached a set of stairs that led to familiar doors. Their brass handles shaped like Lord Martyn's crest, its wood the same as the trees leading to Rockelton. Two men stood on either side, facing forward with arms folded behind their backs. Anna pushed open a door and felt the heat from the Great Hall's hearths envelope her. Opening the door was as hard as trying to force Cole to bathe. The servants remained facing forward. One sneered at her, chuckling at the strain running down her face. She guessed the only reason they contained their anger was to avoid Evelyn's wrath. A tall, sour-looking man looked up from polishing the dining table.

"If you're looking for Lady Wayne," he said. His voice was faint, for he was at the far end of the room. "Find your way to the castle temple."

Anna stopped at the end of the table. Her cloak enhanced the heat from the hearths, sending thick sweat droplets down her forehead.

"Can you lead me to it?" she asked. "I'm not familiar with Kardanhall."

The tall man rested the cloth and polish on the table, wiping his hands on a white apron about his waist.

"It goes against my loyalty to my departed Lord Kardan, but I'd rather no more harm came to his lordship's home. Head out across the hall and follow the cold."

"How do I follow—"

"His lordship kept warm only the rooms in use," said the servant. "By your dress, I'd say you're a hunter. Figure it out."

She left the Great Hall, allowing the man to return to polishing, ignoring the slight riddle in his directions. It was plain that those who served Lord Martyn weren't pleased by their lord's passing. His body had been fused to the brickwork of his castle's keep the last she saw of him. A powdery white mist drifted from the dragon's mouth afterward.

Following the cold proved to be more difficult than expected. She found the kitchen; hints of onion and beef stew gave its location away. Anna basked in its aroma, finding it both welcoming and overpowering. She pressed on towards the temple. Anna returned to the main corridor, eyeing the Great Hall's distant doors before proceeding. The further she went, the more her thoughts drifted back to her grandfather.

The anger for him these past weeks lessened its stranglehold on her heart. Anna saw great change was needed for Lampara and in more than who governed it from the capital. She wished her mind had been different, that she had trusted her grandfather's faith in her abilities. She wished, too, that Norman would not have witnessed the planning of Williamton's suffering. If this had not all come to pass, perhaps Nathan... She swallowed her surging sadness. She thrust her hand into the pouch on her belt.

Anna clasped the pale bear brooch. *Simdorn be with you, Nathan.*

The air grew colder as she made her way down a sloping corridor. A wide set of stairs spiraled downward and out of sight at its end. Lit orb lamps rattled from a strong breeze smelling faintly of mold. She rubbed her hands together, recalling Nathan's complaints about winter on their travels. Wiping away surfacing tears, she remembered Nathan spoke often of spring being his favorite year phase, that its blue skies brought him peace. She smiled, recalling his tale of one spring when, for the first time, Roland met another storm bison. He chuckled when recalling how he had chased the two across a farmer's field.

Anna made it to the bottom of the steps. A door shaped like an upside-down fingernail loomed ahead. She pulled it open and braced against a strong wind. Sunlight splashed against her face, doubling its brightness off the snow. Drawing her hoods tight over her eye it found the place where Lord Martyn had been fused to the keep. His body was gone, leaving remnants of a frozen crater. A bell chimed, sending her senses into a race. She pressed forward through the wind, bracing for a second chime. The temple of Simdorn gave three chimes at mid-morning, two at midday, and three when night fell. It was done for the departed. Sorrow filled her chest. She wished she had woken earlier. She was perturbed that even now the bell's tintinnabulations bothered her.

Mint incense greeted her once inside the temple. A wooden staircase led up to the bell tower. At the end of the room, two windows brought the only daylight. One faced the north, and the other welcomed light from the south. They bathed an altar of granite in their glow. She hugged her chest. Her heart thundered with grief. Anna sent her eye to the floor, fearing to rest it on the altar where her friend lay. Slowly, she drew back her hoods, cupping her hands to form a crescent moon. Her faith demanded it so honor may grace Simdorn. And yet she wanted to curse the goddess for not protecting her friend, for not diverting the men sent to butcher him. She shook her head, nerves abuzz with frustration. Each step weighed on her with a helplessness too late to feel. Anna buried her arms within her cloak, bounding her hands into fists. She passed pews of oak coated in a film of dust, their ends holding steadily lit candles of black wax.

Anna's senses were usually at ease within Simdorn's house. Today they were on fire. A fire with such heat no dragon could match it. Nathan's wounds had been sewn shut with thick black thread. What remained of his chin whiskers had been shaved clean, and his face was washed. Upon his eyes were two small smooth stones shaped like bears and painted white. Anna swallowed, grateful to whoever crafted them. Simdorn's guardians possessed the keen sight to guide the dead to heaven.

A man rose from the last pew on her left. The figure's shadow cast itself over the flag resting upon Nathan like a blanket. Whoever he was, he reached out to rest a hand upon the crest gracing the flag. The hand was long and slender, tested by the look of its flesh. Anna realized it wasn't a man but Lady Wayne.

"I'm glad you didn't miss the midday chime," said Lady Evelyn. Her hand fell from the crest which was of a badger upon its hind legs. "You were keen on keeping close to your friend. I commanded the servants to place you two together and build the fire to last."

Anna remained silent. Every thought trained on Nathan at rest with his hands folded over his chest. She breathed deeply, feeling the flesh of her burns tighten and then release.

"How long was I asleep?"

Lady Evelyn Wayne faced her with tears resting on her sharp cheekbones.

"Three days," Evelyn wiped clean her tears with the back of her hand. "There are men in Lord Martyn's guard who are still in a chilled coma from my dragon. You're one of the few on record to have recovered in less than a month." She allowed a slight smile, resting both hands at her sides. "I knew Brighton's were of strong stock, but you are something else."

Anna's mind drifted back to the barn, of what she knew of the rutoe. Anna shook off the impossibilities and then looked up at Simdorn's statue. The goddess stood barefoot on a plinth, wearing a breastplate of cremstone. She wore a bear's-head helmet with her ageless face within its jaws. Long red locks streamed from the helmet. White robes flowed down and around her body. Anna swallowed, trusting her faith had released her from the chilled coma. She tallied the barn up to her friends' overwhelming worry for her well-being.

"I wish to sit and mourn with you. I hope Nathan understood he made up for my burns," she said. "He would never have guessed, but his misdeeds have done more good than ill."

Lady Wayne gestured for Anna to join her. They sat on the pew in unison, neither moving to begin prayer.

"You have little time left," said Evelyn. "A month at most to return to the capital."

Anna looked to the north window, its light shifting slightly. The cold seeped through the temple's brickwork, telling her winter's months had only just begun.

"I still feel Lampara will not want to be governed by a burned woman," Anna said, rubbing her hands together and blowing into them. "But from how our people live, and how they treat storm bison, someone must lead them to a kinder tomorrow."

Lady Evelyn snorted.

"There's the confidence I knew you possessed. I cannot say you will change anyone's minds on storm bison, but your faith has made you wise enough to mend all else."

Anna tilted her head, leaning back.

"Prime Luther," Evelyn continued. "Has done more for this country's lords than for the average Lamparien. He throws coin at every problem with no thought to the toll his taxes place on the less fortunate. You keep to Simdorn's ways, her use of kindness and concern for the many."

"So, you're saying my choices will gain our people's trust far better than if my face were complete?"

Evelyn nodded. "You have proven yourself skilled as a warrior. Use your mind as you have just done to win the people."

Staring down at her hands, there seemed no reason to be complete anymore. Every thought visited her experiences of late. And though Rockelton may not support her, there was still Natlendton and her home in the Greethumb region to the east. *You were right, Grandfather,* she thought. *And I shall not let Williamton down.*

Anna reflected once again on Nathan, with the flag displaying his crest over him. The midday sun highlighted his pale features. He had been dressed in a leather tunic, its laces the color of walnuts. She thought his house crest should be something much bolder than a badger. Her friend had proven as much.

"I will risk being late for the tournament," Anna met

Evelyn's eye, "but I must leave for the sanctuary and find a wizard."

"I thought you decided your burns have no bearing," Lady Evelyn said.

Anna rose from the pew and offered her hand.

"I won't be going for me."

Lady Evelyn faced Nathan and then gasped.

"The dead must remain dead, for they have earned peace," she whispered, quoting scripture. "You of all people know this is Simdorn's greatest law."

"Yes," Anna said, a sharpness in her tone. "But Nathan didn't earn peace by death in battle, a family illness, or defending another. He was murdered."

The mistress of duels and debates narrowed her eyes, knitting her brow. Anna knew that mentioning family illness wasn't wise, but having Evelyn's support meant the world. Evelyn took her hand, rising with a slight unsteadiness.

"You're right," she said. "Now. How do you plan on making it south? How will you reach the tournament in time?"

Anna bit her lip and exhaled through her nose. She knew only one solution.

"I must face my fear. I must ride a dragon."

ANNA FOLLOWED Evelyn at a brisk pace. The keep towered beside them like an immense drum. It felt like a betrayal to travel without Cole, but her friend wasn't swift enough for the journey. She had visited him on the other side of Kardanhall, where the guest stables contained more straw and feed than Anna had ever seen. The storm bison greeted her in his usual way, and as always knew what was on her mind before the words breached her lips. She pulled her hoods over her face, for once doing so not out of fear of judgement. Only the cold bothered her now, knowing it would grow much worse. Cole's fur was warm when they parted. It had always been what saved her when they were caught in a storm during hunts. At this moment she wished she could crawl underneath him and huddle against his belly.

Across the castle grounds, massive bricks lay strewn. One was wedged in a window off on her right. Lady Evelyn moved with long, sturdy strides, as if her family illness was held at bay. Looming ahead was a tower, punctured from within like a bird's egg. Foulness reached her nostrils, rotten and more potent than any Anna had ever experienced. On the tower's rear side, a cage reached from the top to the base like a set of ribs. Pressed between two bars hung limp the head of Lord Martyn's esant. Anna readied her bow, reaching back for an arrow. A firm grip snatched her wrist.

"You cannot face your fear with intent to kill," said Evelyn. Her green eyes driven and focused. "Besides. Unless you possess strong enough magic, no arrow can pierce the chill protecting a crystalardan."

She shouldered her bow. Its string was wet from her sweat with a slight film of ice over it. Evelyn had made it to the tower's entrance first, her long strides firm with a purpose. The tower doors lay ripped from their hinges and coated in frost over the surface of their wood. Anna pinched her nose, following Evelyn in, slowing her pace. Light filled the tower from above, the very top like broken teeth biting at the sky. Anna noticed the doors to each stall had been smashed in and doused in clumps of upturned straw. Thick beams of dark wood supported the circular formation of the tower. On her left, a ramp climbed upward to more stalls.

"Look there," said Lady Evelyn, pointing to a half-moon-shaped straightaway. "The cold grows worse in that direction. I permitted my dragon to go out to stretch his wings. By my guess, he grew hungry."

Anna cupped her hands, blowing into them. She rubbed her shoulders until some feeling returned to her fingers.

"What if he flew to Rockelton and caused harm?" she asked.

Lady Wayne smiled.

"When you raise a dragon from a nestling, they tend not to wander off. The whistle," Evelyn slipped it from around her neck, holding it up by two fingers, "calls to them when not by their owner's side."

Anna nodded as they went down the straightaway. They found a more open section of the stables. Supporting it on either side, in gold, was the crest of Lord Kardan's house over squared columns of the same stone as the castle. She guessed this was where he kept and bred his finest steeds. Or used to. Blood streaked from every direction like the mouths of dried-up riverbeds. Sunlight streamed from diamond-paned windows crafted using crimson glass. Her heart pounded faster, and tips of her finger were numb. Fatigue compounded over her mind. It felt as though she would return to the coma Evelyn mentioned.

A long, thin line of light ran from the dragon's icicle-spiked nostrils to the base of its tail. Its eyes rested on Lady Evelyn. It lapped blood from its lips with its thick, black tongue. The dragon had formed a bed from smashed wagons and mound upon mound of straw. A gurgle rose through the dragon's throat. It belched a thin white mist as what blood its tongue hadn't collected fell. The blood crystalized and shattered upon the ground. Anna gulped, stepping forward as her toes curled against her feet from the creature's towering presence. She knew that by facing her fear it would disappear, but the winter encompassing the creature left her discouraged.

"What name did you give him?" Anna asked. There was no answer. "I said. What..."

Lady Evelyn was gone. Anna faced the dragon once again. The chill ebbing from his body sent jolts of numbness down her burns. It was opposite the fire of years ago, but the same feeling occurred, that paralyzing fear, a crushing pain in her chest. Anna raised her head, edging closer, shaking off those feelings. The dragon sat on his hind legs and ground his teeth. He sneered suspiciously at her, closing and opening his thick black eyelids.

"I cannot submit to my fear any longer." She stood tall, struggling to reach for her hoods. "I have hidden my face, afraid of what people thought. Afraid of being more than what I believed I could be."

The dragon lowered its long neck from on high. His head drew closer and closer until Anna could touch the bridge between his narrow nostrils. She hesitated for a moment and then drew back her hoods. She felt as though her face might shatter if the dragon came any closer.

"I don't know if you understand my words, but if you can, know that your speed is needed to bring my friend back."

"Touch him."

Anna remained still. Straw crunched as the dragon eased back, eyeing where the voice came from.

"A well-fed animal needs kindness," said Evelyn, resting a hand on Anna's shoulder. "You learned this from Cole."

A low deep hum ran across the dragon's lips. He trained his eyes upon her, their pupils radiating a pale blue. Summoning all her strength, she rested her hand above the icicles reaching inward from the tip of his chin. Anna's eye widened, finding his scales slick, a pale mist wisped from its lips.

"Now, just like Cole, you have earned Thomas's trust," said Evelyn.

"Thomas?"

"My husband's father claimed my brother and I as his own before his passing. He was a good man. He gave me Thomas before dying in the last war. I know no other way to honor a man so kind."

Lady Wayne's words were heavy with pain. Anna let her hand drop, taking Evelyn into her arms.

"Thank you." Anna whispered. "I couldn't have done this without your help."

"You just have," said Evelyn. "Now, let's bring your friend back."

TWENTY-THREE

Men in roughspun tunics grabbed and shoved someone into a short alley. The alley traveled between two mills of faded brick and roofs thatched with faded tall grass. Norman caught a flash from a bronze mouth shield below a green diamond shape. The quiet one pressed her parcels to her chest. Norman took a step from his father's side, searching for someone who could help. He called out to a man leading his horse, but the bustle of carts and passersby allowed no room for his voice to carry. He saw tears run over the woman's mouth shield, her eyes begging.

She twisted and turned in the men's grasp, knowing like Norman, there was no way for her to call out. A whisper from her would bury her alive. He peered up at his father, sucking in a breath. A burning churned in his chest. Norman felt his eyes flicker. Flames erupted over his fists, tingling through his skin. He dashed for the alley. One man drew out a knife as the quiet one's eyes snapped shut. Norman halted within the alley and in a flash all he saw was...

Norman shook himself awake. A canopy woven from black silk overwhelmed his blurry vision. He rubbed his eyes, drawing back his hand from their heat. His skin surged with energy, warming his chest and limbs. He noticed beyond the bed's edge the roaring flames of an immense hearth. He focused on the crackle and snap of its wood, regaining his composure. *I am in Kardanhall.* Rolling over, something crinkled beside his hip. Norman slipped a scroll tied with a black string from under it. He untied it and then unfurled it.

> *Norman,*
> *I have gone with Lady Wayne to Echnumbard.*
> *We leave for the sanctuary in hopes of finding a*
> *wizard. I know less than a month remains to win*
> *the hearts of Lampara in the tournament. My*
> *reason for the search is no longer for my face but*
> *for the friend we lost.*

Norman smiled. "She finally sees that her deeds are what truly matter."

> *You have been given control of Kardanhall*
> *under Lady Wayne's instruction.*
> *Be careful. I don't know what hatred the*
> *servants harbor for you. They hold a grudge*
> *against me, and I do not blame them in the least. I*
> *would advise one way of defense, and it goes against*
> *your nature. They hold great value for Kardanhall.*
> *Threaten it. And your safety will be certain. I hope.*
> *Anna*

Norman sat up to read the letter again, brushing back his hair. Upon reading the line concerning Nathan, his stomach lurched. Resurrection magic saw little success and great heartache. He planted his feet on the floor, hoping Lady Wayne possessed sense enough to discourage Anna from it. And yet he knew if Anna wanted something, there was no stopping her from obtaining it.

He slipped on his trousers, weaving its laces as another thought found him. Anna was right. Threatening arson was against his nature, even more so after what happened to Williamton. The loyalty was strong in Lord Martyn's men's eyes when they had returned to Kardanhall. At no time since reaching it, leaving for Rockelton, and then returning with haste did he trust them. He counted himself lucky after asleep for what seemed ages. He stuffed Anna's note in his pocket. It may act as insurance for his safety, he thought.

Night filled every window, bathing the corridors he passed through in moonlight. Orb lamps flickered on either side of black banners displaying Lord Kardan's crest. Norman shivered as the cold found its way through his boots. It stood to reason a castle required little warmth if its lord no longer lived. He trained his eyes for servants, daring to hope that they would leave him be.

A roar rattled through the windows spaced along the corridor. Norman looked up through a window to find stars. A great shape hid them for seconds and then they appeared once more. Voices echoed from down the hall. Another roar shook loose an orb lamp and clanged against the ground, cracking, rolling, fumbling its oil. Norman followed the voices, grabbing, and raising the lamp.

He stopped short of a corner to find familiar doors. Immense braziers lined the walls on either side, supported by the shafts of spears. The doors were thick and towering, made of dark oak. Men stood before the large gold rings across them. Norman leapt in place at a tap on his shoulder, dropping the lamp. It clanged and spun away, splashing its light across a small hooded old woman.

"This household will heed the instruction of Lady Wayne," said the old woman. A yellowed tooth protruded from her upper lip, "but should Prime Luther suspect something, then the Brighton girl will lose another friend."

Norman met the old woman's milky white eye. His skin shifted to the pinkish flesh of his disguise. His hair rolled up his cheeks, curling to become short and auburn. Straightening his collar, he noticed a hint of gold in the folds of the old woman's robes, the weight of which the fabric seemed to hang. She patted her side, smiling, reaching, and raising the orb lamp. It highlighted her deep wrinkles that reached from her eyes to over her lips.

"Please see you do," he said, wondering what business the prime had at Kardanhall. He realized. "Is Prime Luther here for Anna?"

The old woman nodded. "And it appears you will have to break the news to him. You had best come up with a good story."

The old woman turned on her heels, strolling uneasily up the corridor. Her lamp's light faded with Norman's confidence. He should have shown he was in command and ignited his hand, but his mind got the better of him. A great thrum rattled the walls, brushing the soles of his boots. Norman gulped, peering around the corner. A pair of distant almond-shaped eyes blinked. They glowed orange, warped with red, large enough to swallow him whole.

"Where's Lord Dribble?" Prime Luther breached the darkness, his posture resembled that of an 's.' His armor hung upon his aged person like flower petals in apprehension of their impending fall. His hat wasn't crafted from norlstrell like most primes. It was made of gold fabric, haloed by long red oval gems. "Where is the Brighton girl? That slack jaw bastard was supposed to give her over. Wasn't he, my boys?"

Norman gasped. Two hulking men, one in green-plated armor, and the other in red, aligned with the prime. One possessed a chin thick enough to break down the door closing behind him. His eyes seemed to have no firm direction, shaded by hair a golden red. The man nodded in sync with his brother, who was the same in all but his eyes and teeth. The second man's teeth were cracked and jagged as if he had bitten a granite block. His eyes were wild and darting, as if expecting someone to pounce on him.

"Well?" Prime Luther barked. "Where is he?"

The guards remained still, sweat running down their brows to the gold cloth across their mouths. Norman puffed up his chest and pranced out into what felt like certain doom. *For Anna.*

"I'm afraid, your prime-ship," Norman said, spreading his arms wide with his chin held high. "His lordship is out at the moment."

"And who might you be?" said one son, flashing his cracked teeth. "He's expecting the big man." The prime's son gestured to his father. A jeweled gauntlet guarded his hand. The hand shook despite the sturdiness of his frame. "I want to make the burned girl my plaything."

Norman seethed through his teeth, feeling their points form. Prime Luther chuckled. His prime-ship took three great strides and then settled back into his hunched posture.

"Now, Unter," the prime said, squinting through the

hall's brightness. "You can't sleep with one of your fellow campaigners."

Unter opened a small compartment on his gauntlet. He plucked a tiny spoon from it and inhaled a blue powder through his nose. "Whatever." He coughed; the shaking ceased, but a faint chatter rattled through his teeth. "I bet she'd be a waste of a real man's time."

"That's a good lad," said Prime Luther, turning back to Norman. "What troubles you, boy? Is your future prime too manly for you?"

"No, your prime-ship." Norman could feel his skin shift and fade. He focused on the crackle of the braziers, the dance of their flames. He imagined Anna placing a perfectly aimed arrow in Unter's throat. "Allow me to escort you to the Great Hall. Your journey must have been long and cold."

"Good man," said Prime Luther, gesturing to his sons. "Come along, boys. Perhaps Lord Dribble's scrawny friend can put out a better spread than his master."

Upon entering the Great Hall, a spread, as the Prime called it, spanned the length of the table. Chairs with tall backs lined it, draped with half-red and green banners. Over both colors, a splash of shadowy silk covered a horse of silver. Norman's stomach grumbled once he found a place at the end of the table. Servants received the Prime's cloak. It possessed pale moons along the trim. Two servants each received his sons trench coats. They were of fresh boiled leather, their collars ringed in closely trimmed black fur.

It appeared Lord Martyn had, in fact, wished to impress the prime. At the table's center rested three turkeys cooked to a golden brown and ringed with a yellow sauce. Bowls of roasted red potatoes orbited the turkeys. They were part-nered with apples sliced in such a way Norman swore they resembled the Lamparien governing crest. Prime Luther sat first, hovering over a plate of pure polished silver.

"A fine feast we have here, Lord…?"

"Norman Tilt. I am but a representative," said Norman, taking his seat after the boys did. "As for Lord Martyn, he is returning with Lady Brighton as we speak."

"Good. Slide the potatoes over, Unter."

The prime's son looked up with a mouth full of meat. He grumbled like a disturbed bear. He slurped a dangling piece of meat into his mouth. Norman stifled a bit of vomit in his throat. *Nathan was right,* he thought, slicing a potato and then raising it to his lips. *Luther will definitely be the brains behind either brother should they win.* With a rattle the silver platter slid down the table, scattering potatoes before the prime seized it by the decorative handle.

"I like potatoes, Norman," said the prime, loading his plate and then stuffing his mouth. "I may make those idiots pelt each other for my position."

Norman raised an eyebrow but swiftly hid his confusion. The prime eyed him for approval.

"I've always said if you can put up with a pelting, then you can face anything." The prime chuckled, narrowing his eyes upon his plate. "Even the complaints of the damn council."

"You ought 'ave 'em strung up and hacked to pieces, Father," said the crossed eyed son.

Norman dabbed his lips. "Lampara needs the council. Does it not?"

The sons trained their eyes on him. Norman kept his posture, feigning a smile at them both.

"We need the Wayne woman and the council like we need another rutoe uprising." Prime Luther stuffed a whole potato in his mouth. It opened a jar, the potato rolled off his tongue as he waved at his mouth. "Hot." He spat. "The fools wanted peace with those southern snake riders."

"I have to agree with them, your prime-ship," said Norman. "I've heard about your recent fight with the rutoe. I'm grateful you survived a quiet one's fierce attack."

"Fierce?" said Unter. Spittle ran down his chin. He tossed a bone over his shoulder. "You give those block-headed rat eaters a lot of credit."

Norman released a breath through his nose. He drew from the hearths light to ease his nerves. Fear gripped his throat as he pieced together a response, but the purposeful anger Unter put into hating his people was too much.

"My apologies," he said, avoiding Unter's gaze. "I was taught to be respectful to all who live inside Lampara's borders."

Unter scoffed. "You sound like the Brighton girl's grandfather."

"Enough, Unter," Luther barked. "The young man can think what he wants for now."

"But Father—"

Prime Luther slammed his fist on the table. The hulking boy fell silent, popping open the compartment on his gauntlet. He snorted three spoonfuls of the blue powder. He shook for several moments. The veins on his neck bulged and glowed. Norman watched as he seized the turkey before him. Unter raised it to his lips and tore at it like a wolf a deer carcass.

"Prama dust," Prime Luther said, grinning. "The only good thing to come out of the South."

Norman shook his head to find his fingers digging into the armrests of his chair. The heat from the hearths of the Great Hall no longer soothed him. Their crackle brought only noise instead of peace. His skin itched to shift from the flesh of human to rutoe. And yet death was assured if he allowed himself to be what he was. Kardanhall would become a trap for Anna once she returned.

"How are the potatoes ..., your prime-ship?" said Norman, trying to change the subject. "Are they to your liking?"

Luther wiped his mouth with the back of his hand.

"They're better than last time for certain. Anyway. To business. I await the Brighton girl. I was told she would be here when I arrived."

Norman swallowed, loosening his grip on the armrests.

"Lady Anna is a skilled warrior and hunter. His lordship may have lost her in the woods."

"Her support from the people nearly equals my sons," said the Prime. "I can't have that, not from some girl with no army to stop me. My rule is ending, but when one of my sons wins, it shall be rekindled."

"Will you rule through one of them?" Norman asked, feigning a chuckle. "Is not that against the law?"

"Father," said Unter. "You should wait a bit. This ain't Lord Martyn you be talking to."

"What? Oh, I'm done waiting for that slack-jawed crea-tine." Prime Luther made his hands into fists. Rising, he strolled to the nearest hearth. "You can keep a secret, can't you, Norman Tilt?" He eyed Norman with a softness in his expression. "Anyway, it will be something like that once I remove a few barriers. The Brighton girl's parents were the first hurdle to fall. She will be crushed along with those miserable—".

"Father." Unter barked. "That's too much. Wait, a bit."

A flood of nerves overcame Norman as he watched the prime take a poker from the hearth's rack and waved it at his son. He felt as Anna did but deprived of the warning her nerves provided her. Anna told him her parents had been killed by robbers chasing them through the forests of the Greethumb. He rose to join the prime, but once close enough, he went stiff as a board. His feet rooted themselves in place. A red-hot poker hovered within inches of his face from the prime's grasp.

"The heat doesn't seem to bother you, Norman Tilt. Does it?" said Luther, turning the poker in his hand. "Unter's right. I'm not as sharp as I once was, but I'm wise enough to notice your lack of perspiration."

Great heavy footsteps echoed behind him. Norman turned in time to see a metal wall . He groaned as the towering prime's son grabbed his arms and pressed him toward the poker. He clenched his teeth to remain human. The point of the poker hovered below his chin. His arms grew numb the more Unter squeezed.

"I assure you, Prime Luther," he said. "I am human like yourself."

"You do not need to lie," said Luther, sneering from under his thin white eyebrows. "The clouds rising from the guest stables were clue enough. The man your friend let escape told me about a rutoe possessing power over fire."

"I'm not him." Norman gulped. "I swear—"

The prime pressed the steaming poker into Norman's cheek. Its heat was nothing, but the point sent his flesh to what it truly was. He screamed and pulled away, seething as the poker left a deep cut on its face. Prime Luther pulled back the poker and tossed it away. He rose to full height and grabbed Norman's collar.

"Tell me, rutoe of the ignited ones," Luther pulled him close, "where is Anna Brighton? My son will break your back if you resist again."

Norman heaved and wheezed. His hair tumbled down

his face, and his teeth sharpened, nicking his tongue before eyes flared.

"She is long gone," he said, then ignited the tip of his finger, "as I shall be."

A spiraling, hissing flame shot forth. It struck the hearth, splintering and scattering the wood. Norman shut his eyes at the flash of light. He yanked himself free from Unter's grasp. Prime Luther staggered back. Norman dashed for the doors. The other prime son raced to help his father. Norman halted before the doors. *I cannot open this alone.* He splayed his fingers over its surface and blasted an expanse of flames. The door burned slowly at first. The flames ate away at its thickness.

Shouts and racing footsteps gnawed at his ears from the hall. He saw the guards fleeing with their cloaks aflame. He felt himself yanked back.

"You nearly blinded me, you green whelp," said the prime.

Norman gasped. He couldn't harm the prime, but at this point, being an outlaw was certain. The doors were crumbling, black and fragile. He shook himself free. The prime grabbed him by the hair and yanked. A jolt of pain raced to the roots of his scalp. Norman focused until the long, dark locks of his true self slipped free. He returned his features to human form for a split second, and he dove through the crumbling door.

Stumbling to his feet, ash and charred debris fell from his shoulders. He dashed down the hall, exhaling until he was a rutoe once again. Guards of both the Prime and Kardanhall chased him with raised swords. Norman recalled which way led to the main entrance, knowing a dragon remained before it, but he needed to warn Anna. He needed to find his way south, hoping Cole and Roland still lived. His heart rammed against his chest as he charged the soldiers. Until venturing from Williamton, fighting had never been something he imagined doing. Norman pictured his father, missing him, feeling pride swell in his belly. The battle he learned about in Cillnar was one his father might have fought in. He cast his flames at the feet of those coming toward him, sending them racing for the walls. His father had returned south once Lord William's accountant had made Norman his apprentice. It had broken Norman's heart to be without him, but when news came of a slow-burning uprising in the south, he knew only one rutoe with courage enough to start it.

Nearing the last stretch to the main entrance, no further resistance surfaced. Footsteps echoed behind him, silencing his rising curiosity as he let out a breath. Again, another set of immense doors stood in his way, the low rumble of the dragon breathed through its cracks. Norman slipped behind a brazier, holding steady to one of the spears supporting it. The footsteps grew louder the faster he regained his breath. Two towering shadows raced past him with drawn swords and then vanished around a corner. Norman crept out from behind the brazier, placing his hand firmly against the door.

"Go ahead."

A pang of fear rattled down his spine. Norman turned, allowing his hand to drop.

"You have far more courage than I expected for an accountant," said the prime, drawing a long dagger from a green scabbard at his hip. "Yes. I know much about you. Your father is in my prison."

"I don't believe you," said Norman, raising his hand to the doors. "You could have spoken with Lord William. He had Williamton burned to force his granddaughter to campaign."

Luther drew himself up, sticking out his lower lip as he folded his arms.

"I never would have expected such an extreme measure from a Brighton. I suppose the traitor spilled his guts about me and made campaigning all the more tempting."

"No," said Norman, shaking his head as he faced the Prime. "She wanted nothing to do with campaigning or with you."

"Her actions say otherwise." Luther scoffed. "You may as well surrender where you stand, boy."

Soldiers emerged from the distant hall. Norman last saw the old woman. Their torches grew in brightness, joined by the clicking of spurs. The clicking like the sound of thousands of raindrops against a window. Guards of Kardanhall crowded beside the Prime, swords drawn, their mouths shielded thick gold cloth, wearing dome helmets and long heavy gold cloaks.

"Anna will win the tournament," said Norman, pressing his back against the doors.

"That may have been possible ten years previous," Luther said. A calm in his voice, "but things have changed. I've made certain."

"No. She has greater potential than you know."

"Greater than she knows," Norman thought, hearing the dragon beyond the doors grumble and stomp. His focus trained on the men awaiting orders.

"Take him."

At once, like an immense wave, Norman was swallowed. His arms were yanked back. An icy, metallic feeling snatched and bound them together. Norman focused but failed to ignite his hands. The shackles negated his flames, yet he knew not how. Eyes narrowed with intent filled his vision and then parted as swiftly. Norman leaned back and grimaced as the Prime appeared within inches of his face.

"We'll put him with his father," said the Prime, grinning beneath the brim of his hat. "Perhaps the wish of all fathers will come true, and Huldinarf will die before his own son does." He rested a hand gloved in red leather on Norman's cheek. "He has so little time left as is."

TWENTY-FOUR

I t took much time to apply the dome saddle to the crystalardan without stable boys. The mistress of duels and debates gave Anna instruction, keeping the ice dragon calm with hand motions and the use of her whistle. She stretched her arms to their fullest extent to relieve the ache from climbing up and down the dragon. Anna slid in her seat, taking hold of the edge of its cushion. Near the length of her arms, windows long and narrow lined the dome saddle's sides. The dragon's chill bothered only the soles of her feet as he flew south with them upon his back. Anna had never been in such a small place. She craved the openness of being on Cole's back. She swallowed for what felt the hundredth time to hide her nervousness from Lady Evelyn.

Day had turned to night through the window beyond the council member. The mistress sat a head lower than her, holding firm, long, black ropes. The ropes trailed out a pair of portholes toward Thomas's bridle. Relief washed over her chest, thankful Evelyn had applied the bridle instead of her. The fear still resonated within her somehow, and though she had grown comfortable in the dragon's presence, interaction in so close a fashion would take time.

"We are a day south," she said. "How will you guide Thomas, seeing the day has long since gone?"

Lady Evelyn peered over her shoulder. A small smile on her lips.

"Thomas knows his way about Dar. My father brought him from the southern region of Breezenburg. It's said to be a land of fire and ice, but few journey to. I have been to rutoe lands before. And it shall be day by the time we reach their mountains."

Anna settled slowly back into her seat, finding her eagerness had placed her within a whisper of Lady Wayne. The mistress gave her an assuring nod, facing forward and jerking Thomas's reins. With a great flap like the clap of thunder, he roared and sped faster. His wings rose and fell swiftly in tune with his back. Anna fell forward, reaching to catch herself against the mistress's seat.

"My apologies, Anna," said Evelyn. "Man has yet to invent a way to secure oneself to a saddle, especially one fit for a dragon."

She crab-walked back into her seat. The walls around her felt as if they were closing in. Sweat ran down her brow. "I will manage." She wiped the droplets away, sighing to herself.

"Good. You will need such an attitude when we return to Cillnar."

"If we can in time," Anna said. "I have never seen a wizard and know only what my grandfather described. Do you know what they truly look like?"

Lady Evelyn placed Thomas's reins in one hand, turning so she faced Anna completely.

"No one does."

"How shall we find one then?" Anna gasped. "How have there been no accounts of them besides their deeds?"

Evelyn raised a hand to calm her. Anna's chest heaved. She felt the mistress of duels and debates place her hand on her knee, but the gesture brought no comfort.

"I've heard they change form like the wind its direction." Evelyn heightened the pitch in her voice, giving Anna's knee an assuring squeeze. Her grip was like that of Anna's grandfather, sturdy and firm. "I know we'll find one for your friend. I promise."

"How?" Anna yelled, throwing up her hands. "Nathan died because of me. He died because I thought he was going someplace safe."

Slap

Anna shook her head. The pain wasn't instant at first. She didn't even see the strike coming. She let her jaw hang slack and groaned.

"Did Lord William allow such hysterics?" Lady Evelyn asked, merging her lips into a thin, firm line. "I doubt it very much."

Meeting the mistress's gaze, the pain came not from her blind side as expected. Evelyn was truly an orderman. She fought with honor, as Nathan said in their travels an orderman did.

"No," she said, rubbing her cheek. "He would flick my brow hard. He did so once when his thumb was broken. It took years for me to learn how to avoid such pain."

Lady Evelyn faced forward once more, taking Thomas's reins in both hands. She gave them another jerk, but this time, as his wings gave their thunderous clap, Anna refused to brace herself.

"You will learn to do so with me," said Evelyn. "Now.

Focus on what you want and let us hope our search is swift."

THE SUN REVEALED its light through the dome saddle's windows. It was their second day of travel as Thomas soared over the beginnings of what felt like a whole other country. Evelyn had spoken true about the dragon's speed a day previous. Some mountains reached high into the clouds, while others formed canyons and valleys. Scattered across the valleys were homes, farms, and, on the side of a few mountains were huts entirely of stone. She could barely see them because their stonework blended into mountain sides. Anna rested her hands upon her knees, rubbing them, guilt swelling for being irrational at the journey's start. She rested a hand upon the council member's shoulder. The sunlight highlighted the worn leather of her gloves.

"I must apologize for my behavior," she said. "My grandfather would be disappointed in me."

Evelyn rested her eyes on Anna's hand, then returned to guiding Thomas. The dragon parted the clouds with his roar, sending snow downward from the chill of his breath.

"I was disappointed," Lady Evelyn said, emotion trapping her words for a moment by the sadness in her voice, "but you remind me so much of my daughter. Despite my strong convictions, I haven't the strength to remain so."

Anna gave Evelyn's shoulder a faint squeeze, then leaned close, and folded her arms across her chest. It heaved slightly. Evelyn rested a hand over Anna's. The firm grasp of the day previous was gone.

"I have not seen Emilia for nearly a year, Anna." Evelyn

swallowed deeply; tremors ran through her fingers. "She went out with her wife, seeking to make a change. Emilia said if I was going to stand by while Luther's choices caused harm, then I was more guilty than him."

Anna removed herself from the warmth of Evelyn's presence and rested deep within her seat.

"Does the council have the power to keep a prime from his declarations?"

"No," said Evelyn. "We can only enforce campaign law and remind who governs of what Lampara's traditions demand. We do the same regarding the actions Simdorn frowns upon. My daughter knows I must also be Luther's protector. She believes the ordermen should forgo duty this one time. Allow for assassination to take place."

"The orderman I fought said his fellow guardsmen contemplated assassination," Anna said. "It led him instead to place his name in the final calling."

"I spoke with the man you fought after your duel. He is my eyes on our prime until we return to Cillnar."

Anna sighed.

"My faith in finding a wizard and returning in time is still uneasy."

Ahead through the window a stretch of smooth rock broke through the clouds blanketing their way. It sat before a narrow path leading higher into a mountain ringed by layer upon layer of mist. Immense braziers circled the stretch of smooth rock like a halo struggling to maintain its divine glow. Anna braced herself as they dropped lower. Thomas's long neck aligned straight with what lay before him.

"I know you have many doubts, Anna," said Lady Evelyn. Her voice was low, calm, unlike the nerves mounting in Anna's chest. "The one thing you haven't possessed doubt in is your faith. Use that. Use it as you would your bow on a hunt."

Deep regret thumped against her chest at the choice of Evelyn's words. Anna had made her journey all about herself, barely hearing or paying notice to the struggles of those closest. She thought of Norman. His people were othered from Lampara. Made to appear as both enemies and someone not trusted to share the public with. Her thoughts narrowed to the woman before her, plagued by family illness, and parted from a child fully grown.

The smooth stretch of rock drew closer. Tremors ran through Lady Evelyn's arms the lower Thomas went, but the dragon and dome saddle remained steady. Anna felt unsure whether she should take control or allow her friend to land Thomas alone. The tremors grew worse, sending Anna's nerves on full alert.

"You are ailing, Lady Evelyn," Anna said, maneuvering beside her. "Please allow me to guide us down."

Ahead, their destination was flat and covered in large patches of ice. The braziers on brick pillars reached with their light through the window. Anna rested her hand on the rope. She coughed, choking on her breath as pain boomed in her stomach.

"Do not do that again," Evelyn sneered, drawing back her fist, then threatening Anna with it. "I will not be made a passenger on my dragon."

Anna leaned back, rubbing her stomach. From the corner of her eye, the stretch of flat mountaintop appeared directly below them. Thomas touched down. Through the dome saddle's side windows, his wings slowly retracted, their thick membrane whipping like a thick sheet in strong wind. She turned back to the mistress, finding her quakes had ceased. The dragon clambered to a stop, stomped, and slowly settled onto his stomach. Evelyn stood at half her height and dropped the ropes. She yanked two cords at the top corners of the front window. The door for which it was built into dropped, crunching against the dragon's back.

Evelyn leapt over the steps built into the door and climbed down Thomas's back. She used his shoulder for balance as Anna followed. Her breath returned slowly from the council member's strike. Anna drew her hoods over her head, hiding more from Evelyn than the wind. The hoods felt like a shield against the burning disappointment in Evelyn's eyes.

"This is the second time you've been struck," Evelyn said, checking her gloves. "I trust and admire you. There is little doubt that you will rise to the challenges ahead. I cannot, however, be denied what remains of my independence." She spun on her heel and marched off. Evelyn covered herself with an ankle-length coat, its collar ringed with fur. "Let's be off. You have a friend to resurrect."

OVERCOMING the path where they landed proved slick. Every instinct demanded that Anna ignore her friend's wish for independence. To guide her the rest of their way. But her reflexes weren't a match for another strike, nor had they been for the previous two. Anna pulled her cloak close, snowflakes brushing the ends of her bow strung over her shoulder. Her quiver rattled with each step, signaling few arrows remained, twelve by her last count. Anna wished she had searched for Kardanhall's armory to resupply. She let out a low sigh, looked up, and found her friend had stopped.

"We must keep moving," she said, finding the path

wide enough for her to stand beside Lady Evelyn. "The sanctuary is still a good distance ahead."

"Listen," Evelyn whispered, the wind freeing hairs from her bun. "There is a matter of which I haven't told you."

Anna took each step with care, placing herself so the mistress of duels and debates was in full view of her working eye.

"What is it?"

"The Waynes ... have been smuggling nelka out of the south for some time."

Her jaw fell slack. Both of her hands found the fur lining her cloak. The swift saber-toothed feline was held sacred amongst the rutoe, said to be the size of a carriage and hard to track.

"Must I go alone then?" said Anna. "Why did you not tell me this before?"

"Would you have been able to guide Thomas?" Evelyn checked the knives at her hip, buttoning her coat up to her neck. "You'd have used Cole and not faced your fear. Had I not given Thomas a stable full of potential meals, your chances of finding him agreeable would be nonexistent."

Anna grabbed Evelyn's collar and shoved her. Lady Evelyn stumbled back. Tremors ran down her body as she stretched out one leg, then firmly planted the other. A blade hissed from her sleeve as her eyes narrowed.

"You didn't believe in me," Anna roared, slipping her bow free as she clapped an arrow against it. "All your words have been a lie." She drew back, aiming faster than she had ever done. "I should strike you down and find the wizard myself."

Lady Evelyn frowned, slipping the knife back up her sleeve.

"No," she said. "I always believed in you, Anna. Enough

to take a great interest in you and abandon my duties on the council. Emilia was right. And now I am here to make certain Luther doesn't succeed."

Tension ran through her arms. The cold pierced every layer on her person. Her eye narrowed to a slit but brought little focus against both wind and snow. She swallowed, licking her lips to hold strong against their dryness.

"I truly haven't faced my fear then," Anna said, feeling her arrow's fletching rub against her cheek, begging her to be released. "How much else do I not know?"

Lady Evelyn realigned her feet, dropping her hands to her sides. Anna eyed them for even a hint of something sharp but found them to be empty.

"There is nothing else to tell, except that you are right. You must enter Echnumbard alone."

The arrow went without her say. The string of her bow snapped to attention as her arm dropped, zapped of strength. She called out as a gust of wind closed her hoods, blinding her. There was no cry of pain, nor a heavy thud against the uneven rock at her feet. Anna clasped her hoods, yanking them back.

"I'm grateful for the damn wind for once," Evelyn said, lowering her hand from her face. "I would be gone from this world had there'd been none."

Held firmly in the mistress of duels and debates hand was Anna's arrow. Anna shouldered her bow, searching for words and finding none. She had been doomed from the moment she had entered the Proving long ago. The ordermen possessed speed and training beyond anything she could master. She shook her head, rubbing the stress from her face with a fist. Lady Evelyn held up the arrow, with its fletching first. Snowflakes pounded its shaft, coating its smoothness in white.

"My guess is you will wait with Thomas," Anna said, taking the arrow. "Being my accomplishment was a lie you will be needed for the return north."

Anna shoved the arrow back into her quiver. Evelyn rested her eyes on Anna. They remained still and focused as she ushered the fur of her collar closer to her cheeks.

"Accomplishments are not always done by oneself," she said, breath steaming. "I noticed a set of stairs not far from where we landed. I will await your return there." Evelyn rested a hand on Anna's shoulder. "Good luck."

Anna bit her lip, peering toward the path. Farther ahead, the path was shrouded in mist, but what ground lying before it held hints of ice under mounting snow. The sky had turned gray and grim.

"I guess you are right, Lady Evelyn. Much of what I have achieved of late saw success with the help of my friends."

"Let's put aside titles and manners then." Evelyn smiled. "Call me Eve."

SNOW CRUNCHED WITH EVERY STEP, feeling as though it might be her last. The path had narrowed enough to accept a single traveler. Ice made every need for progress, every step toward Nathan's return slow and uncertain. Anna felt her way with her feet, reaching both arms out for balance. The snow grew less intense once she reached a slight slope. She paused for a moment at a faint echo. Its depth and tone sounded like Thomas. The constant wind kept her from knowing if his roar was out of anger or something else.

Anna found the slope ended as quickly as it began. Her curiosity about Thomas was gone with it, replaced by two towering pillars. Their shape and detail became more and more pronounced as the mist slowly faded before her eye. Anna found a strange sense of calm wrap itself about her. Every nerve didn't buzz, and her anticipation of the worst felt unneeded.

The pillars were marked with symbols carved from red stone. She could not find an answer to how, but every symbol seemed to be the source of this new feeling. The ones upon the right pillar was a fist wreathed in flame like a tree set ablaze. Below it was another fist with one finger pressed to a pair of lips.

Upon the second pillar, a man with long flowing hair evaded a shining red stone with great ease. Below him was a woman with one hand to her brow, and the other levitating a red orb inches above an outstretched hand. Anna passed between them, finding the cold slowly abandon her muscles. Sweat cascaded down her cheeks as she drew her hoods back and removed her gloves, tucking them in her belt. A hiss filled her ears. She looked around for a snake but reasoned that was impossible. Anna gasped.

Grass rose above her boots. The air grew warmer, urging her to remove the cloak of nelka fur Emily had gifted her. She replaced her bow and quiver over her shoulders. She realized once in Echnumbard, not having the cloak might be wise. Refocusing ahead, trees rose, shading her from the sunlight she hadn't seen since leaving the land of Lampara. She moved toward the trees on her left, stumbling back when her feet found no purchase. *But how do the trees stand?*

Anna regained her balance, keeping herself on the straight path ahead of her. Chirping whispered in the distance, joined by the slight rustling of branches. Her mind felt clear like a sky absent of clouds. There was a tingling in her right eye. A tremor from the part of her lips sealed shut from her burns. No one stood ahead, behind or on either side of her, but Anna felt this had to be the work of a wizard.

She looked up, froze, and stepped back at a large shadow. It filled her vision, yet the skin binding her eye shut loosened. She blinked, wincing. A screech left her lips as both eyes drew in the light. They both could open! They both could see! Resting a hand to her lips, they parted and stretched, drawing in the air. Anna let out a laugh that shook her chest. Tears met the corners of her lips. *Clank.* She leapt back; tremors ran under the soles of her boots. Chains rattled, fading into view only to grow blurry by a kick up of dust. Anna dropped to her knees, uncertain even in the calm she felt. She ran her fingers over every inch of her face. It was smooth and...

"I'm... I'm complete."

TWENTY-FIVE

A great, unnerving roar reached Evelyn's ears. She felt her hand begin to shake. Thomas's roar slowly faded into the south's mountain openness. She raised her hand to eye level. Snatching an arrow out of the air was something she didn't believe possible in her current state. She wove a finger through the hole in her glove and winced. She wondered if her friend roared out of hunger or impatience. Blood met the hole in her glove from the arrow's razor-sharp head. *Have I grown that slow?* she sighed, listening for her friend.

Leaving the glove on, she made her way back to Thomas. Her hope for Anna was strong. The girl had been through much since parting from Williamton. Evelyn smiled a small smile. After leaving the Brighton girl within one of the Proving's bathing rooms, it was difficult to imagine Anna campaigning. And yet, without Phillip's race with the cheefox, Anna Brighton may have returned to Williamton or died by the blade of someone far more competent than Nathan Barden.

The snow was relenting. Evelyn wished the wind would

follow its lead. She rubbed her shoulders and squinted. Thomas's immense serpentine outline grew larger and clearer with her quick pace. There was no movement from the crystalardan, no chronic restlessness. She knew from her friend. There was no chill on her cheeks but what the high altitude provided.

Evelyn increased her pace, taking longer strides. She fought the tremors rattling her limbs as she pushed herself. There was no rise and fall of Thomas's back, no crackle as he'd shift his weight with each movement. Evelyn pursed her lips, rubbing away flakes from her wind-burnt cheeks. Every sense readied itself. She knew no man with sword or bow stood a chance against a crys-talardan. She caught from the corner of her vision the dome saddle far from where Thomas remained motion-less. Its metal frame trembled in the wind. Burned and torn fabrics, furs, and wood hung from it as if savaged by a beast.

Unbuttoning her coat, she drew out a long knife for each hand. She ignored their weight. Pain wracked her body like rain against an unfurled sail. Evelyn screamed, pressing her fists to her brow. Thomas was black as the rock about his body. The blues and whites, with each spike of solid ice, was gone from him. His length from tail to head spanned nearly the width of where they had landed. Her friend was one with the mountaintop her feet touched upon. Tears invaded her cheeks, but Evelyn refused to fend them off, withdrawing her fists.

No footsteps filled her ears, nor the crackle and hiss expected from the flames of an ignited one. Evelyn's feel-ings begged her to drop to her knees like a hero in some story. Like anyone may when they lose someone so loyal to them. She missed Thomas's chilling presence, having grown used to it from the moment he hatched. Its persistence was...

Evelyn spun and leapt as a high-pitched cry shook the ground. She collapsed onto her side, dropping her knives. Crackling ran over what remained of Thomas, and then, he shattered before her eyes. An immense dust cloud overwhelmed her, choking every breath. The wind rushed over her, snatching away the dust. Evelyn grabbed her knives, slamming their points into the ground, rolling over onto her stomach. A faint wish to surrender to her family illness pained her. A metallic rattling met her ears from the ruined dome saddle. She stumbled to full height.

She outstretched her arms, jabbing them back at a pair of light thuds. Rutoe wrapped in black bear furs and flowing silks slid under her arms. Evelyn thrusted forward before either were upright. They coughed and choked. Their hands let go of the chain pressing hard against her back. Shackles topped their fists from the chain's ends. She wondered why they would kill Thomas if the mission was her capture. She knelt, pulling free the scarves about either ones face. She huffed, eyeing her surroundings, narrowing her vision. The rutoe before her bore the charcoal black skin of the Swift Clan.

A figure appeared in the confusion. The remnants of dust from her friend's body swirled past him on a strong wind current.

"Do you aim to capture me, rutoe?" Evelyn raised a knife in alignment with his chest, blood, white like milk, dripped from its point. "You must know who I am."

The figure approached at a slow pace. Evelyn kept watch of his hands, his face. She clenched her teeth against the tremors her muscles demanded she succumb to. The rutoe had a mouth shield of norlstrell, held tight to his face by leather straps. His garb was the same as the others, except for a strange breastplate of scales. Scales she had only seen on the hide of infernodawns. His shoulder guards were of a singular claw from the fire-breathing creature. A dragon far larger than the one who damaged Anna's face.

"What have you done with Anna?" she demanded.

The rutoe narrowed his eyes, wrinkling the olive tone of his nose and brow. Evelyn felt a pang in her mind, tearing at her focus. A voice entered it, thick and swift in its accent. *"I know such a person, but not her condition. Yes, I know you, Wayne. I know of your family's dealings with nelka.. The creature is sacred to rutoe, hard to keep safe and breed thanks to those wishing riches from their hide."*

"Am I to stand trial for my family's crimes? Or can I cut you down as I did those swift ones?"

The Quiet One stopped within range of a knife throw. He gazed at the place where Thomas once rested. His silence hung in the wind. The pang within her mind faded, easing away her need to focus, to remain sane.

"Either way," Evelyn said, readying her knives. "I will strike you dead for Thomas."

The rutoe's brow wrinkled. A muffled laugh breathed from under his mouth shield, shaking the ground beneath him. Evelyn firmed her footing, the quaking nothing compared to what she felt in her bones. The Quiet One went silent and still. Heat pressed like a weight against her back. She narrowed her gaze and peered over her shoulder. Three ignited ones approached at a determined pace, their eyes burning, flaring red. Ash lined the diamond-shape of their eyes. A black cord bound their long flowing hair tight to their scalps. Amongst the constant wind, Evelyn made out an enormous fist wreathed in flame on their breastplates.

"You must be the one who killed my friend." She snarled. "I'll end you for that."

The Ignited One in the middle stepped forward. His eyes flared like miniature suns.

"Our border scouts warned us of his coming," he said. His accent was lighter than the quiet one's, though no less difficult to understand. "His magic ruined our crops and thus sabotaged our rebellion. His death was a necessary action."

Snick. The Ignited One dropped to his knees. Blood trailed swiftly down his breastplate. Those rutoe standing paces behind rushed toward her, their fists engulfed in flame. Evelyn dashed, slid, and ripped her knife from the rutoe's throat. Flames invaded her vision as she spun and thrust both her knives through their gut.

Evelyn met the Quiet One's focus, sneered, yanking free her knives. She heard the sizzle of ignited one blood fail to devour the norlstrell metal of her knives. She bit her lip, eyeing what was left of her friend. A small part of his nostrils and jaws held their shape.

"I have taken my revenge," she said, pressing her lips into a hard line. "The Waynes will fund your rebellion. Prime Luther has plans in action to create a dictatorship through his sons."

The Quiet One removed his gaze from her, resting it on those she killed. Her offer came knowing it would repair a mistake. Evelyn had been eager to help Anna, never considering the reach of Thomas's chilling atmosphere. She kept her weapons ready, the rutoe before her taking his time. His feelings were unreadable with the mouth shield, but his silence matched the volume of her own pain. Evelyn watched his attention shift, then narrow upon her. The panging struck her mind again, loosening her grip on her knives. She went to one knee, slamming her knives into the ground.

"The rutoe demand two things before accepting your offer, Wayne," he said, his voice booming within her skull. *"Free our leader for us."*

Evelyn let out a growling scream. Spit flung from her mouth as she rose. The rutoe took a step back, reaching for his mouth shield. The mistress of duels and debates composed herself, rising to full height. All pain from the rutoe's presence within her mind slipped away.

"And the second?"

The Quiet One stepped forward, letting his hand drop to his side.

"Tell us how you came upon the last of the fifth clan."

TWENTY-SIX

Anna kept her fingers splayed across her face. She saw no one ahead, only the faint wisps of her breath accompanied her. Releasing her face made her feel as if being complete would vanish before reaching the arch. Only after she was fully across the drawbridge did she dare to slow her pace. Pain no longer lingered from her wound, nor jabbed at her side when she'd twist or turn. Cobblestones met her footsteps as she came upon a dark tunnel formed in the shape of a triangle. Anna finally allowed her hands to drop, certain her old face would remain absent.

A brief brightness touched her eyes. Anna shaded them both, strangely relieved to be doing so for two eyes now. Scaffolding netted stone structures ahead, and the sun was half in the graying clouds that hinted at coming rain. What structures were free of scaffolding possessed doors without ringed handles, windows without shutters to shield themselves against the harshness of winter. Shoes lay beneath each door, shallow at the heel with a point curving like a hook at their toe. Tiny stones crackled under her feet before

Anna stopped to catch her breath. The air was light and pure, as if it had not been corrupted.

Voices in the distance caught her attention. She used her right eye's peripheral vision. She smiled as, for the first time in years, she saw a light in place of darkness. Anna balled her fists to stifle surging emotions. She needed to remember her purpose for traveling this far, for putting what was no longer a hindrance aside. *But how am I complete again?* She rested her hand on her bowstring. *Is this a trap set by someone who knows me?*

Three rutoe emerged from an alley down the street. The street went for miles, ending at what she believed to be a temple, but not one of Simdorn. Anna raised an eyebrow, guessing what god it belonged to possessed no image. No statue stood upon the temple's pyramid peak, and orbs marked the structure's four corners. She removed her attention from the approaching rutoe. They possessed long dark hair. One had skin the color of charcoal, and eyes a dark blue. He drew back, mimicked by his friends. Of the three, one was a girl of the ignited one clan. Her eyes went dark red, and faint flames raced over her fingertips. Behind her stood a boy with eyes blacker than night, and skin pale like a full moon. The trio wore long, flowing robes matching their skin.

"I'm in search of a wizard," Anna said, offering herself with palms open, not wanting to frighten them further. "Can you tell me where one might be?"

The Ignited One appeared near seventeen to the boys eighteen. She pressed thumb to palm, her flames vanishing. She clasped the pale boy's hand tight within her own and whispered something. His eyes flashed a blazing orange. Anna froze. Swift as hornets, stones rose, surrounding her until there was no escape. They clicked against one another, ever circling and increasing in number. His hand rose, and teeth clenched as if what he did took great concentration.

"You leave," said the boy, bringing the ignited one close. She whispered something in his ear and shot Anna a fierce glance. "Humans put families outside Echnumbard in the mountains long ago."

"Please. I'm here for my friend," Anna exclaimed. "My..." She didn't wish to use her grandfather's name, but if he gave opportunities to rutoe, these three may have heard of his generosity. "I'm Anna Brighton. Granddaughter of Lord William Brighton."

The stones drew closer, hindering her vision like smoke from an untamed fire. Anna squinted through them to find the rutoe had reduced their distance from her. The pale one spoke again, eyes glowing above the hard line formed from his lips.

"That human robbed the rutoe of its fifth clan," he said. "A great battle took them all in a village."

Thoughts crossed paths with memories. Anna remained still, like the banner above the street. Its fabrics divided into colors. She guessed they represented the rutoe clans. The crimson color must have represented the fifth clan. She thought back to the barn in Natlendton. And yet her skin was like most Lampariens, but her hair was neither auburn nor blond. She licked her lips, eyeing the three youths, their distrust solid and dark like the tunnel behind her. The stories of her parents' died intertwined, one of a battle, and the other of them being chased by thieves.

"I wish to find a wizard for my friend," she said, slowly drawing back her hood. The Ignited One gasped. Anna sucked in a breath and shrugged the girl's fear off. "I do not know of the battle involving my grandfather."

The stones dropped at once, filling the air like a sudden, brief downpour of rain. The Ignited One turned her head from side to side, taking two steps forward. Anna wasn't sure what to say. She half wished to share what her mind had pieced together — that she may very well be a survivor of a battle she had no memory of. The Ignited one took Anna's hand in her own.

"We never seen the fifth clan," she said. "Elders have. Yes. You look human yet have hair like ours."

"I thought the same," Anna nodded, then frowned, "but I have no magic like you do. I possess only the skills I learned in life."

The Ignited One ran a long, slender finger down the string of Anna's bow.

"Skills are learned like control of magic. We are learning, but you look like a master of skills."

Anna blushed.

"I still wish I possessed magic like you three," she said, suddenly remembering how her cry of pain had shaken the rafters of the barn. "You are gifted. It took years to be accurate, to learn how to hunt."

The Ignited One left to join the others. Her touch had left Anna's hand warm, like the sunlight against her neck. All three rutoe conversed with one another. Anna noticed they wore the low heel, hooked toe shoes she had seen. The shoes were black, grayed in places by the dust lying across the stones. Finally, the rutoe possessing charcoal skin spoke, biting his lip at first.

"We thought like you once," he said, fumbling with his robes, "but not since Luther Prime sent us to the cold. Not since the man with angry esant kill brave fifth clan and became story all rutoe must hear."

"And now you're in open rebellion against Luther,"

Anna said, summoning what lingered on her mind. "I do not believe the fifth clan are gone." She rested her hand on his shoulder. He flinched at first, but Anna assured him with a smile. "I am campaigning to replace Luther. And if what I believe is correct, William Brighton spared at least one of your fifth clan."

"Who?" all three rutoe said.

"Me."

———

THE ROOM WAS SMALL. Well kept. But still not as spacious as what Anna had grown up used to. The pale-skinned rutoe insisted no shoes be worn in his father's house. She feared to tread on its smooth polished wood floors with her damp, worn socks. Her normal racing nerves were absent during the ordeal. New ones rose with slightly less intensity as she waited. She sat at a table on a stool, which in the north passed for something a boy used for shining boots. Its cushion was a relief on her back, remaining so straightened and stiff in the dome saddle worked a terrible ache through it.

The ignited one, Grenuel, as she called herself, went to put out word for a wizard to join them. Anna cleared her throat, feeling her knees knock against the table.

"A few days ago a friend sent a cheefox to Echnumbard," she said, "but it was intercepted."

"It would not reach here anyway," said the moon-white boy. "Rutoe who rebel keep messages should traitor be their ranks."

Anna bit back her frustration. Even if things had been different, that her wish to be whole remained, no wizard stood a chance of receiving her request.

"What can you tell me about the wizards who found refuge here?"

The two rutoe looked at one another. Their faces offered little in the way of comfort.

"You hear they banished south, right?" said Fradrul, biting his lip with red teeth. "Lamnic know truth."

She faced the moon-white rutoe. His black eyes reminded her of Cole's. A deep emptiness opened in her stomach, making her wish he were here.

"Four are in sanctuary," he said. "They protect and train rutoe while priests join rebellion."

Anna's jaw dropped. She swiftly snapped it shut. Priests fighting was something she never thought possible nor proper. Simdorn's priests kept to prayer, ritual, and council. She swallowed as Lamnic summoned his words.

"Prime Luther offered what you call ... an ultimatum," he said. "Join his army or face banishment."

"And all of them chose banishment?" Anna asked.

Fradrul shook his head. Lamnic drew in his lips.

"Some join and some come here. Others go back to where they came from." Lamnic whispered. "Where that is not even wizards of sanctuary know."

She sat up straight on her stool, reminding herself there wasn't a back to lean against, pondering what she had learned.

"How could the wizards not know where they came from?"

The rutoe shrugged.

"I guess children who dream them to live grew self-loving when old," said Fradrul.

His words made no sense to her. Dreaming someone into existence wasn't possible.

"Is what I understand true?" she said. "A selfless child who dreams can create a wizard?"

Fradrul nodded. Footsteps echoed faintly from the hall behind her. Anna caught only the sound of one person approaching. Though she wished to turn around, she did not want to feel disappointment. A chill lanced over her shoulder. Fingers, short and soft, gave a faint squeeze. She peered over her shoulder, shrieked, and spun off her stool. Her bottom slammed against the table's edge. A child of gray mist let his hand drop to his side. His eyes were placed too close to his nose, outlined in red, trapping their solid black inside a wavering glow. A smile journeyed with haste across the child's face.

"You must be the one Grenuel couldn't silence herself about."

"Yes ... um," Anna said. "I'm Anna Brighton. Did she tell you I'm here for my friend?"

The wizard nodded. His face spoke of him being eight at the oldest. She rose to full height, finding he came up to her chest. He wore white robes with a crest on his chest. The robes shifted and crawled like mist across a bog. Anna kept her surprise behind a blank face. The crest belonged to Nathan's family.

"Grenuel says you believe yourself a survivor of Brighton's raids," said the wizard.

Anna gulped, noticing that the wizard's smaller features reflected Nathan's.

"I believe so. I didn't tell her, but my cries once shook the rafters of a barn. I was in pain."

The wizard stroked his child-like chin with thumb and forefinger. His eyes reflected her face, sending a shiver down her spine. He let his hand drop and grinned.

"How often in your early youth did you use a mirror?

Anna raised an eyebrow.

"Mirrors are for the vain, Simdorn says," Anna said. "I never saw my reflection until after the dragon. I ... was attacked at fifteen. Once I saw half my face burned and eye was sealed shut, I didn't wish to look upon myself again."

"And why do you suppose it took so long?"

"You ask strange questions for what reason I cannot guess!" Anna barked. Her skin grew hot and red. She felt he was delaying her. "I originally went in search of a wizard for myself, but this place has removed what tormented me, and more..."

Her face was red like an apple in the wizard's eyes. Anna raised her hands to find her fingernails black as if dipped in ink.

"What's happening? Anna screamed.

The wizard smiled. He took her hands in his as she trembled.

"With the sanctuary's help," he said calmly, "you are returning to what you once were, Anna."

"But how is this possible?"

Warm tears rolled down her cheeks, blurring her vision, turning the mist making up the wizard into a fog. She swiped her hand across her eyes.

"Columns you passed between to get here possess the ability to heal," said Grenuel, resting a hand on Anna's shoulder. "I came here with bruises upon my cheeks, fearing my mother's fist finding me again."

"Fradual and Lamnic came here after joining the rebellion, blaming their wounds on lack of strength and courage," said the wizard, peering up at them. "Their wounds are healed, but their strength and bravery still waver. Sometimes such things are slow in their arrival."

A tingling forced Anna's eyes shut. They burned for a

moment, pain fading as swiftly as it had come. She opened them to find they were yellow. They shine brightly within the surface of the wizard's eyes. A bright red flared within her pupils.

"Leave me alone!" she screamed.

Anna bound her arms tight to her stomach and dashed down the hall. The ends of her bow scraped the walls when she rounded a corner. There was no one following her, no one to come and slow the onslaught of emotions striking her all at once. The floor grew murky, its smooth brown wood a blur. She looked ahead to find that her vision was clear.

Dropping to her knees, her confusion compounded, as if all the nerves and heightened senses of old had returned. Anna pressed her knuckles against the floor, hearing the rattle of her arrows. Her arms shook and slowly caved.

"You were lied to, Anna."

She turned to find the wizard. His face possessed more definition; faint stubble grew from the end of his chin. His robes remained white, but the crest on his chest was now contained inside a diamond.

"How have you aged?" Anna said, swallowing the pain in her voice. "How did I not hear you following me?"

"Let's stay on point, Anna." The wizard shook his head. "You were lied to. William Brighton found pity in his heart and raised you. You're seeing who you really are."

Anna found herself tempted. Tempted to hide within her hood like she had done for so long. There were no footsteps from down the hall, and for this she was glad. Anna drew up her hood.

"Why hide now?" said the wizard, taking her gently by the wrists. "You must have been doing so for some time, by my guess. It's written in your movements."

She firmed her grasp on the fabric of her hood. Every finger shook, sweat ran down her knuckles. The wizard eased down on one knee.

"You're right," said Anna. "And I stopped hiding long before coming here."

"Good." The wizard smiled. "Now! Who is the friend you wish to help?"

Anna dropped her hands to her lap, focusing on them for a moment.

"Nathan," she said, finding the wizard's lips trembling. His eyes were on the verge of disbelief. "Nathan Barden."

THEY LEFT the house to find the streets busy. Dust rose with the traffic of foot work. Anna found herself in the position of being the calm once again. She held the wizard's hand, refusing to withdraw from its clamminess. He kept his other across his lips, uncovering them when a question surfaced. He led the way some, but with the shock of hearing about Nathan's passing, no exact destination came of it.

Passing an alley ending in a shear wall of jagged rock, five straw dummies wrapped in burlap hung on posts. Five ignited ones aligned with them, reaching with fingers splayed. Flames roared in swift narrow streams, setting the dummies ablaze. One rutoe sneezed. A blast larger than Cole erupted from his palm, scorching the rock face. Anna gaped, stopping herself mid-step. The wizard stormed toward the youthful ignited one. She listened, guessing from his gestures that discipline was being served. The words exchanged were in a language she didn't under-stand. *If I am a rutoe, then why can I not understand their language?* she thought. She listened intently, but the words were too swift to make out. *Grandfa- William Brighton mustn't have thought knowing it unnecessary.*

She cleared her throat and offered a reassuring smile when the wizard returned. His posture was upright, though he came only up to her shoulder. A slow procession of what the wizard said were quiet ones passed, their faces buried in books. They wore olive-colored robes and pressed firmly over their mouths bronze mouth shields. Anna decided against reminding the wizard of her purpose here. The pain in his eyes showed glimpses of a younger Nathan. Memories, by her guess of her friend chasing a storm bison through a field. She kept her face emotionless, sucking back a breath to prevent it from caving in.

"So, you have come to resurrect Nathan? And you think I can do it?" he said. "I will admit my connection to him has begun anew in recent months. My hope was dragged from the confines of despair thanks to it."

"Did... Did you feel it when he died?"

The wizard drifted to a stop, mist swirling and ebbing from the fringe of his robes. He returned his focus to the ignited ones. They had replaced the previous dummies with new ones.

"No." The wizard's voice cracked. "Our connection is through deeds of selflessness. After Nathan reached manhood, our ability to feel emotion, physical pain, ended."

"Are you able to bring our friend back?" Anna said. "I feel with what you know, and the power I am told a wizard possesses, that such a miracle is possible."

He looked up into her eyes. Anna felt her heart take off at a sprint as the wizard with the face of her friend remained silent. The memories she had seen in his eyes were gone, replaced by blackness given no light by their outlining red.

"I would need to leave Echnumbard," he said, stroking his chin. He faced the ignited ones again and then folded his arms. "I will consult the other wizards. You need to understand, Anna. I love Nathan. I miss him. But my place here is of great importance."

Anna weaved her fingers, understanding his purpose in training the young rutoes. The guidance needed was for the three rutoe she had met. Her eyes widened.

"You also risk trouble with Prime Luther," she said, unweaving her fingers, binding them into fists. "The monster banished you like he did the rutoe."

"Oh, ha." the wizard chuckled. "That old man cannot stop me if he doesn't hear of my deeds. My guess is you missed the fine print. Our services to Lampariens are banned. Oh, how word of mouth and decrees on paper color things!"

Messing up her face, she resisted the temptation to thump herself on the forehead.

"Consult the other wizards then," she said. "I wish my friend back and must return to my ... other friend. The Tournament of Primes is less than a week away."

The wizard held up his hands, raising an eyebrow.

"I will be but a moment."

He melted like snow heaped upon a fire, vanishing into the tiny stones in a flash. Anna thought back to Eve and Thomas. She hoped they were well. The last time she had left a friend and mount behind, they had gone missing. She wondered whether Norman and Cole were well. If Norman had taken her advice and purposefully threatened Lord Martyn's servants with Kardanhall's destruction. *Eve shall be fine like Norman,* she thought, *especially Eve.* Anna felt like the mistress of duels and debates could conquer any challenge. There were her quakes to deal with, but from her perspective, Eve's will was too strong to allow anything to hold her back.

The ignited ones' training kept at a steady pace. Anna noticed beyond the smoke and scorch marks blackening the ground, a door off to the left. Stored beyond inside it were dozens of dummies crafted from straw and burlap. A rush thrust back her hair, nearly knocking her off balance. Anna planted her feet, outstretched her arms, the fletching of her arrows fluttered beside her ear. Two pairs of dark blue eyes flashed then vanished where she had met the others. Robes the color of charcoal trailed like a thin streak of smoke. *So that is Lamnic's power. Speed.*

A chill ran across her boots, sending her body into a shiver and her teeth chattering. Anna faced up the street in time to find a pillar of white forming at a steady pace. It shaped into sleeves with many wrinkles. A head emerged from the heavy hood between rolling shoulders. The wizard's eyes flashed dark red as his face faded into focus.

"Let's be off, Anna," he said, taking her wrist. "Time is not on our side, and you have a madman to stop."

TWENTY-SEVEN

P rime Luther had made no move to harm Cole or Roland, and for this Norman was grateful. He observed the craftsmanship of his shackles. They appeared to be made of ordinary iron, yet he could not summon his flames. The glow within his eyes remained faint in the small mirror across from him. His stomach churned from the up and down of the dragon's movements. Bile lined his tongue, urging up vomit, but he took a big gulp. His quarters were at the rear of the vast dome saddle. The dragon who carried it was so large that Kardanhall's courtyard possessed little room to accept its mass. Norman could hear the guards breathing nasally beyond the door. It was as if the man were snoring while awake.

His thoughts were more on Anna than all else. He was unsure if Echnumbard had changed since his father began the rebellion. Had it gone from a place of learning to control one's clan gift to a training ground for soldiers? Did its famed healing abilities find another use beyond the growth of the individual? He knew his friend possessed the strength to deal with change. The message in his pocket proved it.

Planting his feet on the floor, the rug sifted against his shoes. Their soles were worn despite sharing Cole's saddle with Anna during their travels. What he missed most during those many miles were the words they shared. Conversation built upon what he knew of his people. A comforting feeling fluttered within his belly for her greatest passion, hunting. She spoke of tricks she'd learned and those of her own design to trap game. He smiled. Her burns didn't trouble her in those conversations, and now, they no longer troubled her at all. He sighed, eyeing his surroundings. A click, turn, and thud flooded the room with light from the hall.

"Hello. Oh!"

A woman entered with a tray in her hands. Her skin was an olive tone, and her hair was bound back tight with a ribbon. Pressed firmly across her face was a mouth shield of iron matching his shackles. Norman pretended not to notice the lock constricting the shield's straps to her head. He clenched his teeth and shot his gaze to the floor. Prime Luther had given this quiet one a skirt to wear, but nothing to cover her chest. Her feet were without any shoes. She set the tray on a table across from him, turned, and bowed. She padded over to the door.

"Wait," Norman said. "Speak with me. Tell me what you know, and we may overcome Luther's men."

The Quiet One peered over her shoulder. Her eyes were dull, nearly lifeless and downcast. Norman focused on her mind speech, unable to believe he had said such words. Where was there to go *if* they succeeded? The speech came in a whisper, swift and panicked. He ignored the pang rattling his mind.

"Will you need any other services?" she said. *"Prime Luther speaks of you joining your father, but that I am to accommodate your wishes. He says you are a political prisoner."*

Norman edged himself toward the wall at his back. The woman turned to face him, resting her hands on her hips. His chest fluttered. She knelt before him, eyes to the floor, resting both hands to a knot below her navel.

"No," he said, scooting to the bed's edge as he waved her advance away. "I don't want contact of that kind. I wish to free us both, find my father and end Luther."

"That will remain impossible," she said, folding her arms across her chest. *"He has wizards. Traitors to the clans have replaced many of his assigned orderman."*

Norman eyed the door, wincing at the continued contact with the girl. He wondered for a moment what he would do if she left upset. Her eyes were focused on the sharp edge along her mouth shield. The Quiet One's nose bunched above it as if she were ready to weep.

"Luther has terrible plans for Lampara," he said, rising, bringing the girl to her feet. "I need your help in stopping them." Norman raised her chin. Her eyes met his own then darted away. "Can you find the keys to these shackles?"

The Quiet One took his hand in hers, examining it closely. Norman exhaled as she severed their connection. She made for the door in two great strides, knocked, and left. The guard eyed her like a vulture. He smiled at Norman. The guard's teeth were yellowed and caked with blackness in places.

"What 'appened?" he said, chuckling. "You get too 'appy too quick."

"Just close the damn door," said Norman, a slight queasiness overwhelmed him.

Norman slammed the door shut and gulped, exhaling

slowly. The need to vomit disappeared as he realized how bad the guard's breath had been. He sat in the chair beside the table. The chair creaked as he slumped, raising his bonds. They were cold, like the porridge as he ate. He pressed his teeth to his fingers, withdrawing a long, black hair.

Not knowing whether it was night or day, he listened for a change of guard. Samuel was not only an accountant and who he apprenticed under, but a protector of Williamton. A change of guard required a short briefing of one's post. So far with the minutes passing he heard only the guard's breathing and the infrequent roar of the dragon.

He rested his porridge spoon beside the bowl. The wine from the tin goblet did little to ease the porridge down. Norman searched the room for another way to remove his shackles. There was nothing sharp to pick the lock. Anna had mentioned she had rescued Simdorn's priests this way. The spoon's bowl and tip were coated in rust and too wide for what he needed, and the handle was round at the end.

"You back for more short squirts?" said the guard from beyond the door. "What you doing? Get out of m' head!"

Thump.

The door opened. The guard lay across the doorway, shaking and groaning. Blood ran from the corners of his eyes. He tried to raise his head, fumbling with the sword at his belt. Over him, the Quiet One clenched her fists. Her chest heaved as her eyes focused on the guard.

"Come quick," she said, her voice panicked and breathless in his mind. *"I've never done this before."*

"And I have never escaped from anywhere before," said Norman, rising swiftly from the table. "Keep his mind pinned."

"His ... keys ... are on his person." She took hold of the railing against the wall. *"What are you doing?"*

Norman grabbed the guard under the arms and pulled. *The guard must weigh thrice what I do.* "I will look odd roaming the halls with you as I am," he said.

With a great heave, Norman made it inside his room. He snatched the keys from the guard's belt, freed his wrists, and began undressing the man. Norman held his breath. The guard coughed up great plumes of what he could only guess was cheese gone foul.

"This is no time for pleasures," said the quiet one.

Norman removed his clothes, applying the guard's trousers, tunic, and boots before heaving on his evergreen plated armor.

"That isn't my plan."

The dome helmet was snug, and the red mouth shield reeked, but Norman had no choice. He altered his skin, matching the guard's pockmarked skin. A biting feeling doubled and tripled over his cheeks as the marks filled in. The Quiet One dropped to her knees, her breath heavy and muffled. The guard coughed before his eyes rolled back into his head. Norman took her by the hand and helped her up.

"Are you well?" he asked. She nodded, eyeing him strangely as he handed her his tunic. "Let's go before he wakes."

"You are odd," she said, slipping it on. *"Is that why the prime keeps you alive?"*

"No," Norman said. "And he won't be holding anyone else prisoner much longer once I am done with him."

THE HALL WAS LIT by orb lamps of gold. The flames inside the small glass gave off no odor from their oil, unlike others. The wood paneling the wall was polished to a pristine shine and from no tree he'd ever seen. Norman shrugged off the buildup of concerns. There was no time to worry about how Luther had spent Lampara's coin. If Anna won the tournament, he'd demand the selling of the prime's luxuries. The nardans obtained from it given to the people. He raised a finger to his head and tapped it twice. The Quiet One nodded. Norman winced as her voice pierced his mind.

"Should we not hurry?" she said. *"Infernodawns are far swifter than a crystalardan or emnarld."*

"I don't wish to churn up suspicion." Norman stopped them at a corner. Voices met his ears as he peered around it.

Two ordermen left a room, closing the door with smiles swiftly covered by mouth shields. The Quiet One shrank back from him. Her eyes strained, tears running from them as if connecting with him was growing more difficult.

"I apologize. Our actions are something I never dreamed possible."

Norman didn't dare to imagine how long she had been a servant. Been forced to give 'pleasures,' as she called them to strangers. He offered his hand. She crouched and fixated on it as if it offered no guarantee.

"I promise you," he said, swallowing, pushing past the strain of their connection. "You will live through this. I will give you freedom."

The Quiet One sighed, rising to full height. *"I trust you."* She took his hand.

Every hall appeared the same, sconces topped by flickering orbs, walls lined with a brass railing at waist height. Anna had told him during their travels she would let Cole graze when the woods were quiet. She'd walk for some time and listen for an animal to snap a twig or snort at an odd scent. But he wasn't in the woods where an animal could slip up. He steadied himself with every turn they made, steadying them both from the rise and fall of the dome saddle.

He wished he hadn't made such a promise to the quiet one. There was no certainty of keeping it with ordermen patrolling the halls. At the hall's end, there were double doors thick and lined with gold studs. Two large wall sconces bracketed on either side bounced their light off the door's studs. The hall widened the closer they came, cluttered with spade shields emblazoned with the governing crest. Between them, portraits of Luther and his primnoire showed their achievements, one of them plunging their swords into an ignited one.

"Why have you left your post?" said a guard emerging from the left. "I was to swap with you within the hour."

Another guard appeared from Norman's right and grabbed the quiet one. She pulled and stumbled to the ground. Her hands slipped through the billowing cuffs of Norman's tunic.

"Brought aboard to look decent," said the guard, righting her up on her feet and then pressing her face against the wall. "You should know this you whelp. Our departed primnoire made it clear rutoe serving girls don't get that luxury."

"I don't got a clue how she got clothing," said Norman, using the worst grammar he knew.

A quake ran under his feet, scattering his stance. The ordermen kept their balance, adjusting the chainmail beneath their breastplates. They wore the same helmets as Phillip, and over their shoulders were arrowhead-shaped plating. Their breastplates were evergreen and fastened with gold buckles and polished leather straps. There were no stars on their boots, and both kept their mouth shields firmly across their faces.

"Rip this rag from her flesh, you whelp," the orderman sniffed. "Did you finally clean those teeth of yours?"

"Yes... I was sick of you blockheads harping on me," said Norman, slowly taking hold of his tunic. *This isn't right.* The tunic was weather-stained and baggy on the quiet one's slender frame. She slammed her eyes shut. "I've come for a word with his prime-ship."

"For what reason, you rotten-toothed wanker?" said the orderman, pressing the girl to the wall. "You'd best rip those rags off before she thinks we've all gone soft on her."

Norman grabbed a larger handful, narrowing his vision to be more convincing. Her face was compressed between a black leather glove and the wall's finished wood. Her eyes spoke of the promise he had made, the dignity he had given her. And now he was taking both away, as if they were a cruel joke to raise false hopes.

I am truly sorry.

The tunic ripped from her shoulders, summoning a swift breath from her nostrils. Norman realized she must have been clenching her teeth under the mouth shield. No quake sent his hands clambering for support. There was no sudden, harsh blip within his mind, no plea for mercy, or questioning of his sudden betrayal. The Quiet One's back rose and fell in quick succession. Norman puffed up his chest and ripped until the tunic draped from her arms like a ragged sail from a ship's mast.

"Are you seeing our prime about this girl?" asked the orderman, watching him go. He raised a finger. "You can stop. Anymore and there will be no trace of her crime."

The pockmarks on his cheeks and nose wavered.

Norman let go of the torn tunic, bunching his nose, the marks biting with their return. His weighed him with a pain he had no words for. It was a pain he understood too well. They did not share the same skin color or clan gift, but they were above all else rutoe. And in this moment, Norman felt that being human was the worst he had just been. *This isn't the rutoe way.* he thought, thinking of Anna. *She would be ashamed of me.*

"I'll take her by m' self, mates," said Norman.

Norman snatched the girl by her arms. His hand shook as he raised it to knock.

"You know such matters require an orderman present. You'll be interrupting his prime-ship otherwise," said the orderman, who had kept the girl from escaping. "It seems you have not only forgot the rules but also your place."

"And even a dull low-level stooge like you can remember both," said the other orderman.

Something sharp pinched Norman's back, working itself at an angle. At first, it felt like a muscle misbehaving, but soon he had his hands raised. The Quiet One pressed his tunic to her chest. Her face was shrouded in the depths of her long black hair. Its ribbon lay adrift against her foot.

"I knew you weren't that scum sucker," the orderman said. "Can you guess why, Norman Tilt?"

Tingling ran through his skin as his curled chestnut hair lengthened, making his helmet feel like a vice. Norman's eyes flashed a sharp, piercing scarlet. He sent heat over the surface of his fingertips. The knife weaved under the cords that bound his breastplate to his person.

"Because that ugly sow is the cook. No one up here dresses like a common soldier."

"You've been fooled, mate," said the other orderman. He

opened both doors one at a time. "I'll take Enemilu to Unter. They both have business tonight."

The Quiet One stood erect, dropping the torn tunic at his feet. She flashed her long eyelashes, piercing into his mind at such a speed he nearly fell upon the orderman's knife.

"You kept your promise, Norman," she said. She rested a hand on his cheek, digging her chipped nails into its flesh. Norman let out a yelp as she yanked off his mouth shield. *"Keep such a happy thought close when you die."*

Pulling swiftly from his side, the orderman's knife pressed to Norman's back once more. He clenched his teeth. The man's hand grasped his neck like the jaws of a serpent. They moved into Prime Luther's chambers with a speed Norman didn't know he could manage. He gasped, falling to his knees. A dais stood before him. He peered up at a throne carved of the same dark wood as the trees surrounding Kardanhall. A slight shiver ran over him, fading fast with the buildup of his magic. The shackles of earlier had kept them dull and faint within the core of his very being.

"You're far more cunning than your appearance presents," said a voice. "I didn't expect you to refuse a woman's touch before a lengthy prison sentence."

From where the breeze came stood Luther in long robes of red silk. On his head sat not the hat from before, but a wide gold band. A crest, not the governing one but of a beast Norman had never seen in his travels with Anna. It roared above Luther's brow to a full moon made from a white gem. Around the band were four paws tipped with claws of silver, the paws themselves were of a polished gold.

"Keep your eyes on the ground!" Luther barked.

A sharp pinch forced Norman's hands to his face. His fingers dug into his skin as ordermen emerged from the darkness. Orb lamps came to light, leaving a dimness in the air. Taking up a position next to Luther on his throne was an orderman of great height. His olive skin was darker than any quiet one Norman had ever seen. Luther raised a hand weighed down by thick gold rings. Norman let out a gasp, spiraling into a coughing fit.

"Why?" Norman said, pressing his fist to his lips. "Why put me through all this?"

"Because you string bean of slime," Luther twirled his index finger. "I need a good story to tell your father before one of my sons executes him. A future dictator needs something big to set his reign in motion."

The cold went from a breeze to a torrent of chill as a door slid open. Prime Luther pulled his robes close to his chest.

"I would feed you to my dragon," he grimaced, "but the last time I tried that, my dear wife fell to her end."

Two ordermen seized him under the arms, dragging Norman to the door. The cold sent his teeth into a chatter. He balled his fingers into fists, striking both men in the gut. Flames raced over them. Norman yanked himself free and stumbled to one knee. He screamed. Tumbling over, his back met his heel as he stretched out his fists. Norman tried to rise, to ignite his fists once more, but the quiet one had him.

"I will not give up," Norman said through his teeth. "I'll fight you as my father did."

Prime Luther crept down from the dais, rubbing his hands together. The Quiet One narrowed his eyes, forcing Norman to bite his lip. Blood ran down his chin as Luther slammed his boot into Norman's chest. Norman felt his heel slip and slide across the guard's armor.

"Temper those flames, boy," said Luther, reaching out his hands. "I paid good money for all this."

"You have made many poor." Norman gripped the floor, finding no purchase. "You have made them hate all rutoe."

"I will not argue politics with you." Luther pressed harder, sneering at the ordermen rolling on the ground. Their flame licked bodies shook and twisted. "I still have much in my way, and while my sons' rule, I will clear the weeds from the grounds of my country."

It was no use. The Quiet One kept him from using his flames. Prime Luther had him in so compromising a position he could hear his ankle crunching. He eyed the old man, feeling the blood on his chin meet his neck.

"But only one son can win the people and the tournament," Norman rasped. "Just one of your dull-witted children can govern."

Prime Luther let up on Norman's chest. His eyes flared before placing two and two together. Luther smiled.

"So be it, rebel bastard."

Norman's eyes widened. He threw his gaze outside. Daylight touched his brow, highlighting the immense leathery wing of the dragon. It kept the forests and fields out of sight. A horn sounded, long and deep.

"You would see a son die and use the other as a vassal?" Norman said, meeting the prime's weathered eyes. "Is the life of your sons worth so little to you?"

"Throw him out." Prime Luther removed himself from the throne. "I will not be set upon by conflicting emotions."

The Quiet One ceased his pressure on Norman's mind. Their eyes met as the orderman raised him to his feet.

"You cannot go along with this," Norman whispered,

twisting and pulling. "No rutoe would allow anyone to put their wants over their children."

No pain raced through Norman's mind, yet by the orderman's expression, by his deep but subtle breaths, he showed guilt.

"Throw him out! Damn you!" Luther growled. "I don't intend to freeze before reaching home."

With a great heave, the orderman threw Norman and slammed shut the door. Norman tumbled toward the dragon's rolling shoulder. Thoughts of igniting his flames came and went, knowing heat might bring him within inches of the dragon's jaws. Norman gripped and clawed, finding the clouds below growing closer and closer.

Something glistened in the sunlight, round and controlled somehow. Its color nearly matched the dragon's scales for a moment. Norman spotted something thin and brown streaming from it. The disk-like shape swung behind him. Deep down he knew it was strange, but there was only one guess as to what it was. Norman kicked off the dragon's shoulder, turned, and hugged the disk with everything he had. There was a quick dip, but slowly he rose, doing so for a long while.

Once finally upon the dragon's shoulder, Norman lay flat on his back. His chest heaved as the disk slid from his grasp. A figure placed the disk on his head, helping Norman up.

"You sure are brave for a green fella that counts coppers."

"Phillip."

CHAPTER

TWENTY-EIGHT

Anna fumbled with her thoughts, running her fingers down the length of her bow's string. Her mind was more on Eve and Thomas than the direction the wizard led her. She drew her hood over her head, preparing for the cold and the truth to come. There was no certainty the wizard could read her thoughts, no sign of such a power. Lady Evelyn was an enemy of the rutoe, and by the wizard's attention to their lessons, he may not find the mistress of duels and debates a friend. Their steps didn't pass through the tunnel from before. Anna wondered how she would manage the mountains' relentless winds without her cloak.

Instead, they used a door off to the tunnel's right. A mustiness teased her nose once through its threshold. The steps before her were cut in such a way that her feet barely had room for a complete step. The wizard drifted down them, making no sound, leaving a brief residue of mist. His eyes brightened until their path no longer needed the lit sconces guiding their way. The sconces went out all at once. Anna froze, teetering a heel on the upper step while firmly holding her balance with the other. A half minute passed before the wizard stopped at a landing and looked up at her. A slight smile crossed his childlike face.

"We have little time, Anna," he said, drifting up to her like a cloud meeting another. "We cannot travel by whatever means you used. There is a storm upon the mountains."

"How do you know there is one?" Anna said. "Or how I traveled?

"Being that we are high above the rest of Lampara, a storm reaches us first every day. It will then either spare the lands north or hammer them like there is no tomorrow."

She descended a few steps, using the wizard's eyes to guide her, realizing he had ignored her second question.

"I must tell you something ... now, since our journey will not begin where I wish it would."

The light from the wizard's eyes faced toward the landing, returning caution to Anna's movements.

"I left a friend behind before entering Echnumbard," she said, trying to use what light reflected off the walls to ease her fear of tripping. "Her name is Lady Evelyn Wayne."

"Ah. So, that is what caused your break in speech earlier?" the wizard said, facing her once they found a second landing. "I learned of the orderman and her dragon when consulting the other wizards."

Anna gaped. "How do you...? She means no harm to the—"

"Calm yourself, Anna." The wizard raised his hand in a fan motion. "She pays for both her and her family's crimes against the clans, and soon with more than words."

"You must not hurt her," Anna said, taking hold of the wizard's shoulders. Her hands phased through like a traveler wading his way through fog. "She is my friend. I never would have made it this far without her."

"I said nothing of harm," he said, taking her by the wrists. "She funds the rebellion with Wayne coin," the wizard sighed. "I can see the enchantments cleared much of what troubled you and returned you to true form, but your worrisome nature remains."

Anna shook her head. His grip was cold, stronger than expected for someone with small hands.

"I thank you again ... for all of it," Anna said. "What crime did she commit?"

The wizard released her, turning to face a long, narrow tunnel. Its walls were rough, uneven, and cracked in places. No unlit sconces hung on either wall, but a faint white light crept around a corner to the right. He kept at a steady pace, and soon, the lights in his eyes faded to their normal glow. Anna let out a breath, glad for no more stairs.

"It wasn't so much her doing, more a consequence for not remembering the power of a friend's abilities.

"Thomas?" said Anna. "What has his cold done?"

"Let's put away the subject for now, Anna."

"No," Anna snapped. "I wish to know. I have experienced plenty in a short time. I have even conquered my fear of dragons with Eve's aid."

He looked up at her, blinked, sending a thin gray line along the red of his eyes.

"The dragon's cold laid waste to crops," he sighed. "Crops meant for both family and soldiers alike. He... He had to be destroyed."

The light met her chin, outlining the wrinkles of her hood. Words clamored to her lips but swiftly slipped back down her throat, choking her somehow. Anna found killing Thomas an impossibility for anyone wanting to. To be in his presence chewed through every layer she wore without leaving a mark, chilling her to the bone.

"How?" she said. "Eve told me great magic is needed."

"And it was used," said the wizard, folding his arms. His sleeves hung like curtains of snow falling in winter. "Now! Let's make our way."

"Wait," Anna said. "Answer me this, was killing Thomas necessary?"

The wizard frowned, resting his hand to the crest on his chest.

"I wish I possessed an answer for you," the wizard said. "Perhaps when this is over, the rutoe will make up for their harsh decision. For the moment, we must travel to Kardan-hall and resurrect our friend."

Anna raised an eyebrow at the wizard. Her mood was grim and sad for Thomas, wishing the wizard wasn't so fixed on pressing forward.

"I made no mention of Kardanhall."

"You can thank Lady Wayne," he said, turning and leading her further. "Once I told her of you, she mentioned that grim place."

Anna pulled her hood forward, shading her eyes against the sun. Discomfort overcame her, and it chilled her worse than the wind being funneled her way. Her remaining arrows rattled, reminding her more might be needed for what she feared might come.

AN ENORMOUS SERPENT sat on the smooth stretch of rock where she had last seen Eve. It breathed easy against the cold, coiled up in many long, round layers. Folded within every layer were feathered wings of orange and white. A fuzz covered its coils, matching the wings, fluttering with the constant shift of winds. Anna kept her distance at first, hand to her bowstring, wondering where the dome saddle for such a creature might fit. Or if the creature was just as unpredictable as the serpents of the Greethumb region. It was certainly far larger, with a wide hood streaming from the base of its head. She swallowed, finding no part of the serpent not unsettling. Its teeth were like a dog's, pointed at the canines, but not curved like a regular snake's fangs.

"Up on the saddle you go," said the wizard.

The serpent uncoiled itself. Its wings whooshed across the ground as it stretched. On its back, close to the head, was a dome saddle hidden easily by the serpent's great girth. Anna scaled its side, the creature unfazed by her need to use its fur for steadiness.

"What's its name?" she said, peering over her shoulder.

The wizard looked up at her, eyes reflecting sunlight.

"Colbwing," he said, chuckling. "And since I have forgotten to give my own. My name is Brian."

Anna made it beside the dome saddle. It was silver and worn in places. She could hear a faint flapping, as if air passed through a hole somewhere.

"Brian?"

"Nathan Barden wasn't the cleverest with—"

"No," Anna said, opening the saddle door. "I quite like it."'

Backing up, she lowered the door of the dome saddle to find chains. They were rusted, hanging over the back of both seats. Brian drifted in first, taking the front seat. There were no reins or bridle on the serpent's head. After she closed the door, she saw through the window, long thin whiskers streaming behind Colbwing's diamond-shaped nostrils. Brian took hold of them as they slithered through the holes below the window.

"Secure yourself," said Brian. "Riding cobraswifts are far less safe than riding a horse or storm bison."

Feeling the chains against her back, both eyes widened for a second. *It comes together now.* Eve had told her humans hadn't found a way, but it appeared the rutoe were wiser. She removed her bow and quiver, then with some effort she slipped the chains over her head. They rattled against her hood until she secured them about her waist. The wizard nodded, gripped hard the corbaswift's whiskers, and flicked them. A rush pressed Anna's back to the seat. There was a crack like an immense whip behind her. Clamping her hands over her ears, the wizard was unfazed by it.

Within a second, they were among the clouds. Anna gulped, breathing fiercely, unable to take in the roughness of being airborne. It wasn't this way on an esant nor from her recent experience on a dragon. Her heart sank with the loss of Thomas. From how Eve spoke of him, her tone so delicate, the dragon was like a brother to the council-woman. Anna hoped to see her again. For now, focus needed to be placed on Nathan, and then the tournament.

———

A TREMOR RAN down her spine, strong enough to rattle the chains about her waist. They were north within a day, but it wasn't the corbaswift's speed that frightened a tear from her eye. Remnants of smoke wound around Kardanhall's vast keep. The smoke trailed to the one place she had seen destroyed by fire before. *Another ... temple.* Anna drew her hood back. Her hair matted with sweat clung to her face. She brushed away the tear on her cheek. She knew deep down that not even Lord Kardan's servants would set fire to the house of the goddess. Even they knew the punishment for such a sin. *Suicide,* she thought. *No, someone came while I was gone.*

"Where did you leave Nathan before coming south, Anna?"

"I...," The thought struck Anna harder than any blow forced upon her. "We thought he was safe."

"Safe where?" Brian demanded. He leapt up from his seat, grabbing her by the shoulders as his lips trembled. "Tell me!"

"The temple."

Brian collapsed into her arms. Beyond him there appeared only gloom, and within her own thoughts, a journey she felt had been wasted. She wished she had buried her friend out under the open sky. And when spring came, its clear blue would be upon where she laid him to rest. Anna let out a faint gasp. *Cole. Roland.* Whoever burned down the temple must have noticed the clouds drifting from the stables. She reached for Colbwing's whiskers but then hesitated. A faint flash met her eyes as Colbwing glided on the winds, awaiting somehow for Brian to guide him further.

"I will bring us down," she whispered, keeping to memory where the flash came from.

Brian slowly brushed away his tears.

"What? Why? We came north for nothing," he said. "My friend is gone. I knew deep down my magic would have revived him."

Anna slipped off the chains, grabbed Colbwing's whiskers and pressed her knees to the floor. For Brian, she decided to investigate the fire first, hoping the storm bison hadn't been harmed in what was no question an attack.

"Our time is better served getting you to the capital," said Brian, tugging her sleeve. "I love Nathan, but even he knew that in a crisis, time is short."

"I understand," said Anna, whipping the serpent's whiskers. "But deep within me I know something can be gained from us learning more."

She gaped for a moment and swallowed back what she realized. This was the first time she had flown a creature. Not even her... Lord William had permitted her to fly his esant, Sharp Beak. Brian was consumed by his grief. *I must do what I can.* Anna flicked Colbwing's whiskers. They sifted, contracting and expanding within her hands. She raised them slightly upward, the way Eve had with Thomas. The serpent dipped ever so toward Kardanhall. The castle's brickwork was a blur even with Colbwing closing the distance. She firmed her grip, turning them, circling around the temple's collapsed bell tower. Ahead, she pulled up, sending a great roaring hiss into the expanse formed between the curtain wall and the keep. They struck ground, whooshing through the dirt and scattering snow, splitting a stretch of ice. Through the dome saddle, the cobraswift stopped between the bend beginning around the castle. Brian let out a clenched breath.

"We're alive." He whispered in near disbelief. "I was uncertain by your unease."

Anna smiled, finding him lighter in spirits. His childlike face had an immense smile on it, and the red lining his eyes was a bright pink.

"Let's go."

She made for what she saw before, slipping her quiver over her shoulder. A long trench stretched a distance from the tip of Colbwing's tail. Dirt and stones had built up against the smooth surface of his coils. His bright fur met the sunlight, reflecting off the snow like dancing flames. Toward the temple, a shell of its once aged self, glimmered a spearhead. Its long wooden shaft pounded into the dirt. Anna's eyes narrowed. Her heart pounded against her chest; unease sank her stance. Fluttering at length from the spear's head was a scroll.

"Whoever burned the temple meant it as a warning," said Brian, catching up to her. "Let's find out who we're dealing with."

Untying the scroll from the spear, its paper smelled of smoke. Despite the cold, Anna found the parchment warmed somehow by the temple's fire. She unfurled it, catching sight of lingering flames on the seal of both windows to either side of the temple's entrance. *The fire ended recently.* She read with unease bubbling in her belly.

> *Lady Anna Brighton,*
> *I have your rutoe. By the rules set under campaign law, I cannot slow your arrival to the Tournament of the Primes. But since only two days remain, a late campaigner can be disqualified. And with the surprise coming your way, such tardiness is most...*

Anna bolted upright like a startled deer. She went rigid as the chill from Brian's presence pressed against her back. Below the castle's curtain wall, and from amongst the shadows, men in plated armor emerged. Upon their breast-plates, Lampara's governing crest, except it was within the jaws of a beast she had never seen. A beast with a thick mane around its head. Its eyes were like red-hot coals. Anna tossed aside the scroll, clapped an arrow to her bow.

"I don't have enough arrows for them all," she said, drawing and aiming for the closest man. "Can you fight?"

"I can," said Brian, biting his lip, "but not in this form. Can you get us back to Colbwing?"

Every man came at them at once, forming an ever-narrowing arch. Anna loosed one arrow after another in succession. One soared over a man coming from her right. She nocked another arrow, guiding Brian swiftly to the serpent. She realized most arrows grazed their mark. She blinked. Both eyes had been open, and she had been used to being half blind. It had made her one with her bow. Such a great change threw her aim off balance. Clamping her right eye shut, the balance swiftly returned. One man fell to her aim, the arrow passing through his throat. Her pulse quickened to find eight arrows remained. Colbwing roared and snapped as the soldiers doubled their advance. She swallowed her hesitation, nocked, and drew, releasing, and reaching, touching fewer and fewer arrows.

"Can he not defend himself?" Anna said, wincing when her bowstring grazed her arm. "He could clear them away."

Brian shook his head as his lips trembled. Anna could see the frustration on her face within his eyes.

"Colbwing is like a horse," said Brian. "He cannot fight unless trained or possessed."

"Possessed?"

"Yes," said Brian, firming his tone, removing the fear on his face. "Now get me to him."

Anna reached back to find four arrows remained. They circled the inside her quiver as she ran, each moving out of reach, raising her feelings of desperation. She snatched an arrow, wondering why the men didn't attack at greater speed. They didn't close their formation tight like a fist. It was as if they knew she possessed no chance of winning, no chance of escape. Several drew swords as steam rose swiftly from under their mouth shields. She hid her worry behind a stern face. Her hood hung heavy on her head from the heavy, swift snowflakes pounding Kardanhall.

Uncertainty crossed her mind about what Brian meant by possession. A word never meant more to her than what was owned by another. Every thought refocused on the men closing in on them. She fumbled with her last arrow, tensing her fingers over its fletching. A soldier swiped high from her right. Anna ducked, holding firm to the arrow as a slice and crack met her ears. Anna lunged, piercing above his mouth shield, scraping its metal. He stumbled toward the temple, screaming and gripping at his face.

She looked up and froze. She felt her throat close up and mouth go dry. Her chest heaved with pain. Her bow had been cut in two.

"Run" Anna hid her heartbreak, grabbing the wizard's wrist. "There are too many of them."

Brian saw what remained of her bow, pulling free of her grasp, speeding through the snow. Anna felt him leave her well behind as the soldiers chased her hurried footsteps. She shook her head, wishing for time to mourn her bow. The soldiers increased their pace, raising their swords. Anna dodged an avalanche of swipes, rocking on her heels.

"Go! Possess Colbwing before aaah…"

The soldiers grabbed her arms and legs. She felt herself raised, and every breath fled from her lips. They slammed her with great force against the ground. Snow crackled like glass under her head as it glanced off a stone. Her head thrummed with agony. Opening ajar her lips, heavy snowflakes filled her mouth. Anna rolled over, coughed, her head spinning, and crawled upon her belly. A swift, encompassing shadow rose. The soldiers' swords poised at once.

A roar greater than any she had ever heard crashed upon them. The sharp shadows of swords fell away from her. Feet shuffled across the snow, kicking up dirt, clicking small stones against muddied boots. Anna found herself alone. One man removed his mouth shield, eyeing the others as Colbwing blotted out the sun. The serpent reared to strike. Colbwing's eyes glowed. His long whiskers bolted back in jagged lines.

"Flee," said a deep thunderous voice from the serpent's mouth.

The soldiers charged. Colbwing swirled his tail and struck the ground. He gobbled up man after man, shielding Anna with his massive coils. The serpent crushed those out of range of his jaws with a tail swipe.

Anna stumbled to her feet. One soldier lay at a distant and unarmed, bleeding down his face, her arrow buried deep in his cheek. He pulled at the arrow and clawed at a snail's pace toward the temple. Anna approached him slowly, questions crossing her mind. He propped himself, waving her away, but his arm gave way. The coppery scent of his wound met her nostrils.

"Why attack us?" Anna said, towering over the man. "Answer. And I may help you remove my arrow."

"We got sent here to off Lady Brighton," he said, slipping a knife from his boot. He swiped at her, sneering. She kicked it out of his grasp. The soldier shook his hand. "Stay back, rutoe!"

"Does she look like whom you speak of?" Brian asked, his voice thundering from the serpent's jaws.

The soldier crawled away, made to stand, and then collapsed face side.

"She was supposed to 'ave a burned face." He rolled over and shook his head. Blood flowed from under his mouth shield and down his neck. "We thought the girl was here. We was told she'd trespass on Lord Kardan's grounds. That she was a threat."

Seeing where the wizard was heading with things, Anna focused on the soldier, finding him quivering, but not from the cold.

"I know who you seek, and she is no rutoe," said Anna, edging close to him. He swiped at her with his fist. Anna snatched it and threw it aside. "I have no intention of harming you."

She pressed a knee to his chest, laid her hand flat on his face, and pulled the arrow free. The man screamed and groaned, clamping his hand over his cheek.

"Go now. You're free."

"That bloody well hurt," said the soldier. His chest heaved peering over his shoulder to Simdorn's temple. "Thanks, I guess. There ain't no going home after what I've done."

She took the man's hand and pulled him to his feet. The small metal plates on his gauntlet were dotted with blood.

"Beg the goddess for forgiveness," she whispered. "Tell her you will build another temple greater in size."

He met her eyes and found a tear on his cheek.

"Thank you," he said, "for sparing me. I'll make good on the mercy you've shown."

TWENTY-NINE

The deep emptiness remained. Evelyn kept it locked within while amongst the rutoe clan commanders. Their unforgiving eyes glared over mouth shields and clenched pointed teeth. The journey to Cillnar had been quick, and upon a creature neither dragon nor bird. Its speed was greater than any she experienced upon Thomas.

She balled her fingers into fists, averting them from the knives tucked into her dress. *I killed their kin,* she thought, crossing her fists behind her back. *Will they take revenge after their leader is rescued?* It would take nothing, not even a span of minutes, to cut the throats of those in her company. But there were her servants to consider, their expressions weary of her guests. Their minds were likely both on their mistress's decision and the fact that it broke the law. She had ordered them to serve the rutoe wine and avert their eyes. Evelyn couldn't deny it. The commanders were the strangest folk ever to visit her home. That, and with the rutoe who murdered her friend dead, acting against his superiors may lead to unnecessary deaths.

Upon the table before her was a map of the capital. The commanders had marked each point of entry for their forces, ones they discussed in broken common tongue. It was apparent they had thought everything out to the last detail. She leaned against the smooth polished wood of the table, scanning the map, and thrumming her fingers. It was one of her father's maps, browned by cigar smoke and faded in quadrants. To the commanders, the only entrances were the ones possessing the most traffic and protection. She traced point to point with her finger the tunnels she'd discovered as a child. Ones neither her father, the city guard, nor any orderman beyond her and a few others knew.

"You have a plan in place," said Evelyn. "And once Anna wins the tournament, we can take the capital if Luther decides not to accept the results."

The commander of the ignited clan stepped forward, finishing his wine, and setting his crystal goblet on the table.

"We can be, how you say, 'certain' she will arrive on time with the wizard doing the flying. I ... uh, am still uneasy with the last of our fifth clan being raised by Brighton. He crushed our first rebellion and killed her clan. Are you telling the truth? She is a friend to rutoe?"

A faint, sharp pang struck Evelyn's mind. Doing so the commander, but he pressed his lips together while she released a breath through flared nostrils.

"Does being friends with our captured leader's son," said the quiet one commander among them, *"not prove this?"*

"I agree," said Evelyn, eyeing them both, digging her fingernails into the table. "I have seen the care she has for the boy in her actions and words."

"I will trust in that for the time being," said the ignited

commander, resting a hand on the flaming fist on his breastplate. "I worry for the leader's son. You left him at a strange castle with the blacnavinstin's servants."

With a guess such a word must have been a rutoe's way of calling someone a bastard. She remembered the lord's sword at her back, the force of his kick to her legs. The quakes had been too much then for her training to have much effect, even though Martyn Kardan wasn't a young man anymore.

"He took on Lamparien soldiers to save Anna," she said, refusing to wince. "I think we had best push past this issue of trust."

The quiet one commander severed the connection. Evelyn released a faint gasp as the mindful commander pushed aside the ignited one. He slammed his fist on the table, rattling his goblet forward until it eclipsed the Proving.

"You do not get to earn trust of rutoe by tales you did not witness."

Evelyn raised an eyebrow. There was no reason to lie, nor for her to have been in Natlendton to make her words true. She knew the rutoe by their clan abilities, way of travel, and care for nelka. It was apparent that their way of trusting others was far more complicated.

"Then what now?" she said, folding her arms. "Do you wish to gather your soldiers and leave after coming this far?"

The Mindful One glared with eyes bright orange, furniture rose slowly before crashing all at once upon the floor.

"No."

Stepping forward, the commander of the swift clan rested his goblet on the palace. Its location not far from the Proving on the map. And, by what Evelyn thought was sheer coincidence, where his soldiers had set up camp north of the woods.

"No. There is no turning back for rutoe," he said. "My friend knows words pass differently with humans."

The Swift Commander firmed his thick lips into a hard line. His dark blue eyes were soft, calmer than Evelyn saw in his fellow leaders.

"We are in agreement then?" she said.

Rising to full height the Mindful One unclenched his teeth.

"You'd best hope she wins, Wayne," he said.

For a moment, every portrait and piece of furniture rattled. The wood nestled within the hearth collapsed inward, freeing tiny glowing embers.

"Or what?" she said, molding her face until without emotion. "Will you take revenge for the rutoe I've killed? Will you shake my home down to its foundations? I know Anna is more than capable of defeating a few spoiled lords and ladies."

A thud loud enough to make her brace against the table sent vibrations beneath her feet. The paintings and furniture sat crooked, or several feet out of place.

"Fine," said the Mindful Commander. His eyes faded to a soft black. "Now let us focus on freeing our leader."

"Very well."

She drew another map out from under the one of Cill-nar. And as Evelyn explained the layout of Nar-ton prison, the need not to shake her head at the commander came and went. *Men are the same no matter where they come from,* she thought, pointing to where the council had gone to meet Norman's father. *Willing to show their might to threaten those they do not trust.*

EVELYN LEANED HEAVILY on the balustrade. The Proving was separated from her home by hundreds of houses and shops. It was far colder than the previous evening. The plan was already in motion for the commanders to send agents to rescue their leader. She had offered her own skill with a blade, and familiarity with the capital, but rutoe ways were old. Women served only three purposes in a clan, none allowing wives and daughters to become fighters or an orderman like herself. Rising to full height, the removal of her breastplate and gauntlets, which made managing her family illness easier.

"I wonder what they would think of Emilia, of her wife, being willing to lead," she sighed.

Creak.

Evelyn kept facing forward. Her ears twitched under her long blond locks. Letting free the thin knife tucked up her tight sleeve. Faint breaths broke the silence behind her. The room possessed only moonlight and starlight, streaming over the balcony to aid her vision. She didn't require light to make out where the intruder was. And whoever it was must have known whose home they trespassed within. Every manstower within Cillnar was made indistinguishable from the others. The prime and long-passed primnoire didn't wish for their brilliance to be outdone.

"Cross onto the balcony, intruder," said Evelyn. "You won't be given a second invitation."

Her nostrils drew in the smell. "Misnem?" she whispered. She forced every muscle to relax, to ready for the first hint of action. The tips of her fingers held firm the short knife, finding it real, certain, unlike her feelings. A boot thudded against smooth stonework. It broke the rule set by her daughter long ago, one even the servants obeyed. *Even I obey it still.* She felt the coolness against the flesh of her feet. They were growing numb from the cold, but her long thick night robes kept any loss of feeling from becoming absolute.

"I know who you are. Though I find it difficult to believe my senses."

The footsteps came once more, slow, but deliberate in measure.

"I didn't believe you would remember the misnem," said a voice Evelyn had almost forgotten. "I wear it for her, you know."

"And I always found a good wash better than the laziness of perfumes."

Evelyn turned slowly on her heels, finding Emilia hooded and cloaked. Her eyes were incapable of believing what she saw. The words she had said back in the Proving came true. Even in the way her daughter carried herself, she reminded the mistress of duels and debates of Anna Brighton.

"What have you come home for?" said Evelyn, carefully measuring her words, not wanting her daughter to find a reason to leave again. "I must tell you I have changed my position and am trying to stop Prime Luther."

Emelia stepped forward into the moonlight, drawing back her hood and letting loose her long blond hair.

"Finally, you see the old man for who he truly is," said Emilia.

"Yes."

"I come here for rest. Nina will join me shortly."

"How much support have you gained in your travels?" Evelyn said.

Emelia raised an eyebrow.

"So now you are for me campaigning?"

"I was never against it," Evelyn said. "I was uncertain about going against the prime, of what you discovered to be true."

"Father was more than willing to fund my campaign. Are not couples on the council supposed to be in full agreement?"

The conversation was coming to a boil. She needed to bring down the rising anger she saw in her daughter's eyes. She looked so much like a leader. Emilia kept her chin at proper height, her eyes fixed upon Evelyn's. A true leader kept focused on the conversation at hand. *I don't know why it never occurred to me before*, Evelyn thought.

"Our prime has become more powerful, using rutoe willing to betray their own kind," said Evelyn. "I did not want to risk your life, and that of our family's,' by placing coin on the subject."

Emelia smirked.

"That is why I put my faith in the people. They've offered to keep me hidden should our prime see me as a threat to his dimwitted sons."

For this, Evelyn found herself both grateful and guilty. She had not had much faith in Lampara's citizens, knowing how much had changed in recent years. She cast her gaze to the ground, guilt compounding like a wave towards a shore.

"I am here to support you, but also someone who I believe will lead us to a better tomorrow."

"And who may I ask, is this man?" Emilia asked, fumbling with the thick folds of her cloak.

"It is no man but a woman." Evelyn played with the idea of telling her daughter about Anna. She was uncertain if revealing such information was necessary. *Emilia was always the jealous type.* "The woman is from a family long since absent from politics," she sighed. "Her name is Anna Brighton."

"Anna Brighton?" said Emilia. "I hear she is without half a face. How will someone with such a deformity lead?"

"I have taught you better than that. Appearance has nothing to do with strength and leadership. And from what I have heard of late, she has grown in popularity."

The door opened into Emilia's chambers. Nina stepped through to find awkwardness in the room. She nodded and closed the door. Evelyn thought the girl was wise for keeping out at a time like this.

"Place your backing behind this half-burned girl, Mother."

There was a fury in Emilia's voice that Evelyn sensed might strike soon. *End battles of emotion with greater speed than those with a blade.* Her master once said. *For death of the heart is far worse than any man can invent.* Evelyn had felt close to death when she last saw her daughter. It pained her far more than the quakes that left her unbalanced. Tremors rolled through her as she took a step forward. Her balance bent her in a fast motion, bringing the ground within inches. Evelyn coughed at a sudden pulse from her chest. The room felt more stable as she was guided to full height.

"I've not yet experienced the first signs of quakes," said Emilia. "But at no time will I ever allow you to fall, Mother. If you back us both, then there is no reason for us to remain at odds."

The emotion in her daughter's voice was clear and kind. Her hopes went from her belly to her heart in a flash at the thought of no longer being parted from Emilia. Evelyn embraced her with all the strength she possessed.

"And you shall have it." She leaned back, still uneasy in balance, reflecting on the emerald in Emilia's eyes. "Now. I must tell you about the siege."

Emilia gasped. "Siege?"

THIRTY

A cold sweat broke on Norman's brow. The heat flowing through his veins felt like the ice chilling the soles of his feet. There was a deep wish to leave, to flee within the depths of his mind. Norman gazed up at the prison while his trick of skin fluctuated and crawled away with his feelings. The prison towered over the homes of Cillnar, tucked into a corner of the capital, and encircled by fog disguising its true height. Its bear statues were black with a marble sheen, representing its occupants' lack of respect for the law. Unlike the Proving, the statues surrounding Nar-ton prison stood on their hind legs. Their backs were turned to the city as if to keep something terrible inside. Ravens leapt from a window high above the prison entrance with scrolls tied to their ankles. Below the window and between two cracked columns stood guards in armor pitted and rusted. Norman thought that if either man moved, their armor may crumble away.

Beside him stood Phillip, a tall man, wearing a long heavy trench coat possessing fur about its collar. He released a gray cloud of smoke from his lips. His thin cigar at half the length from when they left the palace. Norman firmed up his face and focused on keeping his flesh that of a human's. His hair ruffled despite there being no wind. As if it were eager to return to its long flowing darkness. Norman forced himself earlier to take on a slightly different form. He abandoned his curls for close-cropped hair. His face remained the same Anna had grown to know, adjusting his chin slightly to match Phillip's. He clenched his jaw, sweat ran down his cheek. The minor changes pressed upon his mind like thumbs to a man's eyes.

"Are you ready, Tilt?"

"Ye—Yes," Norman said. A vein throbbed in his neck. "My... My father is in that place. Luther said he had little time left."

"Good," said the orderman, dropping his cigar and squashing it with the heel of his boot. "'Because I won't be holding your hand. This place has more than guards they say."

Norman gulped, bending his fingers into fists to push down his nervousness. Flames ignited over his knuckles for a moment to remind himself of Anna's courage. *I must be like her with my fears.* He shook off his worry, retracting the flames into his knuckles. Norman nodded, following Phillip, doubling his pace. The orderman's strides were long and fast. Norman guessed the man's height and obligation were the cause.. He didn't wish to appear as if he were running, but the snow was nearly at his knees. Once they made it within earshot, both guards crossed their spears. Their eyes widened. Phillip's fingertips splayed upon the door before either had noticed.

"Do you have papers for entry?" said one guard.

"And papers to see a prisoner of our prime?" said the second guard.

"You're both cute." Phillip smirked. "Ordermen don't need no papers."

The guards eyed one another; one tugged at his scarf beneath his chin. He tapped the butt of his spear on the ground to reinforce his point. His dome helmet was well over his brow, and his mouth shield hung limp in the folds of his scarf. Its metal was caked with snot. Norman noticed the light film of frost over the guard's evergreen breastplate. He thought Phillip walking up and demanding entrance arrogant. There was no way such an act could work. However, he had seen citizens seeking refuge from the orderman's presence. The same unease wasn't on the faces of the guards though.

"They do when there's a tournament of primes," said the first guard, signaling his partner. The other guard strolled toward a bell within a hollow. "We've got a few campaigners in here, and my guess is you ain't no orderman. What business does one of your order got with a prisoner?"

Norman stepped forward, parting his lips, but Phillip glared at him. The steel blue of his eyes made Norman's boiling blood feel as if it had frosted over. The orderman sighed deeply. He eyed Phillip's hands. They remained— the guards dropped to their knees, heads jerking back, throats slowly splitting open like waking eyes.

"Was that your doing?" said Norman. "How can a human move like that?"

"You'd be surprised," said Phillip. His knives hissed swiftly from his sleeves, "but this time it wasn't me doing the cutting."

The tracks led down a distant alley, from where the guard had fallen. A light snow began to fall, slowly erasing their existence. A faint trail of red droplets followed the tracks. Norman drew back at a shadow and then snow tumbled from an overhang beside a condemned shop.

"We ain't alone, Tilt."

Phillip raised a finger to his lips, returning it to the hilt of his knife. Norman heard footsteps coming from the left of the alley. Four figures in black drifted from the shadows. At the fingertips of the one leading them, long thin blades dripped blood.

"I suggest you drop the disguise, Tilt," said the order-man, "'cause we're gonna need that fire of yours."

Norman released air from his nostrils as his skin tingled and shifted. Flames outlined his fists, but then he realized who they were up against. *Rutoe. I should speak with them before it is too late.*

"We come to free my father, Huldinarf," he said in rutoeis. "He is the leader of the rebellion against Prime Luther."

The leading rutoe raised his blade-tipped fingers. The others stopped many paces short of the alley's end. She halted within a spear's throw. The rutoe slipped off a black cobraswift helmet. What Norman perceived from the figure's physique to be a woman was a man of extreme slender build. He had sharp dark blue eyes, and charcoal skin. There was a faint white scar down his brow, one eye missing from its socket, and the scar continued to the chin. He held the helmet at his hip. His hair was drawn back and tied.

"You are who he calls, Sheckaldurn?" he said.

Phillip snickered.

"Your father calls you horse droppings?" said Phillip, chuckling.

Norman's green skin darkened. His cheeks burned with embarrassment. Rutoe possessed no list of common names.

Leaders, priests, farmers, whomever throughout the generations were named after the first thing they pointed to as an infant. Norman's family once worked in the fields of a farmer in Lampara's northernmost region. He ground his teeth, remembering that close to where his mother watched him play, a plow horse had defecated.

"Let the subject die," said Norman.

"If I live through this," Phillip snickered. "I might."

The Swift One sneered at the orderman then placed his focus back on Norman.

"We must be quick," he said. "Our forces await the rescue of your father, Sheckaldurn."

"Let's be off then," Norman said. He eyed Phillip, but his presence couldn't instill the fear the orderman possessed. "What did you mean about this place having more than just guards?"

"Touch the doors," Phillip said, pointing a knife at them, keeping his focus on the Swift One.

Norman stepped lightly over the guards. Their faces buried deep in the snow, blood pooled from their throats in long wide arcs. He extinguished a flame-ringed hand, reaching for the door's immense rusted ring. A jolt rushed through his arm, lifting him from his feet. Norman gasped, flying backwards. A grunt let out behind him as he felt a sudden stop. His head cracked against something thin and sharp.

"That's what I meant, Tilt," said Phillip, helping Norman back on his feet. "I figured Luther rigged this place somehow."

"What keeps me out?" Norman said, rubbing his head.

"Being rutoe."

"This is a wizard's work," said the Swift One, wincing as he waved his hand over the door. "Must we trust in a human to achieve the freedom from banishment we seek?"

"I don't much care for that tone of yours," said Phillip, gripping his long knives tight. "You got that skin-changing thing. Use it if you don't want to trust more humans."

Phillip raised his chin, clenching his teeth. The Swift One's blades dug into the skin above the orderman's throat. Norman snatched his wrist, yanking away the razor-sharp blades.

"He gave us the key to freeing my father," Norman growled, pressing the rutoe's hand to his chest.

The Swift One fumed. A flicker of blue lightning raced across his eye.

"We shouldn't have to change our appearance for anyone." The Swift One cast his hand to the snow, clicking his blades, placing his helmet on. "Or any reason. Such magic belongs to the ominous clan and is forbidden."

Norman felt taken aback for a moment. Uncertainty flooded his chest as he looked up at the prison. His father had gone from a farmhand to the leader of a rebellion. Taking risks. Placing him in the care of Samuel, who had taught Norman much. Before leaving the south, learning the *trick of the skin* meant survival to him. His father told him rutoe used it to keep humans from acting rash, from the need for rutoe to use their clan gift in defense.

"I must go alone," he said, rubbing his head, finding no blood. "I will free my father so our banishment may end."

He moved to within an arm's length of the doors. Norman shut his eyes, drawing all focus away from his flames, picturing the man he guised himself as. His chin tingled until pointed and strong like the orderman's. His hair hissed up his cheeks, shortening and fading into its chestnut color. It felt as though a fan of feathers caressed the back of his neck. Both ears rounded off as his eyes glazed over, churning to the color of a mountain spring. Gasps rose from the rutoe in his company. Whispers reached his ears about how his skin was so light and red at the cheeks.

"I'm going with you like we planned," said Phillip.

Norman smiled. A thought crossed his mind, robbing him of focus.

"Will this disguise fool a wizard's magic?"

"You've got only one way to find out." The orderman rolled his shoulders, cracking his neck, raising his fists with both blades at the ready. "After you."

Norman grabbed hold of the handle. Lifting it, he felt a surge of power flow up his arm. He clenched his teeth, fighting the urge to let loose his natural form. Pushing with all his might, Norman felt the door give way, scraping against cracked brickwork. Phillip pushed the other door with ease, gripping both knives in his left hand. A rush of dampness and mold teased Norman's nostrils. He released the door in time to steady himself. The hall before them was long and filled with doors on either side. A spiraling metal staircase led up to where he had seen the ravens.

He released a pent-up breath. His hair fell loose over his shifting ears. The burning behind his eyes pinched his pupils. The rutoe leader entered, followed by the others, finding no resistance from the wizard's magic. The jarring power dissipated from Norman's limbs. His skin phased to its natural green, removing what felt like an overbearing weight. The hairs upon skin stood on end. An ice-blue light surged over the walls, the floor, and across the ceiling at intense speed. A crackling boom sounded at the hall's end. It faded to nothing.

Clattering and rattling answered. Out of the darkness

beyond the hall's end, guards approached at great speed. They wielded swords, and their armor was equally pitted to what the soldiers outside had worn. Norman ignited his hands, charging at them, thinking of his father as he thrusted a heavy torrent of flames. Phillip sprinted, lunged, piercing the throat of a guard. The orderman spun and shoved his knife up into the jaw of a man swinging his sword in a heavy downward motion.

Those among the Swift One's released flames, losing orb lamps from their places, and bashing guards across the face. The Swift One ran in an arc. Norman could not find him until eleven men collapsed to their knees. Men toward the rear of the falling guards fled for the grand staircase.

"We shall find our leader faster by separation," said the Swift One.

"That ain't gonna end well for any of us," said Phillip, yanking his knife from a man's back. "That room above us has got to have something about your leader's whereabouts."

The stairs ahead were wide, parting at the top in two directions. Phillip must have been mistaken. The room sent ravens carrying messages. There may have been a room that revealed where his father was kept. He felt deep in his heart searching for it was a waste of time.

"We shall separate," he said, chewing his lip. "Those guards will return with more of their own. It's a risk, but we must press on."

Phillip shook his head, grabbing Norman's arm. "You're going in blind," he said, jabbing the point of his knife at the stairs. "I'm betting I'm right."

Shouts reached their level, followed by heavy footsteps in equal measure. Norman ignored Phillip's concern, dashing for the stairs. For a moment, there was no one following him, and then the orderman and those of the Swift One's group were at his back. Phillip bolted past him, thrusting a sharp glare at Norman from under his disk helmet. Norman threw his focus onto freeing his father. His brow knitted as they reached the next level. It seemed the stairs reached and spiraled off in two directions for every floor to come.

"You're letting that heart of yours crush that accountant logic," Phillip hissed. "I asked the others to take out the guards. Leave us to do the searching."

Norman raised an eyebrow, deep down agreeing with such a strategy. There was too much eagerness in his heart. And he knew from what Anna said regarding hunting that a rush to find what you seek leads only to trouble.

"You're right," said Norman. The echo of more footsteps reached his ears. "We shall return to the room you mentioned."

Phillip tapped his knife to his helmet in a salute. They raced to the bottom level, pausing in mid-step before another orderman. He was tall, with olive skin, eyes burning a dark green. Norman knew him from Prime Luther's dome saddle.

"Have you come to aid us?" Norman said, peering over his shoulder to find guards at his back. "Or have you come to..."

A piercing sent both him and Phillip to their knees. The Quiet One waved the men behind them forward. The guards raced down the steps, shackles in hand, and then there was a hiss. A hiss like metal across flesh.

"Drop flat," said the orderman within Norman's mind. His mouth shield clanged against the ground.

Norman dropped onto his belly beside Phillip. A great booming cry filled the prison. He clamped his hands over his ears. The shackles dropped without a sound and disappeared into the shadows. Dozens of feet rose at once as a collective thrum sent a cloud of dust over him. Norman coughed, rubbing at his eyes to find the center of the stairs had been obliterated. There was a great gaping void, strewn with bodies, leading to a jagged endless tunnel.

The Quiet One picked up his mouth shield and applied it. A long knife with brown leather woven over the hilt slipped out from his sleeve. Norman ignited his fist, confusion sending a bolt of heat down his brow.

"Douse those fire starters, Sheckaldurn," said Phillip, raising his knife to the brim of his disk helmet, saluting the other orderman. Laughing.

"I said drop it," Norman barked, letting his flames go out. "It's. Not. Funny."

The orderman before them clamped his eyes shut, clasping his hand across his mouth. The ground shook and bodies teetered on scattered debris.

"Okay, kid," said Phillip, once the quaking stopped. "Let's see where they're keeping your dad."

AT ALL CORNERS cages were piled to the ceiling. White and black dung lie clumped upon the bars with squawking ravens pecking at corn in small bowls. Norman found himself wanting another assault upon his senses from the quiet one rather than the constant caws and feathers ruffling around him. He searched amongst the paper stacks, knowing that , like Lord William's financial records, the most recent entries would be on light colored parchment. The search felt like time being consumed in a slow fashion.

There was no organization. No alphabetical order to the prisoner names.

"I can't find anything in this mess," Norman said, removing an ink bottle from atop a stack of papers. "There's nothing but names. There ought to be—"

Beyond him a narrow hall led to more pillars of clutter. There were shelves chock-full of books, molding and disheveled. But what drew his attention away from searching was faint breathing. The ordermen in his company readied their knives, setting down handfuls of lists. Norman crept toward the hall, heart pounding, slowly maneuvering along a wall of cages. Caws assaulted his ears, muffling the breathing. Amidst the room's confusion, a foot appeared, wrapped in rags. Hands reached out, holding a cawing, irritated raven. The man sprinted toward the window ahead.

The ordermen raced to stop him. Norman saw a message tightly bound to the raven's ankle. The man huffed and puffed, maneuvering around a solid oak table. Norman dashed, reached, tripping over a stack of leather-bound ledgers. He gasped. A burst of flames barrel-rolled from his fingertips. The man screamed as the flames consumed him. He dropped the raven and tumbled against an assortment of cages. They collapsed and crunched the more the man tossed about. Cries of pain let out in one voice from the ravens. They squirmed and smashed their way between the bars.

The raven hopped its way to the window. A knife pinned it through the back and into a dusty leather-bound ledger. The knife was the length of Norman's hand, a crescent moon joining blade to hilt, the blade itself capturing the roaring flames. A line of blood ran down its edge and off the ledger. Phillip tipped his helmet to him, yanking the knife free. The flames climbed the walls, consuming the ravens, showering the room in burning feathers.

"Come on, Tilt," said Phillip, grabbing him by the shoulders. "We'll be dead if we don't up and run."

"But," said Norman, grabbing for more papers. Cages collapsed and smashed blanketing the window in a cloud of smoke and dust. "I won't find my father without—"

"We've got to go, kid."

Norman's arms went numb, soon followed by his legs. His eyelids felt heavy as his fingers clawed for more names. The room went dark as he found himself mumbling through globs of oozing spittle.

Norman found himself lying against the metal staircase. A cool breeze sifted its way from under the doors. Its chill nipped his cheek as the scent of smoke filled his nostrils. He rubbed his head. Phillip opened the doors releasing the smoke weaving its way from the room above.

"I had to do it, Tilt," said Phillip, going to one knee beside him. "You had a look in your eye like you didn't mind dying, and that wouldn't help anybody. Not even your—"

"Father." Norman gasped.

Norman stumbled to his feet so fast that his head spun. Pain flooded his temples before he found his focus once again. Behind his father were the rutoe of earlier, their faces concealed within their cobraswift helmets. His father slouched a little. His hair was long enough to cover his chest. The rebel leader's eyes were faded red, and his skin possessed deep and frightening scars. His father looked upon him as if he were discovering a distant memory. His father wore a gray tunic lacking sleeves. His trousers were held up by a thin length of rope.

"It has been," Norman embraced him, "too long."

"It truly has, Norman."

The strength in his father once possessed was distant. Norman could see Prime Luther had fed his father poorly; malnourishment had shrunk the muscles formed from his days of farming and rebellion.

"Now, Norman," his father said. "Let's kill that bastard Luther."

They marched forth from the prison to find the street bustling. Lampariens with golden blond hair and those of a dark auburn flocked from shops and homes toward the Proving. A screech like a blade against blade made Norman wince. He spun to find the Swift One raising his hand, scraping the blades upon his fingers once again. A scream rang out, and soon, a top of the city walls flames erupted. The humans heading for the tournament scattered. Swift ones appeared in a blink within alleyways and the confusion of crowds.

"We've got to head for Evelyn's," said Phillip, dashing west. "Bring your father, Tilt."

"Come, father," said Norman, grabbing his father's arm. "The Waynes can be trusted."

His father yanked his arm back, eyeing the rutoe behind him.

"The Waynes have profited from nelka furs," he said. "You know how important nelka are to rutoe."

"Listen," Phillip said, sheathing his knives. "I helped your son free you. That counts for something."

The weathered form that was his father swirled his fingers into fists, vanishing in concentrated balls of flames.

"Do you think after all Prime Luther has done," the general snarled, "all Lampara's humans have done, that I will trust you?"

The Swift One clasped the rebel leader's shoulder.

"I have no love for the Waynes, General Huldinarf," he

said. His voice was metallic through his helmet. "But Evelyn Wayne now funds our rebellion. She has wronged us and is paying back that wrong in full."

Norman sighed. The street was empty of all humans except Phillip. Upon the city walls faint cries rang out, and flames lit and vanished. His father flashed his pointed teeth at Phillip. His anger simmered. The flames over his hands vanished amongst the scars and blisters across his knuckles.

"That is not enough, my son."

"There is someone else, Father," said Norman. "Someone that will help us win. She means much to me."

"And who is this girl that she will make me trust a Wayne?"

Norman met the burning crimson in his father's eyes. His chest thundered with conflict. There had been so many signs, both recent and in the past. But in the past, uncertainty kept him from summoning the courage to be proven right.

"Her name is Anna," he said. "And she is the last of the fifth clan."

THIRTY-ONE

It was never hard to find him. He always gave himself away, which was both his biggest fault and his best quality. Cole's clouds were nearly invisible in the darkness that was slowly replacing the day. Anna knew she possessed only a night and a day to reach Cillnar. But knowing that her first and best friend was alive meant more than all else. She dropped to her knees and embraced Cole's furry head. The orb lamplight reflected off his silver hooked horns. A change in her appearance didn't matter to the storm bison, as if he recognized her no matter the burns or... It came to her. Anna rose to her feet, finding an unsteadiness in her stance. She had been so happy to see her friend, and discouraged in the wake of losing Nathan, that...

"I cannot return to Cillnar as I am."

She led Cole and Roland out of the stables. Kardanhall loomed like an abandoned ruin. No light filled its windows, and with night almost upon it, the castle resembled a mountain more than anything else. Brian stood at a distance with arms folded, a slight smile on his face, but

there was a strange glow in his eyes. It spoke to her somehow. As if he were trapped in a web that he wished to
escape but couldn't.

"Your reuniting with your friend brings me joy," he said.
The smile on his lips faded fast. "If only I could have done
the same with Nathan."

Silence fell between them both. The truth of failing to
return in time left Anna's heart heavy with grief. And yet
she believed the former lord was in a better place, free from
Prime Luther troubling him again. She sighed. Their grief
would need tending to at a later time.

"I cannot return to the capital as I am," she said. The
thought of returning to her old self felt both insane and
unwanted in her mind. "Lampara's people do not know me
as I am now, and we have no time to find another dra—"

"The effects of Echnumbard's gift cannot be reversed
by my magics either," said Brian. He patted his robes,
reaching into various pockets. "I have one solution, but I
have seen few accomplish it in my time."

As Brian searched, the light of eyes flashed against the
ground. The indentations covered the ground, large and
coated in a light layer of snow. Anna rested her hand along
the edge of one. The indentation she stood inside came to
above her wrist. The courtyard had been trampled by something large. It might have been another crystalardan except
the tracks possessed a curved heel. Thomas had a long back
claw and three long-clawed digits on each foot.

"Someone else was here," Anna said, diverting her focus
from her current predicament, "and rode a dragon far larger
than any I have ever seen."

The thought of becoming her old self returned. It
squeezed at her chest like a hand a ripe fruit. She missed
having smooth use of her bow, but that was gone with her

burns. Her bow was slung across her chest, barely held together by her belt. It wasn't sturdy enough, and neither was her focus.

"My thoughts are more on our current problem," said Brian.

"But this will explain why Norman has not..." Anna clasped her hand over her lips, drawing it slowly away. It felt as if she had forgotten him entirely. "Luther has Norman."

"We must focus on getting to Cillnar then," said Brian, reaching into a last pocket and drawing out a small black book. The wizard flipped through its pages at an unusual speed. "Your friend is in danger, and you have a tournament to win. Ah, here it is."

"Will what you've discovered return my face to what Lampariens recognize? I wish not to burn myself."

Anna dropped the reins within her hands, moving away from the storm bison. The writing inside the wizard's book was in a language she didn't understand. Brian peered up at her with a smile hinting at uncertainty.

"Are you familiar with the rutoe's trick of skin?" Brian asked, resting a finger on a page. "It may help us, but it affects the rutuo of the fifth clan differently than others."

Anna swallowed, knowing what pain it put Norman through. It would only be her face, and yet she had been her true self for a short time. She worried it might be too difficult to maintain the face she once possessed. The return of her overwhelming senses was something else she feared. *If they return,* she thought. They were only useful some of the time and pained her worse than her long-gone wound.

"I will do it," she sighed, embracing Cole, soothing his nerves with his warmth. "What does such magic do to a rutoe like me?"

"You will be at risk of death should your focus not be total. You must be determined when performing such magic," said Brian, eyeing his book once more. He sighed. "Anna. Are you certain?"

Anna exhaled slowly, drawing back her hood. To be the woman she was before bothered her less than what trick of skin could do should she fail. She swallowed the possibility and rested upon who needed her. The rutoe in the south, and, most important of all Norman. Brian nodded, waving his hand over her eyes, instructing her to close them. He told her to picture the face she wished to mirror. Anna chewed her lip. She had only seen what she looked like once. The memory of the burns, heaviness of the burned flesh of her eye wasn't clear enough to fully picture.

"Wait. If I succeed," she said, opening one eye, "is there a way back to being a rutoe?"

Brian frowned, resting his hand within one of her own.

"I'm uncertain," he said. "Survive the tournament and perhaps the answer will come."

She closed her eyes, releasing a shuddering breath. Brian was far too truthful with her. Anna pressed her lips tight, focusing on the darkness of her eyelids. The memory of her face was still faint. What was most familiar came to her. The feeling of complete darkness in her right eye, and how heavy its lid had felt. A crawling ran over it. The cold night air touched her cheeks, reminding her how soothing such a feeling used to be. The crawling ran down the surface of her cheek, warping away at the right side. Anna recalled how limited her speech was with half her lips fused by their skin. Five long years of hiding and hating herself for wanting to impress others, for being disfigured, crept back into her subconscious. *No, I no longer care if others find fault in me.* There were people who accepted her. Nathan, Eve, and Norman.

Soon the right side of her face felt heavy and twisted. She parted her lips, feeling the tug. The pain ran across her face the longer she focused. Her thoughts blurred. The pressures of what lay ahead assaulted her emotions as the fully formed burns fluctuated. She had only to focus on making her crimson flesh the pinkish white of a human. And then all at once balance left her, concentration abandoned her. All the breath Anna possessed came out in a shrill scream.

THE STARS WERE at their brightest, telling Anna the night was at its midpoint. She had learned to tell such things from Lord William himself. He spoke of how Lampara stood still while the stars drifted from place to place, giving their siblings a different perspective of life below. She looked to the woods ahead, and then with surprise she could barely contain Cole. They were on the move at a speed the old storm bison had never reached in all their time together.

She felt something cold and metallic around her waist. Anna sat up straight, finding the pain in her back had slumped over for hours . Peering into the darkness filled her vision with only the light of the moon and stars to give her eye... She rested her hand on her face, flinched, relief washing over her all at once. Anna parted her lips to speak, but like before, half of them were sealed shut. Her right eye pressed against its lid, and for a moment, Anna missed the full sight she briefly possessed.

Anna peered down at Cole. In spite of his newfound speed, his heavy panting released no clouds from his nostrils. His horns were no longer silver but a shining black. She touched his hump. It was white as the moon.

"I'm relieved you survived," said Brian. "I used Colbwing's seat chain to keep you atop your friend."

Anna shrieked, leaning forward to find an enormous smile on the storm bison's thick black lips.

"Once you fainted, I panicked but found life still within you. You truly possess a strong will for someone so young. The ominous clan spent years strengthening their willpower to avoid the death trick of skin can bring."

She ran her fingers over the cold chain. Fur brushed softly against her cheek. There was a long golden cloak over her shoulders. Its hood and collar lined with black bear fur. Anna pulled it tight across her chest. The twisted layer feel of her old face was a comfort somehow. She clenched her teeth, rubbed her head, finding her senses on full alert once more. It increased both her worry and awareness. She smiled and took hold of Cole's saddle horn. All of it was now just something she was used to.

"How far do we have to Cillnar?" said Anna. "Nathan guided me throughout our travels."

He guided Norman too, she thought. Brian raised Cole's head to her, the moon's light reflected within the bison's black eyes.

"With my help, Cole will reach the capital by midday tomorrow," said Brian, returning his focus to the woods. "He is old. Older than us . My magic will keep all fatigue at bay. He will need to be left somewhere safe for a long rest."

"Let's move swiftly then. Cole deserves rest for his friendship."

"Agreed," Brian sent Cole west and then north, trampling roots in his wake. "I sense something on your mind, Anna. Are you regretting your decision?"

"I was for a moment," she said, finally touching her face. "But I long ago accepted myself, accepted my appearance."

She licked her lips, not hesitating, no longer bothered by the thick flesh hampering her speech. The wind ran across her face and into her hood; its chill returned her focus to what lay ahead. A throbbing worry surfaced in her throat for not just about the tournament but about Norman. If Rockelton was any clue to the prime's distaste for rutoe, then her friend... her love, if she dared say it, needed her help.

"I can only hold on to hope that Norman is safe," said Anna, holding fast to the saddle horn. "I would not have come this far without him."

"I understand your feelings for him," Brian said, huffing through Cole's massive jaws. "But worrying for him will make no difference if a prime's son wins the tournament."

Anna stiffened her chin knowing he was right, but Norman had shown her loyalty, friendship, and above all love. Something she had believed for so long would only come from the man who had raised her.

"I shall need to be at my sharpest then," she said. "I don't wish to let Lampara down."

———

CILLNAR WAS GRIM. Beyond the hill Anna stood on, winter had made the days dreary and gray. In the distance, Cole lay on his side, shaded by low branches of pine. His clouds drifted through the branches like smoke from a campfire. It pinched at her chest to leave her friend behind again. Anna had always felt at her best with him at her side. There was some small comfort, though, in that Brian had decided to stay and watch over him. It seemed fair after pushing Cole to his limits. The storm bison's fur slowly faded to the gray she knew. His horns were black only at their tips now.

She made her way to the capital in step with the snow-fall. The sense of danger ahead was reaching a limit, gnawing at the nape of her neck. Anna passed the sign concerning weapons and sighed. She felt naked without her bow and quiver. She dreaded the thought of wielding one of those dueling swords again.

After several hundred paces, the deepening snow had taxed her legs to their limits. She shook the strength back into them, offering both hands at her sides. The city guards acknowledged she was unarmed and waved her through. The immense thick doors thundered open, sending a shiver of dread down her spine. There was still a city to navigate. If Brian hadn't left Roland behind, speed might have been possible. And yet there was no logic in it, a second mount meant a slower journey, and the possibility of being too late for the tournament. *I will return for him someday.*

"Oi, m' lady."

Anna halted short of the cheefox shop.

"Yes," she said, pivoting to face a man bundled in furs before the shop. "I'm sorry, sir. I have no coin for a..."

Ronald. She gasped. He approached at a slow pace, a slight limp in his step. She held back regret, pressing her lips into a hard line. At the Proving, she had struck him in the side, ending their duel. Men were needed to carry him off.

"I'm sorry, Ronald."

"You best be," he said, halting, and bending to catch his breath. "I 'haven't left the capital since our first going about. Thank our ginger goddess, the people 'ere love me."

Meshing her fingers into fists, it was the only thing to

do without breaking into a rant. The goddess being acknowledged so casually grinded at her mind like a stone against beer hops.

"I didn't wish to leave you in such a state," said Anna, every feeling thrumming. "What business do you have with me?"

Ronald stared for a moment. Anna hadn't noticed it on the grassy field of the Proving, but his left eye was milky white. Its pupil a solid black dot. She thought it blind, but it possessed enough focus to demonstrate otherwise. He licked his lips, resting a hand on his chest.

"Oh, just to increase my chances."

He leapt upon her, knife in hand, both crashing to the ground. Ronald punched her across the cheek. Anna spat, kneeing him in the crotch. They rolled in the snow as a crowd gathered. Cheers for Ronald came from the direction of the cheefox shop. Those behind her called for him to leave Anna be. The knife hissed through her hood, catching in the thick fabric, ripping it away.

Anna snatched his wrist, pressing her thumb deep. Ronald ground his teeth; spittle dripped onto Anna's cheek. He cried out and dropped his knife. She reached over, grabbed it, spun it, and thrust it swiftly. Blood dripped and tapped against her chest, running down her leathers. Anna pushed Ronald off, grunting, untangling his arms from her own.

Cheers rose as she eased into a sitting position. Anna found her breath, then peered over at Ronald. She drew her hand away, finding it stained red. Anna climbed to her feet and massaged her jaw. The crowd seemed divided about her victory, the snow gradually ceasing its downfall about them. There were no calls for her arrest. She saw six men on horseback approach from an alley. They wore evergreen plated armor with chainmail dyed red underneath. On their heads were arrowhead-shaped helmets and below their noses green mouth shields.

"She was attacked," said a woman from behind Anna.

People echoed the woman's words as the armored men drew closer. Anna felt the wind bite at her sealed eye, teasing at the skin holding half her mouth hostage. Her hood flapped open and shut in quick successions from a second wind gust.

"You must be the last of the campaigners," said a soldier. A scar split his left eyebrow in two. "It's clear you finished the fight. The tournament begins on the morrow. You may share my horse, or we can summon a carriage to bring you to the Proving."

Anna focused on Ronald for a moment. Lampara had truly changed. Throughout all of Lord William's lessons, facing justice was stressed most. The spectators around her remained divided. Some made claims that she had smuggled the knife inside her cloak.

"I will walk," she said. "Time isn't against me at present, and I must find a sense of Cillnar if I am to lead someday."

Silence fell on the crowd. Her nerves eased as she drew her gaze from Ronald's lifeless body. She pulled her cloak tight about her. Snow crackled, and the wind howled with each footstep. Anna watched the eyes upon her, ignoring whatever thoughts might be behind them. After rounding a corner where once a man boasted about Lord Arthur's achievements, voices rose, breaking the dominance of winter's voice. Were those who witnessed the struggle against Ronald in favor of her now, she wondered.

Anna focused on the directions Nathan had spoken of long ago. The soreness in her legs lessened after she avoided a long patch of ice. She blotted out the final realization that laws meant nothing in Cillnar. In Williamton, crime was infrequent but handled as it should be. Understanding this, Anna slowed her pace to have more time to think. Tension rested its hands on her shoulders, squeezing them, whispering of how it might someday be her duty to restore order. If she won, that is.

THIRTY-TWO

Tying off the final cord to his breastplate, there was nothing left to do but wait. Norman took in Lady Evelyn's thinking room, finding it far more luxurious than Kardanhall. It possessed smooth polished tile floors and tall cylindrical wood columns, topped with the face of Simdorn herself. The hearth was large enough to live within, stocked with wood, the crackling louder than heavy rain against a roof. Across from him the Quiet One stood still like a statue, receiving orders from his father, who paced back and forth. Norman's nerves felt as raw as they had ever been. Every thought was on Anna or the rutoe closing in on the palace. The armor on his person felt useless despite the bold burning fist at its center. His father had him wear it should Luther's men find them.

"Be at ease, Norman Tilt," said Lady Evelyn. "You're safe within my husband's house."

She rose from a tall leather-bound chair beside the hearth. Each inch she rose met unbalanced resistance from her quakes. The mistress of duels and debates released a long shuddering breath, clenching her teeth as she regained composure.

"I forfeited my thoughts of being safe after I saved Williamton."

"What truly troubles you then?" Lady Evelyn moved slowly to a column where a servant's bell hung. She strained, leaning hard against its red wood. "Is it the siege about to begin or our—"

Norman dashed to her side. Phillip leapt from another chair, catching her at the same time Norman did. They guided her to a chair. The orderman nudged the table before the hearth away with his foot. The councilwoman panted as if reaching the final step of a long staircase.

"It's Anna, isn't it?" Evelyn said, straining at an immense tremor down her chest, rendering her legs limp.

"Yes, my lady."

Lady Evelyn Wayne leaned back in the chair, forcing herself to stay upright.

"I think we both know, Tilt, that girl is just fine," said Phillip, removing his disk helmet and setting it on the table. "If Anna can walk away from a fight with me, then she can get north in time."

"Neither of you were meant to die in that duel," said Lady Evelyn, finally slumping where she sat. "You're too set on winning, Brother."

Norman's jaw dropped. Phillip smirked, rising, and shrugging before drawing a long, thin cigar from a pouch on his belt. He took his eyes away from the orderman, casting them on his father. Lady Wayne's servants had given him a shave and haircut. General Huldinarf whispered into the Quiet One's ear. A flicker spun across the olive-skinned orderman's eyes. He had been a spy, from what Norman learned. Meant to follow orders to the letter to avoid doubt from the prime.

"I wish I were with her," said Norman, an emptiness forming in his belly. "I care for her deeply and feel useless in this manstower."

He felt Evelyn's hand on his cheek. It was warm, trembling and slipping fast. Norman held her hand in both of his. A deep wish for a way to heal her surged. He knew only that family illness was in the blood. Unlike sickness caused by the cold of winter, or the ingestion of poison, it couldn't be stopped except by the end of a family line.

"You're a good man, Norman," she said, as warm tears ran down her cheeks. "I feel my time is near. I'm unfortunately expected at the tournament. The prime will not care what state I am in, and to be truthful, he would enjoy me like this."

Norman thought for a moment, finding her strength almost gone. What raced through his mind sounded risky, and though he wanted to join his father in the battle, someone else needed him more.

"I will take your place."

Phillip raised an eyebrow. His cigar fell from his lips, tapping and rolling across the table.

"You want to do what?" said the orderman.

Norman rested Lady Evelyn's hand in her lap and rose to full height. His father parted from the Quiet One, expressionless for a moment.

"This can work to our advantage," his father said. "The palace resists both wizard and rutoe, but the prime hasn't surfaced to face them. Norman. Doing this will place you close to Luther."

Fear clasped his throat at the sudden realization of what his father's next words might be. He'd be able to end rutoe banishment in an instant. A smile formed on the general's thin face.

"The law will see me executed by whoever wins the tournament," Norman said. "If Anna wins, then the duty will be hers."

"That is a chance you must take," said Lady Evelyn. "Either way, you will rid Lampara of a potential dictator."

"And thus," his father said. "Free our people."

THIRTY-THREE

By the time Anna reached the Proving, every one of her senses was on fire. Her head thrummed, and her ears rang no matter how far the explosions were. Dashing toward the bridge, city folk crisscrossed before it on horseback and on foot. Some pounded on shop doors while others hid in the carriages lining the street. Anna stopped at the bridge to catch her breath. The day was near its end as she deciphered that the capital was under attack. Yet despite all the time it had taken to reach the Proving, no one outside the city guard appeared armed or dangerous.

She increased her pace once more, noticing the water below the bridge was solid ice. Ahead, soldiers protected the arena, and esants were perched upon its rim, mounted by armored soldiers. Between the fallen pale bears a familiar face, bundled in furs, drew back his hood and summoned a smile from her worry. Simon Sanderson sat at a table with quill, ink, and parchment. He looked up from scribbling out a name, sighed, and then rose.

"The last to arrive again, Lady Brighton," he said, rotating the parchment to face her. "And without your handsome friend and that storm bison I see."

Anna ignored his second comment, dipping the quill and then signing next to where her name existed in fine lettering.

"The journey had its share of complications," she said.

"Pity," Simon pursed his lips, rolling up the parchment after pocketing the quill and ink. "I hoped to introduce myself too. What was your friend's name?"

"Norman Tilt."

"Tilt," said Simon. His voice sounded overly intrigued when saying it. "Follow me, Lady Anna. Tilt? Such a commoner name for someone lacking the features to match it."

Anna decided against asking what Simon meant. She wanted to go in search of Norman, despite the tournament requiring her attention. Swallowing her assumptions, she held onto hope he was alive and free. The corridor ahead was lit with more braziers than the last time she was here. The straw was swept away, replaced by sweet-smelling rushes.

"Reports have reached my ears that you were attacked," said Simon, unbuttoning his fur collar. "I didn't like that street slug to begin with."

"I had little choice," said Anna, hiding her lack of surprise at Simon's tone. "It does trouble me that I wasn't arrested despite being a campaigner."

"Arrested?" Simon chuckled, leading her up the stairs they used for the champion's platform. "Had you been the aggressor, an arrest would have been deemed appropriate. No matter what strange rumors say of our prime, justice isn't gone entirely from Lampara."

Anna raised an eyebrow; suspicion invaded her mind like a rodent a pantry. Simon turned back to her, unable to peer over his shoulder with the storm bison fur around his collar.

"Hope isn't gone from this country yet, my lady," he whispered.

"I know it isn't, my lord," she said. "I've come to end the strange doings and much more."

The lord smiled.

"You have gone from someone shy and unconcerned to someone who cares. You have my support, Anna."

After several flights of stairs, the night sky greeted them, hindered by lit braziers. The arena was full beyond capacity with tents and ornate pavilions of rich color. The snow began its descent again, and in greater waves of flakes. Anna could faintly hear the explosions dying down, as if the coming storm signaled what Lord William called a temporary truce.

"The tournament will begin at morning's first light, my lady," said Simon. A final distant boom made the lord jump in place. "You need not worry about the rutoe within the city. They think Prime Luther is within their grasp, but he's here. And anyway, the rutoe shall be beaten back to the mountains where they belong."

Simon Sanderson cast his hand towards the ornate viewing box across the arena. Long, rich fabric enclosed the openness it possessed. There was a section at its front set with an arrangement of several chairs.

"I shall find an inn to stay the night," said Anna, drawing over her hood. She ignored the hole flapping open and closed by her cheek. "Goodnight, my lord."

She made for the stairs, snow crunching underfoot, dampness meeting her nose.

"Slow your pace, my lady," Simon called from over her shoulder. "You already have a place here."

Anna returned to the platform.

"What do you mean? I was late, as you said."

Simon waved her over to the railing, pointing at a large yet modest-looking tent beside the prime's box. She gasped. Above its entrance hung a red banner possessing an eight-pointed star. Roaring braziers below it brought a shine to the star's silver.

THE IMMENSE GRANITE steps under her feet were slick with ice. Wind tousled the tent flaps before her, giving thin glimpses of light. Simon had offered to announce her, but she knew Lord William was an informal man. She could see him through the parting flaps, asleep on several stacked cushions, with a lit brazier at either end. He had declared her to no longer be part of the Brighton family. She knew this was true more than by his words, but she still cared for him.

Anna slipped inside, brushing cool snowflakes from her shoulders. Rage was all she felt the last time she had seen him. She had every right to feel that way forever. He was the reason she no longer had parents. A clan. There was still much she didn't know about what she had lost. It made her question at this moment whether she had truly lost anything.

Removing her cloak, she found it was wet and heavy in her hands. Anna set it aside before slipping her gloves off. Lord Brighton may have taken her past away, but he had raised her from a babe. The lord taught her all he knew under the crest of the guiding home star. He did the one thing most important in her mind. Lord William Brighton loved her.

"Grandfather," she said, the word both bitter and comforting. "I have come to do what you believed I could."

His thick gray eyebrows twitched. The blanket on his person rose and fell like a frustrated ocean. Anna remained still, at a distance, the incline of the arena placing her several heads shorter than where her grandfather stirred from sleep.

"Anna," he said, releasing a short yawn. "I never expected you to change your mind. I regret all that I've said, all that I did."

She scaled the small wooden steps in front of the cushions, every thought wishing to double back to the betrayal she had once felt.

"I fled from you with so much anger in me. It took … time, but I overcame my fears."

"Good," said Lord William, opening his arms to embrace her. "I have missed you, sweet girl."

His arms were warm, filled with the same strength she remembered. Anna felt her arms raised to return his kindness, but like in all Simdorn's teachings, no secrets should be kept between kin. She rested her hands upon his chest, looking deep into his eyes, finding only welcome.

"I missed you too, Grandfather," she said, hesitation snatching at her breath. "I have learned where I come from. What I am."

The old lord parted from her, descending the wooden steps until within an inch of leaving. His chin sank into his chest.

"It leaves me with boundless relief not to have woken

with a knife or arrow at my throat..." Lord William turned slowly. From his expression, he had noticed her bow was missing. "I made certain your identity remained a secret. The dragon changed things. I don't know how fire could have done more than burn or, dare I say, kill."

"Perhaps I shall learn the truth someday, but" Her stomach loosened its tightness, "my potential past isn't as important as the life you gave me."

"I can see not knowing still troubles you."

"A little," she said. "But I owe you so much, and not just for the life I had. There is a..."

"I can guess who you speak of, sweet girl," said Lord William, placing his hands behind his back. "I think at this time and place we must return your focus to winning the tournament."

"Then I must tell you what I have learned."

Lord William stiffened his chin, strolling toward her. His feet hissed across the bear rug. "I hope my worst fears haven't come true." he said.

Anna sighed. Her eye went to the ground. The wood burning within the braziers smelled of kory. It was something that always calmed her grandfather into a peaceful slumber.

"If one of the prime's sons wins the tournament, Luther will rule through that son as a dictator."

Her grandfather folded his arms, seeming more bent than usual in his posture. The wind howled outside, teasing his tent's fabric.

"There must be more to his plan," he said, moving to a small table and pouring wine from a decanter. "We've both met those boys. They are beyond what men of education would call dull. Luther would have no trouble manipulating them. However, that still leaves the council in his way."

"The council knows his plans."

"How?"

"Eve. I mean Lady Evelyn Wayne."

Cough. Lord William choked, spitting his wine.

"You put your trust in a protector of the prime?" He wiped his mouth, slamming his glass on the table. The glass cracked in his grip. "She will tell him you know of his plan if she hasn't already." He raised an eyebrow, wiping his mouth again. "How do you know his plan?"

Her words caught in her throat. "I'd ... rather not say. What is important is that we can trust Lady Evelyn. She aided me in learning where I come from."

"I will trust in that then," Lord William said, allowing himself to smile. "Now! It's time we prepare you for the first event, and I know just where to find you a new bow."

THE WIND WAS CALM. Calm like herself, which seemed strange as the sun's light met the rim of the Proving. She stood at its grassy center, the net from last time gone. Tents and pavilions were open, shading viewers from the light fall of snow. Anna felt whole, except it didn't mean her face. The wood of her new bow was smooth, its build light, its rest possessed a new device that kept the arrow steady in quick actions. Her grandfather had even purchased arrows with red goose fletching.

A bow placed her in control. The control she felt was most powerful when on hunts. The targets before her were small, their three rings red, black, and gray. The parchment containing the targets was set against a narrow bale of hay. But what made Anna unrelaxed, even feeling the control she did, were the people on the surrounding field. They numbered four heads deep, some with children upon their shoulders.

"To prove you care for your fellow Lampariens," Prime Luther said, speaking through a speech cone crafted from a smooth dark wood. A gold mouthpiece pressed against his lips. "You must loose every arrow in your quiver. Should you miss, the cost will be greater than execution."

Anna refused to look directly at the prime. Even after ten years, something about him robbed her of the warmth in her blood.

"You must be Anna Brighton," said a voice, light yet direct in word placement. "My mother told me to wish you luck."

The voice came from her blind side. Anna found it belonged to a girl younger than her, possessing shoulder-length blond locks. Her face contained high cheekbones and eyes the green of emeralds. But amongst all that was familiar, the crest upon the fine leathers the woman wore sparked her memory.

"You're Emilia?"

"At your service, my lady," said Emilia, bowing deep. Her bow was of dark wood. From the formation of her muscles, and tightness from the leather of her sleeves, her bow's draw strength must have been high. "Or should I say, in Lampara's service at this current event."

Prime Luther called from his speech cone. "Refusal to prove yourselves in this fashion will end in banishment. Show you care for your people. Do not flee. Do not miss."

"He's a mad one," said Emilia, nocking an arrow.

Grass shuffled, and snow crunched. Anna readied an

arrow, while five campaigners, three women and two men dropped their bows. Beside them, both towering in muscle and wrapped in furs, were the prime's sons. Unter glared at her, elbowing his brother.

"Are you staying, Lady Ugly?" Unter chuckled. His brother whispered in his ear. "My brother says you'd be better off going for half a nardan at a poke and tickle than here."

Strength fled from her fingers. Anna closed her eye as she felt herself wishing to be far away. Her throat went dry, the cold jabbed at her face like a thousand hornet stings. The crowd joined in Unter's laughter, and soon, all she could feel was shame. *I overcame this,* she thought. *I no longer care what others think.* Her teeth slammed shut. Her bow fell from her hand.

"Ignore them," said Emilia. "Here." She handed the bow to Anna. "You'll need this to do it."

Anna rose to full height, hands shaking. The laughter remained within her ears like a lone leaf on a branch during the year's harvest phase. *I've come this far.*

"Thank you," Anna took her bow. "Strike true, Emilia."

The gong's great vibration rang throughout the Proving.

"Last to empty their quiver is a sleepy nutsnatcher." Emilia said. *Poom.* Anna gasped. Emilia let her bow arm drop. "You're looking sleepy, Brighton."

Anna nocked and released in quick succession. She kept her eye on the target, and the target alone. Gasps reached out from those behind the targets. A series of cracks told her arrows had soared over the crowd and blunted themselves against the arena's walls. Faint thuds combined with rushed footwork made Anna guess her opponents were thinning in number. She dared not remove her focus. Her arrow count had started at twenty-nine, and now it was at nineteen.

A scream, deep and guttural, followed a brief chorus of pleas for mercy. "Don't banish me, your prime-ship," said one campaigner. He fled for the exit, grabbed by the arms once within it. A most unmanly scream trailed a soft thud.

Anna gulped. The crowd cheered her name, and soon, it was obvious. At her fingertips, eleven arrows remained. The target before her possessed no center now. She aimed for the next ring, placing each arrow within a tight grouping.

"And there my people," Prime Luther called out once more. "Is our first-round winner. It's ... Emilia Wayne. Wonderful."

Anna let her arm drop, its strength all but gone, unlike the crowd's excitement. She looked to where Prime Luther sat. Rising from her seat, Eve waved to Emilia, sneering slightly at Luther. The mistress of duels and debates seemed shorter. Anna blamed it on the distance.

"You're swift with that thing," said Emilia.

"Not swift enough compared to you, Lady Wayne."

Emilia shouldered her bow and then waved at her mother.

"You need not hide your disappointment," she said. "We have two rounds left. I hear the old man arranged them to please those two idiots he spilt seed for."

Both brothers left the arena in a rage. Lampariens in their way parted like frightened birds in an open field. Two loud cracks and hard thuds revealed the brothers had split their bows in two. Anna smirked. Neither of them had missed, but their arrows were erratically placed.

"I can guess my disappointment isn't as great as theirs," Anna said.

"Now you're learning, Lady Anna." Emilia chuckled.

"Mother said you lack one thing. Confidence. It appears you've found it."

"Yes," Anna said, heading to retrieve her arrows. "I have."

THIRTY-FOUR

The sun was at its highest. Although within the Proving, the heat expected from this time of day was barely noticeable. Those beside Norman shivered in richly woven cloaks, lined with nelka furs of fine quality. Norman strained to keep himself disguised as the mistress of duels and debates. No matter the cold, sweat would not be an issue as he maintained Lady Wayne's elegant features. He let free a small smile. This time Prime Luther would be fooled. There were no hearths to give him away. Norman felt the twitching in his eyes settle to a standstill.

Norman adjusted his posture to keep the long knife in place. Its position rested within a leather sheath in his coat. He gently raised his hand to signal the gong-man high above the champion's platform. It puzzled him how Lady Evelyn moved swiftly in what she wore, and for that matter with more than one knife. The gong sent vibrations throughout the Proving. Below the prime's box, immense doors parted, releasing clouds that filled the entire arena, blotting out the sun in moments. Below faint bleating reminded Norman of only one thing. *Storm bison.*

The grassy field rose from among the clouds and rain. Long black posts secured an immense net around the field, blurring the campaigners upon it. He shuddered faintly, understanding the suffering Anna had described long ago. Norman didn't know if Cole and Roland were alive, but if so, it was better than here.

"Pardon my concern," said the councilman next to him. "Are you well, Lady Wayne?"

Norman shook his head, finding focus once more.

"Whatever do you mean?"

"There was red in your...," The councilman paused with his mouth agape. "Oh, it must have been the orb lamps reflecting in your eyes. My apologies."

"None is needed," said Norman, folding his hands upon his lap. The long, slender fingers of his disguise felt cumbersome, but he had to grant himself credit. His father said Norman was the first rutoe not from the ominous clan to push the trick of skin to greater limits. "I'm excited to see my daughter once again."

The councilman smiled, tugging at his long, pointy beard.

"When will it be done?" he whispered from the corner of his mouth.

Norman eyed him over the fur of his high collar.

"Once Lady Brighton wins, my lord."

Something shattered behind them. Norman turned to find Prime Luther raging at a servant. The boy held a silver tray to his chest like a shield. Wine spread across the tile like an eager storm from the shattered remains of a decanter.

"You'd best hope she does," the councilman whispered.

"We've had this planned for a month. Your aim must be at its best. You seem less plagued by your family illness, Lady Wayne."

Returning his eyes to the Proving, Norman heard the boy weeping as ordermen dragged him away.

"I'm learning to manage it," he said. "Your care is appreciated."

Norman rose. His balance went astray with the thick low heel of his boots. Bringing himself to match the height of Lady Evelyn had nearly crippled him. He rested both hands on the balustrade. Lying across it was a banner displaying the Lampara's silver horse shaded in black. Norman shrunk back a bit at the immense shadow. Great leathery wings snapped, echoing through the arena like a lightning strike. And then a consuming shadow eclipsed the grass at its center, rising and falling, shaking the foundations, and rattling Norman to the bone. Heavy lidded almond-shaped eyes met his and flashed orange. Scales black as pitch covered the infernodawn before him. Smoke trailed from the dragon's spiked nostrils.

Calling out to either Anna or Emilia would end it all. Telling them to move with caution or warning them in any way meant imprisonment or worse. *I wish I had the time to change my voice.* he thought. The trick of skin gifted such an ability, but Norman didn't have years to learn how. He faced the council of affairs in their seats. The councilman with the pointed beard winked at him. He was the only one of them all not to show apprehension this morning. The council knew the real mistress of duels and debates was in no condition to attend the tournament. He found their support reassuring when the stakes were this high.

Norman watched as the twelve to survive the first round surrounded the dragon. Anna appeared out-of-place unlike the others, swinging a long spear tip with five sharp prongs. He could sense it was heavy, its head shaped like a bear's paw. The spear's shaft was long, pale and thick. Norman wished his friend had been granted a choice of weapon, but the prime made tournament rules.

The dragon released a torrent of flames at the two fleeing campaigners. Their bodies melted against the netting, turning its chains red hot. Anna and Emilia thrusted at the dragon's fat, dragging belly. The creature spun and rose on its hind legs, wiping clean in a single swipe another eight campaigners with its tail. Both sons of Luther thrusted their spears into the dragon's chest. It cried out, grabbing for and missing Unter. His brother braced and was knocked across the Proving. He crashed onto the grass, skidding to a halt below the champion's platform.

Norman bit down hard on his lip, tasting blood, skin shifting. Off at the far end of the viewing box, Luther pressed himself against the balustrade. The prime cursed and pointed at the dragon, warning of its approach. Unter eyed his father's foaming anger, dragging his brother to one of the exits. Norman reshaped his face to Evelyn's and smiled. His words had done good. *Luther worries for his children. He doesn't wish to—*

"Unter," Prime Luther shouted. "Finish that blasted dragon. Your brother will keep until later."

A tear ran down Luther's cheek as he said it. The Prime pounded his fists, searching for his speech cone. Norman refocused on the downed brother to find his immense back heaved. His head shifted in the wet grass.

"Go, boy," Luther cried, shaking his fist. "Kill it before you're both eaten."

Norman breathed a sigh of relief at the prime's concern. He saw Anna and Emilia missing. He scanned the field for them, his vision hindered by the net. Blood streamed from the infernodawn's chest in a rich, smoking red, burning the grass below it. And then he saw them rise from behind the creature's tail. The crowd cheered their names as the dragon charged at Unter. The prime's son readied his spear. Anna and Emilia made for him, rolling into the fray and thrusting their spears into the dragon's neck.

He pressed a shaky hand to his chest, backing slowly to his seat. He gasped as his feet tangled in Lady Evelyn's dress. The dragon cried out, planted its immense paws, and then collapsed with one loud thunderous boom. Someone with deft, coarse fingers caught him under the arms. Norman found himself beside the bearded councilman, being asked if he, or in this moment she, was well.

"I am," he said. "I'm just grateful for this round to be over."

"You're gonna need to show us that gratitude at dusk, Sister," a voice whispered.

Norman kept his eyes straight, recognizing the crisp voice, the smell of cigar on the breath of who spoke. "I will, Phillip. I..." He turned.

The orderman was gone.

THIRTY-FIVE

Anna's cloak smelled of smoke. Green streaks blended into its gold fabrics from rolling into the dragon's way. Anna sent it to be cleaned, thinking back to her first cloak, and how the flames tormenting Williamton had consumed it. The returned fear in that moment was gone for good, replaced at present by the coming final challenge. Steam slowly rose from the bath. Its heat drained away, aching in muscles from the first two challenges. The bathing room was the same she used when she had aims at escaping the pressures of campaigning. This time, benches lined every side of the bath, stacked with towels and bathing soaps.

"Nina would be jealous," said Emilia, sinking into the bath until her chin touched the bath's surface. "We've been cramming ourselves into bronze whalebone tubs for a year."

Anna kept to her corner of the bath, a washcloth lathered with soap in her hand. It smelled of ginger. It wasn't difficult to admit how beautiful was. She was far more adventurous than any other woman Anna had ever met.

And to have found the one you will love eternal was quite brave. *Have I found it with Norman?* Anna wanted to believe so, but she was uncertain if he still lived. *He's alive. I know it.*

"Do you need help with your back?"

"What?" said Anna. "No. I need no help with washing."

"You have no reason to be shy." Emilia rose from the water. It was well below her breasts once she was at full height. She pushed her hair behind her shoulders. "I promise I won't do more than wash. Simdorn says when one is married, treat..."

"... a friend as a friend, and your love as your love." Anna finished, smiling as she offered the washcloth. "Take it. You're correct that I am shy."

Emilia began washing Anna's back, making no mention of the claw marks. Cole's quick thinking had stopped the bear's rage. They were the only scars she found no pride in. None of the others had left her with reoccurring nightmares. Emilia plunged the rag beneath the water, scrubbing Anna's lower back. Bubbles surfaced around Anna's chest.

"My guess is you hunt like myself," said Emilia, tossing the soggy rag on the bath's edge. It plopped and flapped, then slid back into the water. "Dammit. I best stick with a bow."

"I do hunt," said Anna, moving to retrieve the rag. "It's the only thing I wanted out of life. Now, I must stop the prime's sons from winning. If they do," she bit her lip, "I don't know if I should reveal any more."

Emilia climbed the short steps out of the bath, choosing a towel from the bench before her.

"I know his plan, Anna. I envy your freedom to be out in the wild, hunting instead of entertaining those of your class. I'm the daughter of a councilwoman and have had the misfortune to mingle with the prime's spawn. Both are dull and river-mouthed."

"River mouthed?"

"You may have another phrase for it," Emilia said, drying off and applying her leathers. They were like Anna's except their plating was thicker. "Anyway, both told me the complete plan. I do not know what the old man will do about the council."

Anna saw what Emilia meant, hoisting herself from the bath, and letting her feet dangle in the water as she dried off.

"My grandfather shared a concern like your own. My thoughts lead to assassination, but your mother is an orderman like Phillip."

A faint bell tolling caught both of their attention. Anna dressed swiftly, struggling with her boots.

"We'll have to ponder what remains of the old man's plan another time," said Emilia.

The daughter of the mistress of duels and debates yanked open the door. Anna grabbed her shoulders as Unter charged past the door. He cracked his arm off a hanging orb lamp. The lamp clanged, cracking against the brickwork, rolling like a burning wheel into the room. Anna poked her head out as Emilia rescued the lamp from the bath.

"I swear to Simdorn," said Anna, "that I heard him cursing his father. Weeping even."

Anna and Emilia dashed down the hall. There was strange blue powered scatter amongst the cracks in the floor. A small evergreen iron plate amongst it, tiny spoon close by. The woman Anna had given her cloak sat against the wall, bleeding from her brow. A small cart transporting privy straw was turned over and smashed.

"His brother died by my guess," said Emilia, ignoring the wet hair clinging to her cheek. "I had a brother once, but our family illness caused my mother to..."

Anna took Emilia's hand and gave it a gentle squeeze.

"I have not seen her since we were in the south. How does she fare?"

Emilia held Anna's hand firmly in her own. They made further progress before stopping in the middle of the hall. Their eyes met, making Anna wish what she saw in Emilia's untrue. Words fled from her mind. Her every nerve felt as if they may ignite with pain. She took Emilia into her arms, hearing the girl's tears tap and run down the surface of her leathers. Anna slammed shut her eye, burying her face in Emilia's chest. Another bell tolled, echoing throughout the halls, but this time she didn't allow it to trouble her.

"Wait!" Anna rubbed the tears from under her nose. "How can your mother be gone from us if she...?"

"Is at the tournament?" Emilia gasped. She took off at a sprint.

"Wait!" Anna said, catching up to her. "We cannot learn who the impostor is now."

"I'm aware," Emilia snapped. "If I have learned anything from my mother, it's that those who *believe* they're clever always slip up."

"And what shall we do until the imposter does?"

Emilia stopped short of a long, narrow passage. Light from the arena reached down it, joined by a faint chilling breeze that nipped at Anna's cheeks. She knew what awaited them on the Proving. It pained her to say the words out loud. All Lampara depended on it, and Anna was uncertain she could step out there and face it.

"We fight," said Emilia. "And whoever lives will reveal the truth."

THE NETS and posts were gone. Braziers large enough for a single man to rest his hut upon burned bright enough to render the crowd hard to see. Day was gone from the sky, but Anna knew the time of day wasn't right. She guessed that a wizard was involved. But what unsettled her most was Emilia being her opponent. To add even greater danger, Unter too was someone she had to fight. Anna focused on her hands for a moment, her back against the wall, summoning courage from every part of her.

Across the Proving, Anna met where Unter's eyes led, finding Luther leering from his prime box, his hands firmly planted upon the balustrade. To Anna's right, she found Emilia for the first time nervous. Her fingers flexed against the arena's granite. Her stance made Anna believe the daughter of the mistress of duels and debates might take off for the exit across the way.

Anna peered over to the prime's box. Eve raised a hand from where she sat. The gong went off, sending vibrations strong enough to rattle the braziers. She balled her fists, taking off at a sprint for Unter, but the hulking man paid her no mind. He charged like a furious bull towards his father. The prime's son pounded his wine cask sized fists against one another, seizing the banner hanging from the prime's box. It stretched and tore, so he yanked it, and ripped it in two. A hard rush hit her side. Anna coughed and collapsed on her back against the grass. Emilia straddled her, raising a fist.

"I'm sorry," she huffed, her long locks a mess. "I saw it in you from the start." Emilia punched Anna in the face. "You can fight." She cocked her fist back. "hunt, and even ride, but what you can't do is lead."

Anna grabbed her fist, and then yanked, throwing Emilia off balance. She heard a crunch, felt the pressure come faster than her grandfather's esant. Blood seeped from her nose. Anna choked, spitting a glob of blood. Anna focused her good eye, but Emilia broke free, and like lightning struck her square in that eye.

"Please!" Anna cried, seeing only Emilia's outline. "Stop!"

"You know I cannot," Emilia said, striking Anna's sealed eye. "I've lost too much, and I won't lose again."

Raising and crossing her arms, Anna bent up, blocking each blow, grabbing hold of Emilia's wrists. Anna pushed with all her might, shaking, and grinding her teeth. She doubled her grip against the anger Emilia possessed.

"You're right," Anna said, seething, "about all but one thing. I can lead."

Emilia withdrew her arms, rounded them, then struck at the beginnings of Anna's shoulders. Anna felt her arms drop. She groaned through her teeth. She found herself falling back, the cheers around her rattling her ears. Unter called for his father to come and face him. A faint voice, familiar in depth, called her name. She watched Emilia cock her fist back, crushing her hopes within it. It was over, but...

Screeeech!

The sound exploded from her lips, vibrating every inch of her throat. Emilia flew back, hands clasping her ears. And within an instant, the girl who bested her with a bow struck the prime's box. A crack rang out, rendering all within the Proving silent.

THIRTY-SIX

It was over. Norman felt his skin shift. His hair blackened. Every part of him felt the impact he witnessed. Anna lay at a distance on her back, calling Emilia's name, twisting, and turning to be upright. He heard the girl he had met long ago fall, but her body found no dirt. No grass is doused with mud. Norman stood with Luther against the balustrade, peering over to find Emilia in Unter's arms. There was pity on the broken-toothed face of the prime's son. Something Norman never expected from a man raised by...

"You!" said Luther, snatching Norman by the collar. "So, Wayne finally met her end. Begin my endgame."

Dozens of footsteps filled his ears as he watched Unter bring Emilia to Anna. Norman's eyes flared bright red, feeling Luther scour his coat, then draw out the long knife from it. Prime Luther struck Norman across the cheek with the pommel of the knife. The crowd across the Proving went sour and vengeful, calling for guards and demanding the prime be arrested. Ordermen flooded the viewing box. A boom shook the arena, swiftly drawing back the illusion of night, casting sunlight against the metal of a dozen disk helmets.

"You won't win," said Norman, wincing at the pain in cheek. He snarled and ignited his fists. "I will not allow—"

Prime Luther pressed the long knife to Norman's throat. The blade breached flesh, smoking, but not melting from his blood. He heard Phillip call out, trading knife strikes until he was forced into the hall.

"I have already won you, green rat," Luther chuckled, sneering at Unter. "Kill the Brighton girl, Unter. Your dictator commands it."

Over his shoulder, the council protested, falling silent at the appearance of knives being drawn. Norman gaped. The ordermen possessed the features of quiet ones.

"Do you not know what this man has done to our—"

"They know, Norman Tilt," said Luther, pressing the knife's tip under Norman's jaw. "And they don't give a damn. I've given every rutoe and wizard under my employ their greatest desires."

"Let them go, Father," Unter roared, stomping toward them. "Your son is dead. My brother is ... dead."

Luther laughed. "Do what your father commands, boy" The tip of the knife sent a trickle of blood down Norman's throat.

"You stupid boy." The prime pushed Norman off. An orderman seized Norman under the arms, drawing him into the shadows. Luther cast his hands up. "It will all be mine once the council is gone. And when I die, you'll get it. And the people will have no choice but to obey."

"Now's your moment to light 'em up." Phillip whispered.

Norman felt himself released, taking courage from the man he thought dead. Flames roared from his fists. An ear-piercing scream rang out as a black outline of Luther twisted and turned within the flames. The crowd fled for the nooks along the Proving, disappearing into its immensity. Norman released a gasp, extinguishing his flames. Before him lay a heap of blackened robes and bones.

The quiet ones looked amongst themselves, withdrawing their knives. Amongst those on the council, the one with his long white pointed beard adjusted himself. He eyed Norman for a moment and then shrugged.

"You're not one for subtlety," he said, "are you?"

"I used to be," said Norman. "I'm an accountant. We aren't ones for theatrics."

"Well, you will have no time for practice. Two campaigners remain, and one of them will be your executioner."

CHAPTER

THIRTY-SEVEN

Anna rolled over, enveloped within Unter's shadow, finding her strength had returned. Emilia's chest rose and fell in quick succession. Anna climbed to her knees to find the Proving was empty except for those within the prime's box. Footsteps crunched and hissed on the wet grass behind her. A pain constricted her stomach to see Emilia twisted and weeping. The daughter of the mistress of duels and debates looked upon her with eyes overrun by pain.

"I... I don't know what that was, Anna." Emilia clenched her teeth as blood ran from the corners of her lips, "but this isn't over. You still have that one."

Unter remained still, looming, his eyes without direction. He wiped his fist under his nose.

"I've got no interest in governing," he said. "My mum's gone. My brother too. And my father was the only brains I had."

Anna felt a hand on her shoulder. She peered over to find her grandfather. His eyes were lowered, and his presence brought her comfort. She rested her hand upon his, all her focus falling on Emilia.

"I must put my friend first before I accept your forfeit, Unter."

Emilia coughed, releasing a raspy laugh.

"You have won, Brighton. Bury me with my mother."

"No," Anna cried. "I am not too late this time. Not as I was for Nathan."

"Anna," Lord William said. "What can you do to stop death?"

"I know a wizard who can help, Grandfather. Go and retrieve your—"

"Shut that mouth of yours, Anna," Emilia cried. "Just tell my wife I fought for her, and ... that I love her. Tell her I couldn't go on living knowing how cruel I was to..."

A shuddering last breath left the girl Anna had known for so brief a time. Anna wrapped her arms tightly around her stomach. It felt as though all she had done was for nothing. She knew Emilia's soul would find her mother's. To die in such a way ensured it. Anna slowly recited the prayer Emily had taught her. It was meant for goodbyes, for being parted from someone with the hope of reuniting. This time it was to show Emilia would be missed. She rose to full height and gasped at who approached. Norman wore women's clothing. The imposter had been him all along.

"I shall honor Emilia's wish," Anna said, facing her grandfather. "I never listened to your lessons of history, or the politics of our country. What do I do now?"

Lord William sighed. A faint smile crossed his lips for a moment. Perhaps, Anna thought, it was pride in her finally embracing the potential within her.

"There will be a ceremony like that of a coronation, except with a medallion," he said. The smile vanished from his lips. "but there is a duty you must perform first, and it shall be most taxing for you."

"And what duty must I perform?"

"You must... You must execute Norman."

THE SWORD WAS heavy in her hands. Heavier than the one she held to duel her way out of responsibility. Norman's neck was thin enough he could slip free of the pale bear guardian's jaws. She had no wish to stop him. No wish to do what was expected of her. Simdorn's law felt like a dagger to her gut. And if she refused to execute her friend, there would be many questions about her competency as a primnoire. The council would have to vote to see who favored her continued governance. If all voted against her, another year of campaigning would be required. And after her display of power in the arena, the council possessed no doubt of her being a rutoe. There was no certainty that her removal or continued governing wouldn't lead to an all-out civil war.

Her palms were slick with sweat. The Blade of Final Finishes, as the council called it, matched her in height. Its long hilt was bound in a coarse brown leather, thick and tightly bound. Those within her presence to make certain she followed through were the council and rutoe commanders. Peace had been struck the day she became primnoire, and by her own orders, the banishment that had lasted ten long years was ended with a pen stroke.

One of the commanders in the finest armor was Norman's father. General Huldinarf had pleaded his son's case before her once she arose a primnoire at dawn. She had listened with tears in her eye, wishing for another way.

Anna prayed while the general spoke of his son's deeds. In the end, she knew the consequences were too high if the law wasn't carried out.

"I, Anna Brighton, am of sworn on duty to bring justice for my predecessor, Prime Luther Brollerfin."

Norman turned his head slowly. His eyes flashed a light red as his lips trembled.

"I love you."

Her grip increased on the sword's hilt. All of it felt as though she were back at the Proving, still ashamed of her burns. The crowd's presence heightened the nervousness in her chest. Executions were made private for a crime of such magnitude, with the bells to announce when all was done. And for this, Anna found gratitude, but still, the task was no easier.

"I love you, Norman." Anna dropped the sword. "I will accept what fate holds because of it."

"You know what this will mean," said Norman. "You will be—"

"I am a hunter, Norman." Anna pulled Norman to his feet. She yanked from around her neck Eve's whistle and blew. The wall behind her boomed and cracked. A second boom scattered the council and commanders. A roaring hiss exploded from the wall, tossing about massive debris. "I think I shall handle life on the run well."

She waved his father forward. He climbed Colbwing as the dome saddle opened. The serpent's eyes glowed as it said, "Are you sure about this, Anna?"

"Brian," she said. "I have never been more certain in my whole life."

PLEASE LEAVE A REVIEW

Customer reviews allow independent authors to continue sharing their stories. If you enjoyed this book, please leave a review wherever you normally would.

Thank you for reading!

ABOUT THE AUTHOR

Andrew Johnston is a fantasy author from southwestern Pennsylvania. He is the author of The Discarded Knight and the Iron Frost Universe. Andrew studies history and spends time with his nephew when not writing.